THE REIGNING QUEEN OF MYSTERY!

In her tenth superb Richard Jury mystery, MARTHA GRIMES again proves that one of 'the best writers of British mysteries'* is American!

"READ ANY ONE [OF HER NOVELS] AND YOU'LL WANT TO READ THEM ALL." —*Chicago Tribune*

"ONE OF THE ESTABLISHED MASTERS OF THE GENRE." —*Newsweek*

"FIRST-RATE . . . Grimes remains a master at delivering the significant detail." —*Booklist*

"STYLISH AND WITTY—FRESH TRIBUTE TO THE CLASSICAL BRITISH WHODUNIT."
  —*San Francisco Chronicle*

"If Jane Austen were alive and well and writing mystery stories today, she'd be Martha Grimes."
  —*The Hartford Courant*

*—*The Orlando Sentinel*

Martha Grimes

THE OLD SILENT

A DELL BOOK

Published by
Dell Publishing
a division of
Bantam Doubleday Dell Publishing Group, Inc.
666 Fifth Avenue
New York, New York 10103

The characters and events in this book are fictitious. Any similarity to real persons, living or dead, is coincidental and not intended by the author.

The author is grateful for permission to reprint the following copyrighted material:

Excerpts from "Carolyn Says II" and "The Kids" by Lou Reed. Copyright © 1973 by Oakfield Music Ltd. All rights administered by Screen Gems-EMI Music Inc.

Excerpt from "Who Says" by Richard Hell. Copyright © 1977 by Doraflo Music, Quickmix Music and Melting Music. Used by permission of Warner/Chappell Music, Inc. All rights reserved.

Excerpt from "Good-bye and Keep Cold" by Robert Frost. Copyright © 1923 by Holt, Rinehart and Winston and renewed 1951 by Robert Frost. Reprinted from *The Poetry of Robert Frost*, edited by Edward Connery Lathem, by permission of Henry Holt and Company, Inc., Jonathan Cape Ltd., and the Estate of Robert Frost.

ISBN: 0-440-20492-5

Reprinted by permission with Little, Brown and Company

Printed in the United States of America

Published simultaneously in Canada

September 1990

10 9 8 7 6 5 4 3

OPM

To
    Kathy Grimes
       Roy Buchanan
          and my cats, Felix and Emily
who have all entered the old silence

No orchard's the worse for the wintriest storm;
But one thing about it, it mustn't get warm.
"How often already you've had to be told,
Keep cold, young orchard. Good-bye and keep cold.
Dread fifty above more than fifty below."
I have to be gone for a season or so.

—Robert Frost

Once born you're addicted
And so you depict it
As good, but who kicked it?

—Richard Hell

Contents

Acknowledgments

When asked where I get my inspiration, I say, "I don't." This time I did.

I would like to thank some people I've never met:

John Coltrane, Miles Davis, Edward Van Halen, Steve Vai, Jeff Beck, Joe Satriani, Ry Cooder, Mark Knopfler, Otis Redding, Eric Clapton, Jimmy Page, James Taylor, Yngwie J. Malmsteen, Elvis Presley, Lester Bangs, Greil Marcus, Jimi Hendrix, John McLaughlin, Stevie Ray Vaughan, Tommy Petty, and Frank Zappa.

And many thanks to some people I *have* met:

Elise Kress and the New Saint George band; Chief Superintendent Roger E. Sandell of the Norfolk Constabulary; Tony Walton of the Hammersmith Odeon; Andrew Moffitt, guitarist; and Kent Holland, who froze in line to get the tickets for Lou Reed's concert.

—and Melrose Plant *especially* wants to thank Lou Reed.

Part One

GOOD-BYE
AND
KEEP
COLD

1

He had seen her earlier that day in the museum behind the parsonage. It was ten o'clock in the evening now and since he had been quite certain he wouldn't see her again, Jury couldn't help but keep raising his eyes to look over the top of his local paper to see if, even now, she had the least awareness that she was being observed.

She didn't. She sat back against the cushioned chair by the fireplace, a glass of brandy beside her on the table, largely untouched, as if she'd forgotten it along with her surroundings. Her attention had been for a while fixed (and it was the first suggestion of a smile he had seen all day) on a black cat that had appropriated the best seat in the inn, a brown leather porter's chair with a high, buttoned back. The cat's slow-blinking yellow eyes and proprietorial air seemed to say that guests could come and go, but it would remain. It had rights.

The woman, however, gave the impression that she had none. The beautifully tailored clothes, the square-cut sapphire ring, the perfectly bobbed hair notwithstanding, that was the impression of her he had got earlier—someone who had stepped down, had given over all rights and privileges.

It was a fantasy, and an absurd one at that. From the few scraps of impressions he had stitched together he was in danger of fashioning the tragic history of a queen forced to abdicate.

He tried to go back to his pint of Yorkshire bitter and the

engrossing column on the sheep sale and the fund-raiser for
the Brontë museum.

It had been in the museum earlier that day that he had
first seen her. She was bending over one of the glass cases
that protected the manuscripts. It was off-season for tourists, a chilly day after the New Year.

The only other people in the room were a waiflike woman
and her balding husband with two young children, all bun-
dled up. In their heavy coats and scarves, the girl and boy
resembled the Paddington Bears they carried. The mother
looked haggard, in her jeans and baggy sweater, as if she'd
just finished up a week's washing; the father, a camera
swinging from his shoulder, was trying to read aloud Emily
Brontë's poem about a captive bird but was dissuaded by the
whines of the kiddies eager to get away from these arcane
manuscripts, grim portraits, scents of old leather and bees-
wax, into the sunnier and more aromatic environs of one of
the local tearooms. "Choc and biscuits" must have been the
ritual treat, for they recited it, in tandem, again and again.
Chocandbiscuitschocandbiscuitschocandbiscuits. Their whee-
dling little voices were rising and would soon turn to shouts
and tears. The mother looked round, embarrassed, and the
father tried ineffectually to quiet them.

The kiddies' whining pleas seemed to awaken the woman
in the cashmere coat to a sense of her surroundings, like one
awakening in a strange room, one she had entered by mistake and which might harbor some undefined danger. Her
expression, indeed, was similar to the one in the touching
self-portrait of Branwell Brontë, imagining his own death-
bed scene. She looked stricken.

She hitched the strap of the leather bag farther up her
shoulder and wandered into the next room. Jury felt she was
just as indifferent to the Brontë arcana as the Paddington
children had been. She was bending over a case, pushing the
tawny hair that fell forward behind her ear as if it blocked
her view of Charlotte's narrow boots, her tiny gloves, her

nightcap. But that examination was merely cursory as her hand trailed abstractedly along the wooden edge of the case.

Jury studied an old pew door taken from the box pews when the church had been demolished. It bore the legend that a certain lady of "Crook House, hath 1 sitting." They must have all had to take turns, back then.

Her slow walk round the display table in Charlotte's room might have given, to a less well-trained eye than his, the impression of absorption. In her eyes was an utter lack of it. The looks she cast here and there were uninquisitive glances from intense and intelligent eyes, but eyes that seemed looking for something else. Or someone. She appeared to be idling there, waiting.

That, he decided, was the impression: her expression preoccupied, the swift, slight turn of the head that suggested she was listening and expectant; there was the air of an assignation missed.

She had certainly not registered his presence; her glance had swept across his face as if it were another Brontë artifact, a portrait or bronze bust. If she were introduced to him five minutes later, he doubted she would remember ever having seen him. Where she stopped the longest and seemed to really look was at the display behind glass of Angria and Gondal, those imaginary kingdoms invented by Branwell.

Then she turned and walked toward the stairs.

Well, he had meant to leave anyway (Jury told himself) and followed her. He stopped on the staircase to look at the famous portrait of the sisters painted by the brother. Jury could see the dim outline, the space once full where Branwell had painted himself out.

The Paddington family had left, too, headed across the narrow street to the tearoom, the children managing somehow to swarm as if there were ten of them rather than two.

At first he thought the woman might be going for a cup of tea herself, but she simply stood on the curb, hesitating as if she were in London at a zebra crossing. The only traffic here at the top of this hill up which the pilgrims toiled was one cab idling by the tourist information center and a boy trying to urge on an intractable dray horse wearing blinders.

A chill wind whipped up the cobbled pavement, bringing with it a taste of rain, and the woman pulled up the collar of her coat so that her hair was tucked into it. Then she plunged her hands into the pockets and turned up the street. He thought she might be making for the enticing warmth of the whitewashed hotel on the corner, perhaps (he hoped, for he could use a pint of something) to the saloon bar there. But she passed it and stopped instead before a narrow house called the Children's Toy Museum. She went in.

Jury stood looking at the façade and then into the dim interior where she was paying for a ticket. He was beginning to feel not only like a fool, but a voyeur. He hadn't followed a good-looking female since he was sixteen, except if a case he was working on required it, and it had been some years since he had had to do that sort of footwork himself.

The little foyer or outer room was crammed with small toys—tops, wooden figures, sweets and souvenirs clustered on shelves. An amiable young man in a Dallas Cowboys sweatshirt and a forlorn-looking girl sat behind the counter, his happy expression and her sad one like the coupled masks of comedy and tragedy. She seemed surprised that here yet was another person over ten or twelve who was handing over fifty pence to go inside and see the toy display. The man smiled as if he approved of such larking about on the part of adults. Jury returned the smile and handed over the ticket money.

Just then a sallow kid with a lick of strawlike hair shooting up on the crown of his head came from the inner room into the outer room, frowning, as if he hadn't got his money's worth. The girl was generous; she realized the problem and told the boy to go back in and push the button. She then instructed Jury in a similar fashion, in case he too was a bit thick about getting the train setup to work. It wouldn't work, after all, unless you pushed the buttons.

He thanked her and followed the boy into the museum.

She was standing at the end of the narrow aisle that ran between the glass walls crammed to overflowing with the detritus of childhood. Stuffed dolls and bisque dolls; elaborately designed dollhouses; mechanical toys and wooden toys.

He wondered, really, if the boy there at the end, standing beside her before the train display, could appreciate all of this. It was, in some sense, a museum for adults. He looked at the replica of a skyscraper built from a Lego set and remembered how much he had wanted one. Against the wall opposite was the most intricately built dollhouse he'd ever seen. Its little rooms were furnished on four sides, and it was probably meant to turn on a mechanical wheel. It even had a billiard room, a green baize table at which were two players, one holding his cue stick, the other bent over the table.

While he looked over this catalogue of childhood, he was aware of the faint buzzing noise of the trains, set in motion by the towheaded lad at the end.

Their backs were to him, the lad and the woman in the cashmere coat, standing side-by-side. Were it not that the lad could have done with a scrubbing and darning, and she so expensively turned out, they might have been mother and son, their coloring was so similar. The trains went round and they stood in a sort of comradely silence, watching. It was the boy who seemed to tire of this first; he walked back up the aisle, brushed by Jury, and left, still frowning, as if the trains, the bits and pieces of miniature buildings, and perhaps toy people and animals hadn't done something clever enough.

Still she stood there, pushing the button that operated the train again. He could see only her back and the faintest impression of her reflection in the glass.

Then she made a strange gesture. She raised her gloved

hand, fingers outspread against the glass, and leaned her forehead against it.

It was as though she were looking at something she had once wanted terribly, as Jury had wanted the Lego set.

It was at that point that he had felt intensely ashamed, felt himself to be a voyeur, an intruder, an invader of privacy. He left the toy museum, feeling he would have to let her go.

"Let her go": certainly an odd, proprietorial way of regarding a person with whom he'd had no contact, hadn't even exchanged a word. Hadn't even, really, exchanged a look, given the glance she had passed over him had probably not registered.

And he was picking it apart, too, adolescently, going back over their mutual occupancy of the two different places as if something might come back to him that would suggest he had kindled at least a passing interest. . . .

It was all one more sign—his doctor would say "symptom"—of just how tired he was.

The only thing to do to stop this adolescent desire to hang about was to walk back to the car park, collect his rented car, and get on with his trip back to London.

He got as far as sitting behind the wheel of the Austin-Rover, letting the engine idle, staring through the windscreen at the almost-deserted car park and the gardens beyond where the children's swings lifted slightly and twisted in the wind.

It had been a lark, a cheering thought, after the wasted week at headquarters in Leeds, to drive the short distance to Haworth and spend the night.

He slid down in the seat, thinking this sudden decision to return was equally ridiculous (and symptomatic, Mr. Jury), since he had meant to stop here overnight. He was just too damned tired to make the four- to five-hour trip back to London. Part of the weariness came from the week in Leeds doing little more than getting baleful looks.

This self-deprecatory notion was all part of the malaise. "*Accidie,* Mr. Jury" (his doctor had prissily termed it, mouthing the word as if it were a tasty new drink). A larger part of this depression came from the knowledge that he had agreed to this assignment to get out of London and away from Victoria Street and New Scotland Yard, where he felt he had lately been bumbling about, making errors of judgment, taking wrong decisions, giving in to uncharacteristic outbursts of temper.

Sitting here now, looking down the slope of snow-patched park where the light drew back, away from the swings, he wondered how much of his recent behavior was actual, how much exaggerated. Nothing dramatic had happened, beyond the occasion of his having got so bored listening to Chief Superintendent Racer's litany of Jury's recent failings (no matter how minor) that Jury had offered to put in for a transfer. What concerned Jury was not the melodrama of this but the lack of it; the suggestion had merely come off the top of his head and he hadn't even enjoyed, particularly, the dilemma it had caused Racer.

Accidie. A holiday, that's what you need. Been working too hard. Then there were the prescriptions Jury had tossed in the nearest dustbin after leaving his doctor's office.

Accidie. It was as good a word as any (he had thought, lying awake at three A.M., which had lately become habitual); perhaps it was better in its foreign-soundingness, defining a condition that his own language was unable to describe. Malaise did not really fit, though he preferred it, for it sounded like a passing fancy, something that could probably be caught lying in the sun on the Amalfi coast and possibly left there, like sunburn.

He could only really think of it in its much simpler guise of depression. In a way, it was a comforting term, for everyone had it, or thought he had it, now and again. It was just that Jury did not feel it would pass off like sunburn or sore eyes. Indeed, he wondered why people seemed to think of it as a condition in which one felt merely dull, stupid, and disinterested in the day's events, when it was actually almost the very opposite. It was an active condition; close to an agony of conflicted feelings and feverish thoughts about one's work, life, ability to fulfill some expectation that was in itself ambiguous, shrouded in mystery. He was not, he knew, ordinarily a contented man. But he was very good at borrowing the expression, the mannerisms, the outward calm of one. And such a façade was helpful, perhaps necessary to his effectiveness as a policeman. What he felt as he lay wakefully staring at the ceiling was that the veneer was chipping.

And it occurred to him now, sitting in the musty car, that he had probably made this little side trip for a day or two of anonymity. Was it this feeling of lack of purpose, of vague possibilities and unformed hours that had made him feel a sense of kinship with the woman in the museum? For she seemed to be wandering here as much as he.

Locking the car again and starting toward the tourist information center with his gear, he felt angry with himself for yet another flight of fancy, totally unbecoming in a man whose whole life was devoted to sifting through facts and, yes, occasionally playing hunches.

Leeds thought he was in London, London thought he was in Leeds. He could not quite expunge the fancy from his mind that he and the woman in the cashmere coat were stopping off in a no-man's-land.

And that was why, when Jury had walked into the dining room of the Old Silent where he'd booked his room, his feeling had been less one of surprise than of justification.

She was sitting at a table in the corner, the only other occupant. With her dinner she was reading a book, and she did not lift her eyes from it when Jury walked in and sat down.

He had his own book. Perhaps it was *symptomatic, Mr. Jury,* that he ate solitary meals with a book more often than he dined with others. Fictional characters, he had lately found, were generally more interesting dinner companions than flesh-and-blood ones. He had the night previously suffered through a small dinner party at the home of an inspector from Wakefield headquarters. The hostess, like a television sponsor, seemed to think any silence at the table was as dangerous to her product as dead air on the telly. Weather, property values in the North and the South, London, the theater, New Scotland Yard—the same old questions and answers ebbing out with the soup and flowing back with the sweet.

So here the two of them sat in the silent dining room, silently reading their books, sipping their wine, buttering their bread. It was ten, which probably accounted for the lack of custom. Several other tables showed signs of diners having departed.

He wondered what she was reading and whether she was absorbed or whether she wanted, as he did, company. Dependable, well-spoken company. He thought he should have chosen something properly Brontë-ish, but he was reading instead a book by the late Philip Larkin called *A Girl in Winter* that fed his mind as well as the roast beef fed his body with its simple plot, elegant style, and sad heroine. It was a calm book.

When she laid her napkin aside, rose and passed by his table (still without seeing him), she had her own book pressed to the side of her leather bag. He angled his head slightly to see the title: *The Myth of Sisyphus.*

Not a calm book at all.

There was no one now in the lounge of the inn but them. A couple who had come too late for the dining room had finished up their meal in that part of the long front room reserved for the lounge bar and left. The Old Silent was a warm and friendly pub: copper and brass glinted; dark wood chairs and benches with flowered cushions were set in configurations around tables that invited the sort of comradely talk that had engaged the couple who had just left.

It was in the saloon bar that Jury was sitting, near the door that led to the public bar through which he heard muted voices. There was no other sound except for the steady ticking of the long-case clock, the occasional spark and sputter of a crumbling log in the fireplace.

There was no reason that he couldn't have taken his drink and moved into the lounge proper to sit nearer the fire. Indeed, as they were the room's only occupants now, nothing would have been more natural than for him to displace the black cat from the sedan chair with some comment about the way cats always took the best seat in the house.

But there was something about her that discouraged such an approach; she seemed so totally immersed, not in that book (of which a page hadn't turned) but in some private world, just as she had been in the museum, earlier. When she looked over the edge of the book, up and past him, she might have been reviewing some inner terrain and, frowning, found something wanting in it, something missing.

Then she would return to Camus, to the same page, holding the book in one hand before her face. Without the coat she seemed thinner. Her hand remained resolutely on the bag planted firmly beside her; the other held the book in such a way it blocked her face. The wrist below the elegant hand—long, tapering fingers—was slightly bony; the gold bracelet had slid halfway down the arm; and the gold band on her finger looked loose.

She was wearing a silk shantung suit, a narrowly pleated skirt and a short jacket, very plain and (he thought) very expensive. The diffused light of the lamp and fire lent the same pale umber to both suit and hair.

For another twenty minutes they sat there. When the clock struck eleven, she looked up. Jury could hear, from the public bar, the publican make his final call for Time. She closed her book, set it beside her handbag, and he thought she meant to rise and leave. But she still sat.

Sounds of the customers from the bar leaving carried in from the small car park; a few of them came out through the lounge.

Then the headlamps of a car dazzled the window before

they were switched off. A door slammed, and Jury heard the approach of footsteps on the walk.

She sat in that rather stern and spinsterish way she had adopted after putting aside her book—hands folded in her lap and feet planted firmly together.

A man walked in the door—a man as well- and expensively groomed as she. He was perhaps in his late forties, the sort who looks fit from exercise (the sort Jury never got) and time spent under a sunlamp. He glanced at Jury without interest.

His attention was concentrated on the woman, who now rose, pushing herself as would an elderly person who has difficulty getting out of a chair. She still held her bag tightly.

There was no greeting, no handclasp, kiss, or even an exchange of smiles. Her visitor sat down without removing his coat, a dark Chesterfield, which he unbuttoned before he threw his arm across the back of the sofa in a careless, even indolent fashion. The fine features, the cut of his clothes, the grace of movement, bore the stamp of the gentleman. Yet the woman still stood while he sat. If his general demeanor hadn't told Jury that the visitor must be on very intimate terms with her, this failure of social grace surely did. He then said something to her and she sat down with a sadly compliant look.

It struck Jury as odd that he had been able to observe so closely the physical details of her person, right down to her wedding band, and yet was not close enough to hear the words that passed between them. The man spoke softly but in a rush. To his low current of words, her own contribution was no more than a word tightly wedged in, much like the bag between herself and the chair arm, breaking in whenever her companion showed the slightest sign of stopping the flow; even then, his hand raised up against her own response.

That what he said was evidently not to her liking was clear from her adamantine look, her glancing away from him to gaze at the fire, and back again as if there was no

place, really, for her eyes to travel. The pale coral of her lips
took on a golden glaze from the light, and her mouth was set
like marble. She looked resolute and unbending.

Having said his piece or made his argument or whatever it
was, he sat back, withdrew a silver case that winked in the
firelight, and tapped a cigarette on it before lighting it. After
waiting a few moments while she stared into the fire, he
leaned forward as if willing her to loosen her resolve, to
return her eyes to his face. Eventually, she did so, very
slowly.

He said something and rose, still with that rather insouci-
ant manner coupled with an air of belligerence.

Her head, gilded by the light, was bent slightly as if she
had been bested or beaten in some serious game. Her arms
rested on the chair arms, hands dangling, one thumb worrying the gold band and the sapphire ring. It was as if she were
considering removing them and putting them in his hand.

Slowly she pulled her handbag like a dead weight to her
lap. She pushed back the leather flap and withdrew what
looked like an envelope or a letter. She had taken it out at
dinner and returned it to her bag again and again as if this
were a magic ritual that must be performed. She stood up
with this piece of paper—letter or whatever it was—and said
something Jury couldn't hear.

Still she held the bag before her like a breviary, its leather
flap back and dangling, as if the thing were now empty,
useless and bereft of a valuable possession.

He reached over, snatched the letter from her hand, and
tossed it in the fire.

For a moment they regarded one another, still oblivious to
any other presence in the room, so intent were they upon
whatever business had drawn them together. The man
turned and started for the door.

She stood there, just her profile in light, the rest of her in
shadow, like a figure turned to stone by an angry god.

"Roger."

It was the first clear word Jury had heard. The man made

a halting sort of turn and she reached into the bag, pulled out a gun, and shot him in the chest. He stood staring blindly as if the shot had gone wild. But in the few seconds it took Jury to stand and overturn the table beside him, the man crumpled and fell.

She pointed the gun down and shot him again.

2

The name of Roger Healey had not registered with Jury
when he had heard it in the inn in West Yorkshire. The West
Yorkshire policeman who had arrested Healey's wife the
night before in the Old Silent had told Jury the man had
something to do with art or music—he wasn't sure what—
except that he was important. The local detective sergeant
from Keighley certainly knew the *family* was important in
these parts, and his ambivalence about arresting one of its
members was clear.

Superintendent Sanderson had no such ambivalence, either about having Jury as the single witness to the murder of
Roger Healey, or about having a member of the C.I.D. of
the Metropolitan Police on his turf. Sanderson was a tall,
rail-thin policeman with a practiced, inconclusive manner
that would throw anyone off guard. In the unlikely event
Jury's testimony would ever be needed, it would carry far
more weight than that of some myopic villager. As of now,
Jury could get off his turf and out of the investigation now
proceeding with the Yorkshire constabulary.

Sanderson would have no difficulty proceeding. It wasn't
even a case of rounding up suspects, of listening to the regulars in the public bar of the Old Silent give conflicting reports of who did what to whom; and the five people who had
rushed in from the bar were clearly relieved that they were
straight out of it. They had stood about in horrified silence

until police had arrived. It was Jury who had summoned them.

And it was Jury to whom she had, just as silently, handed over the .22 automatic. No resistance. She hadn't said a word, had sat down in the same chair, had answered none of his questions, had not looked at him again.

The inquest was convened the following day merely to establish certain facts, such as the identity of the dead man. The identity of the perpetrator was clear.

Her name was Nell Healey and Jury had been right about her relationship to the dead man; she was his wife.

Given the reputation, wealth, and influence of the Citrine family in West Yorkshire, and given her lack of any criminal record, she was released on bail. That, Jury knew, would buy her at least a year of freedom; the case would be unlikely to get to the Crown Court before then, not with all the other stuff on the docket. The only question that had gone unanswered was why she'd done it. But largely it seemed to be the sympathy engendered by her past woes that tipped the scale in her favor.

2

It was those woes about which Jury was now reading in the newspaper that lay on his desk at New Scotland Yard. He remembered the Healey-Citrine names. It had happened eight years ago and had struck him as especially dreadful.

"Really sad, that was," said Detective Sergeant Alfred Wiggins, who'd dug out the clippings, and whose own reading matter was a copy of *Time Out*. "You wonder, how could anybody do that to a kid?" Wiggins was slowly stirring the spoon in his mug of tea and tapping it against the rim with all of the solemnity of an altar boy perfuming the air with incense.

Just as religiously, Wiggins opened a fresh packet of

Scott's Medicinal Charcoal Biscuits, taking pains that the wrapping wouldn't crackle. It was not often that Jury didn't answer him, but this was one of those times, and it disturbed Wiggins (as if it were his own fault) that the superintendent's mood, usually calm, almost soothing, was going sour over this case, and not Jury's own case, either. Thus, Wiggins felt impelled to talk doggedly on, even though it might be better to shut up. And since he was never one much for epigrammatic or witty turns of phrase, he would trap himself into further cliché-ridden sentiments.

Jury's mood was as black as the biscuit Wiggins was now crumbling into a cup of water, and, irrationally irritated by his sergeant's pursuit of some elusive and Platonic Idea of health just as he was reading of the kidnapping of one boy and the disappearance of the friend who had been with him. Jury said (rather sharpish, Wiggins thought), "Most people settle for digestives, Wiggins. And they don't have to stew them in water."

His quick response was triggered less by Jury's tone than by Jury's replying at all. Said Wiggins, brightly, "Oh, but digestives don't really *do* anything for you, sir. Now, this—"

Wanting to forestall a lecture on the benefits of charcoal to the digestive tract, Jury said, "I'm sure it does," and smiled to indicate that he'd only been joking, anyway.

It had happened in Cornwall when Billy Healey and his stepmother, Nell Citrine Healey, had been on holiday, together with a friend of Billy's named Toby Holt.

Keeping his eye on the newspaper, Jury shook a cigarette from a packet of Players and read Roger Healey's statement to the press. It was formal, almost pedantic, full of catch-phrases of grief and comments about his son's prodigious talent as a pianist, so that one almost got the idea that if the kidnapper didn't see to it he practiced every day, it would be similar to a diabetic going into insulin shock. The usual "we will do anything in our power to see our boy is returned . . ."; the usual ". . . police are working round the clock"; the usual.

Except that the stepmother had made no comment at all.

Jury tried to put himself in the place of a father whose child had been kidnapped. He had never had children, but he had been close enough to several that he could feel at least something of what it must be like to lose one. Certainly, he'd seen enough grief-stricken parents in his work. Some had been silent; some had gone in for marathon talking. But none had given a Hyde Park speech. Jury wasn't being fair, he supposed. After all, Healey was a music critic and columnist used to putting thoughts into words; he was an articulate man, and probably a composed one.

The photo of Billy himself looked almost out of place amidst this platitudinous talk. In the old shot of Billy Healey, the camera had caught the boy in a moment when he must have been looking toward something at a distance. His chin was raised, his mouth open slightly, his eyes transfixed and somehow puzzled. The angle of light eclipsed a portion of his face, bringing out the other in even bolder relief, accentuating the straight nose, high cheekbone. He was handsome, pale, his hair brownish and silky-looking. He looked, Jury thought, a little other-worldly, unapproachable, and with the intensity of his expression, unassailable. He looked more like his stepmother than his father.

And of her, there was only the picture in which she was being escorted from the house, and where she must quickly have drawn part of the paisley scarf she wore up over her face. Since her head was also down, the reporters were getting a very poor view. And taking a poor view, given the underlying tone of resentment that Mrs. Roger Healey was unavailable for comment. Her husband had done most of the talking.

The stepmother was good copy; she'd been the only one present, except for Billy's friend, when the boys had disappeared. Given the rather tasteless litter of photos and snaps this particular newspaper had mustered, it was clear they'd like to keep a story of the kidnapping humming along. There were several old snapshots of Billy, angled down the side of the account, one of him with a couple of schoolmates, very fuzzy. Another of him leaning against a fence with the other boy, Toby Holt. Sitting on a big stone slab in front of them was a small, dark-haired girl, squinting into the camera.

"And the chief's not too happy, as you can imagine," said Wiggins, following his own train of thought.

"He never is, not where I'm concerned."

"Wondering what you were doing in Stanbury, anyway."

"It's next to Haworth. I'm a big Brontë fan."

"When you were supposed to be in Leeds."

Jury looked up. "What is this, a catechism? Baleful mumbles."

"You might be witness for the Crown," Wiggins went on, relentlessly.

"Would he rather I'd be witness against? He knows damned well I won't be called as one. Sanderson will give my evidence. It's West Yorkshire's case, not mine."

Wiggins was making a little sandwich of two black biscuits and something slathered in between.

"What's that thing?"

"Charcoal biscuits and a bit of tofu and tahini. I'm a martyr to my digestion, as you know." The whole thing crumbled as he bit down on it; he wiped his mouth with the huge handkerchief tucked into his collar.

Jury looked up from the files and down at the notes Wiggins had made. "This publisher Healey worked for. Get me in to see him."

"Sir." Wiggins's hand hesitated over the telephone. "When?"

"This afternoon. Three, four."

"It's nearly two." The hand free of the tofu sandwich hovered over the telephone. "I was only thinking."

"That it's not my case. You're right. Get me in to see this publishing tyro, Martin Smart." Jury smiled.

Still Wiggins was slowly chewing his sandwich. "The guv'nor's complaining—"

Guv'nor? Racer? Since when was Wiggins calling him that?

"—you're waffling on a couple of cases. The Soho one, for example."

It was a drug-related death, nothing for C.I.D., something the Drug Squad could handle easily. Racer perfectly well knew this. Anything to keep Jury from using his talents in a more attention-grabbing way. Name and picture in paper. Racer hated it.

"I'm sick, Wiggins."

Wiggins put on his best bedside manner. "There's no question there, sir. Pale as a ghost you've been looking. You need leave, you do, not another case."

Jury grinned. "I know. So get me an appointment with Healey's publisher." Jury rose, feeling lighter than he had in weeks.

"I'm a martyr to my digestion, Wiggins. I'm going to see your guv'nor."

3

"Sick leave?"

Chief Superintendent A. E. Racer made an elaborate display of cupping his ear with his hand as if the ear couldn't quite believe it. "*Sick* leave?"

Jury knew that for Racer this was, if not the opportunity of a lifetime, at least the best one that had come along that day: here was a chink in the old Jury armor, a rent in the old corduroy jacket, an occasion that called for much more than telling Superintendent Jury a policeman's life was full of grief, since it apparently was. Jury could almost see the tiny guns taking aim in Racer's mind, trying for a salvo that would never go off.

"You've *never* applied for sick leave."

"Perhaps that's why I'm sick."

" 'Sick leave' is Wiggins's department. He takes it for all of us."

Request denied. Punch time clock. Wheel to grindstone. There're none of us who couldn't use a bit of a rest, *especially me. But you don't see me lying down on the job.*

"Well, he looks sick to *me*," said Fiona Clingmore, who'd come in to collect two big stacks of paper that she was now balancing on her forearms at the same time her eyes were on the booby-trap box Racer had rigged to catch the cat Cyril.

Did Racer really think he could outwit Cyril? Fiona had asked this question as she sat filing her nails into glossy claws. *Gets worse every day, the chief does.*

"If you want me to bring a note from my doctor, I will."

"I'm sure Wiggins can rip out a page from one of his prescription pads. Or furnish some Harley Street letterheads. His desk must be littered with them." Racer smiled his razorblade smile and looked at Jury over folded hands, the thumbs making propeller circles round each other.

Fiona looked from Jury to Racer.

"He's worn out, he is. You only have to look to see he's dead on his feet, practically."

Dressed in her usual black, this one the light wool dress with the tightly zipped bodice and pinch-pleated skirt, Fiona looked like she was ready to crash a funeral service, given the seamed stockings and black hood hugging her tarnished gold hair. Whenever he looked at Fiona, Jury thought of old trunks filled with taffeta tea-dance gowns, ribbon-tied letters, the little paper valentines punched from books that were handed round at school. . . .

Fiona, for all of her shoulder-shrugging, hip-thrusting brashness, was a picture of poignance. He'd better stop thinking about her and the past or pretty soon he'd be walking in his mind down the Fulham Road hand-in-hand with his mother, perhaps watching the wash go round in the launderette. A big dose of nostalgia was not what he needed to cure a big case of depression. Though sitting in Racer's office, looking at Racer's brilliant invention for trapping the cat Cyril helped to assuage *that.* It was a small wooden crate with a drop-screen, activated by pressure of foot or paw, whence the hinges would fold and the screen fall back, covering the box. Inside was a tin of sardines. Racer said he'd got this idea from old films he remembered about hunters and Hottentots (or some other aborigine) where the Hottentots were always falling through holes covered with vegetation into nets that quickly tightened.

He forgot that Cyril—the cat that had wandered into the halls of Scotland Yard seemingly out of nowhere—was not a Hottentot. Jury and Fiona marveled at the pure idiocy of the sardine box-trap. True, the screen banged shut. But all Cyril

had to do was nose it open when he had dined on his tin of
sardines. Thus Racer must have had some vague plan that
he would catch Cyril at it, that he would return from his
club and find claws scrabbling at the screen. If Racer and
Cyril (Fiona had said) ever met, it would be in Hell. And it
would be (Jury had said) a brief meeting indeed, since Cyril
could walk through flames without singeing his burnished
copper fur. Houdini (they had both agreed) would have got
free faster from that underwater escape if he'd had Cyril
with him.

Fiona had two dozen sardine tins in the filing cabinet,
which she was constantly using to replace the ones that
Cyril ate. Cyril loved the box; it was a second home. Slug-
gish from his meal, he would sometimes nap on the can and
Fiona would have to drag him out before Racer returned.
Jury told her not to worry; Cyril could scent Racer's approach from vast distances. The cat could hear him, smell
him, even see him when Racer was pushing open the glass
door of New Scotland Yard. They did not want Racer to
think his contraption wasn't working, or his inventiveness
might take a nose-dive and he'd revert to some other means
of disposal, like painting the carpet with poison.

Yes, thought Jury, the depression was lifting, as he saw
Fiona's eye rove the room in search of the cat Cyril. He was
missing, and Jury knew where he was, though Racer hadn't
twigged it. Jury screened his eyes with his hand in a posture
of sickliness that allowed him to look at the bottom of the
bookcase that Racer had converted into a drinks cabinet.
Tiny tinklings of glass emerged from it. Racer could cup his
ears all he wanted, but he was getting deaf.

The cabinet was fitted with doors easily opened by hitch-
ing a finger (or paw) in the handle. Unfortunately, Racer
would walk by occasionally and kick the door shut. He had
commissioned Fiona to get a lock and key, grumbling
(Fiona'd told Jury) about the char being at the booze bin
again. ("That's what he calls it, imagine? Common, ain't

it?" she'd added, tossing down her nail file and picking up the buffer.)

Inside the cabinet were two or three bottles each of Rémy, Tanqueray, Black Bush and aged Scotch, fallen off backs of vans (according to Fiona): gifts from villains that Racer had done little favors for. There was a miniature replica of a beer keg with a spout and a small cup for catching the whiskey. Right at eye level, if you were a cat. Cyril often wandered from the inner to the outer office in a weaving, wondering way.

"He'll get sick," Fiona had said after one of the booze bin jaunts.

"Cyril? You know he's only doing it to drive Racer crazy."

"Maybe he should have a liver test."

"If you want my opinion," said Fiona, nodding toward her beloved (now sick) superintendent, "a couple of weeks off—"

"No, I do not want your opinion, Miss Clingmore. I cannot recall the last time—if ever there was one—that I wanted your opinion." He was still twirling his thumbs, looking from his secretary to his superintendent with that *got you both on the run, haven't I?* expression.

Fiona pursed her bright red lips and said, hefting the pile of papers, "So you want me to shred this lot, I expect." She quietly chewed her gum and regarded him, poker-faced.

Racer's already alcohol-mottled face flushed a rosier red. "*Shred?* I do not *shred* papers."

"No? What about all them—those—letters to the commissioner last year. You surely didn't tell me to file—"

"Take those papers and your jeweled talons" (Fiona was deeply into nail art) "out of here. And see if that cat's roaming the halls and walking across the forensics lab tables. *Do you hear me?*"

With the weight of the papers, she still managed an indifferent shrug. "Well, I still say anyone that's not had sick

leave in fifteen years deserves more consideration." Turning
to go, she added, "I'll just take these to the shredder."
Fiona exited to the tiny tinkle of glass on glass.

2

Wiggins was still holding a copy of *Time Out* in one hand
and with the other pouring a dollop of vinegar into a glass of
water to which he then added a spoonful of honey.

Jury just shook his head. That Wiggins had got to the
point where he could measure his medications without even
looking up from his reading was proof of a practiced hand
indeed. "I'm not talking Fisherman's Friends and charcoal
biscuits, I'm talking *sick*, Wiggins." Jury was yanking open
the drawer of a filing cabinet. "The real thing, official
sickdom, sicko, down-for-the-count." Jury took one of the
forms from the drawer on his sergeant's desk. "Something
only a week or two in the country can fix. The damned
things have enough copies, don't they?" Jury fingered the
multicolored form.

Wiggins stopped tapping his honeyed spoon against the
glass and looked from *Time Out* to the form to Jury, frowning. "I don't understand, sir."

"Two weeks off, flat on my back. More or less." Jury
scratched his head over the wording of a question. *When
was this illness first evidenced?* He felt like answering, *My
first meeting with Chief Superintendent A. E. Racer. . . .*
He glanced over at Wiggins's desk. The sergeant was slightly
pale. It was, Jury supposed, one thing to be medicating one-
self for a sore throat with honey and vinegar while still at
one's desk; it was quite another to have illness stamped with
the imprimatur of officialdom.

Jury scratched away, half-conscious of the sergeant's
rather ragged breathing. Practicing for the doctor himself,
perhaps? He looked up; Wiggins was looking at Jury sadly.
Across the corner of the entertainment magazine he held

was a banner saying, *The Last Wind Blows.* Whatever that meant. The cover showed the face of a young man, head thrown back, eyes closed, mouth open. Round his neck was a strap holding a sleek white guitar. Across the picture of the guitarist was written *SIROCCO*, the white cursive letters streaming across the cover as if wind were blowing the letters away. "I need a different climate. Warm. Sand, sea, warm breezes."

Wiggins said, "My doctor suggested just that a while back. A year or two ago."

Jury smiled at the fact that now Wiggins sounded somewhat envious. "*What* are you putting down, sir? Not that you don't need time off—"

Jury nodded toward the magazine. "Or Time Out. Nervous collapse, how about that? He certainly looks as if he might have one."

Wiggins flipped the magazine over, looked at the cover, said, "Well, apparently he thinks he is. 'The Last Wind Blows.' It's his last concert."

"Whose?" Jury looked up. Where had he seen the face?

"Charlie Raine's. He's lead guitarist for this rock group, Sirocco. Surely you've heard of them."

That was it. Posters tacked up around London. "Last *concert?* God, he looks like he just started his last form in public school."

"A shame, isn't it?"

Jury penned in another answer to another inane question. "A publicity stunt, more likely."

"I don't know, sir. Actually, when you think of it, success is pretty hard on a person."

Putting aside his pen, Jury said, "We should know."

"What sea and what sands are you going to?" His smile was like the last tiny sliver of waning moon.

"Yorkshire."

The magazine fell to the desk; the pen dropped. They had been across the North Yorkshire moors years ago. It was not the high point in Sergeant Wiggins's career.

"*West* Yorkshire, Wiggins. Warmer."

Wiggins gave him a sickly smile.

Jury rose, stretched, and got out a cigarette. He went round to Wiggins's desk and added, looking down at the picture of the young singer, "And maybe awhile in Cornwall. Don't you have a day or two of leave coming up?" Jury nodded at the form. "Why don't you take it?"

Wiggins took fright momentarily. "I expect you could call that sea and sand," he said with an unusual turn of mild humor.

Jury lit a cigarette, looked at the face on *Time Out.*

"Heathrow was flooded with fans. They had enough police for a terrorist attack. Carole-anne was probably there," said Wiggins.

"Living Hell seems to be her group."

"Oh, that's hard to believe. They're passé."

Sergeant Wiggins often surprised him with a knowledge of unusual or arcane subjects, totally unrelated to his work.

"She's been poring over maps and timetables for a week now in her spare time."

"Is she taking a trip, then? I'll miss her."

Wiggins could move quickly from speculation to a *fait accompli.* And then, Jury realized, so could he. He shoved the form to one side, drumming his fingers impatiently. "What about the Devon-Cornwall constabulary? What did Superintendent—what was his name?"

"Goodall, sir. He's passed away, sir." Wiggins looked into his glass as if it were the funeral wine. "Last year it was. I got a chief detective inspector, though."

"What did he say?"

Wiggins took a large swallow from his glass of honey-vinegar elixir before answering. "Nothing very helpful; he seemed reluctant to go into it. That it had been over eight years, after all. Couldn't dredge up the details off the top of his mind."

"No one's asking for the top of his mind." Jury leaned back, looked up at the ceiling molding. A spider was swinging precariously from a thread of its broken web. "They must have a fairly thick dossier on that kidnapping; even I remembered the essentials, and I wasn't in Cornwall. Couldn't he take the trouble to have one of his lackeys open the files?"

"He was at home, sir. In Penzance. Said I'd got him in from his garden. Staking up some ornamental trees, or something, that a storm had—"

"Swell." Jury thought for a moment. "It's the Devon-Cornwall constabulary." He reached for the telephone. "Maybe Macalvie knows something."

4

The question wasn't whether Divisional Commander Macalvie knew *something* but whether he knew *everything*, a conviction that his Scene-of-Crimes expert assumed he held, and that she was in the process of challenging.

Since Gilly Thwaite was a woman, and Macalvie's lack of tolerance was legendary, none of her colleagues at the Devon headquarters had expected her to last five minutes in the bracing presence of Brian Macalvie.

But Macalvie's suffering others to live had nothing to do with sex, age, creed, species. He had no end of tolerance as long as nobody made a mistake in the job. And he was fond of saying that he understood and sympathized with the possibility of human error. If the monkey could really type *Hamlet,* he'd take the monkey on a case with him any day before ninety percent of his colleagues.

He couldn't understand (which is to say, he didn't give a bloody damn) why people found him difficult to work with. Occasionally, someone who'd actually got a transfer (requests for them had become routine) would burst into his office and tell him off. One had actually accepted a demotion to Kirkcudbright and told Macalvie Scotland was hardly far enough away from him; he'd asked for Mars. Macalvie was part Scot himself, and had just sat there, chewing his gum, warming his hands under his armpits, his copper hair glimmering in a slant of sun and the acetylene torches of his blue eyes turned down a bit from boredom, and replied that the sergeant was lucky it was Scotland because he'd forgot to do up his fly, and in Kirkcudbright maybe he could wear a kilt.

Not everyone on the force hated Macalvie; the police dogs loved him. They knew a cop with a good nose. The dogs belonged to the ten percent of the population Macalvie thought had it together. He only wished he could say the same for their trainers. And the fingerprint team. And forensics. And especially for the police doctors. At this point Macalvie had read so many books on pathology he could have earned a degree.

So ten percent—well, seven on an especially bad day—comprised that part of the population Macalvie thought might possibly know what they were doing. Gilly Thwaite was one, although one would be hard put to know why from the dialogue going on between them when Jury's call came through.

"You're not the pathologist, Chief Superintendent." Gilly Thwaite only tossed him a title, like a bone, when she was being sarcastic.

Actually, he didn't care what he was called, except when *he* was being sarcastic. He said, "Thank God I'm not *that* one. The last time he opened his murder bag I thought I saw a hammer and a spanner. He'd make a better plumber." He shoved the diagram she'd slapped on his desk aside and went back to the same deep immersion in the newspaper she'd chortled about when she came in. "*You? Reading on the job?*"

This he had ignored and he tried to ignore her now. Her argument was perfectly intelligent; it was just wrong. The item in the *Telegraph* was sending up his blood pressure.

Still, she mashed her finger at the diagram, a drawing of the trajectory a bullet might have made from entrance to exit wound. "The entrance wound is *here,* see, *here.* The bullet couldn't possibly have lodged *there*—"

He regarded her over the edge of the paper. "The bullet could've glanced off one of the ribs."

"Macalvie, you can't go into court and say our *own pathologist* is wrong."

"Not going to. I'm going to say he's not a pathologist, he's a plumber."

Gilly Thwaite was shaking her head rapidly; her ordinarily tight brown curls had got longer because she hadn't had time to cut her hair.

"Your hair is turning to snakes, Medusa."

She pounded her fist on his desk so hard the telephone jumped as it rang and she squealed in frustration.

He snatched it up. Anything for a reprieve. "Macalvie," he said.

"My God, Macalvie, are you sticking a pig?"

"Hullo, Jury. No, just Gilly Thwaite. Get out, will you?"

"I just got here," said Jury.

"Her." Silence. "I shut my eyes. She's still here. Go get a haircut." Back to Jury. "I was just reading about it."

Although he was slightly startled by Macalvie's mind-reading, he didn't question it. "Roger Healey, you mean."

"Why else would you be calling, unless you too have some inane theory on the trajectory of a bullet through human organs. She's still here. I've been teaching her about ribs. How every body has them, and there's a heart, and lungs. I think she's ready for her first term of pre-med. I'm flattered. The case was in the less-than-expert hands of Superintendent Goodall of our Cornwall constabulary."

"The chief inspector Wiggins talked to said the case was closed; he said he couldn't remember much about it."

"Billy Healey was walking along a public footpath with his mum—correction, *step*mum, which it seemed to make a big difference to some minds—walking along this footpath about four hundred yards below their house on the coast, an isolated house—"

Jury nodded to Wiggins quickly to pick up the extension. Wiggins did, very quietly, getting out his notebook at the same time.

"—near Polperro. That's about thirty, forty miles from Plymouth— Wiggins. How's January treating you?"

As if that were a cue, Wiggins sneezed and said hello, himself. "How'd you know I was here?" Wiggins smiled at this little magic act of the divisional commander's.

"Nobody breathes like you, Wiggins. It's an especially uplifting sound. Shall I start again?"

Said Jury, "I think I can remember those details. I'll try hard."

"Let's hope so. Anyway, it was around four, maybe a little after, and they were walking. Nell Healey—that's the stepmother—said that they'd been walking the path so that Billy could look for bird eggs. They usually did this in the afternoon, she said, even though they never found any, but it was a fantasy both of them seemed to get a kick out of. Anyway, Billy said he was going in to fix some sandwiches for him and Toby. Toby was indoors.

"The way his stepmother put it, Billy ran and walked by turns over the ground back to the house and would turn and wave every so often." He paused and Jury heard some rustling of papers and what sounded like the click of Macalvie's cigarette lighter.

Wiggins frowned. "Thought you'd given that up, Superintendent."

"I wish you'd join my forensics team, Wiggins. They can't see their own shoes much less through telephones."

"You know what your doctor—"

"Wiggins." Jury gave him a look.

"Oh, sorry, sir. Sorry to interrupt, Mr. Macalvie. He'd just gone back to the house for the sandwiches."

Macalvie continued. "He didn't come back."

There was a pause and an uncharacteristic clearing of his throat, as if something had lodged there. One might have thought the divisional commander was getting emotional.

Wiggins didn't take it this way: "How many packs a day are you up to by now?"

"Into thin air, you'd think. She waited and finally went

back to the house. Thought he'd got caught up in some game with Toby, couldn't find either of them, and then thought maybe he was doing the hide-and-seek bit with her. So for a while she wasn't anxious. And, of course, it's not like losing sight of your kid in the middle of Oxford Street or Petticoat Lane. Then she looked outside, everywhere, and *then* she called the police. Do you want all this detail or just the highlights?"

"I'm amazed you remember all this detail. It wasn't even your case."

Another pause. "Well, let's say I took an interest. A kid being held for five million in ransom money—"

Wiggins whistled, went on writing.

"That's a case you can hardly avoid developing an interest in. And watching Goodall making a right cock-up of it. There was one botched attempt by his men to make contact with the kidnappers. I was detective sergeant then." The tone was a combination of wistfulness and wonder.

Even Macalvie had once been a constable. Even as a divisional commander, he didn't hesitate to do constable's duty. Jury had watched him write a traffic ticket once. Macalvie's net got tossed out and anything that came up he inspected closely. Anyone else in his position would throw back the little-fish cases. Macalvie would dissect minnows. "You assigned yourself to it, more or less?" asked Jury, smiling.

"I got myself assigned to it."

Even as a police sergeant, Macalvie was known to be better than most of the men on the force.

"You know the story about the actual investigation; you've obviously read the accounts—"

"I'd rather hear your version."

"I don't blame you. I got myself assigned to the Healey case because there is nothing, *nothing* as touch-and-go as an abduction. I'd sooner try to balance on razorblades than negotiate a kidnapping. You know the pressures that exist there and the chances of getting the person back. The need for rational thought. Well, it's pretty hard to be rational when it's your kid. And let me tell you the emotions churning round that house could have bulldozed half of Dockland."

" '*I've told you and told you not to come here alone,*' Citrine—Nell Healey's father—kept saying. People love hindsight; we'd rather look back any day than forward. What a scene, what a scene. Blaming the kid's stepmother for not taking better care of him. Then there was the father, Healey, who was pretty much useless, ranting around and yelling at the mother—*step*mother, excuse me—'*How could you leave him alone, Nell? Didn't you ever stop to think Billy might be a target for kidnappers?*' I ask you, Jury. 'Mummy, I'm going to make a sandwich,' and she's supposed to be sitting there wondering if he'll be kidnapped? Okay, I'm not a father—"

Jury smiled slightly.

"—but it seemed to me old Roger could have been offering comfort and succor to his wife instead of hurling insults. Citrine was at least level-headed enough to get down to business. He seemed pretty cool, though it was taking its toll on him, obviously."

Watching the tiny spider repairing its web, Jury asked, "How did she react? Nell Healey? What did she say to all this negligence bit?"

"Nothing."

"Nothing?" Jury frowned, looked over at Wiggins scratching away on his pad. He was better than a tape recorder.

At the other end of the telephone, Macalvie let out a sigh. "Nothing. She was sitting on a window seat, a kind of bay window, and looking out, as if to sea. I thought she was out of it, frankly. In shock, or something. All the while Goodall was talking. He had a very soothing voice, and he was trying to assure Citrine—all of them—that the police were doing everything in their power. He gave the Kidnapping Speech, or what I think of as the Kidnapping Speech: '*Mr. Healey, as we're dealing with a crime that can mean life imprison-*

ment, it's always possible that the victim might be harmed in some way. Naturally, you need some assurance that the boy is still alive—' The Kidnapping Speech went on. How, if Citrine paid this ransom, it would be best to have a detective go with him, the usual crap. Argument over more police intervention further endangering the boys' lives. Argument over marked bills. Argument over police going along. Argument over publicity. Argument over Roger Healey *insisting* on paying, period. Charles Citrine talking to somebody from the bank—there was a V.I.P. there from Lloyd's. It went on."

"But Citrine finally refused to pay up."

There was another pause. "It wasn't Citrine, see."

"The ransom wasn't paid."

"Citrine was directing the Lloyd's person to get the money ready. I was sick of listening to the usual codswallop of junk about 'options' and 'alternatives.' So I said, 'You hand over that money and you're signing both those kids' death warrants.' "

Jury shook his head. "That's the 'negotiation'-type thing we're talking about?"

"Jury, you know and I know, and I'm sure *Goodall* knew the chances. Not just the chances but the game. You know the way people like that think—"

"I wish I did."

"Then I'm telling you: they say to themselves, Now I've got the money, what do I do with the evidence? Especially if it has eyes and ears? At least *until* they get the money, there's a chance they'll keep the victim alive."

"I'm not arguing with you, Macalvie. Tell me the story."

Another pause. It seemed to worry Macalvie if someone wasn't arguing with him. Some people were like that; they needed it just to sort things out. Macalvie wasn't asking for approval; he was asking for consultation. "Okay. The minute I said that, they all started rabbiting on, the biggest rabbit being Superintendent Goodall, who quickly told me to shut up. Actually, he went frostbitten with anger. Roger

Healey shouted at me. It was the 'how-can-you-know?' routine. Citrine looked pretty ashen, but at least he was trying to keep his head. Finally, he said, 'You might be right. But then you might be wrong.' "

"That pretty much covers the ground." He could almost see Macalvie smile. "Then?"

"Then he said he'd pay any amount of money to get Billy back."

"But you changed his mind?"

Silences from Macalvie were unusual. There'd been at least three in this accounting, and now there was another. Jury could almost hear the air hum out there in Exeter. "No. It was Nell Healey's mind. She turned her head from that window she'd been staring through and gave me a look that could cut diamonds. I must admit it even pinned *me* to the wall. Well, you've met her—"

"Just go on, Brian."

"And she said, 'I think you're right; don't pay it.' And then she turned back to the window. Here I thought she wasn't taking in anything, that she was in shock, that—well, let me tell you, that got to me, that did. Apparently, she'd been taking it all in: Goodall's speech, the others' yelling, her old man's intentions—all of it. And hell broke loose. I thought Roger Healey would throttle her right then and there. It was the exact opposite scenario, wasn't it? You see all these films where the wife is wild, tearful, pleading for the rational husband to pay, pay, pay."

"But he didn't. I don't understand, if it was two against one."

"It could have been a dozen against one. She had the money."

Jury sat up suddenly. "I thought it was Roger Healey's or the father's money."

"No way. Those two had some, sure. Healey had a little, Charles Citrine quite a bit of his own. But not five million, not *that* kind of money. It wasn't them the kidnappers were holding up; it was the stepmother. *She* had the money. Her mother Helen's money, apparently, a fortune. Some left to the husband—but he had his own, anyway—a bequest to the sister-in-law, the rest to her daughter."

It was true that the accounts said that the Citrine-Healey family had refused to pay the ransom. Not which one of them. Charles Citrine had been the spokesman; therefore, the assumption was that it was his considered opinion that the police were right; paying the money would do nothing to insure his grandson's safety. Indeed, it might jeopardize it.

Jury's head was in his hand; he was thinking of Nell Healey, remembering those hours during which he'd followed her.

"Eight years later," said Macalvie, "she kills her husband. Why?"

Rubbing his hand through his hair as if that might wake up his brain, Jury said, "I don't know, Macalvie."

Another silence. "That is one awesome lady, Jury."

Thus did Nell Healey join the ten percent of the population Divisional Commander Macalvie could live with.

5

The narrow house in the street in Mayfair was flanked by a jeweler and an art dealer, both of them so pricey that each shop window displayed only a single piece: a sapphire necklace that seemed to float above its crystal display pole; and, in the art dealer's, a single painting in a heavy gilt frame suspended by nearly invisible wires. Mayfair itself seemed suspended in some dimension that escaped the pull of gravity.

Inside the offices of Smart Publishing, Jury found another dimension of light and muted sound—sylvan music piping from hidden speakers that went well with walls painted watery yellow; the rooms, the hallway were relieved only by an off-white that shaded into the pale color. It had the look of meringue, possibly conceived by the editor of the cookery column.

From what Jury could tell in the reception room where he sat thumbing through *Segue,* there were two other magazines—a glossy one called *Travelure,* and an artier number called *New Renascence.* He loved that title. It was devoted to, or divided between, haunts and habitats of the moneyed. Interiors filled with marble, mauve curtains, Kirman carpets, and gloved servants; al fresco scenes by sun-beaded pools; acres of landscaped gardens and deep-shadowed paths through cypress and lacy willows, made for trysts and meditations. A world, in other words, that existed nowhere except between the covers of *New Renascence.*

Segue was by far the most serious of the three, in addition to being the most expensive, the richest and glossiest. No tales of the buskers' lot here, Jury was sure. On the cover was a serious-looking, serious-minded cellist against a backdrop of blue velvet. Jury was trying to place the name, but giving up because he knew he'd never really heard of the cellist, when the receptionist walked in with a cup of coffee. Bone china, not plastic.

She stopped short and asked him his business. He told her he had an appointment to see Mr. Martin Smart. When that failed to budge her, he added (after shoving his warrant card forward), or anyone else who just happened to know Roger Healey—did she, for instance? That sent her quickly to her desk, where the china cup and saucer rattled as she picked up the interoffice phone.

Having got the okay, she said, in a high, strident voice that detracted from a soft, mellow body, that she would take him to Mr. Smart. Three flights up, and they hadn't a lift.

He followed her from staircase to staircase. Her hips swayed nicely beneath the gray silk dress whose shadows shimmered and dissolved as she moved. Otherwise, everything about her seemed to come to points: the tips of her breasts and the tips of her shoes; her chin, her tilted eyes, the wing shape made stronger by artful application of kohl liner; her glimmering hairdo of shellacked, highlighted spikes. She reminded Jury of a small, rocky promontory. As he followed down the hall of the top floor, he felt a pang; it was poignant in a way; for she now reminded him of a thirteen-year-old getting herself up in an older sister's garb, who would have been excessively pretty had she not tried to be glamorous.

She stood at the doorway of Mr. Smart's office, which was empty of Mr. Smart, and said, "He'll be here in just a minute."

Jury nodded. "Thanks." When Jury smiled at her, she smiled herself, but uncertainly, and kept her hand on the porcelain doorknob, swinging the door slightly back and forth, biting her lip, perhaps thinking she might linger there herself for the moment of Mr. Smart's absence. She had very small white teeth. Definitely thirteen, he decided, even though she was thirty.

Jury seated himself in a pricey-looking leather chair that seemed, in its softness, to fold around him. The dark green walls stenciled in old gold beneath an old gold molding, the floor-to-ceiling bookcases, the library steps, the mahogany escritoire that housed a wet-bar, the massive desk, the Italian leather furniture all struck Jury as expecting the imminent return of the CEO. The desk itself was piled with papers and magazines, all artfully arranged in stand-and-deliver stacks. Jury craned his neck to look at the wet-bar. No cat in there; Mr. Smart had settled instead for Courvoisier and hand-cut crystal. The whole office looked hand-cut. Indeed it was the most bespoken-appearing room Jury had ever seen—everything measured, trimmed, and cut to precise tastes.

Jury turned and half rose when one of the personnel (the only one not dressed to the nines that Jury had seen in these offices) stalked in, leaving in his wake a trail of papers, plunked the rest on the desk, and turned to leave, nodding to Jury.

At least Jury thought he had turned to leave. Instead he folded his arms under sweaty armpits and asked Jury what he wanted, in an abstracted and rather unfriendly tone. But before Jury could answer, he'd navigated the lake of the desk, sat down, and reduced everything on it to a shambles within five seconds.

Martin Smart made annoyed clicking sounds with his tongue, murmured he wished to hell she'd leave his stuff alone, how was he supposed to find a goddamn thing? The ordered desk files became a swimming mass. Apparently satisfied, he stuffed a cold-looking, rather shredded stump of cigar in his mouth, folded his arms, and sent papers aflutter as his arms clamped down on them. He said to Jury, "Something I can do for you? Oh, don't bother with that."

Jury had bent in his chair to pick up a few of the orphaned papers that Smart had left in his wake.

"I can find them easier if they're down there. What can I do for you?" he repeated, round his cold cigar. He seemed to be running his hands underneath the papers searching for matches, gave it up, opened a drawer, peered in, gave that up, and asked Jury if he'd like a drink.

"No, thanks. Like a light?"

Smart yanked the cigar from his mouth, looked at its unpleasant condition, shrugged and said, "Why bother?" He put it down on the papers. "You're a superintendent, right?"

"Right."

Mr. Smart pursed his lips and shook his head in wonder. "How'd you get that high? Wha'd'ya have to do to get way up there?"

He sounded genuinely interested, as if he were either doing a bio on Jury or thinking of applying for a job with the C.I.D.

"It's not the rarefied air you might imagine. Chief superintendent, assistants to commissioner, and the commissioner himself. They're all above me. No one's above you."

Martin Smart seemed to like this analogy. He smiled broadly. "Wrong. You're forgetting the readers." He squinted, leaned over his mess of papers, and said, "Superintendent Jury. Jury, Jury, Jury." He tapped a staccato beat with his index fingers. "Where've I heard that name? Oh, hell. You were the one at that place up in West Yorkshire when—"

"Roger Healey was shot." Jury couldn't somehow bring himself to say *murdered*.

Smart clapped his hand to his forehead. He made a quick turn in his leather swivel chair, rolled it over to the green-curtained window bay, sat like a patient in a wheelchair staring out from his hospital prison, then turned and inched the chair back. "Roger." He found a cigarette and a silver-brushed lighter that had managed to go missing under a cover of old *Segue* copies. "Hell."

"You were close to him, were you?"

"Not exactly. He wasn't a staffer; he was a contributor. But absolutely one of the best. First rate. A few times he'd bring in a piece and we'd talk. A nice man. A really nice man. Old Alice out there"—he poked his cigarette toward the hall—"had a real thing for him. All the women did. Well, he was nice to them, wasn't he? Bring round flowers and candy." He knocked some ash from his cigarette with the tip of his little finger. "A damned bloody shame, that was. No one can figure it out."

"Did you ever meet Mrs. Healey?"

"Never did, no."

"Any of your staff know Roger Healey? Aside from the flowers and candy?" Jury smiled to take the bite from his tone.

"Might ask Mavis. Mavis Crewes." He leaned back and stared up at the rococo ceiling molding with a frown that suggested he had no idea who'd done the fancy plastering job or why. "Mavis, Mavis, Mavis."

Martin Smart seemed to have a ritualistic fascination with names. "Who's she, and where?" Jury had his notebook out.

"Managing editor of *Travelure*. Isn't that a hell of a name? I wanted to call it *Travel*, period. Our marketing people—and Mavis, of course—argued there must be a dozen going under that name." He flashed Jury a smile. "Find one. Find one that isn't tarted up with something in the name that's to make you think you're heading for the end of the rainbow. So I suggested calling it *Holy Grail*. You know, I honestly think they'd have bought it. Anyway, Mavis is good at her job; she's been thirty years in the business. I leave her alone."

The implication was that he was happy to have Mavis leave *him* alone. "Is she here today?"

Again Smart's eyes lifted to the ornamental ceiling as he shook his head. "I told her she could work at home whenever she wanted. Naturally, she travelures a lot of the time. She's big on Africa. Kenya. So forth. Her husband was a safari nut. She lives somewhere near Kensington Gardens. Old Alice can give you the address. Hold it." Smart hit the intercom, got old Alice, and scribbled down the information. "Here." He handed the address to Jury. Then he sat scratching his fingers through his hair, hard, making a spiky, stand-up mess of it. It appeared to be his way of reducing stress, something like Churchill and his ten-minute naps. "Since it's clear that the wife murdered him, why are you here? I don't understand."

"Just trying to tie up a few loose ends."

"Having to do with Roger?"

"Not only Mr. Healey."

"Pretty soon you're going to say 'routine investigation, sir.' The papers made a big thing out of the kidnapping of those boys all that time ago."

Jury nodded.

"Does that tie in?"

"I don't know."

"You're a mine of information." Smart washed the sea of papers about for no apparent reason. "You should work on one of these rags we publish."

"Everyone liked Roger Healey, then?"

Martin Smart gave Jury a sharp look. "Far as I know. Shouldn't we have done?"

"Of course. It's just that a person who's universally liked . . ." Jury shrugged.

"A cynic, too." The trick smile showed itself again. "I know what you mean, but I don't know what you're up to. I wouldn't say *universally* liked. There's probably a few concert musicians who could have flayed him, I don't know. The thing about his reviews, though, is they weren't laced with stings and arrows. Edgy, sometimes." He started gathering up papers and stacking them neatly, then stopped and dealt them out as if they were playing poker. "Of course, there's Duckworth."

"Duckworth?"

"Morry. He's American. Rhythm and blues, straight

blues, heavy metal, reggae, New Wave, that stuff. They call it rock and roll."

"He doesn't—didn't like Roger Healey?"

"Means little. Duckworth doesn't like *any*one. Except me. I found him glued to his earphones in the Village—New York City. Let me tell you, it took a lot to lure him over here. I hate that effing word. I only toss him out because you're clearly determined to find *someone* who didn't like Roger. Sounds a bit biased, if you don't mind my saying so. But I'm sure the Met has reasons the mind will never know. Here's Duckworth's number." Again, he handed Jury a scrap of paper, torn from a letter from the chairman of the board, Jury noticed when he looked at it. "It's probably a prison cell."

"The Met appreciates your help. Could I have a look at some old issues of *Segue?*"

"Healey's reviews? Of course." Smart hit the intercom again, spoke to his secretary, then leaned back with his hands laced behind his head. "Superintendent, what *are* you looking for?"

Jury pocketed his notebook, rose, thanked Martin Smart, and said, "Nothing in particular."

"You really *should* work here."

Jury turned to go, turned back. "Would you mind if my sergeant came round in a day or two to talk to some of your staff?"

Smart gazed again at the ceiling. "Hell, no. Send the Dirty Squad for all I care. Liven the place up." He screwed up his face. "Why the hell would she kill him?" He looked at Jury. "Maybe they were having a bit of trouble?" His expression was perfectly serious.

"I expect you could say that." Jury said good-bye.

2

Jury could not quite believe the interior of this house off Kensington Gardens, near Rotten Row. From the outside, it was just another narrow, Georgian building, with its yellow door and dolphin-shaped brass knocker.

But the inside seemed to stretch endlessly and cavernously to this room in which he now sat with Mavis Crewes, a room that seemed part solarium, part enormous floor-to-ceiling aviary full of bird plumage, bird twitter, bird greenery. A tiny, bright eye, opening and closing like a pod, regarded him through the fronds of several palmettos.

Nor was it the only greenery, for round about the room were set tubs of plants, some treelike and overhanging; some tough and flat-leaved; some feathery and ferny; but all suggesting jungle heat and dust. This was further enhanced by the near-life-sized ceramic leopard looking slant-eyed out of the rubber plants, and by the boar's head, open-mouthed and glaring glassily from the wall to Jury's right. Behind him sat a gun case; his feet were trying to miss contact with the zebra rug beneath the table carved from a tree her last husband had carted back from Nosy-Bé. A tree (Mavis Crewes had told him) that was *fady*—taboo. Her husband wasn't superstitious.

He was also dead. Jury wondered from what.

Jury and Mavis Crewes sat in this solarium, surrounded by strange exotic plants, grass shields, spears, and Ibo masks, drinking coffee and Evian water with a cut-glass carafe of whiskey standing by as a fortifier.

Jury kept trying to wave away the thin stems of a hanging bougainvillea. The surroundings that he himself found suffocating, Mavis Crewes apparently found soothing and restful. Between little spasms of speech, the breakings off partly the result of talking of Roger Healey's death, but also partly her own natural abruptness. A tiger's eye stone glinted on the hand that fingered a petal here, a leaf there. There was a chunky diamond on the finger of the hand slowly twisting the glass of Evian water that helped in what Jury imagined to be her campaign to stay travel-thin.

He suspected, given her editorial experience, that she was in her fifties, but she had been coiffed, massaged, starved, and sunlamped down to forty. The latest fashion (Jury knew from glancing into various Regent Street shops) was the safari look: desert colors or camouflage greens, loose shirts and skirts with low, heavy belts, nothing he could imagine any woman found flattering. She wore a bush jacket over a sand-colored shirt and Hermès boots.

In this environment, and with her thin, slightly muscular look, all of that fitted Mavis Crewes rather perfectly. Except, of course, that they didn't resemble mourning, something she had brought up at the beginning of their interview. She hadn't anything black, you see, and she hardly thought it the time for a shopping spree, given the death of her "dear, old friend." If she thought mourning clothes appropriate two weeks after his death, she must have meant to imply he had been very dear indeed. With her swept-back, pale blond hair, he wondered if perhaps she knew black didn't show her to any advantage. The eyes he had thought at first to be black were a murky jungle green.

After the divorce of the first and the death of the second husband, she had stuck her thumb in the pie again and apparently pulled out the biggest plum thus far, Sir Robert Crewes, safari buff, a Knight of the Royal Victoria Order, higher than the OBE her cousin had managed to reel in. Mavis Crewes was very impressed by the title, though knighthoods abounded among civil servants, members of the Royal household, and the foreign service. It was peppered with them probably as a reward for one's going off somewhere (anywhere) to represent the country.

It was not that Jury doubted that Mavis Crewes's grief was genuine; it was just that he wondered how deeply she felt about anything—except, perhaps, the venomous anger for Healey's wife. Although she seemed to refuse to acknowledge her as such: "that woman" was the phrase she used when speaking of Nell Healey.

"Hard as nails," she said now, still twisting the delicate glass between thumb and forefinger as if it were a stem she might snap. She sighed. "That woman."

"Tell me about her, Mrs. Crewes."

"Nell was the second wife." Jury wondered that Mavis Crewes, who had second-wifed it aplenty, could rationalize this. "And not the boy's mother." She threw Jury a basilisk glance.

"What happened to the mother?"

"Went off to the Swiss Alps. Had a skiing accident."

"You think the stepmother couldn't have cared about Billy, then?"

He had said the wrong thing, or in the wrong tone. She sat back again, arms resting on the arms of the white wicker chair, flexing her fingers. "You sound as if you sympathize with her, Superintendent. That's absolutely astounding. But you couldn't have known her well." She gave him a small, cunning smile, as if they'd reached an agreement. "I'm not sure what your role is in this. What are you investigating? That she killed Roger is not open to question. That she managed to be released until her trial certainly *is*. Women like Nell Healey always seem to get what they want. She's flint, she's stone."

Jury hoped his smile would offset his words. "Stone generally meets with hard resistance itself."

"If you're implying *Roger* was hard, you've got it all wrong. He was totally devastated. You didn't know the man. You didn't know his warmth, his charm, his—"

"But you did," said Jury innocently.

She was smart enough to sidestep that. "They'd nothing in common. He loved travel, new experiences, new . . . sensations. He had an appetite for life. She was content to do nothing but stay in that godforsaken part of *York-*

shire. . . ." She looked round at the masks and guns as if Tanzania were more accessible.

"With Billy," said Jury. She flashed him a look. "You've been their guest, I take it."

"Yes. Several times. Charles Citrine thought of Roger as his own son."

"Mr. Healey sounds like a paradigmatic husband, father . . . friend." He let that word hang there. "Martin Smart admired him." He tried to smile, found it tough going.

"Oh, *Martin* . . ." She forgot the Evian, went for the whiskey decanter, giving Jury a dismissive glance. "Martin seems to think publishing's a sort of game; he sometimes hires the most *in*appropriate people—"

"They certainly looked, from the offices I passed, very old-school-tie-ish."

"Then you didn't pass Morpeth Duckworth. God. What a vile person. Do you know I caught him in my office one day with a mop and pail. Cleaning."

Jury wiped his hand across his mouth. "Why?"

"God *knows*. Well, he looks like a janitor, doesn't he? He's done it to others, too. Even Martin. Martin finds it excruciatingly funny. I think Duckworth's going through our files. He's American."

"Oh."

He heard calfskin whisper as she shifted in the wicker chair, crossing and recrossing her legs. "What are you asking these questions for? What's all this to do with Nell Healey?"

"I was thinking more of Billy. That case was never solved. I'm sorry." He rose. "You've been very helpful at what must be a terribly painful time."

That he would leave with so little resistance took her by surprise. "No, no. I'm just on edge." The tan, sinewy hands waved him down again.

Jury sat, gave her that reassuring smile, said, "How long had the Healeys been married before the boy disappeared?"

From the murky depths of her eyes came a glint like a

spearhead. She ran the hand with the whiskey glass over the folds of her skirt, her head down. "Five or six years," she said vaguely.

Jury was sure she knew exactly how many years. The five years between six and eleven would have been awfully important for any child, especially a child with a new mother. But as he felt Mavis Crewes was disengaging, was pulling away from his questions now, he did not want to explore the relationship—or her version of it—between the little boy and his stepmother directly.

"Nell was—is—a Citrine." Impatiently waving away Jury's puzzlement, she went on. "The Citrine family is one of the oldest in the county. Old blood, old money. Charles *refused* a peerage."

If you can believe that. The hefting of her neatly plucked eyebrows implied that Jury must himself find this unimaginable. He kept his smile to himself, this time, wishing his friend Melrose Plant could hear this. "Kindly Call Me God" was his acronym for the holders of the KCMG. The OBE was the "Old Boy's End."

Only the cockatoo, beating a wing and turning round on its stand, reacted to Charles Citrine's crazy behavior as Mavis went on. "Don't misunderstand me, I've nothing against the Citrines. In spite of *her.* Yes, I expect I do resent that they've enough money and influence to bail her out after the arraignment. They can get her out, but they cannot get her off. No question of that!" She took a tiny black cigar from a silver-chased box and accepted Jury's light before she sat back behind a plume of smoke. "He's really quite a fine person, Charles. He's had a lot to do with improving the quality of life up there. In West Yorkshire, I mean. Gotten subsidies for the mills, created work where others seem to be destroying it—well, that's Thatcherism, isn't it? Charles is very public spirited, has been appealed to again and again to sit for Commons. . . ."

And she went on at some length about Nell Healey's father, ending with, "I wrote him a note. I wanted him to know that I sympathize. I thought it appropriate."

The interview that had begun an hour ago with the appearance of a lover's display of grief seemed fast degenerating into a discussion of unemployment and politics. No. All of this talk suggested to Jury that Charles Citrine's high visibility was for Mavis Crewes something other than as a possible political candidate. She must have been ten years older than Healey. And was probably ten years younger than Citrine.

"Of course, it's lonely for him, I expect, living in that enormous place with only Irene. Calls herself Rena. Not much company, I shouldn't think, for a man with Charles's intellect. To tell the truth, in the last few years I think the sister has gone quite mad. Well, that sort of thing usually goes downhill, doesn't it?"

"Not uphill, at any rate. If you're speaking of a psychosis."

"Charles excepted, I'd say the entire family's round the twist. God knows, *Nell*'s testament to *that*." Having given over the Evian water to the whiskey now, she poured herself another glass, drank it off, topped it up, restoppered the bottle. "To tell the truth: I wonder if Roger didn't marry her for it. Money, I mean." She looked at Jury as if he might confirm this, since he'd been in the same room with Nell Healey, circumstances notwithstanding.

"It's not uncommon." His smile was a little icy. "But couldn't he have loved her?"

She tossed back the whiskey. "What was there to love except money? Oh, she's not un*attract*ive, but . . ."

Jury gave a slight headshake. Perhaps she really believed it. "What happened to Mr. Citrine's wife? Nell Healey's mother?"

"Dead." Beneath the tan, there was a rosy flush. "Charles is a widower—" Then she must have seen the implication of this and went hurriedly on to say, "It was probably a blessing that she never lived to see this."

With that hackneyed sentiment, even the cockatoo screeched.

6

The most celebratory activity on New Year's Day had occurred when a sybaritic gang of children from the nearby market town of Sidbury had come to Long Piddleton and somehow gained entrance through the back of the Jack and Hammer, to steal up the stairs to the box room on the first floor. From here they had wriggled out on the beam, dismantled the blue-coated, mechanical Jack, and the lot of them carted the wooden figure back to Sidbury. This had happened three years ago, and it had happened again three nights ago. To hear Dick Scroggs talk, the Sidburyites were only matched by the Newcastle football fans for pure rowdiness.

Marshall Trueblood, dressed no less colorfully than "Jack" himself, was seated at one of the window tables in the Jack and Hammer with his friend Melrose Plant, both of them working away at a large book of cut-outs, and occasionally making sounds of commiseration.

Scroggs, publican of the Jack and Hammer, was slapping over the pages of his *Telegraph* and rolling a toothpick round in his mouth as he bent over the saloon bar. He still hadn't recovered from the New Year's night revelries when the "whey-faced gang of roughs" (as Marshall Trueblood described them) had been surprised by police in a frozen field of coarse grass and bracken, just as one of them had touched a match to some dry branches arranged round the mechanical man that was the pub's pride and joy and the most colorful thing in Long Pidd with the possible exception of Marshall Trueblood. The Jack was rescued with its aqua-marine trousers barely singed and restored to Dick Scroggs.

"It's hard enough to have to put up with the childish pranks of our *own* kiddies," said Trueblood, as he carefully separated a Dracula face from the cardboard surrounding it, "without these rowdies from Sidbury tramping up to the village."

Melrose Plant did not answer. He was frowning over the task of affixing one of the legs to the cut-out torso, his long, elegant fingers trying to work a tiny tab through a narrow slit. "Haven't you poked out the cape yet? I'm nearly finished."

"I mean, the whole thing is too silly for words anyway; I don't see why we have to put up with these childish pranks. When the little ninnies come to *my* door on New Year's Day, I put my hands on their shoulders, turn them about and about and get them all dizzy and watch them go drunkenly off. They think I'm playing. Good Lord." He put a crease in the chalk-white face where the instructions had said *Fold* and handed it to Melrose Plant. "Here."

"Do the cape." Melrose nodded at the big book of punch-out figures.

Marshall Trueblood had found this cardboard collection of put-together monsters and ghouls at the Wrenn's Nest bookshop ("in a fight to the death with some beastly child," for it was the last one). "Do you think we should be doing this here, in public? I mean, she might just come in." He leaned back and lit a jade-green Sobranie and regarded Melrose through a scrim of smoke.

"She won't come in; she's busy packing," said Melrose, who had successfully attached both of the legs to the torso and was picking up the face. "Or, I should say, staring at her trunks and then at the wall. I'm thirsty." He called over his shoulder to Dick Scroggs for another round.

"I can't really believe she means to do it, can you?"

"She's been engaged to him for four years; I imagine she's

beginning to feel rather self-conscious. Have you got the boat?"

"Right here, old sweat." Trueblood leaned a small, canoe-shaped boat against his pint glass. He had found it in a lot of goods acquired at an antiques auction. It had been painted pale blue and bits fixed to the ends so that it looked like a gondola. He had punched out a rat to put in it, which he placed temporarily in the tin ashtray. "Dick! Another round, if you please!"

Dick Scroggs apparently didn't, for he kept his eyes on the newspaper. Finally he gave in to the calls from the public bar on the other side and went round the bar to lavish his attention on the dart players.

"Oh, hell," said Trueblood. "Must we wait on ourselves? That she's been engaged to him, old trout," he continued as he poked out the red-lined cape, "has nothing to do with her marrying him."

Melrose picked up their glasses and went to the bar as Dick came round the other side. "Two more, Dick." As Dick set the glasses beneath the pulls, Melrose turned the paper round. Dick had been in the process of cutting the article about the murder in West Yorkshire from it. He possessed a small, hook-billed instrument for the purpose of sawing odds and ends from papers and magazines. Melrose wondered if he was tracking Jury's career for him, pasting up articles in a scrapbook.

As he released the beer pulls and they stood watching the foam rise on the pints of Old Peculier, Dick observed, "Seems a pity, dunnit? You wonder what'd ever make a woman kill her husband that way." He drew a knife across the cap of foam and placed the glasses on the counter. He was, of course, dying to know if Melrose had been talking to Jury about the case. "Well, I expect the poor woman'd never be quite right in the head with her boy being kidnapped and all. You read about that, I expect?" Perhaps this salacious morsel had escaped Melrose's attention.

"I did indeed. Well, one certainly can't complain in this

case that the police are never around when you need them. Thank you, Dick." He took their drinks and returned to the table, stopped dead as he saw a figure pass by the window behind Marshall Trueblood. "Oh, hell! Here she comes!" The figure disappeared momentarily and they heard the door to the pub open. "Quick! Here!" Melrose shoved the cut-out book and canoe toward Trueblood and slapped his *Times* over the cardboard Dracula.

Whispered his friend, "Don't give it to *me,* damn all. . . ." Trueblood hurriedly shoved the canoe-gondola behind him and the torn pieces into the book and waved it wildly around before sitting on it.

"Hullo, Vivian; thought you were home counting lira," said Melrose pleasantly.

Vivian Rivington looked more as if she'd been counting the days of her life and finding them numbered. Coppery strands of hair had come undone from the loosely braided knot and she blew them from her forehead as she sat down, exhausted. "There's just too much to do, is all. May I have a sherry?" She was looking at Trueblood.

"Of course," said Melrose, giving her a blinding smile and returning to his crossword.

"Well?" she looked from one to the other and then toward the bar, empty except for Mrs. Withersby, who had propped her mop in the pail, and was administering to herself from the optics. "Must I get it myself, then?"

"Dick will be back in a moment. You look beautiful, Vivian." Actually, Melrose thought the mustard-colored twin-set was rather abominable. It drained the color from her ordinarily pearly skin and fought with the coppery hair.

Vivian looked down, as if checking to see if this was herself, and frowned at him. "I do?"

"Absolutely," put in Trueblood. "Very fetching indeed."

"Well, if I'm so damned fetching, will one of you get me my drink?"

Trueblood twisted on the window seat a bit and said,

"You know that dreadful estate agent—Haggerty? Is that his name?—has been asking if you intend to sell your cottage. They are *so* pushy, these people. Of course, proper Elizabethan is rare these days. There's so much of the mucked-up stuff. But I honestly *hope* you're not going to sell, Viv-viv. Though you have indicated that's what you intended from time to time."

She flushed. "I haven't even *left* yet. I'm not leaving for ten *days*."

"Ah! Here's Dick back again! *Scroggs!* Will you kindly see to your customers? Miss Rivington will have her usual."

Dick stuck a cigarette behind his ear and called over, "Tio Pepe's off, miss. Got a nice bottle of port; Graham's 'eighty-two."

"Anything," called Vivian crossly.

"Pushy, as I was saying. Lord, they're after your house before you're even cold in your grave— Whoops! Sorry!" Trueblood held up his hands in mock horror at his gaffe.

Vivian looked at both of them in disgust.

"How're we going?" Melrose put in, keeping his elbow on the newspaper when he saw her eye stray in that direction.

"*We?* I'm taking the train," she said, fingering the piece of white cardboard with the rat's picture. She frowned. "What's this?"

"Nothing," said Trueblood. "People do not ordinarily refer to the Orient Express as 'taking the train.' "

She said nothing.

Melrose knew how she hated to be identified with the lavish life-style of those who thought it was the best revenge.

"That's certainly the way we're traveling," said Trueblood, who moved a fraction of an inch to allow Dick Scroggs to set their drinks on the table.

"That looks," said Vivian, squinting at the rat in the ashtray, "like it came from a book of cut-outs, or something."

Trueblood removed the little cardboard rat dexterously from her fingers, saying, "Plenty of those in the canals, Viv-viv."

As she gave him a murderous look, Dick Scroggs beamed at her and said, "Well, now, Miss Rivington. I expect you're pretty excited, ain't you? Not too long before you leave, is it?"

"Nearly two weeks!"

Dick's smile remained unaffected by her snappish tone. "Not to worry. Pass quicker'n it takes Mrs. Withersby to drink up a pint."

"It's ridiculous," said Trueblood. "A *winter* wedding in Venice. Ye gods. We've been trying to talk her into putting it off until spring."

She looked hopefully toward Melrose. "But I've already put it off several times."

"So what?" said Melrose. "He has plenty of time."

Now she looked suspicious. "Is that a double entendre?"

"I wonder," said Dick Scroggs, getting into the spirit of things, "you don't have the wedding in Long Pidd." Expansively, he waved the hand holding the tray. "A proper reception I could do for you, miss."

". . . very kind," murmured Vivian, trailing a wet circle with her port glass. "But it's impossible, Dick." The sad note of exile was already sounding in her tone.

"They don't travel well," said Trueblood. "The Giopinno family is quite averse to traveling."

Vivian's sudden eruption of temper nearly pulled her from her chair and sent Dick Scroggs scuttling back to the safety of his bar. "You know nothing whatever about the Giopinnos!" She glared at Trueblood, then at Melrose.

Taking care to keep his elbow positioned on the *Times,* he turned to her and said, "We don't?"

"No, you don't. You make it all up. You've conjured up an entire family out of whole cloth. You've manufactured their history to the point where you can't separate fantasy from reality. As a matter of fact"—her tone suggested a final judgment—"you both live in a fantasy world!" This pronouncement seemed to please her.

"Oh?" Seeing the direction of Vivian's gaze, he shot the

hand that had just lifted the glass of stout over the newspaper.

With her fingertips pressed against the edge of the table as if she meant to push herself away from their fatuous company, Vivian lectured them in a schoolmistressy voice. "You sit around in here before lunch and dinner doing nothing but making up stories—"

"Well, I wouldn't say that, Viv—" There was a slipping, rustling sound as Trueblood tried to recross his legs.

"—about Franco's family. His mother is *not* fat with a black mustache. She does *not,* to quote you—" Her tone to Melrose was scathing. "—'despite her ascendancy to this high station, still cook spaghetti carbonara and squid fry-ups for her five brothers twice a week.' Franco's mother is small, a bit rawboned, wears sleeveless dresses and speaks four languages. . . ."

As she continued to set him straight about the Countess Giopinno, Melrose studied her fingertips: the nails looked bitten; a little morsel of skin jutted up from the cuticle round the thumbnail. This all struck Melrose as oddly poignant and he wanted to put his own hand over hers.

"—*not* have 'seven cousins who work the bellows and make little glass horses for tourists to Murano'; *or* 'six uncles with an unflagging devotion to the Communist party'—"

"Your memory is prodigious, dear Vivian," said Melrose, noting that the slight upward tilt to the corners of her mouth lent her, no matter how angry she was, a helplessly pleasant air.

She ignored this. "As for *you*—" The movement of her head toward Trueblood was so sudden she might have given herself a good case of whiplash, and the timbre of her voice, during her recital, had grown reedy, giving the impression now of a child chastising her dolls gathered round the nursery tea table. "—he does *not* have a younger sister who 'climbed over a convent wall and set about disgracing the family name by running off with a traveling circus'; *nor* an older sister who 'auditioned for the mad dwarf in that du Maurier film.' And as for the maternal grandmother's midnight sprees—" Vivian gritted her teeth and set them straight on this branch of the family tree.

Melrose fought a yawn and saw that Trueblood was wearing the vacant expression of the stupid, the insane, or the man whose thoughts are miles away. He wasn't really listening either.

"My goodness, Vivian, did we say all that?"

"Ev-er-y sin-gle word."

Trueblood pursed his lips. "It was Richard Jury who mentioned the dwarf—"

Down came her fist on the table, jumping the rat from the ashtray. "Richard *Jury* has better things to do than sit around fantasizing all day!" she shouted.

Dick Scroggs rolled his toothpick and said, "You read about this latest case up in the West Riding, miss . . . ?"

Melrose was indeed reading about it; he was reading about the crime that very evening while Agatha was at Ardry End, seated on his Queen Anne sofa, stuffing herself with potted tongue and gobbet cakes, and talking about Harrogate.

"I don't see why you won't book a room at the Old Swan where Teddy and I are staying. Teddy would love to have you come, I know; she's said several times how much she'd like to see you."

Melrose's thirst to see Teddy again in Harrogate had been considerably slaked by his having seen her in York. He had agreed, finally, to play chauffeur and drive Agatha there; it would be worth it just to give the Georgian tea service a brief rest. He continued reading the item in the *Times*.

"Melrose, would you *kindly* put down that paper and have Ruthven bring some more maids-of-honor. And why are there no fairy cakes? Didn't Martha know I was coming?"

Melrose refolded the paper. He considered ringing his

friend Jury, but thought he probably had enough on his platter. His aunt certainly had enough on hers. A jam heart, a gobbet cake, and a brandy snap. He put the paper aside and retrieved the latest thriller by his friend Polly Praed from where he had stuffed it between the cushion and the chair arm. *Die Like a Doge* had begun life as . . . *Like a Dog* (so she had told him) with the central character a Seeing-Eye German shepherd until her editor had insisted there were entirely too many mysteries written these days with dogs and cats as characters. It was becoming a cliché. Polly had told Melrose all this, in a rancorous tone as if he were partially responsible, since he himself had suggested a church fête as a setting with some sort of situation involving a terrier chasing after the sack-racers. Perhaps it was his reference to Vivian Rivington and Venice that had suddenly changed *dog* to *doge* and *fête* to *Carnivale*. Thus far ten people in an English touring group had snuffed it in nearly as few pages, falling one against another like a line of dominoes. Polly got more bloodthirsty with every book. Things must be hideously boring in Littlebourne, but he still could not budge her from the place.

"You are being excessively rude, Melrose."

"Hmm?" He looked up from the plight of Aubrey Adderly, dressed as a harlequin and dashing down some waterlogged alleyway. "Sorry, but I did promise Polly I'd finish this manuscript to let her know my opinion."

Agatha mumbled something about "cheap thrillers" and said, "Honestly, you have, over these last months, become wretched company."

"Then why do you desire my wretched company for a week in Harrogate?" He sipped his sherry and resettled himself in the crusty brown wing chair he favored for cold winter afternoons by the fireplace. His dog Mindy slept on a small prayer rug she had dragged in from another room.

In his mind's eye, Melrose enjoyed envisioning this scene when he was shoving his bicycle along in the bitter cold, or standing sodden in rain on the railway platform in Sidbury, or fighting his way through a blinding snowstorm. . . . Actually, he couldn't remember doing any of these things. Still, he liked thinking of himself in these surroundings of Adam ceilings, Georgian silver, crystal chandeliers, and the long vista of the drawing room in which they now were seated, as the rain lashed the casement windows, lightning seared the privet hedges—

He really must stop reading Polly Praed's mysteries. The elements were always in league with the blackguard criminal, huge ghostly faces appearing suddenly on rain-drenched fens, hands scrabbling about in bogs—

"Teddy and I shall need an escort."

Naturally, his purpose was utilitarian. "Whatever for? Nothing goes on in Harrogate except conventions. Large groups of people are always convening there. I don't know what about."

"Nonsense. Harrogate is a perfectly charming place with lots to do: there're the gardens, the Stray, the Baths. You're such a stick-in-the-mud, Melrose. Never used to be."

He didn't? He would have thought, over the years, to hear her talk, the mud was up to his eyeballs.

". . . rather dull. You know, I almost preferred you when you were going through that stage of thinking about marriage."

Knowing he should have resisted any temptation to respond, still Melrose lowered the manuscript and glared at her. If his aunt said things like this merely to get a reaction, he wouldn't have answered. But she was entirely too complacent to bother about baiting him.

"And just what makes you think I've stopped considering it?"

"Don't be silly. With Vivian gone, there's no one about to marry." Now she was up and yanking at the bellpull. "What in heaven's name is keeping Ruthven?"

Anything Ruthven can think of, Melrose supposed. Vivian Rivington had always been the principal threat to his aunt's "expectations" and Agatha, despite her references to the "odious Italian," must have breathed a sigh of relief when the wedding date was set.

"Especially since you ruined your chances," she continued, letting the statement hang in the air much like the silver pot she held while inspecting the last morsels on the cake plate.

Completely disoriented—not an unusual state of mind when Agatha was hard by—he said, "What? What chances?"

"With Lady Jane Hay-Hurt. At the Simpsons' garden party."

"I don't even remember *speaking* to Jane Hay-Hurt. Indeed, I don't even remember the Simpsons' garden party."

"Ha! That doesn't surprise me. You were in one of your churlish moods. Refusing to speak to people, off by yourself, brooding and feeding the ducks."

All he remembered was a garden, colorful frocks, and aimless chatter. That was all. Perhaps he was given to blackouts. Or brownouts. He wished he were in the middle of one right now.

As if Polly Praed's setting had come suddenly to life, curtains of rain lifted and fell across the french windows. His aunt was going on with evident satisfaction about Vivian's forthcoming marriage and the opportunities she seemed to think this event allowed for foreign travel. "Oh, it will be so pleasant to get out of Northants for a while." She leaned back with her teacup and the last of the muffins and rattled on about palazzos and palaces, doges and loggias, canals and campaniles. (She must really have been rooting in her Italian guidebook, he thought.) "So pleasant to be in a place cool, and tiled, and watery."

"If that's all you want, go back to Plague Alley and take a shower."

He returned to the plight of Aubrey Adderly, who apparently thought his thin disguise impenetrable. How many mysteries, Melrose wondered, had been set in Venice during Carnivale? How many bodies went floating down the Grand

Canal? It was all the fault of Edgar Allan Poe and his
godforsaken "Cask of Amontillado."

"There isn't a shred of romance in you, my dear Plant.
It's no wonder you've had so little success with women."
Now that Vivian had finally decided to marry the "dissolute
Italian," the count's prospects had risen considerably in
Agatha's eyes. He was no longer "that impoverished for-
tune-hunter," but "the Count Franco Giopinno of some
prominence in Italian politics" (a contradiction in terms,
Melrose thought). That was now her report to her acquain-
tances, her char (Mrs. Oilings), and the seamstress who was
whipping up a dress for the great event. That the event was
near to hand and Vivian had as yet to issue invitations made
no odds to Agatha.

"Oh, I don't know," said Melrose, studying his empty
sherry glass and reaching for the bellpull. "I wouldn't mind
bobbing around in a canal with Ortina Luna, she of the
liquid eyes."

Munching the end of the brandy snap, she looked at him
narrowly. "Who're you talking about?"

Melrose didn't answer. Unable to induce in himself a
fugue state or go into a coma, he dipped once again into the
pages of *Die Like a Doge,* marveling at Polly Praed's ability
to accommodate her plot, which originally took place amid
the narrow streets and chimney pots of Biddingstone-on-
Water, to the waterier byways of Venice. The original de-
nouement that saw a blind man and his Seeing-Eye dog
chased over the old stone bridge of Biddingstone had trans-
lated itself into the protagonist's fleeing his pursuers across
the Accademia Bridge.

Melrose was fascinated, not by the book (which could
only be appreciated by a blind man), but by its intrepid
author and her prodigious imagination: it did not take wings
and soar; it just bulldozed everything in its path, spewing up
concrete and gravel and clumps of hard earth with no regard
at all for the willing suspension of disbelief. Willing or not,
Polly couldn't seem to care less:

Misfortune had been Aubrey's lot ever since the moment in the Gritti Palace when he had first set eyes on the mysterious Orsina Luna. . . .

Melrose kept his finger as a marker in the manuscript and looked up. The voice-over of his aunt had been sounding all along, rabbiting on about the trip to Harrogate.

". . . a cold luncheon. I think we might take what's left of the Chicken Kiev we're to have for dinner tonight, and perhaps a bottle of muscadet."

Blackly, Melrose regarded her. "Crubeens, marrow pie, and tripe and onions is what we're having. The chicken's off."

The last of the maids-of-honor stopped halfway to her mouth. "What are crubeens? Never heard of them."

"Pig's trotters. Martha does them with an excellent sauce—"

"Oh, be serious."

That, unfortunately, was what he was being. The coppery-haired Orsina Luna on the vaporetto had turned his mind quite seriously to thoughts of the coppery-haired Vivian Rivington who soon might be.

Melrose looked off down the vista. "Let me remind you, Agatha, Vivian isn't married yet." A clap of thunder, a dagger of accompanying lightning obliged Melrose by underscoring this (to Agatha) sinister announcement.

She fairly jumped, either at the onslaught of noise or the implied threat.

Melrose went back to Aubrey, not so easily intimidated.

. . . Aubrey had thought that his harlequin disguise would have helped him to elude his shadowy pursuers, but he realized, as he neared the Rialto Bridge, that this was not the case. The bell in the campanile sounded its ominous gong. . . .

Why was it, wondered Melrose, that the bells of St. Rules just made their dissonant metallic clatter rather than bonging ominously? Probably because St. Rules overlooked Betty Ball's bakery instead of Saint Mark's Square. As he diligently returned to this dismal chase, the voice of his aunt seeped through:

". . . and we decided that the Old Swan is more convenient to the center of things. Besides, it's much nearer the Stray. . . ."

"Charming place," said Melrose, who didn't know what she was talking about.

Suppressing the rising feeling of terror, Aubrey pushed his way through the crowd . . .

"What is keeping Ruthven? Must I sit here all afternoon just to get one or two brandy snaps?"

"I hope not."

. . . pushed his way through the crowd flowing across the bridge. Grotesque masks, powdered and painted faces, costumes of scarlet, orange, blue-licked about like tongues of flame and were reflected grotesquely in the black water of the canal below like some vision of hell. . . .

"It's so wonderful to have all of those acres of green parkland right in the center of the city; Teddy and I shall be able to walk and talk for hours."

Talk about a vision of hell, thought Melrose.

Finally, when they reached the palazzo facing the Grand Canal, the revellers dispersed, flying off in small groups, the trains of the gowns streaming, the capes flowing out. . . .

Melrose yawned. If he himself felt exhausted from all of this hectic running about and suffocating crush, what must old Aubrey feel? He certainly must be thinking about a place to put his feet up. . . . Ah, there it was, of course. The Gritti Palace. Everyone finally fetched up at the Gritti Palace. He decided to make it a point, if Vivian were really determined to go through with this harebrained marriage and he were invited to the festivities, to look out some ratty old pension and leave the Gritti Palace to Aubrey, who had already passed and made a tortuous journey through "nightmarishly twisting streets" to the Accademia. Here he was in another crush of carnival-revellers.

He had, thank God, finally escaped. Aubrey ran down the steps where he saw a vaporetto marked for the Lido. It was about to shove off, and he jumped aboard just as the attendant swung the rope to the dock and pushed away.

Safe!

Making his way to the stern, he stopped dead.

Orsina Luna—mask or no—he was sure it was she whom he had left behind in the palace of the doge.

As the vaporetto picked up speed, the wind tangled her coppery hair and he looked away. The Grand Canal was a tunnel of darkness. . . .

Melrose looked up from the page, glad that Agatha had taken herself off in search of cakes and cucumbers. He could not understand how such drivel (pardon me, dear Polly) could touch something in himself. His eye traveled the length of his drawing room, dim and shadowy in the last of the sun, as if it were that Venetian canal that bore Polly's hero along with the copper-haired woman who was going to end up killing the doge in self-defense and marrying Aubrey.

Well, he was so bored he read the last few pages so that he could give Polly the advantage of some varnished lie about her prowess as a mystery writer. She was, really, considerably better than this lot of codswollop demonstrated.

At least it hadn't yet been published (and Polly probably knew why). Unable to stand it any longer, Melrose flipped the manuscript closed and stuffed it back down between cushion and chair arm, wishing old Aubrey's "sinking feeling" would drop him right in the Grand Canal.

Unfortunately, as Melrose reached for his sherry he was aware of a hollowness in his stomach as the face of the Signora Orsina Luna with her coppery, wind-tangled hair was suddenly replaced by the face of Vivian Rivington with her coppery, shoulder-length bob.

. . . a sinking feeling was the only way he could describe it.

Surely such tarnished prose could not call forth something akin to empathy for old Aubrey as he stood poised on the edge of some hectic—

Oh, for God's sakes, he was beginning to sound like old Aubrey. Or old Polly. Melrose belted back his sherry and slid down in his chair. With both hands he massaged his hair until it stood up in spikes and licks, hoping to work some sense into himself. That was the trouble with all of this maudlin sentiment; it began to suck you in.

His hand tightened on the leather chair arm as he thought of Aubrey's own hand grasping the metal rail of the vaporetto as he stared into the hazel eyes of the signora . . . No, it was Vivian's that were hazel.

And then the images of Vivian started flowing past him as if she too had been painted on the pages of a book: Vivian in her twin-set in the Jack and Hammer today; Vivian looking serene and silky in Stratford-upon-Avon; Vivian in a tatty old bathrobe in that country house in Durham; Vivian over tea, over drinks, over dinner—

His eyes widening as if he'd come upon a houseful of ghosts, Melrose wondered if he had made some dreadful miscalculation. . . .

"Why on earth are you pulling that long face, Melrose?"

asked Agatha, who had thumped back into the room carrying her dish of rum balls. "You'd think you lost your last—what's *that?*"

The racket made by the brass door knocker was violent enough to make the chandelier shudder.

"I don't see why these dreadful children can't stick to the village if they must go about playing pranks, nor why you can't have Ruthven stand down there at the driveway entrance and simply turn them away—"

"Generally, we set out steel-jaw traps," said Melrose, as he heard some commotion and raised voices out in the entrance room and then the deliberate rap, rap, rap of heels across the marble.

Vivian appeared in the doorway.

"It's Miss Rivington, sir," Ruthven said with whatever formality he could muster, but as he followed in her wake like a hound brought to heel, the announcement was superfluous.

Melrose got up quickly, bestowing upon his visitor an absolutely wonderful smile. For once in his life, he believed not in coincidence, but in Destiny. "Vivian!"

Vivian Rivington stood there in a wet raincoat, her hair a mess of rainsoaked tangles, holding out a large pasteboard cut-out.

"Just what in the hell is *this?*"

7

"Wherever you see smokestacks, you know it's shut down," was the cabdriver's brief and bleak commentary on the West Riding mills, once a center of the wool trade. The taxi had dropped him at a car-hire place, and after the sooty valley of Bradford, the monotonous rows of slate rooftops and chimneys marching up and down hills like stairsteps, coming so suddenly upon the open expanse of the moors should have been a grateful escape. Perhaps it was the season; perhaps it was his mood. But Jury saw little to relieve that mood in the endlessness of the moors, the distant hills brown with old bracken and heather, gray with snow and granite.

The Citrine house sat within its own wood of oak, box-wood trees, and tangled vines on the border of Keighley or Oakworth Moor. It was hard to tell where one left off and the other began. The sound of Jury's car lifted pheasant from the dead and nearly knee-high bracken as he drove up the narrow road to the house. He had passed a small stone cottage, perhaps once a caretaker's, but unoccupied now, given the build-up of filmy dirt on its windows. It did not seem the sort of grounds one would bother to "keep up," at any rate. The undergrowth, the dead branches, the moss and vines would simply take over again.

It was a fitting-enough landscape for such a medieval house, fifteenth, sixteenth century probably. Soot-blackened stone, vaulted porch, ranges of timber windows over archways, a turret at one end and a tower at the other. It was very large and looked very cold. Jury wouldn't have wanted to pay Citrine's heating bills. He wondered if it had been in the family forever; he knew the Citrine money had come from the woolen mills. Well, it was hardly Charles Citrine's fault that synthetics had come along.

The room into which Jury was led by a woman servant was not a great improvement over the stark medievalism of the façade. It had once been, he imagined, the "great hall," and still retained most of the size and much of the ambience of one. Its vaulted ceiling lent it a strangely cryptlike appearance. Near one end of the room was the large fireplace with a tile surround and copper hood, certainly not the original central hearth. Beyond this was a long entry screen, heavily curtained to cut off drafts and leading, probably, to buttery or dining room and kitchen. The walls were exposed stone sectioned off by wooden beams. Would he find the stone wept moisture if he touched it?

The furniture was heavy, dark Jacobean. Two baroque and elaborately carved chairs with high backs sat before the fireplace at opposite ends of a long claw-footed refectory table. There were other pieces, a sofa and several easy chairs. On the flagstone floor, oriental carpets were strewn, but their intricate and faded colors did little to add to any overall warmth and life. There were brass and pewter bowls set about full of flowers: mums and Christmas roses. They were sifting their petals onto the surfaces that held them, though, as if they, too, were giving over to the room's wintry look. That relieved this feudalism, but not greatly.

One thing that did relieve it, though, was an oriel chamber in the right wall, upraised and large enough to contain twin grand pianos. The high-climbing lancet windows that arched about this stagelike little room were beautiful.

There was music on one of the pianos. The cover of the keys was down over the other.

Unattended, the fire had burnt low. Why was the room not warmer, in tone if not in temperature? Against the other wall were floor-to-ceiling bookcases in recessed alcoves, and books usually made a room look tenanted, he thought. But these bookshelves seemed to have no arrangement, the books and magazines stacked or merely tossed there without any particular notice, like afterthoughts. Between the shelves was a window seat beneath a high window whose leaded panes should catch the morning sun. He walked over to it and found the view baleful, for it overlooked the downward slope of the moorland hill and the derelict farm, its longhouse, its barns studding the land like empty shells. The only life Jury saw was the black-faced sheep, raising their heads from the bracken.

Charles Citrine shambled into the room—that was the only way Jury could describe it, the sort of careless, shuffling walk the man affected, hands in pockets of baggy corduroy trousers, and wearing a checked woolen shirt beneath a mud-stained denim jacket. From a distance, he had the look of a man who'd been busy in the barn or mucking out a stable; up closer, Jury could see the lines of worry.

He did not extend his hand and looked at Jury with some suspicion. "Why are you here, Superintendent?"

"I thought I could help."

"I can't see how." This was said flatly, without hostility. "None of this makes any sense. Not Roger's death, not Nell's—oh, hell. You might as well sit down. . . . Would you care for coffee?" Citrine sat back in the dark wood chair that had the look of some mythological beast or bird, the feet taloned, the slanted panels ribbed like wings.

Jury thanked him but shook his head. He would have expected more reserve from Charles Citrine, if not outright hostility toward himself, the person who had actually witnessed his daughter's crime. Nor did he seem to care anymore that Jury had, after all, no business being here. Given that Nell Citrine had made no move to get away, her own resolute silence regarding the circumstances, and her apparent acceptance of what she had done would have made an actual eyewitness to the crime hardly necessary. Her own refusal to deny anything would even have rendered circumstantial evidence unnecessary.

Thus Jury's own role was far less vital than it might have been. Perhaps Citrine realized this and that explained his attitude.

Citrine would have been, in any woman's book, a "catch." In his sixties he projected a vitality, a lustiness, even, missing in men half his age. The earthiness born of the land and the casual air he affected born of his work there (though Jury imagined it was more a gentlemanly meddling into the duties of his laborers) were only enhanced by a veneer of sophistication that had come from handling many types of people. In spite of the tensions of the last few days, he had the manner of one almost untouched by the larger world beyond his doorstep. This blend of sophistication, ease, and innocence could be a potent mixture for any woman. Jury wondered if Mavis Crewes had imbibed it. He couldn't imagine the two of them together; Citrine was far more refined and a great deal cleverer.

This room did not encourage ease of manner. Yet Citrine seemed at ease in it—how could a man look comfortable in that Jacobean monstrosity of a chair?—and yet at odds with it, too. The room, the feudal, armorial look of the house, seemed less Citrine's proper milieu than would some South Sea island. His face was weather-burned from whatever farming life he led, and the sunburnt look lent a further crispness to the gray hair shot through with gold and a further depth to the eyes, which had the clear tint of unruffled water in some island cove. Roll up his trouser legs and shuck his shoes, and he could be a beachcomber, a Crusoe happily marooned.

His whole placid presence rubbed Jury's nerves raw.

"Isn't this somewhat irregular, Superintendent? I mean, given you must be the Crown's witness?" The question was more curious than critical, as he regarded Jury with those calm, aquamarine eyes.

"I wouldn't serve as witness, since there's no question of the right person's being arrested."

He looked surprised. "I find that odd. You were the one who saw Nell—who saw it happen." Citrine looked down at the burnt logs, little more than embers.

"Everything I know I told to the West Yorkshire police. Superintendent Sanderson." Not everything. There was really no way to tell it. She went to the parsonage, a tearoom, a child's museum. But how to explain the nuances: the abstracted air, the hand against the glass case of the toy train. And what, precisely, could he say Roger Healey had said or done to provoke such a tragic outcome? Jury had his impressions, that was all. Attitude, aura, evanescence. Sanderson would tell him, with his dry look, that perhaps the Old Silent's black cat was a familiar? To put away his crystal ball.

"There was the appearance," Jury went on, "of an argument. Of a rather serious disagreement."

Citrine had removed a pipe from his jacket pocket, knocked out the old tobacco into an ashtray, and tamped down fresh. He lit up. A fruity-scenting smoke blossomed, uncurled, and dissipated into the cold air. "Given the outcome, I'd say that was probably true," Citrine said dryly and jammed the pipe back in his mouth.

Jury knew he was being deliberately misunderstood. He said nothing.

"I have no idea why this happened. Roger was a devoted husband, a fine man. Spent a lot of time in London, of course, because of his work. And I imagine nothing was quite the same since—" He stopped abruptly.

"If you're talking about your grandson, I know about that. I'm very sorry, Mr. Citrine. I truly am. I'd simply like to know the reason this happened." He tried to smile. "Throw me out any time you feel like it."

Charles Citrine smiled slightly too. "Look, we'd *all* like to know the reason. My daughter won't talk about it. We're not . . . especially close. I think she gets on better with my sister than me. If you want to talk to Irene—" He shrugged. "—go ahead."

"Where would I find her?"

"In the tower. My sister is not so much eccentric as the sum of a number of affects. One is that I have relegated her to the tower, with the bats." Citrine smiled sourly.

Jury's own answering smile was half finished, hanging in air like chill in the room. "And your daughter?"

"I don't know." He studied Jury. "And I don't think it would be a good idea for you to talk to her. I probably shouldn't be talking to you myself; I doubt her solicitors would like it. Who are, as you can imagine, going round the twist on this one. Nell doesn't—" He stopped to get the dead pipe going again. "—care."

Jury watched him coax the pipe back into life and saw nothing in the man's expression that would suggest that Citrine believed otherwise. Yet, it couldn't be true, this assessment of his daughter's state of mind. Yes, it was possible that one might give up on one's own life, might despair of one's own future. But that could only come about through caring very deeply about things having gone wrong that were once in some sense right.

But he was not about to challenge Charles Citrine's statement. "There's no remorse?"

Reaching over to stab at a log with the poker, Citrine looked up. "Not a flicker." He might have been talking about the blackened log. He shook his head slightly, bewildered. "Roger was a very good man, one of the best. I had great hopes when he married Nell . . ."

One would have thought the father would have put it the other way round: when Nell married Roger, or, at least, "when *they* married." His statement made Nell Citrine sound like a rather poor marital prospect. When he paused, staring at the logs that refused to erupt into flame, Jury prompted him: " 'Great hopes'?"

Absently, he held onto the poker, like a walking stick or

cane. Two or three small blue flames licked their way round the logs. "That he would steady her."

Steady her? Jury had to smile. "She seems the last person in need of 'steadying.' I've never seen anyone so self-contained."

Citrine leaned the poker against the stone and sat back. "Impassivity can often seem like containment, can't it?"

The picture of Nell Citrine Healey that was emerging, stroke by stroke—or was it hint by hint?—was not a pleasant one. Remorseless. Impassive. Unsteady. "You're making her sound like a sociopath."

He gave a short bark of laughter. "Good Lord, I hope not. No. Do you know anything about melancholia, Superintendent?"

Jury thought about his own mental state these last months. "Not much. Except as chronic depression. Is that what you're saying is causing this apparent lack of empathy with things outside of her?"

"I don't know. I don't think depression would explain it."

"And her mother?"

"Helen was quite—sanguine, really. A lovely woman." He looked away, dispiritedly.

"This must be very difficult for you." But from the way Charles Citrine talked with as much equanimity as he did about a situation that struck Jury as horrific, Jury wondered how difficult it really was. The man seemed to fit the chair in which he sat admirably, for all that his casual dress and manner were at odds with it. In the meager firelight, Jury saw that in the angle between the horned foot and the seat a web was in the making, a small spider dangled there by its invisible thread.

Citrine nodded, knocked out his pipe on the fireplace fender. "I'm very fond of Nell; but I must admit she's beyond me. I can't fathom her feelings, her reasons for this destructive silence." He sat back again, started fussing with the pipe. Jury wondered why men bothered with pipes; he wondered if all of the attention pipe-smoking demanded served as a safety valve, a distraction from human demands. Citrine said then, with a rather disarming smile Jury imagined endeared him to a lot of people, "I shouldn't be talking to you at all."

"It can't hurt her, can it, in the circumstances?"

Her father shook his head. "I expect not. Sometimes I wonder if she ever had very strong feelings for Roger."

"Oh, she must have."

"Because she married him?"

Said Jury dryly, "Because she shot him. You say all of this is 'beyond you,' Mr. Citrine. But you can't have known them both for so many years and not theorized about the reasons behind her killing her husband."

He had got his pipe going again and the smoke curled away in a cold draft that touched Jury's neck, probably from the rattling pane at the end of the room. "Well, there was Billy, Roger's son. Do you know about that?"

Jury nodded. "And the Holt boy. Still, that was a long time ago."

"Yes. The poor Holts. But he was adopted, I think."

Roger's son. And Toby, but *he was adopted*. Blood ran very thick and water very thin around here. "To a mother, it could have been yesterday."

"The real mother died in an accident when Billy was a baby. Nell was his stepmother."

There it was again.

Why was everyone so determined to point this out? That Nell Healey could only have some diluted measure of a real mother's feelings, the water that could never be as thick as blood? "Let's assume that it did have to do with that kidnapping eight years ago—" Citrine started to object, but Jury forestalled this. "We're just speculating. What could have happened that might have built up over those years in your daughter's mind?"

"You mean, that the ransom wasn't paid?"

Jury waited.

"Surely, if she wanted revenge because we refused—" Citrine made a helpless gesture.

"By 'we,' you mean Roger Healey and you."

"We were only taking the advice of the police, Superintendent."

As Citrine shifted in his chair, Jury's eye was drawn to the tiny spider that plummeted, from its fluttering contact with the leg, nearly to the floor on its silky life line. Jury had never before known a family of such shaky relationships. Blood bonds seemed absent, or appeared tenuous at best. At worst, easily broken.

Citrine didn't know, of course, that Jury was aware it was Nell Healey's money, and Nell who had refused to pay up. The only ones who knew this, as far as Charles Citrine was aware, were himself, Roger Healey, Nell, the Lloyd's banker, and the superintendent in charge. The police sergeant Citrine may even have forgotten: Brian Macalvie.

8

On the other side of the winch, a passageway through the main gate used to give easier access to foot passengers, Jury found the small door to the tower. Above the door on an ironwork standard was a bell from which a string dangled. He pulled it; the bell jangled; in a moment he heard a buzzing sound. Jury looked uncertainly at the door for a while, unable to place the source of the sound. Silence. He pulled the bell cord again, and again there was the same buzz. Then assuming there was some setup here like the security system in a London townhouse comprised of flats, he pulled at the big iron ring. The door opened.

It opened on near-total darkness. The weak light from lamp niches cast Jury's shadow in grotesque, fun-house shapes as he moved upward and around on the stone steps. Thank God, he thought, he didn't suffer from vertigo, or halfway up he'd've been a goner. Round and round he went, stopping once to loosen his tie. He studiously avoided letting his gaze drift to the steps as he felt, rather than saw, something scuttle down them.

Irene Citrine certainly valued her privacy if not her friendships. He was hard put to imagine her girlfriends giggling up these cold steps to tea and bread and butter sandwiches.

A slant of light suddenly broke across the steps, and from round the bend he heard a voice flute a greeting. "Sorry about the stairs and the security system," said Irene Citrine,

who more or less filled, in silhouette, the door at the top,
"but you never know who's mucking about out on those
damned moors, do you?" She took Jury's hand in a hearty
grip and more or less hoisted his six-feet-two frame through
the door.

Irene Citrine—who introduced herself as Rena—told him
Saint Charles had hit the intercom to tell her Jury was coming and to try to control herself.

"Of course, a little gunplay in the local is small potatoes
to the Moors Murders and the Yorkshire Ripper. Still." As
if he were going to protest, she held up her hand and said,
"Sorry, sorry. I'm not all that cold-blooded. Poor Nell is in
one hell of a spot, but we'll get round it somehow. Care for a
drink?" She swept, in her hibiscus-patterned muumuu, to
the other end of the room toward what appeared to be an
old pulpit.

Jury took a moment to catch his breath and survey the
lighting arrangements. Although a couple of floorlamps
splayed cones of light near a sofa, Rena Citrine favored cres-
set lamps with floating wicks and fat tapers. There were
several of these positioned on iron spikes attached to brack-
ets. The oil lamps, though, were lit, and their shadows
reached long fingers across the thick oak table.

Against one wall was a medieval bench strewn with
brightly colored cushions that didn't do anything toward
making it look more sittable. On the facing wall was a fireplace with a joggled lintel and a cornice elaborately carved
with a little row of heads, none of them looking less than
unspeakably insane. Old lancet windows through which lozenges of light burrowed were inset around the octagonal
walls.

A scarred satinwood writing table dominated the room:
covering it were papers, manuscripts, stacks of books, a
typewriter, an Apple II personal computer with an enor-
mously long cord snaking across the room to some source of
electricity Jury couldn't see; ashtrays, each holding a partially smoked cigarette as if each smoke had claimed its own

ashtray grave; a welter of bottles; several canvases in oil leaning against the wall; stacks of books, largely popular novels. On the top shelf leaned little framed photos, snapshots of her travels, apparently.

Jury leaned closer to look at the photos; Rena Citrine on a white sand beach in a bikini (there must have been more under that muumuu than one could guess); Rena on some sort of fishing boat; Rena and another woman holding between them a huge fish; several more of Rena in cafés and a club that looked, with its palm fronds, wicker, and partly black combo, like something in the Caribbean. She was crushed between a man and the woman in the fish-picture, all wearing those overly gay, false smiles one does for club photographers. Hung on both sides of the fireplace and on the wall were posters of the warm sands and sunlit seas that must have been the sources of these pictures. Barbados. Bimini.

Just looking at them made Jury feel colder here in this tower. These pictures against the backdrop of this dark medievalism made him wonder if he were in the presence of some apocalyptic cultural collision.

"How about a Tequila Sunrise?"

Jury's head moved round from the pictures. "A what?"

Rena Citrine was busy with a silver cocktail shaker. "What'd Charles give you? A glass of cold tea or did he hobble to the well for water?" She rattled the shaker from one side to another.

Jury smiled. "He offered me coffee, actually."

"But did it materialize?"

"I didn't want any."

The liquid from the shaker gurgled into a couple of fluted cocktail glasses. Both of these she brought round from behind the pulpit that served as drinks cabinet and handed one to Jury. The drink was a cloudy pinkish lavender. He sipped; he choked.

She gave his back a good thwack. Rena was stronger than she looked, with those angular shoulders and slim arms.

"Straight from Barbados, this lot is. You can't beat their rum."

"I wouldn't want to," he said.

Irene Citrine scooped some papers from one bench and more or less shoved him down on it; then she went round to the other side of the table and sat on the opposite bench, clearing some more papers from the table before her. Through eyes that were tearing from the rum, he looked at her, sitting with her pointy chin resting on her laced hands, staring at him from amber eyes whose irises were wedge shaped, cat's eyes. She had narrow shoulders, their slope increased by the tentlike dress. Her hair was a vibrant red that fell from a center part to her shoulders and seemed to have a life of its own, the way it sprang up and out as if it were plugged into an electrical socket. It was sprigged with gray, and because of the fanciful play of light it looked caught up in a loose net of silver.

"Cheers!"

Jury took the sticky, fluted glass, sipped at a liquid the color of which only Sergeant Wiggins could love, and choked again. His throat was on fire.

"You get used to it. I've been into rum ever since Archie —my late husband—and I went beachcombing in Barbados. Do you like my posters?"

Jury nodded. "Is that your husband sitting in the club, there?"

"Him? No, that was just a couple we met in Bimini. My favorite place. Spent two months there. Archie was camera-shy. Also cash-shy. A fact that Charles never lets me forget. He probably didn't tell you I was married, did he?"

"No," said Jury, his eye resting on the blue and mauve poster of Atlantic waters breaking on the beaches of Bimini. The sunset matched the drink, which he shoved a little way from him in case it was combustible.

"He wouldn't. He refuses to acknowledge a Citrine would run off with a fortune-hunting American." She raised her glass again. "To Archie Littlejohn, God rest him."

"I'm sorry."

"About what?"

"Well, that you lost him."

"Lost me would be more like it. Last time I saw Archie was three years ago when he took out a deep-sea fishing boat off Bimini. There went my last thousand quid. My part of Daddy's money. Dear Daddy was very Victorian and thought women couldn't be trusted with the stuff, so Charles got the lion's share. I have to admit Charles did work for much of his; still, he's one of those lucky people that money just seems to stick to. So . . . Archie floated away and I decided to come back to the old homestead. Well, I was dead broke, wasn't I? We'd spent all my money." She looked round the tower happily. "It suits me. I do a lot of reading, walking, go grouse- and pheasant-shooting with Charles, largely because it irritates him so much I'm a better shot than he is. But, mostly, I have my painting to keep me busy."

Jury squinted over his shoulder at one of the canvases. Cutting across its dark surface was the merest splinter of light. "Not much light for painting."

She shrugged. "Well, my work gains a lot in visual impact in the dark. You won't believe this, but I've actually sold some."

True, Jury found it hard to believe, but he said, "That's grand."

"They don't think so after they get them home and see them in daylight."

Jury looked up at the boarded-over hole in the roof of the turret. "Are you building yourself a skylight, or something?"

She squinted upwards. "That's my passive solar heating. Happened a couple of weeks ago. Some firm was supposed to come fix it." Three Tequila Sunrises had made her, apparently, quite tolerant of the indifference of the contractor. "I get the odd bat or two."

She was picking up the thick candlestick to light another cigarette.

When she leaned across the table toward Jury, the tops of her rounded breasts were thrust against the neckline of the muumuu, in the candlelight white as the hibiscus, and the gold wedges of her eyes flickered. Jury wondered if she knew that her Archie might not have married her for her money after all. "What happened?"

"Helen. Our family weren't exactly poor, the Citrines. But I'm talking about what they take to National Westminster in an armored car. *Real* money." Rena sat back, turned the stem of her drink slowly, looked a little sad. "I liked Helen. She was wooly-headed, extremely pretty, silly, but a good person. Left me a handsome bequest which I managed to run through with the speed of light. All the rest went to Nell. My saintly brother Charles has Daddy's money. Am I supposed to be talking to you?" The "supposed" came out with a bit of a slur along with the smile.

"Superintendent Sanderson wouldn't think so." Jury returned the smile.

"You're better looking than he is."

"So are you." Jury raised his glass as if in toast to her looks, but really to keep her from frothing more of the flammable cocktail into it. "There're only the three of you here now, is that right?"

"Except for the odd servant or two. I seldom venture downstairs except for dinner. That's always good for a laugh. The aperitif, a few acid smiles handed round; first course, trumped-up laughter; main course, squabble; and for afters, silence."

"False smiles, fights, and silence. Doesn't sound too inviting."

"That's when we're having fun. Or were, I should say. Roger—" She looked away, past the fireplace and the posters toward the narrow window. Then she took a cigarette from a little tray, struck a wooden match across the underside of the table, and said, ". . . provided some amusement." Her tone was wry. "He was the essence of a Ralph Lauren advert. Polo. The cologne, not the sport. Although I could certainly imagine him playing it."

"Then you don't agree with your brother?"

"I never agree with my brother, if only on principle. You mean about Roger?"

"Mr. Citrine talked about him as a fine man. Devoted father, husband."

Rena wiped some ash from the table to the floor. "Oh, 'fine.' Whatever that means in Charles's lexicon. Roger was charming—handsome, witty, sophisticated, talented. And shallow. I don't know much about music but I'd be willing to bet he failed as a musician because there was nothing behind the technical razzle-dazzle. I mean, doesn't one need a *soul* or something to be a great musician? Even Billy had more substance. He was a nice enough child if a bit lazy. Sweet, charming—well, that was probably in his genes—but he didn't really apply himself. Unfortunately, he wasn't all that crazy about being a prodigy, which Roger didn't like at all. He could be a real tyrant." She smoked and studied the shifting shadows thrown by the candles. "Not nice to speak of Roger that way, perhaps, after what he'd been through with Billy and that other child, Toby. God. What a decision to have to make . . ."

"What would you have done?"

"Paid up, of course. But then I never take anyone's advice." Her face hardened. "What a bastard."

Jury frowned. "Roger Healey on his own didn't have the money to pay that ransom."

"It might have been Citrine money, but the father, certainly, would have the say. If he didn't insist, then—" She shrugged.

"You don't know the statistics on—"

"I don't care about the effing statistics, Superintendent. Poor Nell hadn't nearly as much say, had she? She was 'only the stepmother.' Well, she was a better mother than most I've seen. There's something about Nell that just reaches out to kiddies. Toby Holt adored her; he did little jobs round the place for which she overpaid him." Rena smiled. "She'd read to them for hours, tell them stories, read poetry, play the piano. She even tried to give Toby piano lessons. But he hadn't any talent." She lit another cigarette from the tallow beside her.

"You think that's why your niece killed her husband."

"She waited a bloody long time to do it, then." She punctuated this by thumping the candlestick back on the table. "Roger might not have been the devoted husband Saint Charles makes him out to be."

"Meaning?"

"Talked to anyone Roger worked with? There's a woman named Mavis Crewes. She's visited here two or three times. Edits one of the magazines, pretended she wanted to do a travel piece on this part of the country. Loved our house. So feudal. Talk to her."

"And you believe Nell Healey found out about it?"

"Nell is *not* dim. Quiet, but perceptive. Then, again, also trusting. Perhaps a bit naïve."

Naïve was not the word Jury would have chosen, not after Macalvie's account. "How does—did—she speak of her husband?"

Rena Citrine smiled slightly. "She didn't."

"But after what happened, they must have been . . . estranged."

"They were probably *that* from the beginning."

"Why, then, didn't they divorce?"

"Roger was hardly here anyhow, and *he* certainly wouldn't divorce the Citrine millions."

"But she—?"

"I expect because of Billy."

Jury frowned. "Billy's gone."

"Perhaps she thinks he might come back."

Jury looked away. "I hope not."

9

It was supposed to have been only a drop-off.

Something in the manner of an agent like Smiley casually leaving his rolled-up newspaper containing the coded message from Control that would forestall the blowing up of the Kew Gardens Flower Show.

Or, thought Melrose, metaphors escalating in violence as the car made the turnoff to Harrogate, like an Israeli or an IRA henchman tossing an attaché case of gelignite out the passenger door without even slowing down.

Unfortunately, Agatha's position in the passenger seat was far more like a steamer trunk than an attaché case, and his carefully planned and simple drop-off ("*Good-bye, dear aunt . . . ah, here's a lad to help you with your bags . . .*" *Thunk! Cases on sidewalk, car picks up speed . . .*) had been completely dished as he'd loaded up the Bentley with her stuff. Why hadn't she just tied a strap round the cottage in Plague Alley and dragged it to the car? Trunk, portmanteau, valise, four hatboxes, makeup case, overnight case (why? when she must be planning on spending a decade), and picnic basket more befitted Lord Kitchener's arrival in Pretoria than a two-week holiday in Harrogate. A few servants in mufti, a whole sweating band of Boers might not have been sufficient to assist Agatha with her "things."

Would she never stop talking?

He was determined not to answer.

All the way from Northampton, it had been Vivian-this

and Vivian-that; Franco-this and Franco-that; the frock she
was having fashioned for her by the Northampton dress-
maker, though clearly she *should* have gone to London and
would have done had Melrose not so stubbornly refused to
visit his bespoke tailor in Jermyn Street . . .

(Where Melrose hadn't been in years, the place dark as a
vault and the tailor withered to the size of his own thimble.)

. . . and what *rags* did he intend to wear to the wedding, then? And whether the Giopinnos would be snobs, the
canals fouled, the hotel touristy, the church drafty, the pi-
geons dirty . . .

(The Pope Polish . . .)

. . . the pasta endless, the Italian men pinching her relentlessly . . .

He was afraid he'd bloodied the inside of his lip when his
mouth clamped tighter on that one.

But largely Agatha's was a running commentary on the
Events of Last Night, as she had managed to extrapolate one
little practical joke into a Roman orgy:

". . . the utter *childishness* of it all! I'd think the two of
you might as well have joined the kiddies invading Scroggs's
place . . . oh, ho, Trueblood! Oh, I can understand that
person doing such a thing . . . always has been a
sneak . . ."

Thus could Agatha rewrite Trueblood's personal history
to fit a single act . . .

"But *you,* Plant! And Earl of Caverness, fifth Viscount
Ardry . . ."

He refused to speak. She'd have the titles whizzing by the
Bentley like an eerie flank of motorcyclists. Was that, please
God, the Harrogate turnoff? Yes. I'll start attending services.

". . . your dear mother, Lady Marjorie. I simply can't
imagine what got into you, I truly can't. Creeping about the
poor girl's property, hiding in the shrubberies, knocking at
her door. It leaves me speechless."

It would take Jack Nicholson with an axe knocking on
her door to do that, he thought, lip buttoned, eyes on the

wide, tree-lined street that led toward the center of Harrogate.

"One of these days I'll find the two of you up in a tree, hammering boards together. Grown men. *Grown* men. And poor, dear Vivian with so much to do—"

Vivian had become poor and dear and wonderful only since she'd actually set a wedding date, thought Melrose blackly, taking his eye from the road for just that second that caused him to swerve to avoid hitting an old lady in one of those electrified wheelchairs that she obviously thought gave her the right to cross against the light, any light—probably have whizzed past the burning bush—look at her go!

"My heavens! You very nearly hit that poor old cripple in the *wheelchair.*"

In the rearview mirror, he saw the poor cripple was giving him the finger as she bumped herself up on the curb. He said nothing.

". . . thoughtless. What if the Oilings woman puts an item in the *Bald Eagle?* Have you ever thought of that?"

The only way Mrs. Oilings, Long Pidd's gossip-cum-char, would know is if Agatha had told her this morning. Mrs. Oilings had refused to help with the luggage as she'd been busy leaning on her mop and catching up on last-minute items. They were driving near the Stray, that wonderful two-hundred-acre common replete with gardens, walks, and streams.

"I can see it now—" Here Agatha drew with thumb and forefinger an imaginary banner-space in air: *"Earl of Caverness and Local Antiques Dealer Take Part in New Year Festivities.* 'Said Miss Vivian Rivington, long-time resident of Long Piddleton who is about to wed the Count Franco Giopinno, "It was tacked to my door. Of course, I thought it must be the children . . ." ' "

He pretended the Jermyn Street tailor had stitched his lips together, fighting his desire to yell *shut up!* Imagine, two blissful weeks without one of the Talking Heads.

As he spotted the sign that pointed them toward the Old
Swan Hotel, she said, "You've done it this time, Melrose."
Agatha smacked her lips in satisfaction. "She'll never speak
to you again."

If only he could get the same result by doing something to
her door.

They had turned up the wet gravel drive, the trees sodden
with the weight of old rain, the air raw, threatening snow.
The Old Swan was a Harrogate landmark, located near the
famous Baths, and large enough for the Kitchener troops, its
floors going up and up. It was at this hotel that Agatha
Christie had reputedly stayed during her remarkable disappearance. Agatha disappearing. Lightning, unfortunately,
didn't strike twice, he thought, as he braked and spat up
gravel.

"This is it, Plant. We're here!"

She said it as if Melrose had suddenly had a fit of hysterical blindness and would zip straight past the entrance at
eighty per. Agatha left the disposal of her luggage to her
nephew and the hotel staff and marched up the steps.

Mentally, he gave himself a pat on the back. He'd won!

Two hundred miles and he hadn't uttered a word. Such
grim determination would have earned him a knighthood
had he not already thrown away an earldom! Four hours,
and she'd elicited no response from him no matter how
much needling, how much baiting. Melrose imagined what
the poor bears must have suffered before bear-baiting was
made illegal, chained to stumps and set upon by dogs. As he
followed in the wake of Agatha's "things"—the trunks, the
cases, the reticules, portmanteaus—Melrose noticed the bell-
hop carrying the hatboxes wore the insolent and sinister expression of Robert Montgomery in *Night Must Fall*.

Really, old man, he thought. Was there a secret spring of
violence in him waiting to be tapped? Axes, snarling dogs,
heads in boxes?

As Agatha took to reeducating the desk clerks as to

the running of the hotel, and attending to the matter of her room's location ("overlooking the gardens, of course . . ."), Melrose plucked a little pamphlet from those set out for visitors. The Harrogate hydros were, of course, famous. He was fascinated by the item on the Countess of Buckingham pitching a tent near one of the wells apparently to get the chalybeate waters before anyone else could. People flowed in, like the waters themselves, in carts and gigs to take these malodorous waters. . . .

Good heavens, Melrose thought, Harrogate was the perfect milieu for Wiggins. Jury's sergeant would be the first to agree that the more offensive the sulfur, the greater its potency and the better the cure.

He looked up and down the long hall, where windows displayed the latest finery to be bought at great expense from the local swank shops. In the enormous and handsome dining room, waiters were moving about putting final touches to napkins and crystal. To his left was a large sitting room that served as bar and a place for tea. Here the tea-drinkers sat about like sticks, what few there were: three couples and one single lady, all middle-aged, looking as if they were caught in some holding pattern between life and death.

One could feel the history of Harrogate pressing heavily in, looking round the Old Swan, sitting here in the cold and sodden January of Yorkshire's West Riding.

God! Would he stop thinking about *Death in Venice?* Melrose shut his eyes tightly to make the vision go away, himself like Prufrock in white flannel trousers strolling along the beach—

"Over here! Yoo-hoo! Melrose, dear! Melrose!"

The fluting voice broke up a vision, like pebbles dashed in water, of himself dying in a canvas deck chair by a bathhouse. He looked about, baffled, and then heard the bellowing voice of Agatha behind him answering the other:

"Teddy! Teddy, dear!"

Hell's bells! he thought. He'd been mentally basking in the Italian sun when he should have been making his getaway. Now he was stuck, that was all there was to it, as Agatha trumpeted by him toward the table where sat the single lady. He was, after all, a gentleman, and could hardly walk out without saying hello . . .

Or could he? Not walk out, of course, but continue his vow of silence? If he could manage to keep his mouth shut for two hundred miles, surely he could play the game for another half hour. He checked his watch as he walked toward the two women. One-half hour, chair to door, the acid test. Could he make a comparative stranger believe that he'd actually taken part in their exchange without saying anything?

"Hel-*lo*, Melrose!" Teddy extended her heavily veined and beringed hand.

With what he hoped was a debonair smile, rather than shaking the hand, he barely grazed the fingers with his lips.

Teddy's tiny black eyes, being lent the glint of shadow and kohl liner, glittered like sequins.

Melrose sat as his aunt said, "Well, practicing for the Continent, are you, Plant? But you'll never scrub off that old moth-eaten country-tweedy look. . . ."

He smiled, choking the desire to ask her if she'd any more adjectives on hand, but merely crossed his unbespoken-tailored gray-worsted-trousered legs, plucked an apple green napkin from the blush pink tablecloth, and sat back while Agatha told Teddy that they were all off to Italy soon.

As they greeted each other, kissing air, and then sat gabbling away, Melrose wondered both how he was to order tea without opening his mouth (here came the waiter) and if this was the same woman whom they'd visited in York. *That* Teddy (Althea, he believed, was her name) had been a heavy, squarely built woman with a frieze of bright orange hair so lacquered that a North Sea gale couldn't've dislodged a wisp of it. *This* Teddy looked a bit gaunt and had given up the henna, apparently, for her bluey-black hair was done in some hairdresser's idiot version of a '20s style, a lot of little wet-looking ringlets like a bunch of mashed grapes.

And she was no longer plain old Mrs. Stubbs, but had snagged—good Lord, were they that common?—a nobleman somewhere in the South of France. De la Roche was her name now. Were there so many loose princes, counts, crackpot kings wandering round that they were ripe for the taking? Which line of thought quite naturally only led him back to Count Dracula Giopinno and that Vivian had shouted at him and Marshall Trueblood she'd be bloody damned if she'd let them come to her wedding—

Slam went the door of her cottage. He chewed his lip. Marshall had a plan for taking the Orient Express.

"*Well, good Lord, Melrose! Absolutely everyone disguises himself on the Orient Express. You should see them trooping about Victoria Station.*"

"Sir?"

Melrose was jolted now from Vivian's doorstep, where he was determined to stand until he molted, by the white-jacketed waiter. He was nearly surprised into a reply of some sort. He merely returned the waiter's smile and got the result he wanted.

"Tea for three, sir?"

After all, waiters in places like the Old Swan were trained to anticipate one's needs. Melrose nodded. He'd really have loved to have been challenged with a menu in Greek, or something. No, that wouldn't be a challenge. All he'd have to do was point.

The waiter returned his nod and said, "The set tea, madame? Or would you prefer sandwiches? Buttered toast—?"

Melrose was absolutely enjoying the small challenge this could present, until the waiter said, "Madame?" Hell, "Madame" would fill up the whole thirty minutes—now twenty-two—just ordering.

"—tarts, of course. Have you watercress sandwiches? Yes, we'll have those with the cucumber ones, too—"

Teddy put in: "Oh, you must try the anchovy toast, dear. It's quite delectable."

"Sir," said the waiter, and swanned away as if Melrose had given him the complete order.

Checking his watch, he raised his time-frame to forty-five minutes, all told, which left, as of now, thirty-one minutes in which he intended to make them believe he had talked when he hadn't.

The *Times* crossword in under fifteen minutes seemed dull by comparison. When he thought about it further, he realized actors could do this very thing: Bogart only needed to narrow his lips, Cagney to grit his teeth, Gielgud to raise his eyebrows, and Gable—hell, did anyone remember a *word* he'd ever said except "I don't give a damn"? Of course not.

Thus for thirty-one minutes, two cups of tea, one finger of anchovy toast, Melrose grinned, grimaced, touched, sat back and forth, laughed soundlessly, leaned close, leaned back, slapped his leg, crooked his elbow, looked intent.

He had become, in half an hour, a brilliant conversationalist.

As they gibbered like gibbons in the bush, he rose, looked pained that he must leave, once again brought Teddy's hand to his lips, and actually squeezed Agatha's shoulder in farewell.

As he walked off, smiling all round at waiters and stone-faced guests, he thought again, *I won!*

He'd make a mockery of speech, a burlesque of words, a travesty of talk.

"Melrose!"

Agatha was bellowing at his back. He stopped, turned. She was waving him back.

Very well.

She was actually being gracious as she said, "But Melrose, you didn't *notice!*"

He raised his eyebrows in question, a thin smile playing on his lips.

"It's *Teddy!* Don't you remember how she looked in York?"

A confidential whisper now from Teddy: "Dear, I've been

completely done over!" Here she spread her arms, then touched her neck, her hair, turned her head this way and that. "There's this marvelous little clinic in Zurich. . . . Well? What do you think?"

He knew he didn't need to do it. He knew he was clever enough to get out of this. After the whole day's efforts, he could have ordered Wellington's troops with a few flicks of his fingers; beaten Connors at Wimbledon with a teabag; left Lester Piggott a length behind with a hobbyhorse.

"Well, Melrose? Well?"

He splayed his arms on the table, looked deeply into Teddy's eyes and said, "Why waste words?"

The gasps and giggles trailed behind him as he left the Old Swan Hotel.

10

Gnawing on a chicken leg that Agatha had missed in her rummage through the picnic basket, Melrose drove through Ilkley.

Trying to circumvent the moors was like trying to get round London on the Circle Line. Every gritty little town seemed to have its moor. Ilkley Moor, Stanbury Moor, Haworth Moor, Keighley Moor, Black Moor, Howden Moor: they were fixed about like railway station stops. Nothing like the North York moors he had crossed several years ago in the snow, a vast expanse of Arctic waste; nor like Dartmoor, a lunar landscape of fogs and slanting rains. Here in Yorkshire's West Riding there was a plethora of moors. Nature, abhorring yet another vacuum, must have said, *There's a space, drop a moor in it.*

And this narrow ribbon of road he'd taken to connect up with Haworth was meant for sheep, not for man—certainly not man in a Bentley. He looked up at the sky, now turgid like brackish water, looked out at the sad-faced sheep and slid down in the driver's seat, his earlier euphoria dissipating.

Face it, you are no lover of Nature. He sighed. The only Nature he seemed able to appreciate was the picture-book change of seasons in his own parkland at Ardry End. Golden autumn, lilac-scented spring . . .

Oh, for heaven's sake; it wasn't like that at all. There wasn't a lilac bush within ten miles.

Was this the right road? It didn't even look finished. Macadamed on one side for a distance, rutted earth on the other, going nowhere, he imagined, but to Eternal Moorland. He pulled over, braked, opened the accordion map. Two moorland sheep raised their heads from the bracken, moved forward slightly, stared and chewed.

Yes, this appeared to be the road. But where was this pub so clearly marked? Any pub marked on a map must be worth a stop.

Good Lord, how self-indulgent. One would think he'd never set foot out of London, so citified did he feel at the moment. He looked over at the two sheep. They looked so clumsy with all that wool, he disliked them. Nor did they seem dying of curiosity to know him.

He tried to refold the map, which remained intransigent to his handling; why was it maps, such neat accordions when you purchased them, would spring apart and seem to grow larger, filling your car, rampant as wild things. Oh, the hell with it. He squared it off and stuffed it, resisting, into the glove box and sat there glooming away.

What was the matter with him? He must get out, stretch his legs, have a brief walk on the moor (very brief), and, warming to this mild burst of enthusiasm, decided to take the picnic basket with him. There might be another piece of chicken or a tart and he was hungry. Agatha had been so busy throwing the debacle in his face, she had actually missed out on some tasty morsels in the basket. He thought he spied a thin slice of salmon rolled around capers and caviar. He set off on his tramp through bracken and rocks, feeling like a true West Yorkshireman.

After cleaning his shoe of sheep dung, wrapping his handkerchief round the rash of bloody pricks on his hand, moving his ankle gingerly where he'd caught it amongst this clump of deceptive, moss-covered rocks, Melrose found a wide, flat stone and sat down to look at the running stream. Or beck, he supposed it was called.

He looked across the snowy patches beside the stream,

past bracken and burnt-looking heather, to a distance where
he caught sight of a woman who, probably because of the
illusory quality of the moors themselves, had sprung from
nowhere. She had simply appeared on the crest of a treeless
hill, snow-covered, walking along it in a cape that billowed
behind her, and nothing in hand that might identify her as a
tourist, a walker along the Pennine or Brontë ways, empty-
handed, going from nowhere to nowhere. The image fascinated him and he watched her walk, a silhouette against the
white horizon, until his attention was called away by a
sound. It was an odd grizzling sound, as if someone were
trying to clear his throat, followed by a sort of cat-cry. He
looked up, saw two birds circling. Curlews sounded like
cats, didn't they? Well, if they were circling over *him,* they
were probably buzzards.

Quickly he returned his gaze to the skyline. The woman
was gone. He lit a cigarette, looked at the coal end, shook
his head. Here he'd come with his picnic basket to commune
with Nature in a Chesterfield coat and with a gold cigarette
case. He shook his head again. Hopeless.

He must take decisions.

What decisions? They'd all been taken for him. Polly
Praed was no doubt right now sitting with her amethyst eyes
glued to the page in her typewriter on which poured forth
the fates of dogs or doges, and Vivian Rivington—

Oh! But wasn't he disgusted with himself? Blame it on
Trueblood; it was all Trueblood's idea. Liar. Trueblood got
the cut-out book, but he himself had gone right along with
it. Well, what fun could you get out of life if you couldn't
devil Vivian, after all?

What he couldn't stand was change. He thought, sitting
here, perhaps he could become a Zen Buddhist. If he
watched the water, if he flowed with the beck . . . Wasn't
that the idea? Weren't they always saying that one must
flow? One must forgo attachments? That life must be considered a running stream and to try to hold water in one's hand
was total illusion? The trouble was, though, that all of this

transience only seemed to apply to friendship, love, and beauty. Not wars and plagues and people one loathed. You didn't see *them* go floating down the beck . . .

So what kind of comfort did *flow* offer? He wanted things to stay absolutely the same, the same little group at the same table in the Jack and Hammer; the same rat terrier outside of Miss Crisp's secondhand furniture shop—

Melrose looked round, for he heard the sound again.

Well, what about the Everlasting Now? Wasn't that a Zen notion too?

He rummaged through the basket and yanked out a chicken wing covered in crumbs of broken roll and knew one of his problems was his total lack of vocation, except for those zombie lectures he inflicted on students of French Romantic poetry. He studied the chicken wing and thought of Rimbaud.

Did he have to choose a genius who'd died at nineteen? At nineteen all Melrose was doing was falling off horses. He was going cross-eyed trying to find bits of meat on the wing and gave it up, tossing it in the basket. Naturally, Agatha had drunk the half bottle of Pouilly-Fumé that his cook had put in specially for him.

He allowed himself a huge, self-pitying sigh. He'd simply got to take stock of himself. . . . Gevrey-Chambertin, Château Margaux, the incomparable finesse of the Montrachets; Chevalier, Bâtard, Chassagne. The ones Dumas had said should be drunk kneeling; the Chablis Grands Crus; the Côte de Girarmes Napoleon loved. And then the port . . . it was more interesting taking stock of his wine cellar.

The noise this time was nearer and more distinct. Melrose left the cobwebbed environs of his wine cellar to squint through the mossy rocks. That mewling noise he had taken as the curlew's was, after all, a cat: it sat there, blinking its yellow eyes, looking starved.

Start thinking of your private stock of port and something comes along to shame you, he supposed. Melrose put the cat in the basket—clearing out the chicken bones first—and lugged it back to the road.

A woman standing at a crossroad apparently waiting for a local directed him to a hamlet the other side of which was an animal hospital. Since she had nothing better to do but stand there and gape at his car, she took a long time about it.

2

The True Friend Animal Hospital lay at the end of an infernal, potholed track of road that ended at a square, gray-stoned building with a cleared-off patch of equally rutted earth meant as a car park. Occupying it were a Ford truck of '40s vintage, a Mini Clubman Estate, a Jag, and a couple of bicycles with wire baskets. A drenching rain had started up right after he'd left the woman still staring after the Bentley. He turned up the velvet collar of his coat and jogged to the unfriendly-looking door of True Friend.

The waiting room was furnished with three wooden benches, one against each wall, and the counter behind which a tired-looking woman in steel-rimmed glasses and hair like a Brillo pad sat with a pile of filing folders.

Melrose's acquaintance with veterinarians was minimal; he wondered, though, why these places always had names like Animal Haven and Loving Kindness when they generally resembled jails and had receptionists like wardens. This one told him that as he had no appointment, he'd have to wait until the *regular customers* were taken care of. Her tone registered her disapproval of his casual and his damp and his rather noisy cat as she nodded toward the benches for him to be seated.

Not that there was any shortage of noise in the room already. A bullterrier and an Alsatian were having an awful row, each straining at his lead to see which could grab a portion of Melrose's ankle first. Some ineffectual snorting sounds came from their master, a middle-aged man with a basin-cut hairdo and a face like a cliffside, who apparently thought he was controlling his charges when finally one lay and the other sat tensely, both with snarls locked in their throats, the bullterrier with teeth bared at a calico cat a youngish couple had wedged between them.

On the other end of that bench sat the owner of the Jaguar (clearly), who appeared to think her foothold on a rung way up the social ladder from the other benchwarmers got her feet far enough off the ground to avoid the drooling bullterrier. Everything about her was glossily groomed: her Chanel suit, her wings of frosted hair, her whining poodle whose snout was pressed to the wire insert of the sort of carrier required by airlines. She did give Melrose a quick, appraising glance, fingered her pearls, and craned her neck to get a better view of the hood of the Bentley.

The two women on the other bench both wore thick woolen coats and paisley scarves over their heads and tied under their chins. In their laps were almost identical flat, black bags. Leaving off what had been a gossipy exchange about some "owld sluther-guts," they turned their wide, pleasant faces, bland as Yorkshire puddings, on Melrose and acknowledged both him and the weather by commenting on the rain lashing the windows. "Fearful poggy the rooads be," said one, giving him a rubber-band smile.

Melrose returned the smile and the nod as he sat himself and the basket on the single unoccupied bench.

The two returned to their exchange, apparently unconcerned that the Skye terrier at their feet was lying with glassy eyes and front legs splayed out and possibly already dead; or that the cardboard box beside the one who had spoken seemed to be moving toward the edge of the bench—

". . . to get 'em to stir theirsen, an' then ah cooms doan t'see t'bairns w'Mickey 'ere . . ."

She nodded at the terrier. ". . . t'lectric an' . . . in

t'Persil. Ah was ommast fit to bust, Missus Malby . . . wi'
t'bairns yammerin' an' . . . roun' 'n roun'."

"Ooh, aye. Pore ting loaks deead i' t' middle, 'e do. Perky,
'ere . . ." And she tapped the box with the airholes.
". . . clackin' away, ahr Tom was . . . caught i' t'mangle,
and ahr Alice yammerin' abaht . . ."

She opened the box and Melrose thought he saw the beak
and top of some colorful-looking bird pop out before the one
called Malby shoved it back in.

The other one clucked her tongue. "Aye, Missus Livlis,
lookin' yonderly 'e is," and gave the room in general a
gummy smile. Melrose interpreted this to mean the parrot
was near death, for these two were certainly into it.

Melrose was fascinated by all of this, for what he made
out was that Mrs. Malby's bairns had stuffed the terrier into
the washing machine (which was apparently an appliance
the Malbys had just acquired) and dashed in some washing
powder. (Sometimes Melrose was just as glad he was bairn-
less.) Whether the terrier had actually gone round at all
before its rescue by Mrs. Malby, he couldn't discover from
their clotted talk, but from the look of it, he'd say the terrier
had been spin-dried. The parrot's fate was uncertain. Caught
in a mangle? It could be Mrs. Livlis (Lovelace, perhaps?)
was not as fortunate as Mrs. Malby and had to do her wash
in an old-fashioned tub and the parrot might have enjoyed
perching on the mangle—

The outside door burst open upon this scene of riot, car-
nage, and washday blues, admitting wind, rain, and a small
girl covered more or less top to bottom in a hooded yellow
oilskin and black wellingtons. Melrose was hoping the box
she held harbored something ordinary, like a litter of kit-
tens. She entirely ignored the yowlings for her blood her
entrance had effected in the Alsatian and the bullterrier as
she marched up to the desk.

Fortunately, the receptionist was finally telling the man
with the dogs to go back and the Alsatian and the bullterrier
more or less chewed and clawed their way across the room,

making passes at the child's boots, though she didn't seem to notice or to care as she set her box on the floor. The flaps were up; it appeared to be empty, so he supposed she was coming to collect her pet. That encouraged him, for he wasn't certain about anything leaving True Friends alive, given the intermittent screeches and yelps he heard coming from the bowels of the building.

Wearily, the receptionist put a question to her—Melrose was too far away to hear precisely, but he picked up on "appointment."

The girl's chin just grazed the counter. She sounded a little thunderstruck when she had to answer, No, and tried to add something about a doctor there.

With that sort of impatience some adults reserve for all children, the grizzle-haired receptionist asked her, "Have you brought in your pet?"

The girl raised her own voice. "No—" Something seemed to catch at her throat.

"Well? What's your name?"

"Abby." The word exploded. "It's my cat."

"And Doctor told you to collect it? Well? What's its name?"

"Buster!" said the girl in a voice raised several notches as she whirled from the counter and marched over to sit on the bench by Melrose, making sure she kept her distance. She sat with her arms hard across her chest, hands fisted, staring straight ahead.

The receptionist just shook and shook her head at this intractable girl and called across the room, "Is he in the hospital, then?" Here she jabbed her pencil toward the ceiling.

"She is *dead!"*

The receptionist quickly changed her tune, realizing that Buster had died at True Friends. The reaction of the customers was predictable: *we didn't hear that; she didn't say that.* Heads swiveled away from the Fury sitting amongst them. The couple with the now-obscenely-alive calico cleared their throats in unison, eyes ranging round the ceiling. Mrs. Malby and Mrs. Livlis had the grace to look truly mournful. The Jaguar owner smoothed her way to the end of her bench, leaned over the arm toward the furious child, put on a mushy look, and tried to engage the little girl's eyes.

Well, thought Melrose, sliding down in his seat, there were always people who liked to check out electrical sockets with their fingers or pull parrots from mangles. He knew what was coming.

Although the little girl refused to look at the well-dressed lady or her beastly poodle, the woman still said, "Never mind, dear; you can always get another kitty."

The Furies, Medea, Pandora could not have unleashed anything into that room more violent than the little girl's expression when she looked at this person. The woman backed physically away from what could have been a fist in the face when the child's dark eyes snapped up and locked with the woman's pale blue ones. And the thunderclap that shook the room just then certainly sounded to Melrose as if God had a few ideas about the fate of the poodle.

It was perhaps fortunate that as the little girl rose in something like a trance to face this woman, the receptionist hurried in with the box, obviously heavier now.

The child took it without a word, turned in her yellow slicker, and walked through the door that Melrose had risen to open for her.

The rain poured from a sky gray-dark as the little girl walked down the road, splashing through puddles.

Melrose had, of course, wanted to transport her to wherever she was going, and wondered what had sent this child on such an awful errand by herself.

But he didn't offer; he felt, for some reason, she knew how she wanted to go, and where; that she must go the way she came, carrying her dreadful burden. Two burdens, he thought, standing there in the door getting wet: her fury and her dead female cat named Buster.

11

As Jury was walking down the Citrine driveway to his car, hoping for a hot bath, a good meal, and a pretty waitress at the Old Silent, he saw her.

At least, he thought it must be Nell Healey. It was at a distance, and down a torturously winding path screened by trees; but he was sure he had seen a woman moving beyond him.

Jury stepped from the drive to the footpath that wound erratically between pines and spiny-branched elms. No wind stirred. It was as if there had been no storm. The wood at dusk was drearier even than it had seemed earlier that afternoon, as desolate and unhappy a scene as could be.

Wretched was the word that came to mind. Oak-galls clung to barks and branches; the skeletal remains of birches lined the gray sky. Jury looked back at the dark slab of the gatehouse, its squints for windows through which no light would show. Drab and eyeless, it looked almost pernicious. Along the path were the stiff remains of wagwort and flea-bane; sodden leaved and congealed between the roots of tree trunks; moss climbed around lichen-slippery stones.

He wondered if there were places that could infect the mind, abrade the heart, corrode the spirit. Why would any-one choose, as she certainly had, to live in such cold chambers, such a severe landscape, which he doubted was much improved by the coming of spring.

* * *

She was standing beside an elm. Standing, not leaning, apparently looking down to the end of the path where a useless gate listed. Useless, because the tiers of stone on either side had nearly disappeared. In this wall that no longer defined any boundary, the gate was redundant.

"Mrs. Healey?"

Although her back was to him, she would have heard his approach over stone shards and fallen twigs. There was no response. But he thought in the moments that followed that her gaze was turned inward, that the wood, path, gate—the entire landscape—was lost on her.

Before he could repeat the name, she swerved a little, looked round at him. "Oh. Hello." She did not pretend that she couldn't remember him, or imagine why she'd be meeting him on this path.

She was holding, incongruously, a handful of leaves rescued from autumn like a small bouquet, as if, having set out to pick some winter flower, this was all she could find. Her skin had a gauzy sheen to it, like her hair. He thought at first the face was made paler by a lack of rouge and eyeshadow; then he knew that what he had taken in the Old Silent for the pallor of illness was not that at all. Her skin had the pellucid look of a child's; her hair was not ash-blond, but streaked here and there with lighter glints and reddish strands; it was variegated, like her eyes. Though the look she gave him was glancing, like cold light on cold water, frozen in the prismatic irises were bits of color like the leaves she held: mottled gold and green and brown with a silvery bloom. Even her clothes were the same colors—dark green sweater hooked round her shoulders, gold silk blouse, brown trousers. It was an autumnal look. In some sort of alchemy, she had absorbed what colors remained. Or, chameleon-wise, was trying to blend in and hide there.

After a moment or two in which she looked from the path to him and back toward the falling-down gate, she said, "I wasn't meaning to be avoiding—" She stopped and expelled a long sigh.

"Avoiding me?" Jury laughed a little. "I'd hate to try to find you if you *meant* to be elusive."

Her gaze went back to the path and gate.

Jury looked down it. "Were you waiting for someone?"

That earned him a flicker of honest interest. "Waiting?" She smiled slightly. "No."

Either she gave the impression of one always just on the point of speaking, or he was so used to people rattling on about their lives that he was uneasy, waiting himself upon her silence. "You seem so intent," he added limply, "upon that prospect." He looked down the path.

Her smile was very slight. "I have none of those," she said, ambiguously and almost irrelevantly. "A useless gate, isn't it? I expect this place was surrounded by a medieval wall. Perhaps that was what was called a *clair-voyee*. . . ."

He moved closer, to a position that would have commanded more attention, if that were possible. She continued in her odd way both to note his presence and to ignore it.

"Mrs. Healey—"

"Nell." Her smile was almost convincing. "We were in close enough contact I think you can call me by my first name." Now, she looked away again, this time at the surrounding elms and birches. "I wonder why you're back."

It was a statement only; she did not seem interested in Jury's reasons. He had the feeling that things were done with, finished, for her. There was no trace of hostility in her tone, and none of hope, either. She looked down at the path, as if studying the groupings of pebbles, leaves, and roots. She seemed deep in thought, but it was not her surroundings that engaged her attention, and not him. She appeared not to care how he answered.

"The reason I'm 'back,' as you put it, is that I hoped you might tell me why you killed your husband."

She opened her mouth as if to reply. He waited for something; there was nothing. Somewhere, he heard the soft thunk of a pinecone. Her profile was to him; her arms folded across her breast, hands resting in the crooks of her elbows.

This fixated pose and refusal to talk did not strike Jury as obduracy. She was not being stubborn. Indeed, she once again opened her mouth as if she meant to answer, then closed it as before.

"Your father says it must have been revenge."

After a few moments, she said only, "Does he?" and pulled her sweater closer. Her voice broke between the two syllables.

Did she sense that she was not smooth enough, not plausible enough to go along with that lie?

"But that doesn't surprise you; that must be the line your solicitors are taking—that and temporary insanity."

A feverish color rose from her neck to her face, mottling the cool skin. But her reaction seemed to stem from something other than embarrassment. The corners of her mouth twitched.

Jury wanted to shake her out of this nunlike placidity and calm acceptance of her fate. And he wondered that she didn't appear angry, or, at least, unnerved, by his appearance. She did not seem even to question it. He went on: "After eight years, that'd be a hell of a difficult case to make—even for someone as clever as Sir Michael."

After a few moments, all she said was, "I expect so."

It was such a flat-out statement and carried such a note of conviction that she mightn't have cared at all what happened to her. Her hands were locked behind her; her eyes fixed fast on the end of the path. Jury looked toward the gate, the *clair-voyee,* and beyond it. There was a bitter little orchard of pollarded trees with shrunken trunks, pencil-thin branches, bony limbs jutting out. In summer, though, it would be different, the trees inviting a child to climb them for the fruit.

"Did your son play there?"

"Yes." It took her some time to add: "With Toby."

It was odd, how she gave only the first name, as if she had an implicit knowledge he'd know Toby.

"Toby Holt."

Nell drew the sweater more closely together and nodded. "They were good friends, which is strange given Billy was twelve and Toby was nearly sixteen. At fifteen, well . . ." She didn't finish. "I actually think he admired Billy. Of course, Billy seemed older, probably because of his music. He was a wizard, he could play anything, really. Poor Toby. No matter how he tried he could hardly make music with a comb. And Abby, they both actually put up with Abby. She was only three. How is she? And the Holts. Have you talked with the Holts? I wonder how they're getting on without him."

Shaking her head, she looked at the ground. Looked and kept shaking her head as if all of this were a puzzle, a mystery beyond her poor powers to comprehend. And strange her wondering how the Holts "were taking it," as if his death had occurred only last week.

There was no question, apparently, that he would see Abby, would see the Holts. He was sure that at that moment she did not even register his presence as a policeman, or perhaps not at all. She was talking, he thought, to herself. At least, she was talking.

Jury was certain that she could see the ghost of Billy Healey beyond the broken walls, climbing a tree. And when he looked round at her again, she seemed to have taken on the aspects of the orchard; she seemed to have shrunken, grown thinner, turned in upon herself. Her clear complexion, even, had developed tiny lines, like crazed porcelain. She had brought a small book of poetry out from her pocket, and her fingers, skeletal-looking to his eye now, turned it round and round.

"It looks"—here she nodded toward the rows of smallish trees—"as if it were freezing to death. But it's only resting. What would be dangerous and deadly is a rush of unseasonable warmth." She paused. "I only know that because of a poem about someone's looking at his orchard and saying to it, 'Good-bye and keep cold.' "

"You seem to find that comforting." A chilly wind sprang up, making a few leaves skitter about with a tinny sound, blowing her hair loose from the mooring of its tortoiseshell comb and whipping a few strands across her face. She pulled them back, like a veil, from her mouth and chin and re-pinned the hair.

"Do you like poetry?" asked Jury.

"Yes." His eyes were on the hands combing back the hair, repinning it. She looked extremely young. "I do because you can trust the language of it. I hate talking."

Jury smiled. "That's abundantly clear. It's the only clear thing about you." If he was expecting this to draw her out, he was wrong. She took her own line.

"Words are like gauze. Semitransparent, easily torn, always frayed." It was a delicate smile, as if it had to be tested. She seemed pleased that she'd said what she meant.

"You're probably right, but it's all we've got, and not many of us are poets. I guarantee Queen's Counsel won't be at all poetic when he gets you in the dock." He moved round in front of her to force her to look at him. "Look, don't you think this silence of yours, this not liking to talk, is a conceit you have that there's some buried truth you might dig up if you could find the perfect words to do it? That the world is deaf and dumb, so there's no sense trying to get through to it?"

He knew the minute the words were out of his mouth he'd said exactly the wrong thing, yet he couldn't help himself. She made him angry. When she turned her face to the path again, he said, "I'm sorry. I have no business talking to you at all, much less . . . chastising you." He smiled a little; he must have fallen into the trap of trying to find the right word and he'd picked one that sounded strange and tasted strange, like sea water. "I'm just sure that there's more to it. Perhaps you've told your solicitors; perhaps the last thing you'd do is talk to me. But I don't think you told them any more than you're telling me. I know there's some other reason you shot your husband."

The silence lengthened like the shadows across the walk. It had grown nearly dark while they were standing here. The purple sky was bisected by a dim band of gold. Drawing her arms up against her breasts, she made a little bridge of her interlaced fingers and rested her chin on them. She had only a small repertoire of movements; they were close and parsimonious, like her words. Since Jury had been talking to her she had moved no farther than the length of his arm. "Why?" was all she said.

He hesitated. He said something else: "You appeared too self-contained for a woman bent on revenge."

She brought her arms down, the hands still interlaced before her. She frowned. "You must be able to see a lot in a few seconds."

"It wasn't just those few seconds. In the dining room, remember, we were both there at the same time."

Slowly, she shook her head. "I was reading a book, that's all."

"Some book. I always leaf through Camus when I want cheering up."

She did not reply to that, but looked up at the purple-black sky and watched two curlews wheeling and making their odd, mulish noise.

"And earlier, in the Brontë museum."

Frowning, she said, "I didn't see you."

"I know. You were much too absorbed, and not in the old manuscripts and ledgers. I also saw you in the toy museum."

The frown deepened as she looked away and then back. "You were *following* me." Jury nodded. "*Why?*"

"I don't know."

She seemed more amused by this than annoyed as she shook her head again, very slowly. "But you said nothing."

And he said nothing now, partly because he was breaking his own code and ashamed of that; partly because the more she talked, the less he did. It was as though there was a small allotment of words, not enough for two people at once. It was his turn to look away, toward the gate and the trees beyond.

"I don't understand." It was as if she didn't much care whether she did or not.

Finally, he said what he hadn't said before, what he knew he shouldn't say, unless he said it to Queen's Counsel. It would then remove any hope—remote as hope was—of Nell Healey's acquittal. "I know you're lying. You and your father. So was your husband."

This brought her head round sharply, a look of honest wonder on her face, eyes wide. In the faded light, the glimmer of different colors could not be seen. The irises seemed to have melded into a goldish-green. "Lying about what?"

"About your motive. Even if you haven't said it, you haven't *unsaid* it. Revenge because Roger Healey, or both of them, took the advice of the Cornwall constabulary and refused to pay the ransom for Billy. And what about your father? Do you intend to kill him, too, out of revenge?" Jury said it mildly.

No response; she became even stiller.

"Your husband didn't have that kind of money. You did. Although the others acted as if it were their money, you were the one who had to sign the check, so to speak. And you didn't; you wouldn't."

Her folded hands came up again to her mouth and her eyes were squeezed shut, as if in this posture she might hold back whatever threatened to come out: tears, words, feelings. Finally, her body went slack again and she asked dully, "How do you know this? The superintendent—" Quickly she stopped, probably aware she was confessing.

"Goodall promised Charles Citrine that the report would be slightly altered? It would make no difference to police which one of you decided, after all."

"The sergeant—" she said, looking at him again with astonishment. "It was the sergeant who told you." Pulling her sweater closer—it was much too cold now for just a sweater, but Jury doubted she noticed it that much—she said, "I remember him very clearly. His name was Mac-something. . . ."

"Macalvie. He's not a sergeant any longer. He's very high up, a divisional commander. Same as a chief superintendent."

"Then you're high up, too."

Jury smiled. "Not like Macalvie. God isn't higher up than Macalvie."

It amazed Jury that she was actually smiling. Not only because she hadn't before, except for a tentative one, but that she could smile over Brian Macalvie. "You don't hate him? For giving that advice so bluntly."

That she might be expected to hate him seemed to puzzle her. "Why should I? I didn't have to take it. And the advice was pretty much what police had been giving all along; the other officer was saying the same thing in a most unconvincing way. The sergeant had a great deal of force and intensity; he was probably placing himself at risk, too. I got the feeling he was absolutely sure he was right."

Jury smiled. "He'd be the first to agree."

"He didn't seem conceited."

"Oh, conceit has nothing to do with it. He's just very much in touch with his own talents—and they're considerable, believe me. That you didn't get Billy back doesn't mean he was wrong. But you must have thought sometimes that if you'd paid that ransom . . ."

She moved away from him and seemed to be concentrating on the black bark of an oak. "It's all over. But it was over before; I haven't much of a case, as you said."

Jury walked to the tree, leaned his hand against it. "I don't think our knowing will make any difference."

She frowned up at him. "He'll be subpoenaed, and you're—"

"The official police report said the 'family' refused to pay the ransom. The point is: Macalvie—and I—might be more interested in justice being served. But you—" Jury shrugged. "—I'm not sure you're interested in it that much. You give me the impression of someone who's carried out a very difficult task, at last, and damn the consequences."

Since he had moved into her line of vision there and was big enough and close enough to eclipse her view, she had to look at him. She stared at his sweater, his raincoat, and avoided his eyes. "You think I'm cold-blooded." Her expression was sad.

"No. 'Remote' isn't 'cold-blooded.' "

She stood looking at the twisted trees, saying nothing, drawing the silence round her as she did her cardigan.

"Good-bye, Mrs. Healey."

"Good-bye."

He had taken a few steps down the path when he heard her say, "And keep cold."

12

The woman at reception at the White Lion Hotel wore an expression that suggested she must take full responsibility—was "most terribly sorry"—for the hotel's not being able to accommodate him. When she returned from an inner office, "just to make sure there's been no cancellation," repeated her apology twice, and dabbed at her raw, red nose, Melrose was concerned that his sudden appearance at the White Lion and his subsequent leave-taking had caused some gust of tears, some upheaval on the part of the hotel staff over the discomfiture of prospective guests. But the chilblained nose and smudged eyes were not owing to an emotional onslaught at Melrose's being turned out into the cold. She had caught a chill and was feverish. She made suggestions: the Black Bush across the street? No, he'd been there already. Stupid of him not to book a room in advance.

"Whatever for? Haworth in January, the rooms generally go begging." She seemed fearful that he would take upon himself the charge of stupidity when his outcast condition was already a great deal for him (and her) to bear.

Beginning to feel like the dying cast of *Les Misérables,* Melrose tried to raise her spirits with assurances that the tourist information center next door would find something for him. The clerk looked despairing, and as Melrose smiled and smiled and then left, he wondered if the people of Haworth had been more infected by Brontë gloom than by virus or murder.

* * *

While the attendant at the information center was helping a middle-aged woman, Melrose roved the small room and plucked up pamphlets, a guide or two, and a few gloomy monochromes of the surrounding moors and the village. One of these, the scene of Haworth parsonage and grave-yard, he thought he would send to Vivian just to let her know the sorts of places he was hanging about in since their last meeting. In his reconnoitering of the racks he was fol-lowed by a pie-faced boy of perhaps ten or twelve, who was carrying a large bag of crisps and licking a purple lolly en-closing a band of bilious green that went round and round in an hypnotic circle, probably the unwholesome child of the woman at the counter. The boy had expressionless eyes, blank as coins, and, having nothing to do, meant to occupy himself by getting this sticky sweet closer and closer to Mel-rose's cashmere coat.

"Branwell Brontë?" asked Melrose, as if the lad had ques-tioned him. He then read, as loudly as he could, Branwell's commentary on the Lord Nelson, which was appended to a photograph of that famous pub. " 'I would rather give my hand than undergo again the malignant yet cold debauchery which too often marked my conduct there.' " Melrose paused, looked down at the ill-mannered lad, and, in a mea-sured, distinct tone, said, "Well, I don't know where he got his drugs, do I?"

The woman in the turquoise get-up, whose long, sallow face was further elongated by the height of the black turban-like thing she wore, turned quickly and said, "Malcolm!" in a deep, almost basso voice. She gave Melrose a hooded look and clutched Malcolm to her side, a grip from which Mal-colm broke with alacrity. Melrose was more his style.

On the wall above the counter was a huge blowup of a photograph of the ruins of the old farmhouse Emily Brontë was said to have used for her Wuthering Heights. The other woman, round-faced and with a yellow bubble of hair and a tiny voice, was asking how good the road was to this site.

When the patient woman behind the counter told her that there was no road, that she'd have to *walk* the moor for perhaps a quarter of a mile, she turned to Melrose, as if for reassurance and said, in her whispery voice, "I can just look at the picture for a bit, then, can't I?"

"Absolutely, madam. That is precisely the way I climbed Mount Kilimanjaro. With my camp at its base, a large map, and some drawing pins I went straight to the top. Read Hemingway for atmosphere. After all, why have the reality when you can settle for its appearance? Why substance when you can walk in its shadow? Why, for pity's sake, waste time? It is all we have."

The cherub-faced lady looked moonily at him. "I never . . ."

Melrose was sure she hadn't. He walked to another turn-stile of postcards, followed both by Malcolm and the smol-dering, suspicious eyes of the Beastly Boy's mother.

"We're not going to that dump"—Malcolm nodded to the photograph of Top Withins—"*we're* going to Hadrian's Wall, we are."

Melrose turned the stile and said, "Well, you'd better hop it then. That particular dump's in Northumberland."

"Mum knows 'im."

Melrose turned from the picture of Haworth's cobbled street. "What? Who?"

"Hadrian. The Emperor Hadrian." He mashed a handful of crisps into his mouth and waited to see how the moun-tain-climber would take this.

Melrose walked away.

The Beastly Boy followed. "See, she sees things. She can read cards and she sees ghosts. She's got like second sight."

Obviously not, or Malcolm wouldn't be here. Melrose stared. "Go away."

The Beastly Boy stuck out his tongue, a purple and green surprise, and was dragged off by his mum at the same time the beehive blonde collected her maps and charts and smiled brightly at Melrose in a good-bye look.

Melrose finally had his turn at the counter.

There were several places that she could suggest, all B & B's, though. "There's Mrs. Buzzthorpe; she does a lovely full breakfast; there's only the one room there and it would be quiet. If anything is quiet round here now." She ran her hand across her unquiet brow. "I expect you know—"

"I was really looking for something like an hotel or inn. There's the Old Silent, I understand." At least, that's where Jury said he was staying.

The poor woman clutched her sweater about her and said, "Ah, but that's where that grisly *murder*" (she made a meal of the word) "happened." Her voice had dropped to a hissing whisper as she leaned across the counter. "Two days ago, it was. A man murdered there. I expect that's why it's hard to get accommodation." She wrinkled her nose in distaste. "Thrill-seekers."

"But is it booked?" asked Melrose, himself lowering his voice to a whisper.

"'Twas closed by Keighley police for a bit. I can ring up." She did and had to report that its few rooms were taken. She went down her list again. "Weavers Hall. That's very pleasant." Doubtfully, she looked at his clothes, the silver-knobbed walking stick, and out the window at the Bentley. Hopelessly, she smiled. "I'm not sure it's quite your line, though."

"I'll take any line at all at this point. Where is Weavers Hall?"

That he was so amenable to what she seemed to regard as her starved selection made her go about her maps and pencils with alacrity. "It's just here, near the reservoir." She stabbed her sharp pencil at a point in the map a short distance from the village. "That's the road off to the right after Stanbury, which is a mile away. Altogether, not above two miles."

"You're very helpful; thank you. Does this place do meals? Has it a restaurant, that sort of thing?"

Her look was baleful, as if just having got him sorted out, she must now disappoint him. She put in quickly, "But Miss Denholme does a nice evening meal."

He smiled. The expression "evening meal" always made him think of beef shin and creamed potatoes, for some reason. Well, he would dine with Jury, anyway, tonight.

"Is her wine list extensive? Never mind," he said, when the brown eyes rounded in surprise. "Only kidding."

13

The Beastly Boy was engaged in the torture of a gray cat when Melrose came upon him on the grounds of Weavers Hall, directly after he'd parked the Bentley. He cursed himself for a fool for not having worked out that the lady at the tourist information center could well have directed the family here, as it was one of the few accommodations left.

Behind a large, flat rock, the center of a pile of smaller, crumbling pieces of stone, the Beastly Boy was more or less sitting on the cat, trying to force salt-and-vinegar crisps down its throat, at the same time bonging its head with what appeared to be a rolled-up poster. A huge bag sat up against one of the stones. The cat struggled and whined miserably. The boy had his back turned, and a band of pale, flaccid flesh showed where his Banana Republic T-shirt had ridden up and his jeans had ridden down.

Probably owing to one of those portable stereos that sat against a wire fence and from which blasted forth rock music, the boy didn't hear Melrose's approach. Behind this fence, chickens scratched, ducks weaved drunkenly, and a rooster walked about apparently baffled.

The stereo was one of those that the young seemed to walk like dogs or carry about on their shoulders (having no other burdens). When he heard one walk by him on a London pavement, he always thought of it as a tribal call, one of the tribe on Regent Street signaling to his kind over on Piccadilly, perhaps. This one was putting out a musical hash consisting of (it sounded like) a couple of hundred cymbals and a thirties Chicago shoot-out.

Sitting on the flat stone was a bottle of lemonade that the boy reached up for as the cat tried to squirm its way from under him, and Melrose saw that he meant to force this too into the cat's mouth. He immediately pulled his walking stick from the leather straps of his suitcase, flicked it under the wrist that held the lemonade, and sent the bottle hurtling through the air, to land with a thud on the earth by the fence. Some ducks, beating their wings, waddled over to see what was going on.

The boy let out a yell, and the red flush across his face suggested the onset of a tantrum. He was up and fairly twitching with rage. The cat got up from its splayed position and shook itself.

"That's *my* lemonade!" But his eyes were on the innocent-appearing walking stick, actually a cosher, a leather tube filled with tiny pellets. Melrose was leaning on it looking at the broken, crumbling stone pile.

"Been to Stonehenge, too?"

The boy glared as well as he could, considering the thick-lensed glasses. The cat stopped looking muzzy and torpedoed down the road toward the outbuildings—a barn, stables, and a small stone cottage. A dog the color of bracken and snow like a border collie was barking at the cat's approach, either urging it on or warning it off. Melrose imagined a platoon of dogs would look safer to the gray cat than the company of the Beastly Boy, who was now looking at Melrose and mashing crisps into his mouth ferociously. Around them, he said, "You're stupid."

"I'm also bigger." Melrose tapped the cosher against his palm.

As he took a step backward, the boy's spider-lashes fluttered several times. He seemed to be thinking, and a hard job he was making of it given the face twisting like taffy. "I'm telling Mum."

"Oh, do. Then Mum will come to me and *I* can tell *her*. Mum and everybody else at this place."

The boy's eyes narrowed; he looked in the direction of Melrose's car and said, "Our car's better than yours."

Melrose slipped the walking stick back through the flaps of the suitcase and said, "Let's swap." He picked up his case and was about to turn on his heel when the boy turned up the volume of his stereo and shoved it toward the fence. The chickens were clucking and dithering about and the ducks rushing to the other end of the fenced enclosure.

Oh, for the Lord's sake, thought Melrose. "Stop that," he said.

"Thought maybe they'd like a front-row seat for Sirocco. You don't even know what they are, do you?" he asked smugly, over the blast of music.

"A hot wind that comes off the Sahara. Good-bye."

"Stupid!" the boy yelled at his departing back. "It's one of the best rock groups in the world!" He waved the poster. "I got front-row seats!"

Melrose kept on walking. He hoped Peter Townshend and rock stars like him were still breaking up their guitars, setting their drums on fire, et cetera, so that the pieces and burning bits flew into the front-row seats. As he was nearing the stone path, he looked to his left and saw a small girl coming from the barn and stables. He squinted. It was the Fury, the child he had seen at the vet's. Her black hair glittered like a helmet; she was wearing a white shawl that nearly reached her ankles and a dress too long for her.

If she saw him, she gave no sign of it. Given the determined walk and the look on her face, he seriously doubted she saw anything else but the object of her fury, there by the fence. She was carrying the gray cat over her shoulder like a bag of meal.

Several ducks left the barnyard brawl and rushed over to a corner of the fence nearest her as if they sensed something was coming, preferably dinner; and the rooster staggered over, planting each claw on the ground, digging in.

Seeing her, the boy let the stereo slide from his hands, music still playing, and tried to back straight through the fence. No escape. Melrose, like the ducks, could smell something in the wind as the girl set the cat down by the pile of stones. The cat calmly washed its paw, all threat of danger apparently forgotten under the protection of its patroness.

Melrose dropped his suitcase and started toward her as the Fury stepped closer to the boy. Did this little girl live every day on the cliff's edge? he wondered.

Apparently so. Before he could reach out, the arm was winding up, and she threw a lightning punch at the boy's chin that cracked when it landed.

The chickens were going crazy; the rooster was stalking like Frankenstein's monster; and from the stereo came frantic applause, whistling, and cheering voices that built to a roaring crescendo. The boy slid down the fence and let out a howl that mixed rather well with an ovation that should have broken the portable stereo to smithereens.

"Stop that!"

The voice pulled Melrose round as if by physical force and he saw, running from the doorway of Weavers Hall, the turbaned woman in the turquoise outfit, the Beastly Boy's mother. She startled the gray cat, who sensed more danger coming and bolted down the road. The chickens thrashed about, colliding, just as the venomous woman screeched at the little girl. Melrose lost that precious moment in which he could have strong-armed her or even tripped her—anything to stop her before she gave the Fury a backhand slap that should have knocked the child to the ground, but didn't even bend her. The child stood there, stubbornly planted with feet apart and refusing to go down for the count.

He bent down beside the little girl. "Are you all right?"

She nodded, frowning at him, not in displeasure, but as if she were trying to recollect where she'd seen him before. She did not have, as he had first thought, brown eyes. They were a deep navy blue and, at the moment, glazed with tears that didn't fall. She gazed off toward the hills beyond, mindless of the scarlet splotch on her face, like the ineradicable mark of a witch's hand. Her eyes were squeezed shut and her mouth downturned.

"Yuk, yuk, *yuk!*" She stamped her feet as if they were caught on hot coals. Then she whirled about and ran off in the direction of the barn, her arms raised, the shawl fluttering like wings. She'd stop and whirl like a dervish, then run again as if God's wrath followed her, her white shawl flying, hair black as sin.

14

While Melrose watched the white shawl disappear into the barn, a woman had come out on the walk and was sweeping the flagstones. To see her there, also wrapped in a shawl, a dark one, long enough to reach to her shoes, and engaged in this homely task, made him feel the world had suddenly righted itself. And yet when she righted *her*self Melrose had the eerie feeling he had seen her before as the woman walking across the moor. Her posture, the determined look in her eye, the long shawl, all contributed to this sense of déjà vu.

Besides that, she was attractive in a sullen sort of way. He could not see her eyes, as they were downturned to her task, but her hair was mahogany and her skin as clear as the little girl's. Indeed, she looked like an out-of-date edition of the child, like last year's fashion, the quality still there, the seams frayed. The little girl's mother, most likely, she worked with the intensity of one whose last chance had come to prove herself.

Suddenly, she looked up. "Oh, sorry. I was thinking about something." Even the smile was tense. "Are you Mr. Plant? That the tourist board rang up about?"

Melrose nodded. She was a random beauty, as if everything were there, but hadn't been got quite right, like the early stages of a portrait the painter had given up on: the eyes well spaced, but the irises a washed-out blue; the mouth full, but tilted down at the corners; the complexion clear except for a few barely discernible pockmarks, the legacy of a childhood disease.

She reached out her hand. "I'm Ann Denholme." She started to pick up his bag, but Melrose immediately took it himself.

"The family who must have arrived before me—may I ask their name?"

They walked through the big oak door into a hall filled with dark wood and faded turkey carpeting. "The Braines, mother and son." She looked with disgust toward the upper rooms. "Only just got here and already there was some sort of fight out there between the son and Abby, and she threatened to pack up and leave." She had removed the shawl and hung it on a peg inside the door. Now, she had her arms crossed and was rubbing her elbows, looking troubled. "He's absolutely beastly, that boy—"

Melrose smiled and nodded.

"—but Abby doesn't seem to be able to understand that she can't treat guests as she pleases."

"Abby didn't start it; I did."

Ann Denholme was leading him down a hallway and stopped to look back. "You?"

"Me. The son's the type who'd tear the wings off Clouded Yellows and lovebirds." They had come to the landing. "When I came round the house—" Melrose stopped. It wasn't because of some sense of honor that he refused to tell of the peccadilloes of others; the reason (he told himself) that he did not rat on people was because he was rich and didn't need to. Amazing what a bit of money could do toward solving life's little problems. "I reprimanded him."

As they walked the long hall past several doors with handsome walnut frames, she asked, "For what?"

So the Beastly Boy hadn't told; he wouldn't have wanted Melrose's version to come out. Besides, Melrose could stalk the halls with his cosher at night. "He was annoying the chickens. Which room is mine?"

"The chickens?" She regarded him doubtfully as she

opened the door and stood against it, her hand on the knob so that he could precede her.

It was a Victorian room, overstuffed and crammed with its four-poster bed, button-back velvet side chairs, double bureau, long curtains with heavy tie-backs, washstand, faded sprigged wallpaper, gold fan in the empty fireplace, pottery on the mantelpiece. Charming, nonetheless, possibly because of its busyness, as if a little old lady in flounces and cap had fussed about adding yet other pieces of unnecessary ornaments.

As he unbuckled his case and threw the straps back, he said, "I saw your daughter at the vet's today. True Friend, I think it's called."

"Abby's not my daughter."

Her tone, he thought, was chilly. "No? But she looks exactly like you and since she lives here, I assumed . . ."

"She's my niece, my sister's girl. That would account for it, I expect." Her eyes were fastened on Melrose's dressing gown of silk paisley, a gift that Vivian had brought back from one of her Italian jaunts. "That's beautiful. I love materials, though I can't afford that kind." That she was sitting on his bed, admiring his dressing gown, struck Melrose as a bit odd, however flattering it might be. Things seemed to break out rather suddenly at Weavers Hall—fights, sex—like a rash.

There was a brief knock on the door frame and a ruddy-skinned woman, probably in her late sixties and with a pansy-shaped face, said, "Mug of tea, sir?" She held a thick Delft mug toward him.

Said Ann Denholme, "Thank you, Mrs. Braithwaite." Her voice was curt. But the woman seemed to take it in stride. She made a tiny curtsy and took away the same smile she had brought with her. "I always serve tea in the drawing room downstairs about this time, but I thought, in the circumstances . . ." Her voice trailed away.

"You mean, that I might want to avoid Mrs. Braine and her son." Melrose was mildly annoyed that he was being told to keep to his room and stay out of further trouble. "On the contrary, I'd be delighted to join the other guests for tea."

"You would? There are only two others. I doubt you'd find much in common with an elderly major and a slightly . . . um . . . decaying Italian princess. Or so she says." Ann Denholme smiled to let him know her assessment of her guests was good-humored. Then she said, "I must tell you, the mother was extremely upset over Abby. And you."

"Miss Denholme, I must tell *you* that I am *not* upset over the Braines. The son should be a ward of the state."

Ann Denholme colored slightly, obviously realizing she hadn't gone about this in the right way. "Of course. Mrs. Braithwaite's taken in the tea now. I can just have her fetch another cup."

"Here's my mug—" He held the Delft blue mug aloft. "—that'll do."

"No, no. I'll just tell Mrs. Braithwaite . . ."

"Please don't bother. I'm meeting a friend in two hours for dinner at—"

But she'd already left the room.

Melrose sighed and shook his head.

He should have ratted.

Discordant piano music, as if a cat were prowling the keyboard, came from the drawing room.

The piano was somewhere behind the open door. He could not see it but knew that the Beastly Boy was the one slamming away at it. The mother allowed this racket to continue, sitting over there before the fireplace with a lap desk full of playing cards. Another occupant of the room, herself seated on a chaise longue, was a handsome, sixtyish woman dressed rather formally in lavender silk.

Melrose couldn't imagine anyone more turquoise than the Braine woman. She had sloughed off the balloon of a jacket, but was still wearing the tight blue-green pants. However, she had added a few more items to her costume: spike-

heeled shoes with an ankle strap, also turquoise; drop earrings of blue and green glass that looked like bits from broken bottles; a heavy lathering of turquoise eyeshadow. Melrose put on his gold-rimmed spectacles as he moved farther
into the room, nodding to the ladies, and coming to rest by a
floor-to-ceiling bookcase. He noticed that a book lay splayed
open on the piecrust table by the Beastly Boy's mother.
Surely not (thought Melrose). *Yes it was. The Turquoise Lament* by Mr. John D. MacDonald. The ensemble was complete—no, it wasn't, for now Mrs. Braine was stuffing a cigarette into a turquoise holder. She was the most turquoise
woman he had ever seen. This was relieved only by eyes,
hair, and turban, all black.

Master Malcolm had stopped for one blessed moment, but
was poising his crablike fingers over the ivories, when Melrose said, with a twitching smile, "Play it again, Sam."

Malcolm, momentarily stunned, wheeled round on the piano stool. "Wot?"

There were traces of an accent surfacing that spoke not of
Chelsea or Kensington but of Shoreditch. "Merely joking.
Well, *this* is a charming scene!" he said heartily, moving to
the fireplace and warming his hands.

The aristocratic lady in lavender glanced over the top of a
slim volume (read, Melrose thought, precisely for the purpose of glancing over) and regarded him shrewdly.

Immediately after Melrose spoke to him, Master Malcolm
slid from the stool and inched toward Mummy, who sat
glaring at Melrose, and, with her arm round her son, mut-
tered comforting words like "Lovie," and other endearments
that made Malcolm look as if he'd rather be out kicking
dogs.

"Are you playing solitaire, then? Ah, the Tarot. Well."

Ramona Braine stared at him from coal-pit eyes and said,
"Taurus."

"I beg your pardon?"

"You. Born under the sign of the Bull. Stubborn, given to

rages. Though you can be loyal. I knew there would be trouble. I felt it. And more to come. Much more."

They might have been sitting in a caravan, given that fairground-gypsyish tone she used. Since she put no time limit on the trouble, the prediction was safe enough. "I'm an Aquarian, actually." He smiled.

"Just barely," she answered, gathering her cards together. And then she looked round the room as if some effluvium were forming, and mentioned the chill when she'd crossed the doorsill. "Mark me," she added, drawing Malcolm to her.

"Ah, leave off, Mum." The boy broke from her entwining arms and lurched over to a chair where he sat with his hands stuffed in his pants pockets and his chin on his chest.

The Turquoise Lament rose, adjusted her several wire-thin blue bracelets, and commanded Malcolm dear to come along.

They trooped out of the room, Malcolm not forgetting to give the keyboard one last thunderous pounding, before he turned and glared at Melrose. *So there.*

Although the first landing on the piano keys had made her start in her chair, the self-contained woman by the fireplace had not changed expression, had merely turned another page of her own book.

But with the exodus of the Braines, her relief was evident. She laid the book flat on her lap, and expelled a sigh. "Well," she said. She managed to invest the word with a world of commentary on the horrors of family life.

Melrose was still standing by the bookcase, running his finger over the MacDonald oeuvre. The titles were fascinating, each with its separate color. The woman on the chaise was wearing an extremely rich-looking dress of lavender silk with a ruched silk velvet bodice. From the bodice the dress fell in a pillarlike line. It was hardly the sort of thing Melrose expected to see here in a fancified bed-and-breakfast establishment. Wings of silvery hair, blued so that in the firelight they picked up the shade of the dress. Ah, yes, he thought, his arm on the bookshelf, definitely *The Long Lavender Look*. The lady's own book was as elegant as she was: small, narrow, the leather tooled, the leaves gilt-edged. She drew the ribbon across the spine to mark her place, closed the book, and sighed again.

"Do you think there might be another tot of sherry in the decanter?" Her voice was arch. Looking from Melrose to the ravaged tea-sherry-chocolate assortment on the rosewood table, she smiled slightly.

He lifted the decanter, saw little more than a golden film across the bottom, but reckoned it would be enough for a glassful. "I'm sure Miss Denholme will be happy to give us more." He managed to shake half a glassful from it and hand it to her.

"Oh, yes, she's most obliging, but I dislike being a pest."

Melrose doubted it, although he liked this woman's sparky manner. "That doesn't sound very pest-y to me, especially when her other guests left the whole tray veritably in tatters."

"They're only staying two nights, thank God. One cannot pick and choose one's clientele in this business, I expect. Since I've been here, the selection has been egalitarian, at the best of times. At the least, well, I shan't comment."

"And how long have you been here?"

"Off and on, over . . . um . . . twelve years. Mostly off." She sipped the sherry and made a small tray of her hand on which to place the stem.

Melrose had not thought Weavers Hall might be a stopping place for such a woman. "You must like it, then."

"Not especially. Might I have a light?" She had drawn a small cigarillo from a chased silver case.

Melrose smiled and obliged, saying as he lit her small cigar, "That gown you're wearing is quite beautiful."

She looked down, apparently admiring it herself. "Thank you. It's a Worth. Frankly, I think half of the world's problems could be solved if one dressed well. Dior, Givenchy,

Worth." She sighed. "If they'd all been sewing and cutting during the time of Henry the Eighth, his wives wouldn't have had so much trouble. Especially Anne Boleyn. My dear! Did you *see* that dress? You obviously understand how important the right cut is," she added, looking at Melrose's jacket. "*That*"— she nodded at the blazer—"is the sort of garment that can be a *disaster* if taken off a rack." She shuddered. "Major Poges—have you met George Poges? No? I'll say this for him: he dresses well. He also makes this place more bearable. Unfortunately, my husband is dead."

Wondering why she spent so much of her time at this unbearable place, Melrose said, "I'm very sorry." He plucked a cigarette from his own gold case.

"My late husband was of an old Italian family, the Viacinni di Belamante. By luck, I am the Princess Rosetta Viacinni. But call me Rose. I was born in Bayswater." Her smile was wan, a little self-deprecating. "And you are—?" She cocked her head.

"Plant. Melrose Plant."

"And are you here for long, Mr. Plant? Are you walking the Brontë way? Are you climbing to the oxygenless heights of Top Withins so that you can faint near its crumbled remains? Are you a Pilgrim?"

"No Pilgrim, no." Melrose grinned. "Quite beautiful country though, isn't it?"

He had seen little of it except for his gloomy meditations by the stream.

"Beautiful? My God!" Her eyebrows rose.

In a bored way she turned her head toward the fire, and Melrose saw she must once have been far more a beauty than this countryside. That beauty had retreated somewhat behind the creased brow and the heavy-lidded eyes, but remained in the high cheekbones, the straight nose, and the elegant posture.

"Viacinni di Belamante?" Melrose looked at the snake-eye of his cigarette, and said, "An Italian nobleman, was he?"

"Oh, yes. A wonderful man, though somewhat fanatical

in his politics. He had, surprisingly, a passionate love for England. It was here that I met him—"

As she talked about her dead husband, Melrose could only think, *oh no.* Would these Italian noblemen be crossing his path now, always, wherever he went? Would he see them strolling in Kew Gardens? In a bookshop near Northampton? Punting on the Cam—? Was he crazy? When had he seen *anyone* punting on the Cam? It was as if Vivian's deciding to marry one were similar to symptoms one associated with a dread disease: they turned up everywhere—in casual conversation, on Underground signs, in newspapers.

"So," she was saying, "through a little luck, a littler bit of beauty, a great deal of social grace, and a greater deal of finagling, I became a princess." She spread her hands in childlike and disingenuous wonder.

A basso voice that preceded its owner into the room proclaimed, "I heard that, Rose. 'Little bit of beauty,' my eye—" A tall gentleman entered. "You'd have all London at your feet if you'd only go there more often."

Melrose was uncertain as to whether good manners dictated his rising from the sofa for Major George Poges's presence—it could only be Major Poges, despite the mental image Melrose had formed of him. Major Poges he had mistakenly pictured as a stooped, withered army pensioner, black-suited and with rows of antique medals, a plastic shopping bag, and a drool.

This Major Poges (who now sat on the sofa opposite Melrose like a rider who had mounted a horse) had an exuberant self-confidence and a good-humored manner that would have made one overlook any imperfections of face, figure, or clothes. The thing was, there weren't any. Melrose calculated he must be in his late sixties or early seventies, but he was one of those men whose looks, like the Princess herself, were ageless. The taut, slightly ruddy skin; the chilly, but startling blue eyes; the neat gray mustache; the appearance of privilege that he did not exercise when he talked; his

perfectly cut tweeds—all of this called up other images in
Melrose's mind:

He had seen Major Poges before, oh, not *this* Major
Poges, but his counterpart: at Wimbledon, seated center
court in white duck; at Newmarket races in a tweed jacket
and cap, binoculars trained on the starting gates; in white tie
and tails at the opening of a concert at the Royal Victoria
and Albert Hall; at the Proms; in the early mists at Vis-
count-Somebody's estate in Scotland, sighting along his gun
at the bird which simply hung against the light-veiled, malt-
colored sky for the sheer delight of dropping as a sacrificial
dinner for Major Poges; in pinks galloping over a sea of
grass, a warren of fences, his bay leaping hedges with the
Quorn or Cottesmore; or cantering along Rotten Row or
deer-stalking on the Isle of Mull; at Traquair House, Ham-
bledon Hall, Brown's Hotel . . . Major Poges was the England there would always be, the essence of anthem.

What in hell was he doing here? In this once-glorious,
now shabby house whose owner catered for the likes of the
Beastlies.

"Where's the sherry?" Poges asked, grabbing up the decanter by its long cut-glass neck as if he meant to throttle a
crane. In disgust he sat down and drew out a leather cigar
holder, offered it round, even to the Princess, who merely
smiled, wiggling her cigarillo. *No, thank you.* He settled
back, tapping the tips of his shoes with his swagger stick,
and frowning. Then he looked up. "Aha! The sherry has
found its way down the gullet of the Braine person—ye
gods! Have you ever seen so much color? Turquoise, at that.
Did she set fire to an Indian reserve?" He ripped away the
brown paper from his package and brought out a bottle of
Tio Pepe.

Vivian's favorite drink. Melrose flinched.

"Reserves, one must always have reserves." He poured
each of them a glassful. He had his smoke, his drink, and he
sighed with relief. From what, Melrose wasn't sure. He
hadn't been down the mines or at the mills all day. "You

know why this village is glutted with tourists, don't you, Mr. Plant?"

"No, I don't. Seems off-season."

"My God, hasn't anyone told you about what happened at the inn down the way? About a mile. The Old Silent. Woman shot her husband and we know her." He was pleased as punch.

The Princess sighed. "I was *about* to tell him, Major. There's one *more* story you've beaten me to."

He feigned distress. "My dear Princess, I *am* sorry." Meaning he was one-up. As she was about to speak, he went on. "It's all very strange, and I cannot believe the woman is deranged, not to look at her face; and do you know she's been—"

"Been here," snapped the Princess, turning upon Melrose a self-congratulatory smile, having stolen the story right out of the Major's mouth.

"You know this woman, do you?"

With a little gesture of his hand, Major Poges graciously allowed the Princess to answer.

She sat forward on the chaise and leaned toward Melrose. "I can't say I know her well, but I do believe she's a friend of Ann Denholme. She didn't mention it? The entire village is aghast; the Citrine estate is only about two miles from here."

"Two and one-half," said the Major, uncorking the Tio Pepe again. "I walk about Keighley Moor nearly every day." He refilled his and Melrose's glasses; the Princess put her hand over hers and shook her head.

"Miss Denholme said nothing, no."

Major Poges turned to the Princess. "Well, I doubt she would, Rose. Don't you find her an altogether secretive woman?" To Melrose he said, "When I asked her where the marmalade had got to this morning, she reacted as if there were some subterfuge at work, some double-meaning, as if one of us was running spies—"

The Princess laughed and shook her head. "What hyperbole! He always talks like that. We cannot depend on anything you say, George."

He smiled sheepishly and raised his glass. "Can't help it. Life is so damned dull otherwise. But I expect you're right." The sheepish look suggested that he had no intention of stopping, however. "Only, you must admit Ann Denholme seems to see life as a locked box of secrets. Sexual, I hope." His mustache twitched.

"Hope away," said the Princess.

Given his brief talk with her earlier, Melrose would say that Major Poges's metaphor was right on the money. It accounted for the literal, rather steamy bodily presence of Ann Denholme, yet mental absence—the rather remote look, the look of a woman who was not really there.

The Princess leaned even farther forward, her eyes no longer milky-gray but glinting like steel shards. "What I understand from Ruby—she's the maid and stumbling server of our delectable meals—was that Mrs. Healey would bring her boy here to play with Abigail. That's Ann's niece."

But Abby couldn't have been more than three or four then, a strange playmate for a twelve-year-old boy. Still, given that it was the Fury, she was probably interesting even at two.

"A terrible tragedy, that. Mrs. Healey's son and a local boy from Haworth were kidnapped. I can't imagine you haven't read about it. It was in the *Times,* after all," said the Major, thereby questioning Melrose's possible taste and wiping out every other newspaper on Fleet Street.

Before Melrose could extract any more local information, Ann Denholme stuck her head round the door and announced dinner. It was eight o'clock.

"Hell," said the Major sotto voce, shredding his cigar in the big ashtray. The Princess sighed. Both of them were just revving up for a wonderful gossip. Raising his voice he said, "Thank you, Miss Denholme. I was wondering, though, if we are all to be seated at the long table." The tone suggested they damned well better not be. "I cannot envision dining with Master Malcolm." He gulped down his drink.

"But you've taken tea with Abby, Major Poges."

He snorted, got sherry in his nose, and pulled out a huge handkerchief. "My God, madam, that is apples and oranges. Your niece is human—in a strange little way, granted—but the Braine boy is a swarm of wasps. He better hadn't land on *my* plate."

"It's a very long table, Major, as you know. They'll be sitting at the other—"

"Rubbish. I'm sure the boy keeps an air gun for just such occasions. Oh, very well, come along, Prin——" He stopped short and stared at the person coming through the door now, upon whom Ann Denholme bestowed a welcoming smile.

Since the person was in the process of removing a huge black helmet—cyclist? dare-devil stuntman? driver?—it was impossible to tell whether it was male or—

Female, definitely. An absolute mess of long hair the color of oats she shook out like a mane, dangling the helmet in her hand. She was dressed, or swathed, in black leather, collar to toe. She had apparently held up a hardware store, for she had so many metal chains round her neck and hammered metal earrings and bangles encircling her wrists she clattered through the room like Marley's ghost.

Ann Denholme introduced this young woman as Miss Ellen Taylor. The Major bowed, the Princess murmured, Melrose smiled. Miss Ellen Taylor was totally self-absorbed; she had a vague smile that she hung on various points in the air, never quite getting round to the three guests.

Major Poges bent over to put out his cigar and said, very low, to Melrose, "The Eagle has landed."

The Princess, her hand on the door, smiled at Miss Taylor and said, "I heard Dior was bringing back the bomber's jacket: that is a *fascinating* ensemble."

Melrose declined the Major's request that he join them. He had to meet someone in Haworth.

And anyway, the curtain had just gone up on the next act.

15

Weavers Hall appeared to be a cabaret or theater in which the curtain rises in folds and cascades down. The sofa was a front-row seat; all he had to do was wait to be entertained as one act followed another. The trained seals should be along any moment now. He smiled.

Miss Taylor was too busy studying the bookshelves to see the smile. All of that black leather simulated, indeed, a seal-like hide. It was supple; it glimmered wetly; light caught in its pliable folds as she bent, rose, bent again to remove and replace various books.

In a dismissive tone, she said, "God, but someone here sure goes in for mysteries."

An American. But "heah shoe-ah"? He did not, however, have some stereotypical image in his mind of Americans as always dressed in black leather and riding motorcycles and having loud voices and hard accents—as Miss Taylor certainly did.

He put hers down to nervousness, for some reason he couldn't explain, as she threw herself down on the opposite end of the sofa, with some loud talk about the weather, the brittle air, the ice-patched road, the ruts that had nearly thrown her. The helmet she stashed on the floor and was wrenching her long hair about as if she meant to strangle herself with it; from a secret little pocket (the leather jacket had many) she drew some hairpins which now bristled from her mouth like thorns as she plucked them out and stuck them here and there to bunch her hair up and back. Around them she said loud, indecipherable things ("Chrisbu'thr'snurumin'lage"), while Melrose made umms and ohs in his throat. In the streak of light from the anglepoise lamp, he imagined the oriental carpet rippling, the floorboards tremoring slightly from the voice that was still loud despite the strictures imposed by the hairpins.

Ellen Taylor was extremely attractive, although she hadn't done much to enhance the qualities that made her so. The bountiful hair could use a good wash, the hands that fooled with it were oil-streaked and nail-bitten, and the only makeup she wore was on her eyes, with too much shadow, as if overdoing them made up for underdoing everything else. Her lashes were so heavily mascaraed they looked like tiny, dry twigs that hid rather than enhanced the dark brown eyes beneath.

What interested him even more was her ambivalence: her voice was raised as if she meant to separate herself from others; at the same time, when she could easily have chosen a half-dozen other places to sit, she had plopped herself down by Melrose.

Far from projecting her chosen image of Brash Young American, Melrose thought she was more a play of light and shadow. He wished, though, that she hadn't chosen shouting as her vocation. . . .

Ah, but it wasn't, he discovered when he asked her if she was touring or just what?

"I'm researching my next book." Having bunged up her hair into a sort of large blossom, she scooped down on the sofa and pressed her head against its back. From a zipper pocket in the black leather jacket she pulled out a packet of Benson and Hedges cigarettes and shook one out for Melrose, then one for herself. When her loops of linked metal necklace clanged and the hammered bronze earrings clapped, she sounded like someone on a chain gang.

"Book? You're a writer, then?"

She nodded, exhaling a bale of smoke that hung in the air

between them as she turned her head to look at him from under lowered lids and lashes. "I am hot, *very* hot in New York ['New Yawk'] at the moment. And you know what it is to be hot in New York ['New Yawk']." Her face turned away from him as she inhaled deeply.

"As a matter of fact, no."

Her eyes widened as she turned her cheek against the sofa to give him a splendid, startled-doe look.

"Say again? Do you mean you've never been to *New York?* God, where else *is* there?"

"Well, speaking of God, there's Rome."

Her nose wrinkled. "Are you kidding? The pope's there."

"Last time I heard, yes. How about London?"

"Too provincial."

"Moscow?"

"Come *on.* Moscow's just a logo and a pose."

That took care of any future summit meeting, at least, so he changed the subject. "I don't believe I've read anything by an Ellen Taylor; but I'm not up on hot young New York writers." Quickly, he added, in case he had sounded offensive, "But that's no reflection on your hotness. I've just never got much further than Rimbaud."

She considered this. "He's not bad."

"I believe he was quite hot at the time."

"Wouldn't surprise me." Some more exhaled smoke fogged the air. "Anyway, *Taylor* isn't my writing name. It's Tamara."

" 'Ellen Tamara'? Hmm. Perhaps you've not been published in Britain?"

"Not *Ellen,* just Tamara. One name. Like Cher or Sting or Dante." She appeared to be searching the table for a clean glass, and seeing none chose the Princess's slightly smudged one, which she wiped out with a napkin.

Melrose stopped in the act of filling the glass she held out to him and considered. "You left out Michelangelo."

"When I was writing under my own name I couldn't sell a damned thing. Couldn't even if I wrote like Hemingway.

The which I resemble, incidentally." As she searched up an ashtray, the chains and bracelets clattered.

"Ernest? Or Mariel?"

Another lungful of smoke billowed out as she laughed.

"Very funny. Fortunately, I can take a joke. Fame hasn't altered me, nor 'custom staled my infinite variety.' Despite the celebrity, I'm still a humble person."

So then was Cleopatra, he did not say.

"No, once you get bitten by fame, you're ruined. My editor said, 'In your case it would take a rabid dog.'" She raised her glass as if toasting her editor. "He's very supportive like that."

"He sounds brilliant."

She shrugged. "But he thinks I should go back to writing the way I did before."

"And how was that?"

"Not so experimental—straight narrative, more or less. Gothic type. A little like Brontë, a little le Fanu, a *soupçon* of James."

Melrose had just then taken a sip of sherry and choked. "*Henry* James?"

Slapping him on the back, she said, "You okay?"

"No." His throat felt grainy, his voice rusty. "No. You'll have to do an emergency tracheotomy. *Look,* no one writes like Henry James now, and Lord knows no one *used* to write like Henry James, except Henry James. And how is it you manage to include him in your Gothics Unlimited list?"

She turned her head so sharply the metal earrings clinked against her face. "Say again? What about *The Turn of the Screw?*"

He had to admit that was a bit Gothic.

She studied her nails to see, apparently, if there was anything else to bite. "And there's *Portrait of a Lady.* You've read that, surely." Now she was chewing on a morsel of thumb.

"Of course."

"I rest my case."

"On *what?*" He started chewing on his own thumbnail. Was she mad?

"You must not've understood it," was her oblique answer.

It really was too much. Was this gritty, poorly spoken girl actually educated, knowledgeable, informed, and—surely not—talented?

She had checked the watch that was far too heavy for her bony wrist and was saying, "Well, got to vamoose. I thought maybe I'd have a meal in the village. Maybe at one of those hotels."

She rose quickly and jammed the black helmet over her head. With her small face peering out from the black dome, she looked a little like an astronaut who'd been hanging around so long she'd shriveled.

Melrose stood up. "I have to be going myself." He gathered up his coat and stick and followed her out the door.

As they walked across the stone courtyard, Melrose looked in through the mullioned window of the dining room where, at one end of the long table, were seated the Princess and Major Poges; at the other end, the Braines. Yet the panes were cloudy and the window so ivy-clad that the faces and forms bathed in the dull gold and rose light were broken into wavering squares—a blur of turquoise, a wedge of dark wool, a glint of a lavender sleeve. Having seen them in action, Melrose found it odd seeing them in this ornamental light. They seemed to dissolve and reform in the fragmented patterns of a kaleidoscope. Around the table, fluttering and disappearing and returning was the maid, Ruby, in a crisp white apron. Ann Denholme appeared in one of the panes and then fell away.

". . . and only twenty-nine, and I'm a millionaire. Can you believe that?"

"Why not?"

"I'm too *young*, goddammit," she said, kicking a stone back toward the pile.

They had come to her "bike," which took Melrose utterly

by surprise. He was expecting some fancy ten-speed; what he was looking at was a BMW approximately the size of a baby elephant. "You mean you ride *this?*"

She sighed, lit another cigarette, and shook her head. "No, I walk it on a leash." Then she went on about early fame as she looked up at a night sky as smooth and black as onyx and just a few cold stars that looked eons apart and probably were. The moon was full and bright and luminous. From here the dining room window looked as illusory as a cascade of rainbow water. From the barn, whose outlines melted into the sky, came a series of hectic barks, and a dog came out of the darkness into a patch of moonlit ground. It was the border collie he'd seen earlier. The dog looked a bit too sharp for Melrose's taste; he preferred his own dog, Mindy. ("Your Ralph Lauren dog," said Trueblood, "countrified, under all that tangled nap, true gentrification.")

From behind the fence, in the chicken-duck enclave came an occasional warm cluck. It had been an eventful day for the wildlife, thought Melrose. Tomorrow they'd probably want to visit the Tower of London. Closer now, the dog barked again.

"I believe we're witness to the curious incident of the dog in the nighttime."

But Ellen was still immersed in disturbed dreams of her own success as she lit a cigarette with a Zippo and clicked it shut. "I'm a *millionaire.*" She cast a sidewise glance at Melrose to see if he was properly impressed. "In pounds," she added. "On one book," she added, taking no chances.

"That *is* astonishing. What's the book? Was it your first?"

"My second." Ellen appeared to want to bury the first. She leaned back against the bike, ankles crossed, a model's pose. "It's about New York City: *Sauvage Savant* it's called. It's very hot in L.A., too, incidentally. But, naturally, if you're a hot writer, it's always going to be New York, isn't it?"

"Sauvage Savant," Melrose repeated. What a pretentious title. That must be the price one pays for being a hot, young

New York writer. With what he thought was a with-it little grin, he said, "I expect there are a lot of 'literary savages' in your city?"

"Say again?"

"I'm referring to the title."

"It's a deli in Queens."

The collie, who had stationed himself a few feet away, cocked his head, in a wondering way. Melrose was trying to sort out the various New York boroughs. He could not position Queens on his mental map. "I see."

He was quite sure the dog knew he was lying, given its expression. It was absolutely still but fully alert. Its silence was impressive; its stare, rather harrowing. If it couldn't read minds, it could probably read lips.

"What happened was, the owner's French, and the sign painter is his cousin, French, too. Don't ask me what they're doing in Queens. François—I call him Frankie—wanted a clever Frenchy sign. It was supposed to be 'sausage' but his cousin just couldn't make the connection. Who could? A knowledgeable sausage on your rye with mayo? Frankie's a real horse's ass, which is why I like him. He knows I'm really the rage in New York, and he's expecting me to turn his deli into one of those clubby places, you know, like the Algonquin, where Dorothy Parker hung out. It was really when I hit it big that he worked up this 'savant' business. He parts his hair in the middle and wears an apron up to his armpits and has a straight mustache I think he just inks in with a ballpoint. Well, there's not much going in Queens by way of published writers; and I'm not Dorothy Parker."

He was a little taken aback by this modest assessment of her own writing skill. "Who is?"

As she pulled the strap of her helmet tight, she said, "See, I wanted to do something different; I couldn't stand one more book about Manhattan. I will personally vomit outside Doubleday if I see a window display of one more book about Manhattan. I'm doing all the others: it's to be a sort of trilogy, no, a quartet, I guess. . . ." She pondered this as she studied the night sky.

Why was the dog looking up there too? Melrose wondered. Had the collie and Ellen some affinity?

"The Bronx, Staten Island, Brooklyn, Queens. Maybe I'll toss in the Jersey shore."

"That's not New York." Melrose touched the collie's paw with his cane, to see if he could get a reaction. He didn't.

"Who can tell anymore?"

Melrose shifted his walking stick from one hand to another, thinking of this exotic city, so huge that part of it was an island surrounded by other islands and boroughs, each a kind of city in itself. He was wondering if perhaps he shouldn't take some sort of inventory of himself: was he spending too much time with his port and paper before the fireplace? Shuffling about his village until he would drop dead of a stroke across Miss Crisp's chamber pots? Or in Agatha's cottage in Plague Alley . . . ? *Pull yourself together,* he told himself. Then he smiled. It was time to rewrite his will. He did this every half-dozen years or so to drive Agatha to distraction. He was holding back that wonderful nugget involving primogeniture until she got totally out of hand—

"You all right?" asked Ellen, whose gloved hands were rubbing the handlebars. The noise of the engine ripped through the frosty air. "Your face looks funny." She squinted. "You've got great eyes, incidentally. Really green."

Melrose knew his eyes were green. But great? He opened his mouth to thank her—

"Like scarab beetles."

He closed his mouth. As she gunned the accelerator again, he said, "I'd be happy to offer you a lift"—he pointed toward the Bentley, moonraked and glimmering, with the reservoir shining off in the distance—"only I'm not going into the village. I'm meeting a friend at a place down the road."

"Was it the inn I passed?"

"Probably; it's called the Old Silent."

"Well, maybe I could get a bite there."

Melrose cursed himself for mentioning the inn. "Ah, I
. . . don't think so. It's more or less off limits; it's a crime
scene, you see."

The noise stopped. "Say again?"

He wished he hadn't said once.

"So how come you're going there? If it's closed to the
public?"

"I, ah, I'm only meeting someone."

"What happened? What crime?"

"A man was killed there a couple of days ago."

"Killed? You mean *murdered,* don't you?" She frowned,
as if the culprit stood here in the moonlight before her.

"Well, yes, I expect you could say that." He had the lunatic notion he was including the collie in his answers. The
dog's ears had pricked up; he certainly looked as eager for
details as did the girl.

She shook her head, muttering some imprecation to the
skies or the gods. "Jeeeezzz. Well, you're obviously not going to talk." Suddenly, her head swung round. "You're a
cop, aren't you?"

"No, absolutely not—"

"Hell, all this time I've been hanging around talking to
the cops."

The collie yapped when the motor roared again.

"Look, I'm *not*—"

"Stranger!"

The call came from the direction of the barn; Melrose
looked around quickly to see the dull glow of a lamp, one of
those ancient oil lamps, upraised, casting only a blur of light
along the ground.

He could not have been more astonished if suddenly a
highwayman, masked and cloaked, had stopped Melrose's
coach. There was no threat in this voice: it was clearly

pitched enough to cut through the noise of the motor Ellen kept revving up.

As the dog whipped round and streaked like a swimmer through the ground mist toward the lamp, she asked, "*Who* is that?"

"A little girl. Her name is Abigail, I believe."

"She lives here?"

Melrose nodded. His eye followed the lamp that looked disembodied, hanging on an invisible arm.

Ellen kicked the motorcycle into action, said *See you,* and streaked away much as had the dog, each going in the opposite direction.

He watched her down the drive until she and her BMW were swallowed up by the corridor of trees. Through their trunks he could see a skin of moonlight on the reservoir.

Then he turned his head toward the black, ivy-latticed window, wondering, in a momentary surge of anxiety, if he'd imagined the fuzzy gold-lit interior, the patches of color, the underwater movements. But no, of course not: it was lit, though the silver and turquoise were gone and the only movement came from the maid. He could see the black patch of her dress moving from pane to pane, as lights went out, one after another and it, too, grew darker. And then the moon, like the interior lights, suddenly went out, behind a cloud, as if Ruby had thrown a switch.

Melrose lit a cigarette, more he thought to see the flame spurt up than because he needed a smoke.

As he got in the car and quickly flicked on the headlamps, he heard the voice again—*Stranger*—and the crisp bark of that dog.

16

The Old Silent sat just off the Stanbury road, surrounded by moorland. Across the blackened heath dry-stone walls ran off to remote hills marked by low witch-shaped and wind-blasted trees. Melrose had never seen a gaunter landscape by day or by night. Coming upon the inn over a dip in the road, he thought it wore the truncated, free-floating look of the courtyard he had just left.

When he pulled into the car park, he saw the Old Silent in a more normal light: a well-tended, whitewashed and black-timbered building with a courtyard for tables in better weather. Closed for the twenty-four hours following its un-likely venue as a crime scene, it had now, he imagined, gained in celebrity for that same reason. The car park was choked at nearly ten o'clock. He saw through the amber-lit windows the customers crowding the public bar.

Inside was warmth and a quick return to normality after the scene he had left. Melrose took his drink through to a lounge with a fine stone fireplace over which hung a painting of the inn and in front of which sat one of those high-backed sedan chairs. A porter's chair. He had always wanted to hold court in one and waited for the black cat, the chair's present occupant, to move. The cat had other ideas.

While he waited for Jury, he moved about the lounge and looked above flickering lights and little shaded lamps at pic-tures and brass ornaments and an account of the origin of the Old Silent's name. Melrose sighed. It was one of those

Bonnie Prince Charlie tales. The inn was yet another of those historic places that had offered Charlie refuge and (in this case) the "silence" of the locals. Given all the stopovers the Young Pretender had made, Melrose wondered how he ever got to his destination. He'd certainly clocked up a lot of traveling time. Melrose closed his eyes and imagined the prince traveling with Agatha. The Old Silent would have gone nameless. . . .

"You always sleep on your feet?"

He knew it was Jury, but he didn't open his eyes. "I was thinking of Agatha." He felt the hand clasp on his shoulder.

"No wonder."

They had studied the menu and decided upon Pike in a Blanket.

"Because I am enamored of the name," said Melrose Plant to Richard Jury. "I picture the pike," continued Melrose, "tucked in a little woolly square with a safety pin."

Over a plate of oxtail soup Melrose finished telling Jury the events of the day, and was surprised that in the telling of it, all of those events had indeed taken place in one day. "To think that only this morning I was having coffee in Harrogate with Agatha and friend. Of course, Agatha does have a certain lunar quality. Distant howlings in the woods behind Ardry End . . ."

"This soup is great," said Jury, smacking the pepper shaker all around it.

" 'This soup is great,' " repeated Melrose with a sigh. "The only person I know who has a more poetical turn of mind than you is Divisional Commander Macalvie. I expect while you were hanging round the Citrine place and I was being vastly entertained at Weavers Hall, Macalvie solved at least three cases."

"Four," said Jury, holding up his fingers. "One battery, one murder, two break-ins. I'm going to Cornwall; I want to have a look round the Citrine property."

"You think the answer is there?"

"I think the question is there."

"You sound like Gertrude Stein. Policework is surely more straightforward than that."

"Straightforward?" Jury shook his head. "I only mean I have the feeling the wrong questions are being asked. But that's nothing new. You said this George Porges—"

"Poges."

"If Major Poges likes to walk, why don't you walk with him? Might learn something." Jury looked up from his bread roll.

"Because it's exercise. I don't mind the sort of exercise that's a means to an end, such as cycling along to the Jack and Hammer; I just dislike the sort that appears to be an end in itself. I saw today, running along the Pennine way, a jogger. This one was in flaming red, *neon* red. Now, I ask you: three of the gloomiest minds in literature, bless them, set their accounts of despair, desolation, broken hearts, on these moors. Bleak as mines, barren, rocky. How dare someone in flaming red *jog* across them? She was probably carrying a piece of natural grain bread and a bottle of Perrier for weights. So what do *you* do, Richard? Running? Racquetball? Ten laps round Nelson's column?"

"Nothing. Of course, I think about it—"

Melrose pointed a finger at him. "Ah! You see, we both follow in the true tradition. We are men *who think about* exercise. That, Jury, is a lost way of life. Even Trueblood has a rowing machine in his den."

"That's just to get a rise out of you; Trueblood's not so stupid he'd use the damned thing." Jury looked round. "Where's that fish in blankets? I can hardly wait."

"But I can see," continued Melrose, his thoughts on Long Piddleton, "that it's moving in. Oh, we have no joggers yet; but I had a look-in at the post office stores. Where I used to see Weetabix I now see fruit-almond-coconut-pasha-wheat-germ cereal. It's the hound at our heels—all of this jogging and eating goat's milk cheese—when one could have a succulent piece of Stilton and a glass of Cockburn's port—it's all part of upward mobility. If I have to be mobile, I want it to be lateral."

"So do I," said Jury. "Here comes our waitress."

She set their plates before them. The "blanket" turned out to be parchment. Steam had ballooned its glazed surface and the waitress held her sharp shears over Melrose's portion. The waitress Sally slit the crisp steam-filled parchment and released an aromatic mix of wine and herbs and garlic and (Sally whispered) a bit of brandy. It would have cleared the nostrils of even the most intractable sinus sufferer.

"This would keep your sergeant out of doctors' offices for the next ten years," said Melrose.

"It smells absolutely wonderful, Sally," said Jury, with an equally wonderful smile.

She turned quickly and rushed off, the kitchen door swinging shut behind her.

"Nell Healey was a friend of this Ann Denholme?" asked Jury, after a few moments of solemn eating.

"I'm only telling you what Major Poges and the Princess said. Perhaps they got it from the moribund Ruby, I don't know. Or perhaps Ann Denholme mentioned it; I would imagine all of the publicity would have had the whole of Weavers Hall talking." Melrose raised a spoonful of the fish liquor to his mouth. "The only thing this lacks is a soupçon of Old Peculier. It's rather good; it's rather pleasant to have your before-dinner sherry, your dinner, your after-dinner brandy all wrapped up in parchment. Saves a great deal of time."

Jury had nearly finished his meal. "Go on about the Hall."

"It's like a minstrel show. 'Tamara,' pardon me, 'Tamawa,' what a pseudonym. From New Yawk." He put down his spoon. "Except . . ."

"Except what?"

Melrose shrugged. "The place is eerie. . . ." He started to say something else, didn't know what he wanted to say, and shrugged again. "I don't know. 'Eerie' is the wrong word. I don't know the right one. Uncanny? No." There was a return of the anxiety Melrose had felt when he had stood in the courtyard lighting a cigarette for the sake of the flame.

"Don't worry about the right word. What was the feeling?" Jury pushed his plate away.

"Must you look so intense? I've given you a running account of the last three fun-filled hours at Weavers Hall." Melrose described the scene.

"The details might not be as important as their effect on you."

"You, a superintendent of police saying *details* might not be important? You want feelings?"

"Why don't you just say the first thing that comes to mind?"

"Tristesse," said Melrose. "Obscure," he added. "A gulf, a sadness, an obsessive sadness."

Jury pushed back his plate, folded his arms, and thought of Nell Healey.

"You know Nell Healey actually shot her husband," said Melrose. "It's not a question of innocence or guilt."

"It's a question of motive."

"But do you honestly think knowing that will save her?" Melrose frowned.

"Yes."

Melrose took out his cigar case. "Sounds to me as if she doesn't want to be saved. What if she feels so guilty about not paying the ransom for this boy that she no longer cares what happens to her?"

"Then she'd have killed herself, not her husband, who was, according to Macalvie, absolutely beside himself when she refused to pay. Roger Healey was far from being a pauper; he was well off, but he didn't have *that* kind of money. Not big money. Neither does Charles Citrine. And the money wasn't the only question, either; it was the rotten dilemma of what would be in Billy Healey's best interests." Jury took a cigar from Plant's case. "Then, of course, Billy was Roger's son; he was only Nell's stepson."

Melrose paused in the act of lighting their cigars. "'Only'? Good grief, you're one of those espousers of the theory that blood is thicker than water?"

"Of course not. But nearly everyone pays lip service to that old shibboleth. The media would have had a high old time had it ever come out that it was Mrs. and not Mr. Healey who'd made the decision not to pay. Here's a woman rich as Croesus who wouldn't ransom her stepson. What does that look like? The evil stepmother looks in the mirror and sees the face of someone more beautiful. The competition, in this case, isn't Snow White, but her husband's son."

"I can think up an even chillier scenario."

Jury nodded. "Only I saw her standing in that wood like someone in a trance; she was looking at an old gate between stones that no longer served a purpose, where Billy Healey and Toby Holt used to play. The look was so intense that I swear I wouldn't have been surprised to see that boy materialize right before my eyes. Perhaps he had, before hers."

They both turned when a heavy, slightly stooped man with a checkered cap and an old brown cardigan, a trowel in his hands, came shuffling up to their table. His look was one of perpetual discontent, the narrow, tobacco-blackened line of his mouth downturned like a bulldog's. Glaring from the silver dish of vegetables to Jury and then Plant he asked, "'Ow's them runner beans, then?"

Apparently, since the Old Silent's dining room was catering only for them that evening, all of the help had the run of the hall. This person before them would stand his ground and chew his tobacco until he'd got a report on the state of the vegetables. "Excellent. And you're Mr.—?"

"Oakes. Jimmy Oakes." He was picking up the dish and ruminating, apparently, upon the state of the runner beans. "Bad crop, it be."

"But these were very tasty, Mr. Oakes."

The man shrugged and let out a whistle of breath. "Summat grundgy they be. Got 'em in Ha'erth."

"I don't understand, Mr. Oakes. You're speaking of your *own* crop having failed?" asked Melrose brightly.

"Thass it. Bad. F'got ta plant 'em."

He shuffled off with his trowel.

"Roger Healey," said Melrose, looking after Mr. Oakes, "what sort of person was he?"

"Straight as an arrow, according to everyone I've talked to. People who worked with him loved him. Charles Citrine thinks Roger Healey was one of the finest men he'd ever known and blessed the day he married his daughter. Nell Citrine, you see, was thirtyish, unmarried, and—to use his word—'unstable.' "

"Does that mean Miss Citrine was in and out of mad-houses or had a difficult time choosing the correct sauce for the veal? When a man calls a woman 'unstable' it generally means she doesn't agree with him."

Jury mopped up the last bit of liquid with a piece of his bread roll. " 'Slightly eccentric' he said."

"She didn't share his political views, in other words."

"I appreciate that you defend her without meeting her. Do you have any of those cigars?"

Melrose took a leather case from his breast pocket. "I haven't met her, but you *have;* you said nothing about 'unstable' or 'eccentric.' "

"The strange thing is, even with her killing her husband in the lounge of an inn . . ." He lit the cigar and shook out the match. ". . . she didn't strike me as anything but normal."

Except, he didn't add, *for the silence.* Jury crossed his arms on the table and turned the cigar in his mouth. "Citrine is an extremely low-key, affable man. Hands in pockets, walks and talks with a sort of self-deprecating air."

"So does our Mr. Oakes, but that doesn't make me want to trust him with my bean planting."

"Why is Nell Healey the blight in this crop of perfect people? Daddy sits down over drinks and tells the very superintendent who's witness against her she's unstable; Roger is a white knight and beloved of all. Except for the aunt."

"A notable exception, perhaps."

Jury made a circle with his wineglass and thought of Rena Citrine. "The aunt dislikes the family *except* for Nell Citrine. Though she strikes me as so self-engrossed she wouldn't do a hell of a lot by way of saving her."

"That's three for our side, though."

"Actually, four."

Melrose smiled as he watched the sweet trolley lumbering across the oak boards, Sally behind it. "Who's the fourth?"

"Brian Macalvie."

"How could he *possibly* remember her after a brief meeting eight years ago? Pardon me. Divisional Commander Macalvie never forgets." As the trolley came closer, he saw an enormous glass bowl of trifle wobbling about.

"He referred to her as 'one awesome lady.' "

"Good Lord, that's better than the Queen's patronage. So the cause is not lost."

"When it comes to Macalvie no cause is lost. As long as it's his."

"What'll it be, gentlemen?" asked the Old Silent's manager, later in the lounge.

"Pike liquor," said Melrose. "Or if that's unavailable, a glass of Rémy. And coffee, thanks."

The telephone brr-ed insistently as the manager looked a question at Jury. "Just coffee."

"Old Silent Inn," said the man into the receiver, rather grudgingly, as if he feared the name would bring a new onslaught of inquiry. He then turned, handed the receiver to Jury, and went about serving up the cognac.

"Just hope to God it isn't Racer."

It was Wiggins. "How are—" Jury decided not to complete the routine *how are you;* for Wiggins, the question was never routine. He settled for "Hullo, Wiggins."

Lack of inquiry notwithstanding, Wiggins proceeded to

tell Jury both how he was and how the weather was, the two states being mutually dependent. "Right rotter, it is, here, sir. Winter rain. You know what that's like. . . ."

"I'd never noticed a difference between winter and summer, Wiggins. What have you—?"

"There definitely is, sir." Patiently Jury waited for him to complete the forecast for both Wiggins's bronchitis and his personal rain. Wiggins finally realized that the point of his call was the investigation he had undertaken in London and not the state of his health. "Sir, there's good news and bad news. Which do you want first?"

"Any news."

"The bad news is that not one single person I've talked to has anything negative to say about Roger Healey. I've talked to ten people on the staff of that magazine, and they all say the same thing, different words. Roger Healey was to them a marvelous person, an incisive critic, a practiced musician. Several of them said little Billy was close to a prodigy, and his father was that proud of him. This all came up when several of them mentioned how Roger was a tower of strength and a monument to grief over the boy's loss. . . ."

To Jury, such strength in the face of heavy loss seemed a bit appalling, a bit stone-cold, just as Wiggins's clichés implied.

"—but what's strange is that even the people, at least the three I talked to, whom Healey had cleverly insulted in his column didn't bear him any grudge or dislike him. The librettist, for instance, whose experimental opera Healey had dissected with a good deal of blood-letting actually laughed and said himself it was a rotten piece of work. His opera, not Healey's column."

Plant had taken his glass and coffee over to the fireplace where he was trying to knock the cat out of the sedan chair. "Did you talk to Mavis Crewes?"

"No, sir. She said she saw no reason to, as she'd enough of Scotland Yard and its insinuations. What did you insinuate?"

"That Nell Healey wasn't a combination of Scylla and Charybdis. What about Martin Smart?"

"I did. He was quite pleasant about it, though he didn't understand why I was there, since you'd already been."

"Incidentally, does Racer know you're questioning people?"

"The chief superintendent never thinks I'm working at all, sir," responded Wiggins with no hint of rancor.

Jury could hear crackling sounds in the background that could have been anything from a wrapper on a packet of throat lozenges to a crumbling of black biscuits. The persistence of telephone sounds when talking to Wiggins was like snow on a tape with the volume turned up.

"Now, the flutist, name of William Browne, was a bit more grim; still, he had to admit that Healey hadn't attempted to trash him: there was one piece out of the five he'd played Healey had liked in part."

"Sounds pretty trashy to me, one out of five."

"But I've read these reviews, sir. I have to admit that Roger Healey doesn't *appear* to be out to get the subject, or to be grinding an axe. His negative criticism is almost apologetic."

"Which would be an effective way of putting someone down."

Wiggins was silent. Then he said, "You appear to be somewhat biased against Healey, if you don't mind my saying so."

Jury smiled slightly. "I don't mind. And you're right." Jury was watching the black cat's progress round the sedan chair and Plant's attempts to ignore it.

"Though, actually, there might be something in what you say."

"Thanks. Go on."

"As I was saying about this piece in *Segue:* it was a review of a charity concert. Healey is handing out plaudits for most of the participants except for the oboe player and one other. Listen: 'The event of the evening was the appearance of Stan

Keeler of Black Orchid. I say "event" because of the awe in which this "underground" group is held by its devoted (fanatic) fans. Mr. Keeler displayed a formidable technique. Surprisingly, his technique is what he so often buries in Black Orchid's rare appearances aboveground. Black Orchid is the most exhibitionistic group to walk on a stage since Peter Townshend and The Who. I joined the audience in its applause for Mr. Keeler's rendition of his most famous song, "Main Line Lady." I applauded because Mr. Keeler didn't do a couple of lines right on stage.' My point is, sir, that not even Stan Keeler was much bothered by that."

"You mean you talked to him?"

There was a dramatic pause—or perhaps Wiggins had only turned to the hot plate and the kettle to refill his cup. "I certainly did, sir. Went to his flat in Clapham. He's got some kind of crazy landlady who protects him from the press, from reporters. I mean she's weird."

"What was his opinion of that review, then?"

"He laughed and had another drink. He was lying flat out in the middle of the floor. Said it helped him to think." The pause suggested that Wiggins himself was thinking things about this behavior. "Keeler just didn't seem to care."

"What about the good news, Wiggins? Or was that it?"

"Something like that, but more so. When I was in the magazine's offices, as I was leaving, I met a chap walking down the hall. At first I thought he was a janitor. Jeans and a black T-shirt. Carrying a mop and pail."

Again Wiggins paused as if waiting for Jury to agree that, yes, such a person might have been a janitor. "See what you mean. But he was one of the staff."

"Yes. He's the most popular columnist they have. He's their Pop person. You know—jazz, rock-and-roll. His name's Morpeth Duckworth. I thought I recognized him because his column's always got a little picture of him over his by-line. I stopped him and asked him about Healey's death. 'His wife did the greatest service to musical criticism ever done,' was his answer. He was just leaning on his mop and smoking I think it might even have been grass. I mean, in the offices—"

"You're right, Wiggins; go on."

"Of course, I asked him what he meant. What he said was—" Here Jury could hear the rasp of pages quickly turned. "—he said, 'Healey's generous contributions to this magazine have done a lot toward shining shit.' But this bit is more to the point. 'Healey was the quotidianal phony of the music world.' Then he picked up his mop and bucket and went on down the hall. I definitely think you should talk with him. Only—"

"Only what?"

"Well, if you don't mind me saying, sir, I think you better educate yourself just a little on the rock scene. To understand him."

Jury smiled, as much as Plant's manuevers with a rolled-up *Country Life* as at his sergeant's injunction. "Why bother, when I've got you? Terrific job, Wiggins. For the first time in this investigation I feel there's some hope. Mr. Healey may not be tapped for sainthood, after all. Maybe we can get him down off the monument. You did a good job."

"Always glad to be of assistance," said Wiggins, sounding almost priggish. But Jury could tell from the tone and the rhythmic tapping of the spoon against the cup that Wiggins was himself elated by the compliment.

"I'll definitely see him. Anything else?"

"That's the lot, sir."

Jury was about to say good-bye, when he remembered the earlier interview. "Wiggins. How did you manage to get past Stan Keeler's landlady?"

"I more or less collapsed in her hallway."

Jury frowned. "What was the matter?"

"I pretended I was ill."

17

The lop-eared dog Stranger had been busily digging about in the ice-crusted earth when, upon seeing Melrose's approach down the road from the Hall, he had immediately stopped to go and stand sentry at the door of the stone barn.

At this hour of ten in the morning, Abby Cable was going silently about her tasks together with another little girl, whose name was Ethel (Melrose heard)—as in "Ethel, you didn't get this mash right *again*," and "You can't stick that into *stone*." The first complaint was directed toward a small tub with a spoon sticking up in it, the second toward the figure of Ethel, standing on a chair before a poster.

Ethel was the same size and probably the same age as Abby Cable. Stubbornly, she returned to trying to push a drawing pin (or so it looked to Melrose) into the corner of the poster. The luckless pin merely bounced out and the corner curled downward again. The other top corner held, since it was pinned to the wooden frame of the barn door, the walls made up of blocks of millstone grit.

Seeing it was useless, she jumped down from the chair, the face turned toward Abby a study in frustration.

Ethel's color began and ended in her light red hair. Her complexion was as pale as anything Melrose expected to see this side of the grave, dotted here and there with tiny buttery freckles. She had an etiolated neck set on small sloping shoulders above a white shirtwaist, a long white apron, and white stockings. She made Melrose think of a pint of cream.

Ethel nearly glowed with neatness, as if she'd been licked clean by cats. This was in contrast to the Fury, who, although at the moment living in the eye of the storm, still looked mud-splotched. Perhaps it was just the contrast; Abby was wearing her wellingtons and a dark dress made of wool stuff and, this morning, a black shawl, as if there were no length to which she would not go to prove she was plain and grim.

Melrose observed them from the distance of the shadowy doorway, since Stranger had now been joined by a much larger dog, smooth-haired, about the size of a Scotch deerhound, a hundred pounds, give or take. It slouched over to see if anything interesting was happening and stood there giving the impression that it wasn't any more eager to develop a more intimate relationship with this person than the border collie was. It annoyed Melrose that his championing the gray cat did not seem to admit him into the closed world of other animals. The cat itself was stretched out in a pool of cold sunlight and showed even less interest in his savior than did the dogs. They sat side-by-side, looking up at him.

He was not sure whether it was a barn or one of the old long houses that provided shelter for both people and animals. The roofbeams were high with heavy crucks and, at one end, three rows of loopholes that allowed for needed ventilation (given the somewhat pongy dung-smell coming from the other end) and on this brighter-than-ordinary morning tossed confettilike patterns of sunlight on the floor.

At the other end, off to his left, where Abby seemed to be ministering to a cow, was the byre with wood-framed slate boskins that partitioned off the animals: in this case, the pony and donkey he had seen earlier behind the barn.

What must have been the old threshing floor lay between doors on either side of the barn. The door across had been boarded up. Melrose stood on a large slate floor with small rugs strewn about to make it appear homey, he imagined.

In front of a stone fireplace were a makeshift table (an oblong board across two sawhorses), a heavy mahogany chair, and a high stool. He concluded this was the dining area, and the kitchen was beside it: here was a table covered with oilcloth on which lay a loaf of bread and some meat and cheese. Refrigeration was left to the window ledge, where a bottle of milk sat beside a square of butter on a plate. A kettle hung on an iron rod that swung into the fireplace.

Against the end wall to the right was a creaky-looking cot covered in a layer of quilts. Beside it was a crate piled with books and a lamp.

But what especially struck Melrose was the number of posters and prints decorating the walls—Dire Straits, Elvis Presley. The recent acquisition that Ethel had labored over was a poster of the rock group Sirocco. Indeed, it might have been that same glossy one lately in Malcolm's possession. It was tacked up beside a smaller scene of a Cornwall cliffside and beside that one . . . oh, hell, Venice. Venice floating in its unearthly way, distant across the water. Insubstantial as it was, it still looked more real than the Cornwall cliffs dashed with high plumed waves. . . .

A very large and beautiful poster in a baroque frame that Melrose was certain was one of the Magritte "empires of light" hung above the book crate. To see it in a barn—but then Abby Cable appeared to make her home in this place— was strange indeed. Strange as the picture itself. It showed a house with a lit window and a streetlamp glowing in darkness; yet above this was a clear blue sky with clouds. He had seen it before reproduced on cards.

Having been admitted, apparently, to this sanctuary, Melrose was not quite sure what to say, and so said words he would gladly have chewed up and swallowed once they were out of his mouth: "Well! This is certainly a pleasant barn!"

Abby Cable turned upon him a look that might have been fashioned by the toilers at Stonehenge, a look that had come down through the ages by way of Antigone and Lady Macbeth, a look that had worn itself into the fabric of the world. A look that barely suffered fools to live. As if that weren't enough to stop a train, it had to be that deep blue that is often falsely, if poetically, attributed to Aegean seas and island skies.

"If you like barns," she said. Then remembering apparently he had saved her cat, she said, "That's Ethel."

Ethel was much more forthcoming, probably because it allowed her to drop the odious paddle and come to have him look her over—her ruffled shirtwaist, her fancy ribbon. She smiled up at him and showed two missing teeth. "We're having tea. You can have tea with us, can't he, Abby?" There was no response from Abby, who was busy trying to adjust the straps of the oat bag to the pony's head. Ethel adjusted the bow in her hair and seemed to provide the answer to her own question by announcing: "I'm older than Abby."

When no congratulations were forthcoming from Melrose, and no sign from Abby that she had heard, Ethel flounced over to the oil-cloth-covered table where the loaf of granary bread sat and continued cutting. "That's my dog, over there." Ethel pointed with the breadknife toward the big dog. "It's not a plain sheepdog; it's a Kuvasz." She emphasized the word carefully, looking at Melrose to see if mention of this marvelous breed would stir him. When it didn't appear to, she went on (by rote, he thought, as if the child had memorized a book): "They were owned by the King of Babylon who made laws for them. That they couldn't be killed or bothered. Long, long before that the King of Summertime breeded them. My dog's Hungarian and his name is King."

Abby Cable squinted in pain at this account of the dog's pedigree. "I told you before there's no King of Summertime. There never was. And his name's *Tim,* not King. *Tim's* what it was when you got him."

Melrose's smile reached from one to the other. "It's rather delightful, though, you must admit. The King of Summertime." When the Fury looked at him he realized he'd made a tactical error. "But I do agree. I mean practically speaking I doubt there's such a person." He wondered what it was, though, or who, that Ethel had confused with "summertime." A king of Sumeria? That must be it.

"I told you he wasn't that stupid," said Abby, dragging the feed bucket over to the donkey.

Melrose didn't know whether to be flattered she'd apparently been telling Ethel about him or wonder just how stupid, if not that stupid, he seemed.

Ethel, mouth clamped in a narrow, angry little line, cut away at the cheese.

"It's just rough sandwiches," said Abby. The tone was neutral. She came out of the stall and latched the door. When it shut Melrose saw that here was another poster. Each animal had its own favorite, apparently. He couldn't see the cow's, but the donkey's was an old Dylan poster and the pony's was that American singer who, he thought, had died. Ricky Nelson.

"Thank you very much, but as it's only a bit after ten, I don't think I could handle a sandwich. Certainly not after that huge breakfast your aunt gave me." Since she had said nothing by way of encouragement here, Melrose added, as the kettle screeched, "But a cup of tea would be very pleasant."

While the pony made mushy noises, content with his bag of oats, Abby stood back from the stall, hands on hips, regarding either Ricky Nelson or the horse. Since her back was turned, Melrose couldn't tell which. Ricky, apparently, for she said, "We have to take your poster down, Ethel."

Knife in hand, Ethel whirled. "It's *my* poster."

"It's my barn."

Ethel wailed, "I love him."

"It's too bad," said Abby, firmly. Melrose thought he discerned an echo of the words that had been hurled at the vet's receptionist when she added, "He's dead."

Stranger sat up, sensing a confrontation.

"He's in *heaven,* then," whined Ethel. "He's singing up in

heaven. And I can marry him when I get there." Her high little voice trumpeted forth with the triumph of a Gabriel.

Matter-of-factly, Abby answered, "Who says there's a heaven?" She squelched a bucket of feed over to the door and sat it down in readiness for the chicken yard.

So appalled Ethel must have been at this heretical statement that she could think of no response. She slapped two plates down on the cloth-covered sawhorse table, bouncing the bread and cheese, furious. Then she dragged over the wobbly stool, apparently meant for Melrose, and thumped it down at one end of the table.

Abby gave Ethel a pained look. "That's too little for him. He can have my chair. I'll get the other one."

Before she collected the chair, she stood upon it, reached in her pocket, and brought out some chewing gum. Holding back the top corner of the poster as she chewed, she then stuck the doughy stuff to the stone and pressed the corner of the poster in place.

Ethel, red-faced, stuck her tongue out at Abby's back and, when she heard the voices at the door, quickly tried to regain her princessy demeanor. He could see, though, that she was searching for a killing last word. "Well, then you'll *never* find my hiding place. I was going to tell you—"

A lie. Even Melrose knew that.

Abby kept herself rigid. "You can't have a hiding place in my barn."

This was a longstanding argument, clearly, cut off by the voices outside. An elongated shadow that fell across the threshing floor doubled as the man and woman separated at the door. Abby thumped at the corner of the poster one last time and clambered down from the chair.

"Hullo, Abby."

"Hello."

The gentleman and lady standing there spoke simultaneously, the woman with a little more authority than the man, who seemed, although smiling, less certain of his welcome.

Abby merely turned from the poster-fixing, returned the

greeting glumly, and went back to resticking the chewing gum.

"Having tea, are you?" the lady said, looking from Melrose to Ethel, to the makeshift table and back at Melrose at the same time she dropped the hood of her coat from bronze-colored hair vaguely streaked with white, whether from age or highlighting he couldn't say; she appeared to be in her forties, and was dressed in some long, loose, patch-work-bright garment that the Princess probably would have approved for sheer flamboyance.

When Abby didn't turn from her work, the woman walked over to the wall, turning to say "Rena," when Charles Citrine had introduced her as "Irene." She held out a small package to Abby that was (Melrose heard her say) ". . . from Nell."

Abby looked at the brown wrapping and slipped it in one of the big pockets of her skirt.

Melrose caught snatches of their—or *her*—conversation as the brother spoke casually to Melrose about the weather, the country in January, and Weavers Hall. Citrine (with a nod of his head in some direction back there) said he lived in an old house "across the moor."

Irene Citrine stood there conversing with Abby. Although *converse* was hardly the word, since Abby's end of this conversation was uncompromisingly monosyllabic. Melrose made out that the box was from "Nell, who specially wanted you to have it . . . had she tried rubber cement to hold up the poster? . . . a handsome poster. . . . Who are they? . . . Nell's sorry she couldn't . . . Nelligan's flock is . . . need anything . . . ?"

They were wandering in decidedly unlabyrinthine avenues of conversation, given Abby's answers:

"Thanks."

"No."

"Yes."

"Rock band."

"Well."

"Yes."

"No."

In other words, a typical Abbyesque exchange with someone she was indifferent to, although she appeared to prize the gift if not the giver. Melrose thought the giver was surely trying her best.

Charles Citrine was trying his, too. Citrine was a man who would be tagged "affable" straightaway. In these circumstances, however, the manner was strained. The man's thoughts were elsewhere; the pale blue eyes fixed on his sister and Abby, at the same time he exhausted the conversational possibilities with Melrose about the weather, the countryside, the Hall.

It was, perhaps, simply a more mannered version of Abby's own responses to Nell Healey's aunt.

Once the Citrines had gone, Abby walked to the byre and then back to her "bedroom" and then over to the table, where she exchanged the thick chipped mug Ethel had set out for Melrose for a fluted cup and a mismatched saucer with tiny blue flowers.

"*Well?* What *is* it?" demanded Ethel. "What's the *present?*"

"I didn't open it," said Abby calmly.

Ethel fluttered her hands excitedly. "Open it, open it."

"It's in my hiding place. Get the kettle." Abby sat with her hands folded.

Grimly Ethel swung the kettle from the rod with a thick cloth and poured it into the pot while Abby settled herself on the low wooden chair. Since Ethel's seat was the stool with a cast-off cushion, their relative heights round the table were wholly disproportionate. Melrose felt as if he might be looking down from that heaven that Abby disclaimed any knowledge of.

Abby poured the tea, Melrose's cup first, plunked down the pot, and picked up her sandwich. These were indeed "rough" sandwiches, ill-cut portions of cheese between hunks of bread.

"Well, this is a welcome relief from the morning's events."

When Abby looked at him, apparently doubting great things had come of a morning at Weavers Hall, he wished he could stop being so hearty.

There was a ritual silence as they drank their tea. The two dogs had each been given their meal and Stranger took this as a signal to relax his vigil and lie by the fireplace. Tim had left in search of something more inviting than this inactive person.

Abby divided her attention between her plate and the empty air round Melrose's shoulder.

Ethel, despite her prim neatness, turned out to be a noisy eater, chomping her cheese, slurping her tea, and beating a tattoo with her heels against the stool. Having hit upon one more thing to madden her friend, she said to Melrose, "I've got things hid in this barn and Abby don't know where."

Given Abby's stony look, she apparently believed it. "You can't have a hiding place in somebody *else's* barn. I told you."

Ethel simpered. "Well, I do. You don't know, I could keep a gun there." She then started in, nonstop, on the murder at the inn.

"Blood all over—"

"No, there wasn't." Abby's voice was a flat-out contradiction. "Stop talking about it."

But given the sacrilege earlier paid to the dead singer, Ethel was clearly going to get hers back. Crumbs gathered in the corners of Ethel's mouth as she went on: "She *shot* him. Splat!"

"*Ethel!*"

Melrose himself would have hesitated to continue, faced down by that pair of eyes, but Ethel was going to turn the knife. Anyway, it wasn't every day such juicy gossip came along in this isolated region.

"We wasn't to talk about it." Abby's voice was level but her look would have stunned the animals in the stall.

"That Missus Healey, she's *your* friend."

Ethel, Melrose saw, for all her milky-whiteness, her ribbons and ruffles and dimples, was a small fiend, sitting there with that hair of fiery licks, the upright kitchen fork like a trident.

"And she can't come here, *can* she? Because your auntie won't let her."

This was delivered in a snide, singsongy voice meant to engage and enrage her hostess. Ethel was bringing out the big guns. "And anyway, *you* got the pictures of dead people"—she motioned with a nod of her head toward the crate that held the books—"right over there. I saw them *all*. There's pictures of that little boy, Billy, and his friend." When there was no response to this, she said, "They're terrible, my mam says. Says they just let that little Billy *die*. I saw all the pictures of you and him and the other one, that Tony."

"Toby." The correction was automatic, issuing forth from some brain and mouth not Abby's own.

Melrose interrupted. "I suggest you stop talking about things you know nothing about." He shoved his chair back, looked at Abby, wondered if she were some sort of magnet for negative planetary waves. Ever since he had first seen her, she seemed always to be bedeviled.

Although she said nothing, the vibrations issuing from her stony posture made the table appear to quiver, the dirt floor beneath them vibrate; on her face was the expression Medea might have worn on Jason's return.

"Go home," said Abby.

"We're having the funeral. You said we were."

It was then that Melrose noticed the small black-draped box by the bed. A votive candle, unlit, stood at one end. Buster. Melrose looked away.

And Abby merely repeated, "Go home."

"But we've *got* to bury Buster! Or she'll start smelling up the whole barn."

The air, Melrose thought, should have been redolent with

the smell of Buster, given the cat had been there for twenty-four hours.

"Go home," Abby said again, in that same atonal voice.

Ethel tossed down what was left of her sandwich and got up, haughtily, as if to say it made no odds to her whether she stayed or went. But as she pushed her sleeves into her coat on her way to the barn door, she issued one parting shot.

"And if there's no heaven and we just turn into vapors, then just where's *your* mother, *I'd* like to know!"

Abby's eyes were turned to the old beams of the roof. "With Ricky Nelson."

Part Two

THE
KING
OF
SUMMERTIME

18

Lost cause was a term that never applied to any case Brian Macalvie was working on; it often extended to the people working under him, however.

Often, but not always. The female voice Jury heard coming from the forensics lab at the end of the corridor belonged to Gilly Thwaite, Macalvie's Scene-of-Crimes officer.

When Macalvie saw Jury appear at the open door, he motioned him in with an impatient wave of his hand as if Jury were an overdue referee.

Not that Macalvie needed one; he was standing in his usual posture, hands pushed in trouser pockets and shoving back the raincoat he seemed never to remove, and chewing gum at a rate roughly equivalent to the fast-talking Gilly Thwaite. Across the lab table she leaned into him like a heavy wind.

Jury sat down in a white enamel folding chair and tipped it back, watching Macalvie stand there like the tree that wouldn't be uprooted. She was trying to face him down about fingerprints, or the lack of them, in the case they were working on.

". . . no partials, no latents, only elimination. For the sixth damn time. Nothing!" Her big black-rimmed glasses took over half of her small, triangular face like goggles.

Gilly Thwaite was more than usually edgy, thought Jury. She was smart enough to know that what Macalvie's co-workers thought of as the chief superintendent's "arrogance" was better described as his simple confidence that he was right ninety percent of the time—which he was. Macalvie allowed a margin for error or natural disasters: flooding of the River Dart, the collapse of Exeter Cathedral, the disappearance of the Devon-Cornwall coast, or worse—information withheld from him. This was why Gilly Thwaite was being defensive, Jury knew. She suspected that Macalvie was going to pull the rug out.

"The toilet seat, Gilly? I mean *under* the toilet seat. Even a bastard that could shove an old guy's skull in can be very fastidious about—"

"Yes! Under, over, inside the tank. . . ." She came close to slapping him with the folder she fanned in front of his face; Macalvie brushed it away as if it were a mosquito. "Look, you seem to forget I'm *not* your print expert—"

"Be grateful for small blessings, Gilly," said Macalvie round the cigarette he was lighting. "Let's get to the call box on the corner. At thirteen-five a call was made to that number. At thirteen-ten the old guy was killed—"

"Two call boxes, Superintendent, *two.*" She held up two fingers directly in front of her chief's eyes.

Macalvie's expression didn't change, so she finally dropped her hand. "I'm talking about the *only* one this villain could have called from and got to that house in four minutes." He shrugged. "But if you insist on two possibilities, it's still the same thing, it'd just take a little longer."

"Those call boxes were dusted for prints; do you think between the whole team we don't have at least one brain . . . I take that back." It was hard to make Gilly Thwaite's face flush, but Jury saw the blood rising along the neck.

"Either of them credit-card phones? Phone-card phones?"

Wiggins, who had been scrutinizing a row of phials on one of the tables for either cures or diseases, looked over at the two.

"Regular call boxes." Gilly Thwaite pretended to be shrugging this off because she knew it was important and she'd missed something. Jury could almost see her mind racing, sprinting round the course trying at least to keep abreast, if not ahead, of Macalvie's nag.

He stood there chewing gum while she didn't answer. "You thought of calling Telecom?" He tapped ash into his hand. "Probably make their day, a couple crowbars, an axe or two . . ."

She stood there frowning, saying nothing.

"Think about it." He looked at his watch as if he were timing her, then started toward the door.

"Why do you have to play with your people's minds, Macalvie?"

They were on their way down the corridor to his office.

"To find out if they've got any. She's one of the few who does. What's wrong, Wiggins?"

Sergeant Wiggins was looking decidedly puzzled as he slowly unwrapped a tin of Sucrets. "What? Oh, nothing. Nothing."

The office was cold because Macalvie always kept a window open whatever the season. Since he never seemed to remove his coat—he was out more than in—the cold didn't bother him. Jury was surprised to see the window festooned with scraggly blue and brassy-orange tinsel, the sad remains of the passing season. The late sun reflected and refracted it on Macalvie's copper hair and when he turned, sparked his intensely blue eyes. God did the lighting for Macalvie.

He had plunked himself into his swivel chair at a desk full of ashtrays, folders, and coffee mugs that could have gone to the lab; amidst this buildup of what Jury imagined was the residue of old cases that Macalvie refused to close and therefore to let anyone file, he pulled out a folder it would have taken his secretary a week to find.

Wiggins hunched down in his heavily lined raincoat and looked unhappily at the open window. He pulled his thick gloves from his pocket and put them on, staring at Macalvie. Hint-wise, it wasn't of much use; Macalvie could never understand disturbances of the body so long as the mind was in first gear.

Jury hadn't bothered taking off his coat, either, and hadn't bothered sitting down because he was too busy staring at the photos Macalvie had spread out, facing Jury. "What's this, Macalvie?"

"Pictures." Macalvie reached down into his file drawer, stuck a pint of Glenfiddich on the table with some paper cups, leaned back, and propped his feet on the desk top. "Photos of remains. A boy and his dog."

"What are you talking about?"

"Look at the photos. They buried the dog, too."

Jury's head came up. "I'm not one of your team, Brian. You don't have to wait for me to catch up with you. If you're talking about Billy Healey, he was never found, and Toby Holt was killed by a lorry. This isn't Dunstable races, and I don't care if I win, place, or show. I just want to show up with something when the chips are down—"

"The chips are always down. Have a drink." He started pouring small measures into cone-shaped cups.

Wiggins, who ordinarily looked at liquor the same way he looked at lizards, actually drank his down neat, choked, pulled out his lozenge tin.

"No, thanks," said Jury, waving away the drink. Leaning on the divisional commander's desk, his hands splayed, he said levelly, "Listen to me: you're a chief superintendent, a divisional commander, not Sam Spade—you even call your secretary 'Effie'—and you act like Joe Cairo and the Fat Man are going to come walking through a bead curtain. You run a department, Macalvie; you're not Spade or Marlowe. So stop pulling cards out from behind your ear, okay?"

Wiggins quickly pulled out his charcoal biscuits, anodyne for anything—digestion, anger—and shoved one toward Jury. Jury took it without thinking, stuck half in his mouth, and chewed the dreadful thing. No wonder Wiggins was almost always sick if this is what he thought would cure him.

Macalvie sat wide-eyed, feigning wonder . . . feigning concern . . . just feigning. "You through?"

Jury swallowed, choked, and reached for the paper cup Macalvie was taking up. He took a drink and said, "I can only *assume,* since you didn't tell me anything, and since I'm here on the Nell Healey business, that somehow you've discovered the boy's body. *How,* I don't know."

Macalvie looked surprised. "How? I just kept on searching, Jury." *Why wouldn't any cop do the same?* his expression asked.

Jury scanned the police photographs of skeletal remains, human and what appeared to be animal, taken from all angles, first lying in the grave, later carefully removed and placed on the ground, out of it. "Nell Healey doesn't appear to know you've found anything."

Macalvie took his feet off the desk, made a neat stack of the photos and replaced them in the brown envelope, which he handed to Jury. "You want to tell her, Jury?"

Wiggins coughed, sucked his lozenge noisily, and looked from the one to the other. Macalvie was out of his chair, jamming a tweed cap on his head. "Especially since you don't know the whole story? Come on; we're going to Cornwall."

Wiggins shoved his lozenge under his tongue, and said, "Well, it'd help if you *told* us the story." He sneezed. "Sir."

Jury smiled. "Be sure you leave the window open, Macalvie. You never know when *He* might call you to fly out of it."

The window shut with a bang that splintered the old paint at the corners. "You guys are a treat."

They passed the desk of Macalvie's secretary, whose eyes were bent on an embroidery hoop. "Will I see you again?" she asked, sucking a finger that she seemed to have stabbed with the needle at her boss's appearance. "Or should I just leave up the decorations till next Christmas?" Her face, as chiseled as a square-cut diamond, turned to the ceiling molding, round which were festooned more dull and dusty strands of tinsel. "Sergeant Thwaite called to say Telecom is having your service at home disconnected."

Macalvie's cap was pulled down somewhere in the region of his nose. "I don't have a home; I don't have an office; I don't need a secretary. So long, Effie."

She seemed to be considering this, as one hand left the hoop to scratch almost meditatively, like a cat, under one armpit. "Then can I take down that bloody tinsel and moth-eaten wreath?"

Jury smiled at her. "We could all do with a bit of glitter." He looked at the faded gold loopings and smiled even more broadly. "I take it the decorations aren't your idea."

The hoop was forgotten, lying on her typewriter, a decades-old IBM. Her smile was as wide as the wreath. "His. Every year, he wants the damned stuff up."

Wiggins made a sound between a giggle and a sneeze as Macalvie's coat disappeared round the door.

Jane leaned her square chin on her equally square fingernails. "And every year he gives me the same present."

"Bath salts," said Jury, solemnly.

"Bath salts," said Jane with an added touch of glamour in her smile. "Crabtree and Evelyn."

"Good-bye, Jane."

She brought her fingers to her palm a couple of times in a good-bye wave.

19

"That's okay, Wiggins, I'll drive," said Macalvie as Wiggins was quickly trying to capture the driver's seat.

Jury got in the passenger's side while Wiggins stowed himself into the rear seat and appeared to be offering up a prayer.

Macalvie twisted round and said, "We can take the A-thirty-eight, but the shortcut across Dartmoor's better. No traffic."

Obviously recalling an earlier drive through sheets of rain and hemmed in by stone walls (no stone of which Macalvie had left unturned), Wiggins brought out his big gun: the vaporizer.

Macalvie gave Wiggins a look of disgust. Jury nodded at the road ahead. "Take the A-thirty-eight."

Macalvie shrugged, tore away from the curb.

When they hit the roundabout, a black Lamborghini with a woman driver dripping jewels and a fox fur cut him off, gave him a finger, and took the car up to ninety as she sped onto the motorway.

"Lady, lady," sighed Macalvie. He yanked the blue light out and shoved it on top of the Ford.

"Brian we're going to *Cornwall.* You're not—" Jury was tossed against the back of his seat as Macalvie jammed the pedal down.

"Following her, we'll get there a hell of a lot faster." He smiled broadly.

Wiggins had a coughing fit and Jury just shook his head as the Ford closed in on the Lamborghini. "You're not a traffic cop, for Christ's sakes."

"So what? There's never one around when you need one." The Lamborghini finally pulled over. Macalvie braked on the shoulder, got out a ticket book that he kept stashed in the glove box, and said, "This won't take long."

Macalvie, Jury knew, loved being a copper. The possibilities were endless.

Looking through the rear windscreen, Wiggins said, "Do you think he might have been a deprived child, sir?"

"No." Jury was blowing on his hands. "But his parents were."

"There's one old Lambo won't be hitting the highways for six months." He whistled and drifted out into the traffic.

An hour later, they were flying by a brightly lit Little Chef that Wiggins eyed longingly, as if the wind stirred up by the traffic was wafting the aroma of plaice and chips and beans on toast down the motorway through the driver's open window.

Macalvie had been giving Jury the details of the scene, eight years ago, in the house on the Cornwall coast. They were the same details, but Macalvie liked to get everything right at least twice before he moved on. "You should have heard them, Jury—Healey and Citrine—when she refused to pay up. I thought Roger Healey was going to take the poker and let her have it. Daddy wasn't quite so violent, but it looked like a cardiac arrest was imminent. *'Are you insane, Nell? He's my son!'* or *'My dear God, you've got to. He's like my own grandson.'* No one seemed to think Billy Healey was *her* anything."

Macalvie was trying to honk an old charabanc out of the fast lane, but it kept on rattling right along. Through its dirt-smeared rear window, Jury made out a group of people who looked to be in some sort of costume. Finally, the Ford pulled into the inside lane and Macalvie slowed down, hunching over to have a look. A wide, white banner on the side of the old bus announced the Twyford English Country Dancers. They seemed to be singing; they were certainly clapping in time to something, and sounded drunk as lords.

"I think maybe they got an elephant driving."

The elephant smiled down at the Ford and raised his plastic cup.

"Oh, hell," said Jury.

The blue light went back up on the hood. "You want that horse's arse out here on the *highway,* Jury? No wonder old people are always getting clobbered on zebra crossings. It's probably your effing C.I.D. running them down." He shouted at the charabanc and waved it to the next exit.

"You must admit, sir," Wiggins said to Jury, as they careened to a halt in the car park, "Mr. Macalvie's right. Can't have this sort of thing on the roads."

The sergeant smiled up at a blue neon sign missing one of its letters: CAF.

To Jury none of the riders looked a day under eighty as they spilled out of the bus, still singing, still clapping, still boozing.

" 'Ello, 'andsome," cried a lavender-haired lady as she grabbed Wiggins's hands and tried to dance him sideways down the car park.

An old man who looked less sturdy than string was squatting down, arms crossed over his chest, doing something that looked more Russian than English. They wore frilled shirts and braces.

Jury smiled and disentangled himself from three wiry ladies determined to drag him into a set as Macalvie was having a fine time with the huge driver with sepia curls who, in the tight trousers that looked from behind like two moons, wasn't having problems with his sexual identity since he clearly didn't care.

Macalvie was shouting like a football coach: "Now you" —he shoved a ticket he'd written into the elephant's jacket

pocket—"can dance your little toes and tambourines right
in that caff and don't even *think* about coming out until you
can walk a straight line on your bloody *hands.*" He walked
over to Jury. "Get that dedicated look off your face, Jury.
We'd've had to stop anyway; Wiggins needs his cuppa."

"So here's what happened."
The three were trying to ignore the " *'ello, luvs,*" the
waves, the brandishing of paper napkins from the long table
with its speckled-blue Formica top on the other side of the
café.

Three coffees to go was not Sergeant Wiggins's idea of a
proper tea-break, to say nothing of a meal; he had time only
to snatch a Kit-Kat before they were out in the fog again,
slamming the car doors, Macalvie splashing the coffees with
a burst of acceleration.

With the divisional commander, there were never any
qualifiers: no *I think*'s; no *a possible theory might be*'s; no *in
my opinion*'s. Jury shook the hot coffee from his hand and
let Macalvie go on, despite the fact they'd got halfway across
Devon and still no mention of the police photos of the skeleton.

"So here's what happened. Billy Healey goes into the
house to make his tea—tea for Billy and Toby consisting of a
couple of loaves of bread and ten pots, according to Mum."
Macalvie smiled slightly, as if he were one of the family or,
at least, a distant relative. "So he's in the kitchen with his
dog, Gnasher. He's got the kettle on the hob, he's sawing the
bread in slabs, spreading it with an inch of currant jam, milk
out for Toby, and butter—" Macalvie veered into the outside lane.

Said Wiggins, looking longingly behind him as another
café receded in the highway mist, as the car advanced on the
turnoff signposted for Ashburton, "It's amazing you remember these things. I mean about the currant jam, and so forth.
You might as well have been there."

Macalvie couldn't have agreed more. "Too bad for

Devon-Cornwall I wasn't. By the time I managed to get to the house, it was clean. That whole kitchen—not to say the rest of the house—should have been gone over on hands and knees."

"I agree," said Jury. "Go on."

"Nell Healey said even the vitamins were lined up: calcium, C, A, whatever. That was the place I thought she was going to break down. She was always nagging Billy to take calcium because he was violently allergic to milk. And she thought like most kids he was fibbing when he said, sure, he'd taken them. But they were lined up in a row."

They were in Wiggins-territory now—not Ashburton, but allergies. He crossed his arms over the front seat. "It can play hell with a person; I should know."

Jury had lowered the window and was tossing the undrinkable coffee from the paper cup. "You're not allergic to milk, Wiggins." He turned to see Wiggins take a brown bottle from his coat pocket dispensary.

"One-a-Day." He washed the capsule down with his coffee. "It's especially important when you can't stop for a proper meal. Which happens all the time." The tone was dark.

"Yeah. Well, obviously something interrupted Billy Healey's little meal eight years ago," said Macalvie. "Someone walked in and surprised Billy. And the someone got a little surprise himself when Toby came in from wherever he was for his tea."

"He could have been in the kitchen, too."

"No. They took photos." Macalvie's tone was grudging. "The slice of bread with the jam had been half eaten; the bread with the butter hadn't been touched. Neither had the second cup of tea. So Billy starts the tea-making and probably tells Toby, wherever Toby might have been, and within, say, that fifteen or twenty minutes someone comes in the kitchen door. The kitchen was at the back facing the dirt road. It was someone Billy Healey knew."

"That's a hell of an assumption, Macalvie."

"Then you haven't been paying attention—well, what's this, then?"

A sable-brown car flew by in the inside lane. It must have been doing a hundred.

Jury winced. "Macalvie, that's a Jag. It's an XJSC, V-twelve engine. Top of the line. We're in a bottom-line Ford V-eight and you're not going to catch—" Jury's words were lost on the wind as Macalvie hit the accelerator.

20

The cottage was half-buried in long grass and weeds; the garden looked more in need of harvesting than pruning and surrounded a small, square, cream-washed house that looked as if it were more functional than livable. It only needed a neon sign or big letters to pass for one of the motorway cafés.

A tall, thin, quarrelsome-looking girl opened the door to Macalvie's fist-pounding. Jury would have thought he was raiding the place rather than visiting it.

The girl's sallow frown looked cast in bronze and her unfocused brown eyes were set in deep sockets. She had a dishcloth over her shoulder and was lugging a Hoover. She informed them the *perfesser* was having his evening meal and they could go on back. With the handle of the Hoover she pointed, more or less, to a room at the rear and then went off.

Dennis Dench was eating quail and salad, washed down with a half bottle of white wine.

Each tiny bone had been placed in a bone dish, not haphazardly, but rather with attention to the underlying structure of the small fowl. After greeting Macalvie, who made an unconvincing apology for disturbing Dr. Dench's meal, Dench went back to the quail. He did not gnaw at the leg bone, but chewed the slivers of meat carefully.

He greeted Jury, and, once up, put his napkin down.

Dennis Dench took one last sip of wine and said, "Hullo, Brian. They're not the Healey boy's remains."

As they left the dining room, Dench looked back over his narrow, sloping shoulder at Macalvie. "You should know that; I've told you half a dozen times."

"Oh, sure." It was Macalvie's deadpan tone, the one he used when he wasn't going to argue a point.

They passed down a cheerlessly white, though well-lit hall toward a door at the end, and Jury paused to look at a large print that supplied about the only color in the house he had seen thus far. It would have to be an O'Keeffe, the one of the cow's skull.

"Nice, that," said Dennis, coming back to stand by Jury. He fiddled with his thick glasses as if they were an out-of-focus microscope. "Very good." He stepped back a bit, cocked his head, frowned slightly. "Well . . . as good as a painter could get in that particular line."

The basement laboratory was no more antiseptic than the rest of the house, although it was considerably more interesting. It had not an O'Keeffe but a Daliesque quality in its display of bones, leathered skin, objects floating in large jars —all less horrific than surreal. There were two skeletons in full bloom, if the bright red carnation between the ribs of one and the daisy chain round the collarbone of the other were an indication.

Dennis Dench shook his head. "Minerva's always doing that."

"Minerva?" asked Sergeant Wiggins, who turned from his inspection of a jar.

"One who let you in. Thinks it's all a bit of a giggle."

Jury couldn't imagine the young woman who let them in giggling about much of anything; her skin was the color of the ashy mask contoured over the frame of a skull.

Plucking a starched white jacket from a hook, Dennis said, "I've told her a dozen times the lab needn't be hoovered, but she still insists the floor needs scrubbing and the 'skellies' dusted. I think she's named them. Naturally, she doesn't touch anything else because I told her I would put her in the tub there"—he nodded toward something like a washtub—"and then her skelly would be scattered over Salcombe estuary."

"What are you putting together?" Macalvie nodded toward the long white table with a Formica top where a sand-box rested on one end and, on the other, the threatening tub. Bones protruded from the sandbox, apparently drying; in the tub of viscous liquid, other bones were being divested of remaining flesh. Having pulled on his surgical gloves, Dennis pulled out several smaller bones and plunged them into another bath. The hanging light was dazzling, a false sun. "Jason at the beach?" asked Macalvie, chewing his gum.

Dennis addressed Jury. "I told him not to drag you all the way here from Exeter."

"You're well known, Dr. Dench. It's not a lost trip."

Dennis Dench gave Macalvie a pursed little smile.

"Call him Denny," said Macalvie, walking over to a cabi-net and knocking on it as if he expected someone or -thing in there to open up. "Let's see Billy Healey's skeleton, okay?"

Having dipped the two bones in the tub, Dench now stood them up in the sand and said, "You can see the skeleton, but it's not Billy Healey's."

Macalvie was trying to open the cabinet door. "Just be-cause I don't have a degree in osteoanatomy doesn't mean I haven't read up on it. Who the hell built this cabinet? Dr. Caligari?"

"The skeleton's over here, Brian. You never did have the patience of Job."

He removed the white cloth from the skeleton of a child that Jury would have guessed to be preadolescent. It was restored except for a few fragments that lay in a neat semi-circle beside the leg. Beneath the child's skeleton were the tinier animal bones.

Macalvie stood, hands in pockets holding back his raincoat. He nodded toward the bone fragments. "You can't jigsaw those in?"

"Wouldn't be worth it. There's probably been warpage anyway. They wouldn't tell you anything more."

Wiggins, having had his fill of pickled things in jars and the range of photographs tacked on the wall, came over to have a look. Running his hands over his rib cage, he said, "Seems everything's there." He might have been making comparisons. "What's the most difficult thing to determine, Professor? From the skeletal remains?"

Macalvie snapped, "Age."

Dennis Dench looked away, pained. "How many times do we have to have this argument, Brian? Age in a child is the *easiest* thing to determine. You know perfectly well—from what you've *told* me you'd read—complete epiphyseal fusion in a skeleton is found only in adults." He turned to Wiggins and Jury: "In this case, it was fairly easy. It's a skeleton of a subpubic male Caucasian of between fourteen and, I'd say, sixteen. The Healey boy was only twelve."

Macalvie shook and shook his head. "Don't tell me you can cut it that close."

"The devil I can't; except for some environmental variants, bone fusion can be traced in a growing child with exactitude from year to year."

Macalvie said, generously, "Okay, even if I give you that—"

"And what about the odontologist's report? Everything points to this as the skeleton of a boy older than Billy Healey."

Jury said, "You mentioned environmental variants. That would include malnutrition, wouldn't it?"

Dennis frowned. "No sign of that here, though. You're referring to the Healey boy's allergy to milk products?"

"I understand Billy Healey had to take heavy doses of vitamins and calcium. . . . There was some doubt as to whether he took all he was supposed to."

Answering for Dennis, Macalvie said: "No actual signs of

malnutrition, but that doesn't exclude the bones as being those of the Healey kid."

"Brian, I hate to remind you: I've written three books on the subject."

"I know. I've read them." He was standing in front of Dench's desk running his finger over bindings. Quickly he pulled one out, flipped through it, found the column he wanted, and said, "I quote: 'Ossification centers are often difficult to recognize and sometimes lost in an immature specimen.' " As Dennis raised his eyes to the ceiling, Macalvie flipped the pages again. "Here you've got a case of a youngster whose height could be determined only within *three inches.* That's a hell of a variable, three whole inches."

"Oh, come on, Brian. All anyone has to do is watch a games match at some school to see a boy of twelve can be as tall as one of sixteen. And the difference in Billy's and Toby's height wasn't apparently that much. An inch, inch and a half. Anyway, we're not talking stature here, we're talking *age.*" Dennis's look at the skeleton was remorseful, his hand drawn down the long femur bone in a gesture that suggested it was flesh and blood he touched.

"You're forgetting something, Denny. Let's *assume* you're right about the age," said Macalvie. "The only thing you're basing your conclusions on is one little thing—"

"It's not a little thing. Each epiphysis fuses with the bone shaft at a particular age—"

"Can you forget that for just one damned second while I go on?"

"No." Dennis carefully realigned the femur of the dog with its pelvic bone.

Carefully, Macalvie leaned his hands on the table just above the skull and leaned over the small skeleton. "Jesus, but I'm glad you're not on my forensics team—"

"So am I." Dennis politely stifled a yawn. "You've got a thick skull." He ran his eyes slowly over Macalvie's face. "Literally."

"You're working in a vacuum, Denny. I'll tell you why I'm right—"

"You're wrong."

"Because, number one"—Macalvie had moved over to the rack of test tubes and pulled two from its pronged fittings—"these soil samples. Now, the vicar of that church told you, although you've conveniently forgotten, nobody's been buried, to his knowledge, in that disused graveyard for forty years, and here we come up with soil removed and replaced long after that. I sent this stuff through forensics—"

"Thought you didn't trust them." Dennis had stepped back to look, sadly, at the small dog's skeleton.

"They didn't know what it was for."

"I could tell you the same thing they did."

"Maybe. Since you seem to know everything. The disturbance of this soil and its constitution shows that the grave was dug within the two-year period when a nearby mineshaft was excavated because we've got traces of zinc and other substances in the soil. That's one. Two: in those two years not one preadolescent male Caucasian went missing from the area without either returning voluntarily *or* having been found *or* the remains having been found—"

Wiggins turned from his study of the markout of the gravesite and frowned. "Pardon, sir, but isn't there a fallacy in that argument? What about cases not reported?"

"All right, I'll give you that. But we're still talking about a missing boy and a dog buried together in a structure obviously fitted out to sustain life. Until somebody pulled the plug." He was talking to Wiggins over his shoulder, his hold on the table still secure as if Dench might drag it out from under him.

Macalvie went on. "To say nothing of that deserted cemetery being found within a quarter mile of the Citrine house. And with all of this evidence, you're standing there and talking about a possible *three- or four*-year difference in *bone fusion.*"

"That's right. And I'm dealing in facts; you're dealing in

induction. You're adding up a lot of information and coming to a conclusion. But a piece of your information is missing. Ergo. Erroneous conclusion," said Dennis calmly.

Macalvie shook his head quickly, like a swimmer clearing water from his ears. He glanced at Jury, who'd been leaning against the counter. "You've said sweet nothing. How do you rate the chances that two kids with two dogs could have been buried secretly in that time frame and so close to the Citrine house?"

Jury had had his eyes on the tiny skeleton of the dog under the boy's feet—for his mind had encased them in stone like the effigies he had so often seen in the churches and cathedrals—lord and lady, earl and countess—with a little dog, and sometimes two, cushioning their feet. And he remembered the position Dennis Dench had inferred; the bones of the dog had been lying atop the skeleton of the boy. While part of his mind stood aside and looked at the problem objectively, he himself could hardly breathe and his own eyes were no longer dazzled by the glare of the hanging light, the fluorescence, the almost screaming whiteness of the walls, the Formica. They had grown steadily dimmer, though his ears had taken in everything the others were saying. At the same time he watched the light fading like headlamps sweeping by in the fog and the then total darkness. He could hardly breathe. Which of them had used up the last of the oxygen? The child? The dog? He had had the dog, at least. The dog that Jury doubted had been sealed in the grave for companionship.

But who knew? Who could possibly tell what a mind so warped would do? "I was wondering about Toby," Jury finally said in answer to Macalvie.

"Toby? Toby's dead. You read the report."

"He was fifteen."

Dennis Dench laughed his short, brittle laugh. "Convenient, that would have been for me."

"It was certainly convenient as hell for the kidnapper.

The only witness dies in an accident? Talk about coincidence."

"Believe me, I did," said Macalvie. "According to your police there wasn't a single reason to tie that lorry driver to Toby. The lorry was actually *stopped* at a zebra crossing—I didn't know they did that—and the kid bolted across it when he started up. It was dark, raining, he swerved. Too late."

"That's another thing. What in the hell would the boy be doing in London?"

"Running. Is there a better place to hide than in a crowd?"

"The natural thing for a kid to do is run home."

Macalvie sighed. "Not if there's somebody at 'home' who knows you're witness to a kidnapping."

"That's your theory, Macalvie."

"So what's yours?"

"I don't have one."

Macalvie went over to stand beside Wiggins who was studying the photographic mockup. He unfolded an old newspaper clipping and laid it on the counter beside the partially reconstructed photograph. The picture in the paper wasn't a studio pose; it showed a young boy with a puzzled look, his hair covered by a woolen jacket hood like a monk cowl. He was squinting. Macalvie studied the picture for a moment and said to Dennis, "I couldn't tell me old mum if her eyes were nothing but silver discs; mind if I change this?"

"Yes." Dennis was covering the small skeleton.

Even while asking the question, Macalvie cut a piece from a scrap of paper, penciled something in while looking at the clipping, and put the tiny strip on the photograph. "Give me your scarf, Wiggins."

With some reluctance, Sergeant Wiggins unwrapped the brown scarf as carefully as a doctor removing bandages from a patient who'd just had an eye operation.

Macalvie arranged the scarf around the skull in the photo,

simulating the newspaper picture. He put the rest of the scarf over the left-hand side of the face and what remained was a fuzzy, but reasonable facsimile of a face.

"If that isn't Billy Healey, I'll turn down the promotion to assistant constable."

Dennis tucked the covering round the skeleton of boy and dog, as if, in the ordinary way of good nights, he were putting them to bed. "Since the chief constable hasn't offered it, it's not much of a bet."

Macalvie grinned. "Thanks for letting us take up your time."

They walked back through the dining room where the dishes still remained, together with the bottle of white wine. Dennis Dench took three glasses from a sideboard, set them on the table, and said, "You've got to taste this. It's superb. Chablis Moutonne."

Holding it up to the light, Macalvie rolled it in the glass as Dennis Dench rolled his eyes at Macalvie.

"He knows as much about wine as he does about bone fusion," said Dench.

Macalvie sipped, rolled the wine in his mouth. "Full and direct. Subtle bouquet, though a bit violent. Admirably dry —what do you think, Wiggins?"

Wiggins sipped it; his mouth puckered. "Very dry, sir."

"Bone dry," said Jury.

2

"The guy's a genius," said Macalvie, as the three of them stood near the car. The rain driven in from the estuary blew Wiggins's scarf back; he snatched at it, clearly not wanting to lose it twice in one evening. "Too bad he's so stubborn," added Macalvie, slamming the car door.

"How far is it to the Citrine place?" asked Wiggins, staring out into the cloud of rain.

Jury turned to answer. "No farther than it'll take to hand out three or four tickets, probably."

Jury, sitting in the back seat, wondered if the Devon-Cornwall constabulary fitted out all of its official cars with tape decks or whether Macalvie had managed one just to listen to Elvis.

After twenty miles, they were leaving "Heartbreak Hotel" and entering into a memory of a bright summer's day, purely temporary; bright summer's days usually were.

Wiggins, sitting beside Macalvie in the front seat, had been going on about telephone kiosks for the last fifteen minutes or so, probably (Jury thought) in an attempt to lead Macalvie round to explaining Gilly Thwaite's own call box and Telecom's part in it.

"It's like the red double-deckers. Landmarks, those red call boxes are, and they're taking them all down. Only leaving up a few, for nostalgia's sake, probably. I'm surprised there're those in Exeter still standing. Like the one Miss Thwaite was talking about. . . ."

No comment. Macalvie was singing along with Elvis about the empty chairs, the bare parlor.

"A crying shame," said Wiggins.

"What is?" asked Macalvie, as the parlor and doorstep of "Are You Lonesome Tonight" vanished like the flying landscape.

"That the kiosks are coming down. The government's only keeping about two hundred of the K2's—that's the regular one, like the one Miss Thwaite was talking about. . . ." Wiggins paused. No response. He went on with a sigh. "I always liked the Jubilee one. A bit fancier on top. Very valuable that would be now." Wiggins's laugh was more of a giggle. "Don't think you'd find Telecom trying to break one of *those* call boxes open." There was no answering comment from the front seat. One would have thought those two never used the telephone. Wiggins's sigh was huge this time. "If you wanted one, I mean one of those King George boxes, you could actually buy one. Cost you over a thousand quid, maybe two. There's a firm exports them. They refurbish them. Americans probably keep 'em in their halls. Cast iron, post-office red. I wonder how the American call boxes work. How they get the coins out—"

Jury turned and gave him a look. "Bulldoze them." Jury shook his head, turned back again.

Wiggins was undaunted. "Antiques dealers are buying them up and selling them, too, if you can imagine."

"I can imagine anything about antiques dealers." Macalvie pushed the eject button and Elvis came out.

Jury was trying to think about Dench's bones as he watched what he could of the dark landscape Macalvie was fast leaving behind, and with it, one of the new eyesore–call boxes Wiggins so abhored, telephone encased in its acrylic surround. Suddenly, the car was rocking with heavy metal.

"My God, Macalvie. Turn that down."

"Led Zep?" Macalvie half-twisted his head to the back. "You don't even like Led Zep?"

Even. Jury the musical stick-in-the-mud. "And keep your eyes on the road."

"Beautiful voice, he has, that Robert Plant," said Wiggins, *da-de-da*ing "Stairway to Heaven."

"And Page's guitar. That bow work is cosmic, *cosmic*. I don't go at all for the noodlers, Edward, Yngwie, those guys."

Noodlers?

"Oh, I can't agree with you there, not at all. You can't call them just speed freaks. Yngwie's got progressions as classical as they come," said Wiggins.

Yngwie? Edward? Were all fans on a first-name basis with their idols? "What about Charlie?" asked Jury.

Again, Macalvie twisted round. "Charlie who?"

Jury sighed. "*Raine.* Don't you keep up with the current scene?"

"You talking about that group that's in London? I've got something here."

To Jury's dismay he took his hand off the wheel to scrabble amongst his tapes, slid one in. A voice, clear as the frozen night, was in the middle of a song.

> . . . *sky*
> *was blue above*
> *the trees but only*
> *for a while*

It sounded to Jury as if it were going the way of Elvis's bright summer day. The light gave way to darkness, summer to winter, stone walls to the ravages of time, cliffs to the lashing of waves. It reminded Jury, in some way, of the *clair-voyee.*

> *I watch the streetlamp*
> *Down below*
> *I watch you turn*
> *I watch you go—*

"Well, well, well," said Macalvie, killing the tape as a low-slung sporty number shrieked past the Ford on this otherwise deserted stretch of road.

Wiggins was thrown back as Macalvie accelerated.

Jury sighed.

3

The Citrine house was stark white against the sky and a hundred feet or so from a cliff along a solitary stretch of the Cornwall coast. A frozen gullied road was not meant to encourage visitors. Nell Citrine Healey had been the only one who had used it; she must have liked her privacy. It was privacy, Jury thought morosely, that had worked against her.

The rear of the house faced the end of the dirt road. They went in through the kitchen door, unlocked, unbolted.

"Doesn't anyone bother to lock up?" asked Wiggins.

"She probably thought there wasn't anything of value left to take," said Macalvie.

Wiggins looked away.

They stood in the big kitchen with Macalvie looking down at the long oak center table as if he could see the sandwiches—the one half-eaten, the other untouched—and the pills still sitting there. Macalvie pointed to a row of mullioned windows. "Billy wouldn't have heard—"

"No one could have known Mrs. Healey wasn't *in* the house; that she was *out*side was mere chance," said Wiggins.

"Of course. So if it was someone known to her, and she *had* been there, say, in the kitchen, whoever it was could simply have said they didn't want to drive the car any farther down that road. But they wouldn't deliberately announce themselves by coming down that road. So Billy wouldn't have heard anything. Anyone could have walked right in, but it was someone he knew, I'm sure."

Jury leaned back against a Welsh cupboard of wormy chestnut and folded his arms, looking at the kitchen hearth, the chairs pulled up to it. It was the sort of spot that could have seduced anyone into having a cup of tea. "If you could only remember, Macalvie, that you weren't here; that you weren't in this kitchen." He looked out at darkness.

"Then what's *your* theory?"

"I don't have one."

Wiggins came in from the front room, saying, "They've a piano, a baby grand—Good Lord, sir, shut that door!" His look at Macalvie was severe as he pulled the lapels of his overcoat tightly round his throat.

Macalvie shut the kitchen door.

As he would have recognized the outfitting of the kitchen, Jury would have known this room from Macalvie's description. In the center was the writing table where Charles Citrine must have been sitting, talking with the police superintendent. Over there was the window seat where Nell Healey had sat staring out to sea. There were no sheets, no covering, over the furniture. In spite of the rising damp and the passing years, the room still had the look of its occupants having left just minutes before: an open book lay facedown on a coffee table; the pale cushions of an armchair still bore the impression of an occupant; the logs were laid and ready for lighting; sheets of music were stacked on the piano. Until one noticed the spine of the book was cracked, the pages stiff with age; the sheet music yellowed; the piano layered with dust.

Said Wiggins: "They must have taken music pretty seriously to have a grand piano in a house they used only a short time out of the year."

"Billy was supposed to be some kind of musical prodigy. The piano"—Macalvie nodded toward it—"was the father's idea. Healey was a frustrated concert pianist who was probably living out his fantasies of being Rachmaninoff through his kid. My bet is he was a real slave driver. Anyway, the kid didn't use it."

"How do you know?" asked Jury, not terribly surprised by this time at Macalvie's clairvoyance.

"There was no music on the stand; the cover was down; I ran my finger over it. Dusty as hell." Macalvie smiled. "He didn't practice here; she didn't dust. Says something about them, doesn't it, the way they were."

The smile was in place, but it didn't reach his eyes, Jury noticed. Then the smile vanished and he walked over to the french window giving out on a view of waves they could hear but couldn't see.

"She likes you, too, Macalvie." Jury smiled at his friend's back. "You should go and see her. I'm sure you wouldn't have any trouble getting round Sanderson."

There was no answer.

"I'm having a look upstairs. Brian?"

Without turning, Macalvie said, "Billy's room is at the top, the guest room next to it. Toby used that."

While Wiggins visited the guest room, Jury went into Billy Healey's. As had the living room, this one still looked lived in, as if all of his boy's things had been left in just the way he had placed them. Cricket bat lying across a carved walnut chair and a cap hanging on its finial; stacks of magazines and paperback books slipping and sliding along the far wall in a drunken wave; fossils and chipped seashells on the bureau, one especially good specimen lying on a bit of torn paper with the penciled inscription, *Chessil Beach,* the paper browning round the edges, beginning to look more like parchment. But the focal point of the room was outspread on the faded oriental rug at the foot of the bed—a complicated intertwining of metal tracks, miniature buildings—or pieces of a Monopoly set used for that purpose—and an electric train. He stood looking at it for a few moments chewing his lip. Then he knelt down, unable to resist its lure, and punched the starting button. The slightly rusted engine slowly and laboriously started chugging along the track, entering a mossy tunnel of a papier-mâché hillside.

He let it run as he went over to the books against the wall, sat down on the floor, and looked them over. Jury could almost see the years of Billy's life changing with the books. Picture books, the William books, comics. He must have named his dog Gnasher after the one in these old "Beano" strips. Then came *Oliver Twist, Treasure Island,* nothing by the Brontës—perhaps he got too much of that in Yorkshire —and some poetry. Jury recognized the small paperback of American poetry as the same one that Nell Healey had been holding. He pulled it out, thumbed through it to Robert Frost, noticed as he did so there were a lot of underlinings, marginal notes that surprised him. Apparently, his stepmother had had a decided effect on his reading. He found the one called "Good-bye and Keep Cold," and read it through twice.

> *But one thing about it, it mustn't get warm.*
> *How often already you've had to be told,*
> *"Keep cold, young orchard. Good-bye and*
>   *keep cold . . ."*

Jury put his head in his hand. He went on looking through the book and stopped at a poem of Emily Dickinson, also heavily underscored. His eye was immediately drawn to the line, *"It was not frost, for on my skin I felt siroccos crawl . . ."* The word *sirocco* was underlined twice and in the margin written in a loopy scrawl, "desert wind, hot."

"I used to have one, but not this good of a one."

Wiggins's voice brought Jury round. "What?"

"Train, sir." Wiggins was kneeling by the track. The engine was going through the tunnel, probably for the dozenth time. Jury had forgotten the train. "It was a contest, it was, to see who could collect the most pieces. I was the only one had a British Rail Pullman car. What sort did you have, sir?"

Jury had risen, still with the book in his hand. "None. What's a 'sirocco,' Wiggins?"

The sergeant looked up from the miniature metal station, frowning. "The band, you mean?"

"No. I mean what *is* it? What's it mean?"

Wiggins shook his head. "No idea. Funny name, come to think of it. They're usually called things like Kiss of Death, or plays on words like Dire Straits. Good name, that." Wiggins got up. "The guest room's all tidied up. Nothing there that seemed helpful."

"I'll have a look." Jury frowned. "Do you still have that issue—"

Wiggins looked back, standing in the doorway. "Of what, sir?"

"Nothing," said Jury. "Nothing."

4

It had started to rain steadily during the short drive to Macalvie's cemetery. *Macalvie's cemetery:* the graveyard that surrounded the disused church appeared to Jury to have little purpose anymore than that which Macalvie had brought to it. It surrounded the church unevenly on three sides.

They squelched through mud and high grass, stepping, Jury imagined, on graves whose stones had slowly slipped so far beneath the ground that one could barely see them. When they'd nearly reached the wall, Macalvie beamed his torch downward, kneeled, and removed the canvas staked across the grave.

It had been carefully staked out by Dennis Dench. Markers showing the position of the body were still there. The site was clear of vegetation for a foot round the site. There was little else to show that a body had been exhumed from the opening, that it had not been dug for a burial yet to come.

Except (thought Jury) that nobody came here anymore. He squinted through the dark at headstones leaning at odd angles, nearly hidden by tall grass and weeds. The rain fell steadily.

Wiggins stood at the bottom of the grave staring down, the package that was Dench's book between his gloved hands like a Bible. He made no move to rewrap the muffler that a sudden wind had disturbed; he said nothing about the weather.

Jury looked up from the gravesite to the old wall, crumbling like the wall round the Citrine house in West Yorkshire. What in heaven's name must have been going through that poor woman's mind in her interminable watching at the gate that listed like these gravestones in that deteriorating wall? What scenarios had she devised for the death of her stepson?

That she was hopeless of ever seeing him again was clear. She was not watching that small frozen orchard waiting for a miraculous reappearance, waiting for the boy to climb down from the tree in which he'd been hiding. It enveloped her like fog, the sense of hopelessness.

In her darkest imaginings of the way he died, could Nell Healey possibly have imagined this?

An owl screeched. They all stood looking down into the excavated grave, filling with rain.

Wiggins did not complain about the weather.

21

Melrose refused to open his eyes when he heard what must have been a mug of tea placed on his bedside table. He shut them more tightly still when the curtains on wooden rungs were slowly pressed back and the window raised. Why on earth did people seem to think one could not move without the morning tea, and that one's private bedroom was Liberty Hall? Nor did he hear the footsteps of the Person recede. The Person must have been standing in the room—the slow breathing seemed to come from the direction of the foot of the bed—staring like a ghoul as he slept. Nothing could be more unnerving except perhaps lying in a trench with the enemy standing over you wondering if you were, indeed, dead.

Finally, he heard skulking steps, the door gently close.

After a few seconds, he opened one eye to sunlight and a fine day and a cow staring at him, ruminatively, through the window.

Melrose threw back the covers and didn't give the cow the satisfaction of knowing he had spotted it.

Major Poges and the Princess were the only ones at the table when he entered the dining room. Ruby had just served Major Poges his boiled egg. The Princess was drinking coffee and sitting several chairs away down the other side of the table. She fluted a good-morning to Melrose.

Ruby, her hair pulled back from sallow skin and a face

like a lozenge—mildly palliative—recited a rather extensive menu to Melrose, including mutton chops. Melrose ordered tea, toast, and porridge. Solemnly, Ruby took the order, collected some of the used crockery, and took herself off.

"And bring some more hot water, Ruby," the Major called after her.

One could tell a great deal (Melrose had always liked to think) about the way a person approached his boiled egg. Major Poges did not behead his (as did Agatha), but tapped and tapped the top gently all round with the back of his egg spoon and peeled it.

From her end of the table, the Princess called down, "We're the last. Or you are. It's nearly ten."

"Miss Denholme appears to be very liberal with her mealtimes."

"*And* her food," said the Princess, whose plate, from what Melrose could see, did not attest to this. It was empty. "She caters to one's tastes." The Princess raised her finely chiseled face to the ceiling and exhaled a stream of smoke. This morning she was dressed in rose wool with one of the Weavers Hall shawls (this one of magenta) gathered about her arms and fastened with something pricey that winked in the sunlight.

"She's also quite a decent person, if a bit on the broody side. When I came here the first time, she was off nursing her sister—Iris, I think her name is. I understand the doctors feared the poor woman would have a miscarriage. I have never had children, myself." Her tone suggested she couldn't understand why anyone would.

"They'd have turned out to be Malcolms, every one." The Major scooped up his egg. "Doesn't come on as the motherly type, not to me. Why'd she take over the child? Doesn't seem to care much about her. As for catering to your tastes," the Major went on as he jammed up a toast round. "What taste? You scarcely eat anything." He turned to Melrose. "She will only eat what is quiet and needn't be cut."

He called down to her: "For God's sakes, come to your usual place and sit down."

Her expression declared that this was the opening for a rejoinder she'd been dying to make. "I am sitting down here, Mr. Plant, because I do like my morning cigarette. And it is *beastly* manners to smoke whilst others are eating. So I've been told."

Sotto voce, the Major said, "Oh, shut up." Then to the Princess, he called again, "We refuse to sit here and yell. I complained once, *once* when you were smoking that cheroot. Come back to your usual chair."

"Ah!" she exclaimed, rising. "Thank you *so* much."

Melrose smiled as she made her languid (and supposedly underfed) way down the table to the chair at the Major's left, which he had risen to hold out for her. The Major's sigh was huge and resigned; he reeked of martyrdom. Her *thank you* simply breathed of feigned deference, as did her paralytic smile at him as she slid into the magisterial chair.

"Now the one who fascinates me is the Braine woman. She's quite loopy, that one. Did you know she was on her way to Hadrian's Wall? She claims to be in touch with the Emperor Hadrian, which must be difficult as he's been dead for several centuries." The Princess leaned closer to Melrose. "Second sight is what she claims to have. Knew there'd be a murder near here, that's what turned up in her 'magnetic field.' She was 'drawn here' by some irresistible force."

"Second sight so often turns out to be hindsight, I've found," said Melrose. "I imagine she predicts further trouble."

Major Poges looked mildly surprised. "She did. How'd you know?"

"I didn't. But isn't it always safe to predict further trouble? Won't there always be?"

"No wonder Malcolm's the little beast he is. They're off, she says, to meet Hadrian's spirit. Tomorrow. Noonish." She flicked some ash onto a plate. "And people think killers are crazy."

"Is that what they're saying about this woman who killed her husband? I'd imagine there'd be a great deal of speculation there."

"Speculation, yes. The family's very old, very county," said the Major. "I've met them. Well, him. Charles Citrine. Done a bit of shooting with him."

"The Gun, here," said the Princess, nodding toward Poges, "has never brought back anything for our meager table."

"Stop calling me that. Just because a fellow likes an early ramble on the moors and a bit of shooting—"

"His kill-to-cartridge ratio is about one to one thousand."

Melrose smiled. "This Charles Citrine—"

He was interrupted by Ruby's coming in with the tray, setting Melrose's porridge and tea before him and the hot water before the Major. She then set about collecting the dirty dishes as if she were nicking them. For some time she held a goblet before her with an abstracted air, frowning at its blood-red glass, then quickly set it on the tray and picked up a plate with several mutton-chop bones on it and nearly ran from the room.

"Is she always like that?" asked Melrose, plugging a large square of butter into the center of his porridge and watching the melting rivulets trickle off.

"She's a goose. Pay no attention to her," said the Major, digging in the jar of marmalade.

"I hadn't thought of the porridge," said the Princess, leaning to get a better look at Melrose's bowl.

Major Poges looked up sharply. "Don't give it to her. She's right onto it, Mr. Plant, but don't give it to her." To the Princess he said, "If you want porridge, *ask* for porridge." He slammed down the marmalade pot.

A delicate ribbon of smoke trailed upward as she said, "One can't keep the kitchen open all day, Major."

"Ha! Then have a boiled egg." He shoved the silver dish toward her.

The Princess reared back slightly, her mouth in a moue.

"If you want to waste your time tapping and cracking and peeling, go ahead. And then one nearly has to *carve* round the white to get it out as if one were a sculptor. No, thank you. You don't seem to be having such a fine time with yours." She leaned closer to his plate. "Look at all of the tiny bits of shell—"

"You're the *laziest* damned woman I know." He put down his spoon and snapped his paper open, back half-turned to her. But he wasn't finished with his recital. To Melrose, he said, "Nearly everything is too much trouble for her to eat." Secretively, he leaned toward Melrose as if the Princess weren't there. "Do you know what she dined on last night? A plate of creamed potatoes, mashed swede, and one forkful of peas. *One!*" He held up his index finger.

The Princess stuck out her tongue at his back, then rested her chin across the back of her hands in an artfully contrived pose. "One can hardly eat peas after they've left the heap, can one? I'm not about to chase them."

Major Poges nearly buried his face in his crushed paper. "When we were in London once I made the mistake of suggesting we dine at Wheeler's. Is there *anyone* who thinks Dover sole is hard to eat?"

"Yes. They never fillet anything properly. There's always the odd bone large enough to drive through the heart of Dracula." She sipped her coffee and inhaled deeply.

Melrose wondered if he were to be forever reminded of Vivian's upcoming marriage.

The Princess sighed. "The only implements one needs are a blender and a Cuisinart. That's all I have in my kitchen."

"Kitchen?" Major Poges looked up from his newspaper to stare at her. "What kitchen?"

"Major, you know I have a house in London."

He shrugged and went back to his search of the paper. "Oh, *that.* Surely, the kitchen was boarded up long ago. Ah, here's an item. You wouldn't think they'd be burying this killing at the inn toward the back of the paper, would you? I expect it's because there's nothing new. They've merely taken the old stuff and given it a good shaking."

The Princess stubbed out her cigarette and laced her hands beneath her chin again. "I find it very interesting that the accounts go on and on about the husband's marvelous reputation. And his 'courageous' refusal to pay the ransom all those years ago. It's as if *she* were straight out of it. The few times I've spoken with her, Mrs. Healey struck me as rather reserved, but certainly not a stick, and certainly not without a bit of steel in her spine."

Melrose finished his tea. "It sounds as if you're a little suspicious of the husband."

"Good heavens, I question anyone who is reputed to be flawless. Anyway, it sounds chauvinistic, the courageous husband and the wife who was apparently struck by the vapors. It was as if she had nothing to say in the whole matter. Well, she finally said it, didn't she?"

"A person'd think you *approved* of what she did." The Major folded his paper, fanwise.

"Oh, I do. So dramatic. No sneaking about trying to pick him off in a dark alleyway. Her solicitors would have to be idiots not to get her off."

"Get her *off*? The woman killed him in plain sight of a detective."

She answered the Major but looked at Melrose. "That makes no difference. It's the motive. The man refused to pay that ransom." She waved another cigarette in Melrose's direction.

Melrose lit it for her and said, "That wouldn't stick, would it? Had she done it right after, or six months later, or even a year, I imagine they could plead extreme depression."

The Princess rose, gathering up her cigarette case. "I wasn't aware there was a statute of limitations on despair, Mr. Plant. It's snowing again. There goes my afternoon in Leeds. Will you be dining with us? I surely hope so. It does make a change." The flowery scent trailed behind her as she left the room.

Grumpily, Major Poges watched her go. "Damned woman. Gets the last word in, you can be sure of that. Well, *I'm* for a walk. Snow or no snow. Care to join me? Mr. Plant?"

Melrose looked up. "Oh, sorry. No, I don't think so. I was just wondering, have you seen Miss Taylor this morning?"

"Not this morning, not since I heard her shoot through the night on that motorcycle probably mashing everything in her path."

"That's just it: wouldn't we have heard it when she came in?"

Major Poges checked his watch, shook it, held it up to his ear. "Who said she did? She's from New York, after all."

He turned and left the room, murmuring something about bullying Rose into joining him on Stanbury Moor.

New York or not, thought Melrose, there was hardly anything in Haworth to be getting up to. He sat there, feeling decidedly uncomfortable, staring out at the slow fall of snow. It might have been five minutes or fifty, as he brooded over collisions on icy roads, when he was more or less brought round by the voice behind him.

"Are you coming, then?"

He turned from the window and saw Abby Cable in what looked like proper gear for an Eskimo. He could barely see her face; he could feel the glare, though, like ice struck by light. "What? Coming where? Have you built an igloo?"

There was a silence. Her face was muffled in scarves, shawls, and something feathered on the edges that moved with her breath. But he felt the penetrating stare. "To find the sheep. You said you wanted to."

He had? When he didn't jump from his seat, she said, "Good-bye, then."

Adults lie. That was in the tone, pure and simple, something she was used to.

"I don't know what to wear for this adventure."

Silence. The Eskimo turned. "A coat would help." She

left the doorway to which Melrose rushed. "Can't you *wait* for three minutes?"

She opened the door to the great snow-swamped outside. The dog Stranger sat there with snow on his coat. "Okay," she said, flatly.

As he strived with his wellingtons he could hear the clock ticking.

22

He felt ridiculous tramping along with a crook in his hand.

"You need it," she had said. "That stick-thing won't do you any good."

It wasn't, he had said, a "stick-thing." It was a nine-teenth-century cosher. Finding out it was a weapon had stirred Abby's interest. She'd hefted it, inspected it, asked if police had used it to kill people, and seemed disappointed that that hadn't been the cosher's primary use. But her attention ripened again when he added that it was, of course, possible to strike a mortal blow. Why? he asked her.

The question went unanswered as they'd set off in some northerly direction to the rear of Weavers Hall.

"I don't see why we can't keep to a well-worn path," Melrose noted irritably as they'd been stolidly walking for twenty minutes. What he suspected was the last of civilization had been left back on the Oakworth Road where a red telephone kiosk stood quietly alone. He saw two paths criss-crossing like long dents in the fresh snow. The snow wasn't deep; it was merely forbidding, given this landscape.

Her sigh at the hopelessness of taking along this person untutored in the ways of sheep was rather exaggerated and punctuated with a swipe of the cosher, which she had appropriated, and with which she dealt mortal blows *(swish!)*. "Sheep don't use paths. I expect you don't know nothing about sheep."

Must she begin every comment regarding the possibility

of some small fund of knowledge on his part into a total lack
of faith that he had any? *I-expect-you-don't* this and *I-expect-you-don't* that?

"I certainly do. I know that under the outside coat is an
inner one that keeps them warm." Melrose wished *he* had an
inside layer, as he worked the hand holding the crook to
keep the circulation going. His fingers felt like ice-packed
twigs.

But she trampled on his small bit of sheep-knowledge,
saying, "People think they're stupid. They're not. Come up
against some stroppy old ewe and you'll see." It was almost
a challenge as she pointed the cosher in the direction of a
large, black-faced sheep some distance away.

"Is that so?"

Abby did not answer rhetorical questions; clearly she felt
there was no reason to replay her statements. He got it; he
didn't get it; it made no odds to her. Melrose imagined that
whatever information he did manage to get from her would
come out dry as cold toast, unlaced with jam. She was certainly not one to embroider like Ethel.

"You never know where Mr. Nelligan's sheep are. They
wander off."

"Who's this Mr. Nelligan, anyway?"

In answer, Abby turned and pointed with the cosher in
the direction of a hillside that could have been a mile off but
was probably closer. In this landscape, judging distances
was an art in itself. "That caravan over there."

Melrose shaded his eyes, looking toward the distant hillside where he thought he saw a small structure, smoke curling from its roof. "A caravan with a smokestack?"

"He cut a hole in the roof."

He didn't bother questioning this. "Then why isn't Nelligan out here saving his *own* sheep?"

"He drinks poteen. Once he had over a hundred sheep got
down in a gully. Stranger rounded them up." She shook her
head, clearly implying that if it weren't for her dog they'd all
be down in a gully.

They plowed on, heading for a broken wall "yonder." It occurred to him that he didn't even know what this egregious errand was for. He stopped. "Where are we going?"

"Wherever Stranger goes," she said, looking up at him. Beneath the circle of the hood her eyes shone out, a dark and fathomless blue.

"We're following the *dog?*" No reply. "My own dog follows *me.*" This was not technically true: Mindy's residence by the fireplace was seldom interrupted by anything so banal as a "walk." Well, Mindy was old. And so, he felt, was he. Another ten minutes of it and he would grow a beard of hoarfrost. He wrinkled his nose; his nostrils seemed to be glued together from the cold dry air.

The landscape was like the negative of the landscape he had seen last night, standing with Ellen (and where *was* Ellen?) outside of the Hall. A dead white moon against a black sky, the silvery reservoir beneath. This sky was sickly pale, the clouds low and leaden and the blackened moor beneath the covering of snow, bracken, and heather so dark and withered the ground looked singed, as if they had come upon a moon crater. Melrose was fond of the natural setting of his own house, its woods and lanes; the grand view, the scenic vista. Sometimes, sitting in his comfortable chair before the fire watching Mindy vegetate, he had felt he should jump up, get his binoculars, and rush out and watch birds. A country gentleman of good breeding and lavish means should certainly be more involved with his natural surroundings. Melrose compromised and kept his binoculars on the floor, occasionally picking them up when something flew by the drawing-room window.

"Where are we?" he asked again, his eye searching this waste of snow for some marker, some directional sign. A while back they had crossed a beck (precariously, he thought) whose waters, replenished by yesterday's melting snow, curled over choked roots and around stones.

"Nowhere particular," said Abby.

He stopped, jamming the crook in the snow, and said, "You really mean you don't know, correct?"

She regarded him coolly. "You're not lost."

The dog ran, spewing up snow, toward an old drystone wall.

He *felt* lost. "I should have brought an ordnance map." He watched her tramp on ahead of him, toward the wall and the dog, brandishing the cosher. For her it was probably a jolly old adventure, some kind of game. It occurred to him he still didn't know precisely what their goal was. "Wait up, for heaven's sakes. *What* is the object of this communion with the moors?"

"I expect you wouldn't like it if you were in a tomb, buried alive." The blue eyes were looking stormy.

It sounded like one of the Braine woman's inscrutable comments on Hadrian's troops.

She clicked her tongue, and Stranger started a patrol of the wall. Wind had caused the snow to drift, and the dog was nosing slowly along, sniffing. "Here, poke with the crook."

"I take it we're looking for sheep. Good grief, if any were trapped in there they'd be dead."

"No they wouldn't," she said matter-of-factly. "I expect you don't know their breath makes airholes—"

"Oh, be quiet." But he did as he was bid and tried to hold on to his temper. He'd never get anything out of her if he drove her deeper into silence. The crook met with no resistance; what, he wondered, were they to do with these entombed sheep, should they find any? Stranger had reached the end of the wall and turned, panting.

"That's all right, then," she said. "There's another wall yonder."

"So you *do* know where we are."

"More or less." Slogging along, she held the cosher above her head like a bayonet. There was another wall up there. Stranger ran alongside of it, raced back, sat down, and at the clicking of her tongue darted through what was apparently a hole in the wall.

They approached it. "Well, we can't get through there, obviously."

"It's a cripple hole," she said, disregarding his statement. Carefully she lay Melrose's stick near the hole, got down and crept through on her hands and knees.

The last he saw of her was a mittened hand coming back to claim the cosher and whisk it through the hole. Then there was silence.

He looked at the size of the cripple hole, remembered how big the black-faced sheep was, and imagined he could get through it, if he manuevered on his back or his stomach. He called: "I'm much too big for this cripple hole thing."

No response. His voice was borne away by the wind; he heard its distant echo, or thought he did. No sound came from the other side of the wall, not even the bark of the dog. He cupped his hands and let out with a "hallo, hallo." He whistled as if the dog would come at his bidding. Who was he fooling? That dog wouldn't pay attention to Attila the Hun.

He knelt and peered through the cripple hole. No tracks led away from it, of girl or dog. Blast it all, where was she? Except for wind soughing through the stand of evergreens over there to the east, the silence was engulfing, and the clouds appeared lower, the sky chalkier, the curlews circling in ever-narrower patterns, as if they meant to settle soon, like vultures. Oh, for heaven's sakes, it was merely an illusion created by the godforsaken moor.

"I'm heading back!" he shouted irritably as he planted his crook more firmly in the snow. Why should he continue on this senseless venture? He'd got precious little information for his trouble, all of those monosyllabic answers. That bit about the dog Stranger constituted, for Abby Cable, a parliamentary address. Must have been two, three sentences. "Well, *good-bye!*"

There was no response although he thought she was probably just the other side of the wall, doodling in the snow, drawing rough pictures with his walking stick.

Still. One never knew whom one might meet. He thought of the black-cloaked figure striding across the moor. Furthermore (he rationalized, as he tossed the crook through the hole and lay down on his back, arms outstretched to gain purchase on the stone), they were probably not too far from the Citrine estate.

God. He flattened out, heaved his way through the cripple hole, to which the sheep smell and sheep's wool clung. Then he rose and shook off the snow.

They were directly on the other side of the wall, Stranger working one end, Abby the other. Melrose walked beside the snowdrift to the place where she was poking with the cosher.

"Use your crook," she said.

"You heard me calling. Why didn't you answer?" Irritably, he poked the crook into the drift.

"You said you were going." She shrugged and looked at him, eyes narrowed as if against something heavenly bright or hellishly unsightly. "You're still here, aren't you?"

He resisted the temptation to raise the crook. To hear her talk, one would think she were clairvoyant. What she expected to happen, would.

"I'd sooner talk to the dog. Did you get him as a pup?"

"No."

He sighed, watching Stranger snuffling at the drift of snow. "Well, how'd you get him?"

"He came by," was her no-frills answer.

The dog was pawing away, sending up fans of snow.

"I should think a border collie smart enough to round up a hundred sheep down in a gully would be missed."

Abby appeared to be giving this some thought. In her flat-as-a-pancake voice she said, "Maybe nobody cared." Then as the dog kept shoveling away, she added, "He's found one."

The highlight of the morning for Melrose was to be pulling and yanking a sheep from what must have been its snow tunnel. The ewe didn't seem the worse for wear as Stranger herded it out of the snow.

"Now, what do we do?"

"We don't do nothing. It does for itself." She turned and tramped up the moor, headed, probably, for the wall in the distance.

Since he was getting nowhere putting questions to her he hoped would elicit answers that might deepen into some conversational foray about her life, about Mrs. Healey, about anything, he decided to be direct, even if the subject was grisly. He supposed the little wall Abby Cable had built between herself and the world was as resistant to grisliness as it was to snowbound animals.

"That's a terrible thing that happened at the Old Silent Inn, isn't it? It must have upset you quite a bit." If it did there was no sign of it. Her small face held to its contour of stony silence just as those distant outcroppings of millstone grit held to the horizon. "Since she's a friend of yours and your aunt's." He tossed that in because he wondered, indeed, if the two women had been friendly.

"I don't think so."

"Don't think *what* so?"

"She's a friend of Aunt Ann's." She made that little clicking noise with her tongue, and Stranger, who had gone so far he showed only as a dot in snow, turned and ran back.

"Oh? I thought Mrs. Healey came to visit your aunt."

"She came to visit *me.*"

The sheer force of her anger hit him like the wind, one of those winds that "wuthers," that rakes the snow and slants the trees. "Billy and Toby and me, we were best friends."

Then she turned and tried to run but could do no more than lope along, shrouded in her heavy garments.

"A dead lamb," she said, when he'd caught up with her. She stood looking at the small thing, its legs tucked up. For some time she stared down and, then, in her usual business-like manner, covered it up with snow.

"Look, don't you think we've had enough of death and blight for one morning?"

But she'd already followed the dog down the wall into a wind that had stiffened enough to bend the stand of pines off to the east. What an execrable place; what execrable weather. If Cathy Earnshaw had wanted to be flung out of heaven to get back here, it must be a cold heaven indeed. Melrose looked upward and thought with longing of the public house not far from here, surely. Shading his eye with his hand, he turned from the high moor and looked down-ward. Was that some pub on the road where cars, tiny in the distance, were parked like beetles? If they weren't always stopping for entombed sheep and pathetic dead lambs they could make it down there in another twenty minutes. Warmth! Light! Hospitality! Yes, the picture he conjured up was the very shape and color of good fellowship: the rubi-cund, accommodating publican; the hearty regulars round the bar; the dark brew, polished pine, glinting brass, rosy glow of mullioned windows . . .

Where was she, for God's sakes? The wind sent up coils of snow with a snakelike hiss. He saw her and the dog Stranger way off at the end of the wall and was a little surprised at the relief he felt. He called. No answer.

In the habit by now of following her instructions, he walked toward the two, aimlessly poking the damned crook into banked-up snow, wishing almost he could jab some sheep where it really hurt, thinking *Aha!* when it finally met with resistance. He hunkered down, rather proud of himself, and started shoveling the snow off with hands that he was sure were frostbitten beyond saving. He uncovered a patch of dirty pink snow and black sleeve. He rose very quickly.

The sleeve was frozen stiff, the fingers of the hand jutting out curled as if the hand had tried to gain purchase on something. Life, perhaps. He stood there blinking, staring down at the frozen hand much as Abby had looked at the pathetic body of the lamb.

Hardly aware of what he was doing, he looked for the motorcycle, as if he might find it, black and shining, leaning against the drystone wall.

He hadn't seen Ellen; *no one* had seen Ellen since she had vanished last night down the drive against the backdrop of dark sky and silver reservoir. . . .

It was an image that he knew would haunt him for the rest of his life. Furiously, he swept away snow from the arm and the face.

Ann Denholme's eyes were open, the sockets partly filled with snow. The face looked heavenward, the dark hair he could see gray with frost, and spiky, looking almost like hair that had whitened overnight from some dreadful shock. Her coat was stiff as ice, but when he lifted her arm slightly, the cold wrist was limp.

Melrose looked off to his right, saw that Abby and Stranger were slowly making their way along the other part of the wall, and started covering the body.

The snow was mucked about, but he thought or hoped the wind would hide both his handiwork and the blood scent. He could hardly have the poor child (for now he so thought of her) discovering the body of her aunt.

As they neared him, Stranger's head lowered to the bank, sniffing, sniffing. Melrose pretended to slip and fell down across the body. Perhaps his own scent would cover hers.

Stranger, he was sure, could smell death.

But although the dog seemed interested in pawing about the place where Melrose sat, Melrose gave him a few rough pats and tried to turn him away. Stranger was not about to be turned.

Abby tilted her head and then shook it slowly, giving the Clumsy One a look of utter disgust, whether at his falling over or at his idiot attempt to make her dog respond to ordinary commands, he couldn't say. Abby looked at

Stranger, made some tiny sound in her mouth, and the dog froze in position.

Both of them stood there within two feet of Ann Denholme's snowy grave, locked in place like players in that old childhood game of Statues.

How in the devil was he going to get them out of here? Not only that, but get either to the inn or the telephone kiosk back there on the Oakworth Road? He wondered if this was the way she looked at that lazy shepherd, Mr. Nelligan.

Melrose got to his feet and played for time by arranging his overcoat and shoving his (gangrened, he was sure) fingers through his stiffened hair. All the while he was rehearsing and rejecting various ruses. Finally he said, "This is too much for me; we must return to the Hall." How pompous he sounded.

Not that it made any difference. Abby stood with her crook in one hand and his cosher in the other, both plunged into the snow like crutches. The damned dog was going to hypnotize him with that eye of his. Melrose felt slightly light-headed.

"Well, go on, then," said the little cripple with a huge frown.

"Very well." Melrose took one step, then stopped suddenly as if he'd just remembered something. "Oh, incidentally, I know where Ethel's hiding place is." *Oneandtwoandthreeandfour* he counted as he walked away.

On the *four* they both shot past him, jammed themselves through the cripple hole, and took off toward the Oakworth Road, spewing up snow.

23

"It were a dreadful thing, but there's no way to help you, I can see," said Mrs. Holt, irritation flickering across her broad features. "It were painful enough at the time."

Without police dredging it all up again, her look at Jury said. Since her eyes, as she sat in the overstuffed chair across from Jury, were trained not on him but on the ashtray on the table between them, Jury thought the source of the fleeting look was not the fate of Toby Holt but the cigarette Jury had stubbed out immediately upon entering the room. Given the rabbity sniff of her nose, he was sure of it. Owen Holt, large, square-faced, an unhappy-seeming man, looked not directly at Jury, but across his shoulder, apparently out of the window. His eyes were the grayish-blue color of denim and washed out, like faded jeans.

Mrs. Holt had opened the door of the terraced house in Oakworth, dressed in a coverall, head turbaned, and holding a rainbow-hued feather duster and a chamois cloth in a white-gloved hand. Had they not now been sitting in her grimly tidy parlor, where her husband Owen seemed himself to be a visitor, Jury might have taken it for a window display to entice the passersby to snap up the three-piece suite on hire-purchase. The sofa and two armchairs were covered in a hideous, multicolored pattern with fringed throw pillows that just missed matching the blue, pink, and yellow zigzag design. All of this fought with the old-fashioned sepia-tinted wallpaper covered with tiny bouquets whose cinched stems trailed fluttery little ribbons. The fake coals in the unusable fireplace might have been nicked from the same window.

But what particularly struck Jury about the Holt parlor wasn't this discordance of paper, paint, and pattern: it was the absence of ornaments and the lack of pictures. There were no mementos, no little groupings of figurines; no framed photographs or bits of embroidery; no books, only a thin stack of magazines lying on the coffee table. In the corner cupboard was china that he doubted had been used in many years. The one hint of frivolity was a glass- and wood-beaded curtain that hung in an alcove at the bottom of the staircase.

"The Social come round," said Alice Holt, in reluctant response to Jury's question, "and said they'd got this ever-so-sad case of a little boy that'd been orphaned . . ."

Her voice trailed off as the hand shot out almost of its own volition to pluck the ashtray from the table. "And as Owen here'd talked about wouldn't it be nice t'have a bairn round the place . . ." She rose to dispose of the odious ashes. "T'other person talks, but who had the care?" she said elliptically and she whisked from the room holding the ashtray at arm's length.

Owen Holt had either got used to his wife's doing the talking, or he was congenitally a silent man. His contribution to this conversation had been spasmodic. But now he said, "Quiet he were. Meant to adopt him. Never did, officially. But always did think of him as me own." He was still looking somewhere beyond Jury, still taking in the scene beyond the window.

The long-case clock ticked in its spastic rhythm, a little like Owen Holt's speech, and Jury was quiet. Then he said, "I'm sorry. It must have been particularly difficult for you, having to . . ." His mouth formed the word *identify* but no sound came with it. *Identify the body.*

Jury's mind clouded. Like a double exposure, the image of Owen Holt looking down at the boy lying in one of those

rows of refrigerated compartments pulled out like a big desk
drawer was overlaid with the remembrance of himself staring down onto the rubble of the flat that night so long ago,
looking at the outstretched arm of his mother, the cupped
hand, the black velvet sleeve, his own frenzied attempt to get
the plaster and wood away from her, while more kept falling. Her hand seemed to be making just that gesture it so
often had, when she held out her arm and motioned for him
to *come along, now.*

As if some fierce photographer kept letting off the flash,
the image would come back sharply after all these years
when he looked at a woman's arm outstretched just so.
What had driven him nearly to distraction was that his
mother had been alone.

" 'Twas." Holt nodded slowly, over and over. "And Alice. Alice never stopped cleaning since that boy died."

It shook Jury a little, that his own estimation of Alice
Holt had been so superficial. Her husband had wrapped up
in that one observation what drove the woman to this frenzy
of housekeeping, always trying to keep things straight, to get
things back to their proper place, to keep her mind swept
clean of the detritus of the past as she swept her parlor clean
of the dust of the present. And again, he thought of the
rubble.

Alice Holt returned, took her seat, picked up the feather
duster like a defensive weapon, and went on. "It were only
to be for a little while. While things got sorted out for the
child. With Owen and the arthritis he'd had to leave the
mill. We'd got trooble enough without another mouth to
feed." She was staring at the particular place on the coffee
table from which Jury had picked up his notebook and pen.
"Of course there's the orphanage. But . . ." Furtively she
reached over and polished the end of the coffee table where
the notebook had lain.

Jury's throat tightened, remembering the bleak corridors
of Good Hope, where he had spent six years of his life. But,

at least, he could remember the faces of his dead parents. That had been more than many had, more than Toby Holt had.

"So we had the lad for all his life," Alice was saying as she traced the base of a lamp with a white-gloved finger and squinted at the tip.

"A short life it was," said Owen.

It was as though she eclipsed the life altogether by ignoring her husband's comment. Instead she shifted to the Citrines. "You don't find *them* taking in poor children. *Them* that have the money—"

Jury interrupted what promised to be a litany of complaints. "I take it Toby and Billy Healey were great friends."

"The best," said Owen.

"Better Toby'd never seen any of that lot. She put ideas in his head. A bad influence, she were."

Owen Holt waved her comment away, smiling with forbearance.

"What sort of ideas?"

"Musical, she told him he was, like her own boy." With the multihued duster, she pointed. "Why, I'd like to know? Toby was tone-deaf if ever a child was. It were Billy that could play piano and anything else handed him."

An unexpected chuckle came from Owen Holt. "That was just to make Toby feel good. But he did try."

"Pigheaded."

The phrase might have been meant to define Toby, Owen, or even Jury himself, since she was glaring at him.

Studying Jury with suspicion, eyebrows scissored together, she said, "You're from Scotland Yard in London. What's Scotland Yard to do with that Healey person getting killed in the Old Silent Inn? We got our own police. Only time I ever remember Scotland Yard coming up here was about that Peter Sutcliffe." Alice Holt seemed to think Jury was mounting a police investigation as mammoth as the Yorkshire Ripper case.

"Nothing like that," he said vaguely.

She started fussing with a small stack of magazines, already neatly stacked. "All I know is what I told police back then. It's the Citrines you should be asking. Cold-blooded lot. It weren't enough they wouldn't pay the ransom for their own boy; they got Toby killed, too." She stopped in the act of running the glove round the grooves of a piecrust table.

" 'Twasn't their fault, Alice."

"No? If he'd not gone on that trip with her he'd be alive today!"

"Very attached to Mrs. Healey was Toby," said Owen, seemingly unaware that he might be fueling his wife's jealousy of that attachment. "Do you know he even tried to plant a garden in that grit soil. Determined lad. And Mr. Citrine's been good to us, letting me work when I can hardly hold a rake."

"Conscience money, that's all—"

"Be quiet," Owen Holt snapped in what Jury thought was an uncharacteristic display of bad temper. He stared down at his crippled hands.

Jury looked round the room again. The large television, the fridge he'd got a glimpse of earlier, the good china (albeit unused): knowing what he did about the generosity of the welfare state didn't necessarily mean the Holts had other income, but there seemed an abundance for a man who hadn't been able to work for several years except at odd jobs on the Citrine estate . . . then he remembered Nell Healey's comment that she'd done what she could. "I'm sure they must have felt responsible for what happened. I can understand an annuity of some sort after what you'd been through—"

Alice Holt sat up straight. "We don't accept charity. It was Toby's—"

"Alice!" Again, Owen Holt warned her off.

"Well, I can't see what's wrong with it." She said to Jury, "It was just ten thousand she set up for a trust fund for the boy's education. After two weeks, and Toby missing, and—"

Here, she raised her eyes to stare at the ceiling, not, he thought, at the rooms above but to keep the tears from falling. "—dead. She changed it over. The trust I mean. Told us to use it for ourselves. . . ."

Owen Holt merely shook his head. "Police aren't interested in all that." He looked belligerently at Jury now. "It's our affair, that."

Sharply, his wife looked at him. "You drank near half of it away." She seemed to think Jury now was her ally. "Drink and gambling, that's a fine thing. Up there at the Black Bush, with that lot you played cards with. Not one of them with two pence to rub together and freeloaded off you."

Holt started rocking his chair as he shook his head again. "I told you a dozen times, 'twas because I just went kind of crazy over the boy being gone. You don't see me doing it no more, do you?"

"No." Alice Holt sat back, putting down the duster and dragging off the white glove, which she held clenched in her hand, like a flag of truce. "No, I expect you don't." Defeat, not over an argument lost, but of a life, was heavy in her voice.

Owen Holt turned his head again listlessly to gaze out of the window, and Jury wondered for a moment what the pose reminded him of. Nell Healey came back to him, standing and gazing at the orchard.

Like her, Owen Holt might have expected Toby to materialize out there working in the gritty soil, managing finally to make a few flowers grow.

24

Jury forgot the dead telephone receiver in his hand.

He had been staring for some moments now through the small squares of glass in his door of the call box, some of them fretted with frost and six of them cracked in one way or another. He had counted them.

When he left the Holts it had been drizzling. Twenty minutes later it was raining. It had started just as he had got into the kiosk. The cracks and the rain distorted the cobbled street and stone wall opposite, the figures running through the rain under newspapers.

The message at the Old Silent had directed him to call Melrose Plant, who had told him what had happened.

As he listened, Jury wondered if it were he, if it were his own blurred eyesight that was causing the squares of glass to waver.

He was furious with himself now, after Plant had rung off, for not asking for more particulars. His hand was latched, still, in the handle of the door of the call box, as if he had just closed it, as if he had just been going to make the call.

At least he had managed to stop his fast-moving thoughts, broken and running like the figures in the rain, long enough to compliment Melrose in getting the little girl out of there, away from what would have been a terrible trauma.

Abby, Melrose had said, could handle trauma considerably better than he himself.

* * *

Jury hung up the receiver.

Two murders in four days.

He hoped Nell Healey had an alibi.

He passed more than a dozen police cars angled along the Oakworth Road at this end, some of them with two tires in the ditch like abandoned vehicles.

Even though it was hours since Melrose Plant had called the local police station, there were still two cars with blue lights turning, in the car park of the inn a good mile from the point where the others had stopped.

"Look who's here," said Superintendent Sanderson mildly without turning his face from the snow-covered moor before him.

"I'm on holiday, remember?"

"Ah. Well, January *is* a popular month for holidaymakers here in Yorkshire. Almost as popular as the Lake District." Sanderson was making a bellows of his cheeks, trying to suck some life into a cold cigar.

There must have been two dozen of Sanderson's men in the distance, which meant there were more of them farther away whom Jury couldn't see.

And this was five hours later.

Jury stood there, looking off in the same direction. "Isn't the Citrine house somewhere over there?"

"About a mile from here, as the crow flies, and as you know."

"I don't expect another murder on her doorstep—if I can put it that way—is going to help her."

Sanderson took the cigar from his mouth and said, "You can put it any way you want, Superintendent." He looked at Jury and smiled grimly.

Jury persisted. "Mrs. Healey barely escaped jail after her husband's murder. The Citrines knew Ann Denholme and so did Roger Healey, I imagine." He drew his eyes from the moor and turned them on Sanderson. "You'll have her in custody within twenty-four hours." He made no attempt to keep the rancor out of his tone as he turned to leave.

He was surprised to hear Sanderson say, "Very probably."

At least, thought Jury, watching the man drop his dead cigar into the dirty snow, Sanderson wasn't smiling.

Melrose Plant frowned at the wire fence and wished the ducks would stop waddling up every time he came out into the forecourt. He was standing by Jury's car, looking over at the police constable who'd been left behind by Keighley police.

"Try and remember as much as you can," said Jury. "Sanderson certainly isn't talking to me." He was looking down at the ordnance map Plant had brought out from his jacket pocket. "By that wall there," said Melrose. "About twenty feet from the cripple hole."

"How much could you tell about the condition of the body?" asked Jury.

Melrose was standing shivering in only a cashmere sweater, hugging his arms about his chest. "My knowledge of the state of rigor mortis is pretty much limited to when Agatha stops talking. It begins around the jaw, doesn't it?"

Jury nodded. "Top to bottom. It couldn't have passed off; that would take upwards of thirty hours. More, in the cold, probably."

"The wrist was limp. So she musn't have been out there all that long. The last person who saw her was Ruby, on her way to bed last night, about eleven. Ruby thought it odd she wasn't about at breakfast this morning."

"Telephone calls?"

"For her?"

"Or made by her, last night, this morning." When Melrose shook his head, Jury said, "Then I'd calculate she was shot sometime this morning, fairly early. It would take the rigor somewhere around twelve or fifteen hours in this cold. It's unlikely she'd go out in the middle of the night along the moor." Jury looked up at one of the windows. "Who's that?"

Melrose followed his gaze. "Malcolm. Taking in everything, no doubt."

The boy's face was mashed against the casement window, the grin distorted into a gargoyle grimace above a lanky gray cat lying on the sill.

"I don't see why we must go through this dreadful business over and over again," said Ramona Braine, more to her carefully arranged cards than to the company in general, who had, given Jury's introduction into their midst, started in again on the murder of their landlady.

"I do," said the Princess, returning her silvery gaze to Jury. Her voice was eager; in order to make room for this new person to sit, her hands scooped back the gored skirt of her handsome rose wool dress where it had been fanned out on the chaise. "You're a friend of Mr. Plant? How lovely."

Jury smiled noncommittally and took a seat beside Malcolm, supine on the facing sofa, to Malcolm's great surprise. The maneuver, though, clearly pleased him. He dragged an Ertyl plane from his pocket, this one a miniature Spitfire, and pretended not to be impressed. Scooping the plane through the air, he sent it upward, accompanied by blubbery lip-vibrations to simulate the sound of its engine.

Jury accepted a cup of lukewarm tea from the pot, sat back, and let them tell him about the dreadful business of the morning. The Princess and Major Poges cut across and contradicted each other's reports at every opportunity. For a good quarter of an hour this continued, with Ramona Braine, who Melrose had told Jury had been hell-bent to get to Northumberland, now apparently content to stop over and make hindsight prognostications. "I knew the moment she said she was a Sagittarius . . ."

"Place overrun with police, you'd think we were all suspects," said George Poges.

"I certainly hope so," said the Princess, extending her cup to Poges for a refill of tea.

Jury looked down at Malcolm and his drifting Spitfire and asked in a joking tone: "And where were you when the lady disappeared?" It was Jury's experience that children were ordinarily overlooked in police investigations.

Malcolm stopped the plane's midair plunge and looked up at the new person, open-mouthed. "Me?"

"Umm."

Spirit world in abeyance, Ramona Braine thrust herself forward in her chair, nearly overturning the wooden board she was using to hold her Tarot cards. "In *bed,* of course!"

Jury ignored her, as did Malcolm. Malcolm, clearly thrilled by a total stranger's interest, was having nothing to do with this bland asleep-in-bed alibi. His eyes narrowed and a tight little smile pinched up his lips as he slid closer to Jury. "*When* this morning?" It rang out on a note of triumph.

Of course he would have ingested his share of *Cagney and Lacey* episodes, like every other kid in Britain.

Jury gave him a comradely tap on the shoulder, "Good question." He looked at them all.

"Oh, five-ish, wasn't it?"

With feigned contempt Malcolm said, "*Five-ish?* You wouldn't catch them on *The Bill* saying '*FIVE-ish.*' "

Poges shouted, "This isn't one of your telly bloodbaths. This is *real* life!"

Given his mother, Jury imagined Malcolm's confrontations with real life were somewhat limited.

The Princess said, "Oh really, George. Stop sputtering at him. The poor child doesn't know anything."

"That so?" Malcolm *vroooom*ed his metal plane downward. "I know enough to know you're lying." Silence. "Not you," he said, directing his gaze at the startled face of the Princess. "Him. The Major." Then he started making figure eights with the airplane.

Not even his mother could make a sound at this announcement, work her mouth as she would. They all sat about looking waxen, except for Plant, who was smiling and lighting one of his small cigars.

"What in God's name is going on here?" George Poges started to rise from his chair. "We're not going to believe the rantings of a malicious boy—"

Malice took precedence over murder in Ramona Braine's cards, clearly. "Don't you go calling Malcolm names, you nasty old bug——"

"*Please!*" said the Princess, touching her temples.

Vrooooming his plane up and down and having a fine old time sending everyone into a state of nerves, Malcolm was holding on to whatever attention he could get and seemed delighted by whatever names might be called.

Jury reached over and caught his wrist and eased the plane from his fist, ignoring Malcolm's banshee protests. "I'm just parking this for a minute." Jury took a brass box with a tiny drawer from the side table and slid the Spitfire inside. "In the hangar."

Although Malcolm scowled mightily, he took the box-hangar and fiddled with it, but was clearly enjoying this new man's being in on his game. Jury thought that in Malcolm's young life, probably, he'd never actually realized his potential for power over adults other than the crass kiddies' methods of making noise, kicking furniture, and sending cats up trees. Malcolm pointed at the Major as if the boy were a witness in a courtroom drama. "*You* never told police the truth. I was standing outside that window—" and here he pointed to the sill whereupon the gray cat snoozed.

"Spying!" said Major Poges, rising from his chair with steely eyes.

"I seen you early this morning go out the back with that floppy hat on and your galoshes and your . . . gun." Malcolm slid down, looking a bit frightened.

That slight pause before he mentioned the gun made Jury wonder if this was a chancy embellishment.

"Where were you, Malcolm, when you saw this?"

"Malcolm! I *forbid* you to say *one more word!*"

"Why? I didn't do nothin'," said her son, reasonably. "I was up in my room. I got a perfect view of that moor back there." He made it sound like the kitchen garden. Gravely, he pulled down his T-shirt and sat back, adding, for good measure, "Prob'ly on the way to the gun butts."

Major Poges opened and then closed his mouth.

"Absurd," said the Princess. "Absolutely absurd! Major Poges would *not*—"

But he interrupted her with a weak smile. "It's all right, Rose." He said to them all, "The boy's telling the truth. Nothing sinister in it, though. I couldn't sleep and thought I'd just have a tramp across the moor to see if I could bag a grouse."

"You were headed for the shooting butts, then?" asked Plant, looking at Jury.

"No, no. Need a driver to put the birds over you for that. No. I was for Keighley reservoir. It was dead dark—this was about four-thirty, five, and I planned walking into the light. I reckon I was there an hour or so. A snipe or two settled, but no pheasant or grouse. I'm not that much of a shooter, anyway; I probably would have missed the damned birds, or tried to." He smiled wanly. "It was just exercise with a sense of purpose behind it. After an hour I turned back." He took a swallow of his sherry. "It was a little after seven, as Master Malcolm can no doubt verify." Now, there was more humor than bitterness in his tone.

And Master Malcolm seemed to have lost interest in the Major's predicament, as the boy was more concerned with moving his Spitfire in and out of its new airplane hangar.

"You should have told that to Superintendent Sanderson," said Melrose.

Poges looked a bit ashen. "First thing that flashed through my mind was that I might have been in the vicinity where Ann Denholme was killed and here was I, carrying a shotgun. All right, I must admit I fibbed."

Said the Princess, waving her cigarette holder: "Naturally. Who wouldn't?" She held the holder in the direction of Melrose, who moved to light it.

Ramona Braine's eyes came up as her hands stopped sweeping above the cards. "How did you know she was *shot?* When that policeman questioned me, he didn't mention that." She smiled meanly.

The Princess's smile was even meaner. "The man told *me,* darling. And I passed it on to Poges, here." She sighed and swabbed her silky, silvery hair up with her hand. "I managed to worm it out of him, somehow." Then she offered Jury a smile as dewy as her pearlescent holder, which was arched toward the ceiling as she put her elbow on her knee and swung a slim and slippered foot.

"Rose is only trying to protect me. I'm touched." His tone was quite sincere.

Ramona, earrings wobbling, had suddenly lifted her eyes heavenward and intoned: "Danger is all about us—"

The Princess looked at her, bored. "Must you flush out the spirit world to pick up that little nugget?" Ramona Braine gave her a furious look, put aside her lap desk, and pulled Malcolm from the sofa. Malcolm was less than eager to follow his mother from the room.

She turned her lowered lids on Jury. "George is always taking walks. He has indulged more than once in beastly early-morning ones. I know because once I went with him." She shuddered slightly. "Six A.M. We saw some sheep. I wasn't aware that living creatures were up at that hour—"

"Rose." George Poges gave her a look and went on: "I expect that because I knew she'd been murdered out there and because my mind was on guns . . ." He shrugged and added wryly, "Though I do hope Superintendent Sanderson won't take that association too far."

"Aside from Malcolm, no one saw you?" asked Melrose.

The Princess was about to speak, but quickly shut her mouth.

"Not that I know of."

Jury leaned forward to replace his teacup.

"Perhaps someone saw you. That might help you."

Poges shook his head. "Out there on the moor 'at that hour' if Mr. Sanderson is to be believed." George Poges smiled grimly. "My route—that ordnance map of yours, Mr. Plant. Let me see it for a moment." Melrose took it from his pocket and handed it over. The Major sketched in a few lines. "Here's the way I walked." As if he were looking to Melrose to champion his cause, he handed it back. Jury glanced at the dog-legged penciled line.

"Stand of pine, shooting butts. There's the wall and up farther the reservoir. It's my usual route. Ask Abby."

The Princess's hand flew to her mouth. Then she said, "Abby. The poor child. Has anyone given her so much as a thought?"

"I have," said Melrose Plant, sadly.

Mrs. Braithwaite had come in teary-eyed to clear the tea things away and was surprised to see a new guest in their midst. Or in the wake of the Princess's exit and announcement that she must have her nap. She was followed by Major Poges.

"You should have told me, sir, there's a friend of yours come to tea. Well, I must make some fresh." Ever the good servant, though she wiped at her eyes with her sleeve.

"Never mind, Mrs. Braithwaite," said Jury, quickly commandeering the tea tray. "I'll just carry this for you."

"You didn't," called Melrose, as Jury left the room, "happen to run into a motorbiker?"

2

Jury fared better in the kitchen with his hand clamped round a very hot mug of coffee and a small coal fire burning in the chimneyplace. On either side were two chairs losing their stuffing, covered with faded India cotton throws. The aromatic coffee mixed with freshly baked bread rolls diffused through the room like the steam coming from the kettles and clouding the windows. It was five o'clock and nearly dark.

"And what I said to her was, 'I got enough to do without the evening meal . . .' "

His attention had slipped away from Mrs. Braithwaite momentarily. She had given him his coffee and started in complaining about the cook, Mrs. Hull, who, upon arrival of the Yorkshire police and news of the mistress's death, had fallen down in a lump.

". . . gone all keggly-like and jubberin'." Mrs. Braithwaite snorted her disgust at such persons who couldn't rise to an occasion. " 'That lot's still got t'be fed, don't they?' I says to 'er. Got me own grief, I do, but not to make things worse, I go on, I says."

"It must be a trial to you, Mrs. Braithwaite," said Jury. "Some people simply fold up in a crisis." The housekeeper was a round sort of person with short thick arms. Steady and stout as a fireplug and always ready to do her job. The arms hadn't stopped reaching and waving and opening cabinets and cupboards in the ten minutes Jury had been letting her bash about the kitchen. She had already had her private cry over the owner's death; the tissues ballooning the pocket of her apron and the reddened eyes testified to that.

"Yes, indeed 'tis. All of them police about, and up in the mistress's room, crawlin' all over." She lifted the lid of a heavy kettle and the escaping steam clouded over the acorn windows.

"I appreciate the coffee, Mrs. Braithwaite. Sorry to put you to more trouble."

She wiped her hands on her apron, protesting it was no trouble, not for a friend of Mr. Plant who was a "fine, dacent gentleman" and wasn't it dreadful Mr. Jury'd come for a visit and found all of this?

Jury thanked her, smiling inwardly that she didn't seem to find it odd Mr. Plant's friend had stationed himself here before the fire in one of the heavily cushioned chairs, inviting her, as if he were host, to join him.

"Why don't you have a coffee, yourself? Let the lot of them send out for fish and chips." He rose. "Come on; sit down." And he took her arm and led her to the chair opposite. She sank into it with a look of relief, fanning her flat, round face with her hand. "I'll get the coffee." He took a companion mug from the sink, poured the coffee, and asked, "Got anything to put in this?"

"Bottom shelf, cupboard near the door," she answered, her eyes on the burning coals.

Jury brought over her brandy-laced coffee and sat down. "How long have you been working here, then?"

"Nearly twelve years. Just bring over the bottle, will you? I could do with a proper drink. And there's glasses on that shelf, too," she called to his departing back.

Jury poured the drinks into little balloon glasses and set the bottle down. "I'm sorry about what you must be going through."

The seriousness of his tone threatened to provoke more tears. But she wedged her hand over her mouth and held them back. Under control again, she said, "Whyever the poor girl bought this place is a puzzle. Had it for a dozen years. She must have got it on the cheap. The Denholmes are London people; why'd she want to live out here in the wilds? There's many a time I've thought of going back to Harrogate—ever so lovely it is—but I'd've felt I was letting her down. I don't think Miss Ann had all that much business sense."

Jury thought for a moment, and said, "What about her niece?"

Mrs. Braithwaite looked up, slightly surprised that the conversation had taken this turn and said, "Abigail? We call her Abby." She looked up at a few snapshots stuck round an old mirror in need of resilvering and said, "That's her, with her Aunt Ann."

Jury got up and looked at the snapshot. Small as it was even with the light silhouetting her outline, he could still see the strong resemblance between the little girl and the aunt.

"Why did Abby come here? What about her own mother and father?"

Warming to the fire, the brandy, and the turn of the conversation (something to keep her mind off the death of Ann Denholme), Mrs. Braithwaite leaned forward and said, "That'd be Ann's sister, Iris. And right strange that were. Poor girl, she'd had two miscarriages already and her doctor wanted to see she got proper nursing." Her manner grew even more conspiratorial as she went on: " 'Twasn't the husband who could do it; he had his job, after all. That Iris was a pale, thin little woman; sometimes I thought I could put my hand through her. Ann went off for six or seven months to take care of her. And three years later, after poor Iris died, Ann took on Abby. Trevor came here—Trevor Cable, Abby's Da. I'll have another little sup of that brandy, thanks. He didn't want her, or felt he couldn't do for her, apparently. He seemed to think Abby needed a woman about."

"And was Ann Denholme fond of her niece?" Jury asked as he poured a little more into her glass.

"Fond? Well—I expect so." She seemed alarmed at the notion that such a question would arise. "Ann was a broody type. All those long walks on the moors . . . ," she ended uncertainly. Then Mrs. Braithwaite sniffed. "It's not because she's been turned out, if that's wha' yer thinkin'."

"Why would I think that?"

The question went unanswered.

From the cooker came the abrasive sound of a clattering lid. As Mrs. Braithwaite grumbled and struggled from her chair, Jury said, "Never mind, I'll see to it."

"Oh, would you now? It's that soup. If you'd just give it a stir and turn down the gas."

"What do you expect will happen to her now?" Jury asked, his back to her as he stirred the thick stew. "Back to the father? Or will Social Services step in?"

As he returned to his chair, he saw her face hot with anger. "Not back to *that* man, not if I've a breath left. Oh, no." Vehemently, she shook her head. "He doesn't want her, anyways, is what Ann said."

Jury waited awhile, made some small talk about the countryside then said, "You've certainly had your share of bad news in these parts. There was that killing at the Old Silent Inn—"

"Yes. Terrible, that is, about Mrs. Healey. Mr. Citrine was over here just this noon to pay his respects. Brought over a brace of pheasant."

Jury looked at her, but her head was down. "Charles Citrine was a particular friend?"

"I wouldn't say 'particular.' Ann knew the family; and Mrs. Healey would come over here with . . ." Her hand wedged over her mouth again as she squinted down at the coals, spitting, turning to gray ash. "That poor little boy, Billy."

"Billy?"

With her forearm she wiped away tears, ignoring the ball of tissues in her pocket. "I niver did understand it, sir. Such a *nice* man was Mr. Healey. He fairly doted on that son of his. It must've nearly killed him—" She stopped suddenly as if she'd realized a truth inherent in this, though not what the truth was.

"I would imagine the same could be said for the mother—" Jury checked himself.

"Oh, yes, yes," she said quickly. "But she wasn't the *real* mother, was she? I mean, I know she was that fond of the boy. But she couldn't have a *real* mother's feelings."

Jury felt himself grow cold. He leaned over to freshen her drink; brandy didn't seem to affect her that much. "I've taken up too much of your time." Jury rose.

But from the way she held on to the hand he offered, apparently she didn't agree. "Would you just give that stew another bit of a stir?"

25

A black and white collie sat just outside the double door to the barn, using its nose to track the weather. It looked curiously at Jury, but did nothing, except to turn and follow him in, keeping close to Jury's heel.

The sun was nearly down; light cast squares upon the ground that stretched across the center of the barn. The large doors at the other side were tightly closed, cracks stuffed with cloth. To his left, in the rear and in the shadows, was the byre from which came rustles and the lowing sound of a cow. Part of a stone wall held a fireplace, and in front of it were a table and mismatched chairs. There was an old sink beneath another small window.

At the end of the barn opposite the byre was a cot, layered in quilts. Beside this bed an upturned crate served as a case for books and a few records and beside it was a record player, older even than his own. On a low stool at the foot of the bed was the outline of a box beneath a black drapery. It appeared to be a little larger than a shoe box. A small table lamp stood on the crate, the light fanning out through the open circle of the shade over the bottom part of a big framed print of a house amidst dark trees. It was no more out of place in a barn, he thought, than the faded travel pictures of Venezio (which reminded him, for God's sakes, to call Vivian) and a view of the Cornwall coast, the frilled waves lashing the cliffside. Between them was an empty space with blobs of gum, as if another picture had hung there. Venice and Cornwall were faded, but the one of Elvis in his younger days appeared in mint condition.

The little girl came out of the shadows of the byre, rolling up a poster that she held against her stomach. She was making a long and solemn job of it. Although she did not acknowledge the presence of a stranger in her barn, her downturned eyes so firmly engaged with her task, he felt she knew he was there.

"Hello," Jury said.

She didn't answer; instead she concentrated on her rolling-job, stopping now and then to shove in the ends. Then she said, "I'm taking down Ricky Nelson."

"The singer, you mean."

The dark head nodded, still downturned. "He's dead." There was in her tone a finality that would have silenced any sentimental remark about finding comfort in mementos. She looked over to the hearth where lay the new poster pinned down by a hammer-weight on top and the sleeping dog on the bottom. The corners at the top curled inward. "I'm putting them up in his place." "They" were the members of the Sirocco band and, however they measured up to Ricky Nelson, they were, at least, alive. That seemed to be her estimate of the affair. It was the poster he'd seen further enlarged in the window of the record shop in Piccadilly. It was a rather austere and studied pose, Charlie Raine leaning against a leafless tree, which was the focal point, and the four others, looking off in other directions in an otherwise blasted landscape.

Ricky Nelson had died some years ago, but perhaps in what looked to Jury like Abby's very patchwork past, events stitched together from piecework left behind by others—she had only recently come to realize that something else was gone from it. The mismatched clothes she wore fit the image, too: the somewhat muddy white shawl that reached down her back to her ankles, the zigzag-striped jumper and brown wool skirt, its hem covering the tops of old boots.

Thus when she raised her face to give him a grim look, Jury was startled by its beauty. Her eyes were a deep blue that sea beyond Cornwall could never match. She said: "I don't think it's right to have a poster up of somebody dead." Here he saw her glance quickly toward Elvis pinned to the far wall near whom the Sirocco poster had been fixed. "I don't care if Ethel's mad. It's my barn." From a pocket hidden beneath the shawl, she took out a wad of stuff that looked like tangled string, found a rubber band, and rolled it carefully over the poster. Then she returned the blue eyes to him, apparently waiting.

"Do you want me to help you tack that up?"

She was not, clearly, to be fooled by some offer of help. "I expect you're another policeman."

Under that blue stare, he felt more like a suspect. He smiled a little. "Was there one here before, then?"

"Two. They kept asking questions. One was nearly as tall as you. He asked me did I like rock music." She looked at Jury, waiting.

He might be taller, but was he smarter? "That's sort of obvious, isn't it?" She didn't verify this. "I don't ask a lot of questions."

"They *all* ask questions." She was still clenching the rolled-up poster and Jury could see a slick of sweat from her palms where they'd moved up and down. "But they never tell you nothing. Except Aunt Ann had some kind of accident."

The words came out slow and fine, as if they'd been ground like grit from millstone. She had found the lie in them.

Silence filled the barn, broken only by the shuffling of the cow in its stall.

"I've got to give it its medicine," she said quickly, the sick cow a welcome distraction from the topic at hand. "You can watch."

* * *

"Sometimes I have to take care of Mr. Nelligan's sheep." She gave Jury a quick look to see, apparently, if he believed in this vetting of animals by a person so young.

"Who's he?"

Abby stoppered up the bottle and got down from the stool. "He lives out on the moor in an old caravan. He doesn't take care of them at all." She picked the poster from the dirt floor. Jury looked at the two doors of the empty stalls. On one was a poster of Mick Jagger, on the other, Dire Straits.

"I'm putting this away," she said, walking over to an old steamer trunk. She bent down and unclasped the tarnished brass buckles, lifted the lid, and carefully placed the poster in it. Then she stood quickly, a furious look on her face, and let the coffin lid thunk down. "We're having our tea," she said, turning to the fireplace, where the collie now lay, beside the larger dog, paws outstretched, eyes drawing a bead on Jury's every move.

Jury smiled slightly, assuming that "we" meant Abby and the dogs.

"You can have some too," she said, without a clue as to whether she looked forward to this addition.

"Thank you." In the grave preparation of the tea things, Jury said nothing; he doubted he could penetrate her thoughts, as tangled as the load of strings in her pocket.

"I've only got tea bags," she said, lifting the top of a box of P&G's and setting several of them on the table.

Jury smiled. "If they're good enough for Prince Edward they're good enough for me."

Gazing at him over a little dish of buns, she looked puzzled.

"There was a picture in the paper over a year ago of Edward going to his first job—he wants to be an actor. He was holding a box just like that." Jury nodded toward the P&G box.

Still frowning, she dropped three tea bags in the pot. "Well, if I was his mother I'd see he got a proper tea." In a pique of anger, she plunked a bun apiece on two small plates. "He's all she's got left."

This sad estimation of the sinking family numbers at the palace forestalled any comment on Prince Charles and his brother and sister. Those three were married and gone. "It must be hard on the Queen watching her children grow up and move away."

She fiddled with her shawl, said nothing.

Jury looked round the walls of the barn. "You have some very nice posters and pictures."

After she'd wetted the tea, she said, "Ethel gave me the cat one." Abby pointed to a picture, one corner curling in for lack of a drawing pin. Her tone was uncertain, and she glanced at the trunk, as if the gift from Ethel was a task as yet unfinished in her mind, still causing her a muddle. The picture was one Jury had seen several times before—a popular and sentimental interpretation of childhood; a little girl in a thick, rich frock, holding a bowl of milk in her lap. Her dimpled smile was directed at an assortment of starveling cats meant to look sleek and rather rich, all waiting for their dinner.

It must have reminded Abby of her dog, for she picked up the enamel pitcher and poured milk into a tin plate by the fire. The collie went busily to work on it. "She gave it to me probably because she thinks that girl looks like her. Ethel has reddish hair in curls like that. And white skin." Abby pulled her cheeks out with her fingers, distorting the heart-shape to something cartoonishly plump. "It's round, her face is," she said through tightly drawn, rubber-band lips. "Ethel's my best friend. What do you think?" she asked, waiting for the verdict to be handed down. That Jury and Ethel had never met presented no problem to Abby. He should be able to decide from a combination of her description and the picture.

He rose from his seat and walked over to the picture. The

child there was snub-nosed, dimpled and too prissily dear to be believed.

Until Abby cleared her throat, he hadn't realized she'd come up behind him. "Ummm." He cocked his head this way and that and said, "She looks sticky-sweet. And she also looks underneath as if she'd dump that basin of milk over that black cat that's clawing her dress."

"That's Ethel," said Abby. She walked away.

Jury's eye took in the rest of the barn at this end: the corner with the cot and the crate that held a stash of books and comics. "May I look at your books?"

"Yes," she called over to him. "But I wouldn't look at *Jane Eyre*."

"No? Why not?"

"If you want to be sick."

But *Jane Eyre* seemed to have got some rather thorough handling, despite its sick-making propensities. He leafed through it and saw the many downturned tips of pages. It was a heavy old volume, illustrated.

"This one's better," she said, kneeling down to remove the black drape from the box that Jury could see now had held boots. She lifted the lid and pulled out a small book. "Mrs. Healey gave it to me. Her aunt brought it. I wish she'd come instead."

It was the book of poetry Nell Healey had been holding when he saw her on the path. And it was a duplicate of the one in Billy Healey's room. He thumbed through it. Many of the same markings were there, and the same notes in the margins. "This looks like it might have been a favorite book."

"It was." She took it back, returned it to the box, refitted the black cover.

Jury frowned. "Why do you keep it in there?"

"It's a hiding place. Come on." She rose and pulled at him, still crouched down.

"Why is the box covered in black, then?"

"Because it's for Buster's funeral. She died."

She? "Was she a pet?"

"My cat."

Jury was fascinated. "Did you bury her?" Abby seemed surrounded by death.

"Not yet. *Come* on."

Back at the table, he watched her pour milk into her cup and add four teaspoons of sugar. She poured the same amount of milk into his and added the same four teaspoons of sugar.

Silence seemed to crowd him as they each took a sip from their mugs and then sat back looking into the milky depths as if some tea-leaf fortune might be forming down there. The Queen might not make a proper tea, but Abby had at least torn the tea bags open and tapped the loose tea into the pot. It was covered with a towel in lieu of a cozy. Jury's mug had a picture of Winchester Cathedral on it.

Abby lifted her head to look straight ahead of her and Jury followed her gaze. She was plucking at her shawl and staring at the little cot enclosure, the bookcase or, he thought, above it at the massive framed print.

"Where did you get that one, Abby?"

She looked away. "Billy's mum. Mrs. Healey." Then she turned a dark look on him. "You never found him."

Her look did not suggest she was holding him personally responsible. But he was a policeman and he must bear the weight of the failure of his fellows. "I know."

"He's gone. He's dead. He was my friend, him and Toby. We used to play a lot over there at his house. We climbed trees."

In the starved orchard. Yet, she could have been no more than three or four.

"So now I guess I get sent to Lowood School," she said, sitting stiffly. He opened his mouth to reply but she didn't give him a chance. "Well, if they think I'm stupid like Jane Eyre, they'll see. There's no headmaster that's going to hang a cardboard round my neck." Her eyes narrowed, her mouth tightened, as if the grisly scene were being enacted right before her. "And if they think they're going to make *me* walk round and round out in the rain like that dumb Helen—" Swiftly she fired a glance at Jury. "Stranger'll be outside that wall and he'll get me out. I'm not walking round and coughing in the rain." Here she mimicked a coughing fit. "And *then* that Helen just lies in bed dying and smiling like the angels are all sitting there feeding her Kit-Kats." Furiously, she shook the black bobbed hair. "It sounds like Ethel."

How long had she sat beneath that lamp poring over the details, hearing the rain on the old barn roof, the rain in the courtyard, the rain in her mind?

Jury looked at the collie, sitting up, its ear perked, sensitive to some sign of distress. "This dog looks smart enough to save anyone."

Abby was collecting the plates. "Except Jane Eyre. Nothing's smart enough to save her. She's hopeless." She held her cup as if it were a great weight in her rounded hands.

"Like Ethel," said Jury. The corners of her mouth quirked upward.

Jury looked at the painting on the wall on the other side of the barn. It was large enough that the details were clear. "I like your painting."

Putting down the plates, she said, "It's my favorite." After a little silence while both looked at it, she said, "Why's it dark at the bottom with that house and those black trees like it's night, and the sky's blue above like it's day?"

Jury shook his head. "I'm not sure," he said. Her expression told him he'd better come up with something better than that.

Her voice rang out, "It's like a church."

"I don't see what you mean."

Abby leaned closer. "The *tall tree* looks like a *steeple*."

He cocked his head, staring at the painting. "No, I don't think so." He felt her sidewise glance, heard her chair scrape back. Then she marched round the table to stand directly in front of him, the table between. "A steeple," she said again, raising her arms and pressing the palms of her hands together to illustrate, her cheeks glowing with the intensity of her conviction. Jury moved his head to see the painting, but she did a sidestep that blocked his line of vision. She had made her point, taken her stand, and no comparison with the real article was necessary.

Jury blinked under the sheer force of her blue eyes.

When he didn't respond, she dropped her arms. Then she came round the table and clenched his sweater sleeve, pulling at him. "Come *on!*" He allowed himself to be yanked from the bench at the same time she made a clicking sound with her tongue, and the dog rose immediately, alert. She was to deal a stunning blow to this man's perceptive powers, and a witness was needed. Stranger followed.

The three of them faced the painting, "Empire of Light." Since she was to be guide in this museum, he let her continue:

"There's that streetlamp. It's right in the middle." Then she was silent.

He glanced down at her, saw she was chewing her lip, her arms folded tightly across her chest, her fingers plying the loose threads of shawl. Stranger looked up at Jury looking down as if he too wondered how this would extend her church analogy.

"You're right about the streetlamp and the lighted windows." His eye traveled from the night below to the day above, a sky of light but vibrant blue, a pattern of white clouds drifting, and he wondered about the limits of his own mind. Of his compulsion to turn a whole into parts, into symbols and emblems. It was his job, in a way. The whole he couldn't see; he worked with bits of mirror, slivers of light. *What was he last seen wearing? Identifying marks? Routine investigation.* The streetlamp was the focus here; but if you looked at it too long, would it suddenly switch off? The painting hung in comfortable silence, perfectly accessible if one looked at it the right way.

Her voice, in a higher register, broke into his thoughts,

insistent: "It's better than Lowood School." Turning sharply, she stumped over to her crate-bookcase and hefted *Jane Eyre* to her chest with one arm, the other hand, finger wetted, shuffling through the pages with a furious energy of its own. Proof found, she marched back. "Here." She shoved the book forward, her finger stabbing the face of the master. He was thrashing a child with his cane.

The picture spoke for itself. Wordlessly, she sat down on a milking stool, head bent as she flailed through this awful book, searching out further horrors.

Jury kept his eye on the painting as he said, "They can't send you to Lowood School. You're too important."

Immediately, the rustle of pages stopped. He could feel her looking at him, but when he turned his head, her own head dropped her face almost flat against the open book, as she traced a line with her finger and pretended not to hear him.

He said, "Perhaps you'll live in the 'Empire of Light.' " That he knew would be a notion so outrageously exciting that she could quarrel it down.

Her head snapped up and the beguiling look of patience-being-tested-to-its-limits returned. If he was such a nit, she would have to be practical for both of them. "*People* can't live in *pictures*." She then lowered her head and sifted through the pages until she found another illustration to live in.

"It's not as nice as your barn, but it might be just as real. You might be living in one of those lit-up rooms." He nodded toward the painting.

"If it was real, you can bet Ethel would be living in the other one," she said to the book in her lap. "Besides, it's dark there."

"Very dark in some way." He walked over and sat down in a rocker. From his pocket he drew a packet of Orbit gum. Sliding a stick out, he said to the crown of her head (still bent over the book), "Would you like some?"

Abby looked at it, took the stick and seemed to study it to

see if it was her brand, thanked him, and then took a dented metal box from the crate. She lifted the lid and put the gum inside. The box rattled as she returned it to the shelf. "He's all right, I expect," she said, turning the book so that Jury could see the illustration of the doctor who (the caption read) had come to tend Helen.

"Yes." He rocked for a moment, as he watched her roll the page from the corner down, first with her finger, then with the palm of her hand, slowly. "Well, I can tell you something else that will probably happen, though it's not nearly as good as the 'Empire of Light.' Happen to you, I mean." Jury shoved a stick of gum into his mouth and waited as her face came slowly up. "It's much better than Lowood School, though you still might not like it much." He scratched his head. She put the book on the bed. "You see, your Aunt Ann owned the Hall. Now it belongs to you."

She snapped shut *Jane Eyre* as she had the lid of the metal box. Her face, for the first time, melted into a childlike, wide-eyed surprise. "I can't. I don't own anything except Stranger and the things in here." She shoved the book away and absently started scratching behind Stranger's ear, which had perked when the dog heard its name. "I don't own anything," she repeated, and her face whitened with the dreadful thought of something she couldn't handle dropped in her lap like the book she'd just discarded.

"You'll be able to do anything you want, almost."

"I have enough as it is." She retrieved the metal box and held it on her lap, her hands locked over the top.

"You wouldn't really have to do much. Nothing would really change. Cook would still be here, and Mrs. Braithwaite. And Ruby."

Quickly, she looked up at him, her eyes narrowed as if assessing the desirability of Ruby staying on as one of her staff. Then she said, "I know one thing. If I owned this place, there's certain people would have to leave."

"Such as?"

"Malcolm!" Again, she managed to turn her face to putty by pulling down on her cheeks with her fingers so that the red underlids of her eyes were visible.

"He tried to kill my other cat. The earl saved it. I expect he's all right."

Jury thought she meant the cat until the lid of the box came up and, after rummaging about, she handed over a card. It was one of Plant's. Title, address. A trifle nicked round one edge because Lord Ardry was no longer Lord Ardry and he carried them only for emergencies. Jury smiled. "I know him. He's definitely all right." He handed back the card.

Abby took it absently, pondering over whatever valuables she had inside the box. She drew out a locket and held it swinging hypnotically from its golden chain. "Billy's mum gave it to me."

It was pure gold, twenty or twenty-two carat, he thought. Jury snapped it open and saw, side-by-side in a double frame, two boys looking out at him. That they resembled one another was owing to the slightly fuzzy sepia tint of the photos, to their similar smiles and sweaters. Another look told him that the one on the right was older. Four years would make quite a difference at eleven and fifteen. What a treasure, he thought, for Nell Healey to give away.

Jury said, "It's Billy and Toby, isn't it?"

"We were all best friends. I always went over there to play with them and climb the trees. From the top of the highest one—it's this *big* giant tree—I could see everywhere." She raised her eyes, looked at the old beams of the high roof, and grew almost breathless thinking about it. "*Everywhere.* All of the moors and Haworth. Goose Eye and Keighley. Even Leeds," she added, considerably expanding her horizon. "I've never been there," she added flatly, and sifted again through the box.

How much was remembrance and how much fantasy?

Jury handed back the necklace and, wordlessly, as if this were a solemn rite of exchange, Abby handed over a white envelope, dirty around the edges with fingering. The inscription was written in flowing letters, the postmark was faded. He could make out *Venezio* and the year. It was the same year that Billy and Toby had disappeared. The notecard inside was a duplication of the Magritte print.

He looked up. She shrugged its importance off and said, "You can read it."

" 'Dear Abby, I like this picture. Love, Nell,' " Jury raised his eyes, but she was looking everywhere else and pulling back her black hair, twining it tightly as if she were going to pin it there, then letting it fall and giving Stranger some brusque and vocal command which seemed to surprise the dog. Immediately, he went to the door of the barn to stand lookout.

Then Abby slid off her cot, pounded her booted feet about on the rug, and kneeled down to mess with her records. "I expect you'll have to go now; after I listen to my record I'm going to have a lie-down," she said.

"Okay," said Jury, rising.

"I've got three Ricky Nelsons—or Ethel does—and one Dire Straits and two Elvises."

Brian Macalvie's all-time favorite. He smiled. "I've got a good friend who likes Elvis."

"He's dead." She put the needle on a few bars into the song. Elvis was singing "The Impossible Dream." They listened. "What's an 'unrightable wrong'?" She pointed at the record. "And if it's something so bad you can't put it right, then why's he trying to do it?"

She wasn't angry; she was anxious. Surely there had to be an answer.

Jury stared at the record. He thought for a while and said, "Because some people never give up, no matter what the odds."

One puzzle answering another. This, apparently, made total sense, for she returned to her ever-so-slightly deprecating air and asked, "Don't *you* have a card?"

Jury pulled out his wallet and handed her one.

As he looked back she was studying it, hard.

26

Melrose was flooded with relief.

Trying to break the sound barrier, the motorcycle ripped up the rocky road and came spitting to a halt in the gravel outside of the drawing room. The room itself vibrated and the gray cat went rolling off the sill when Malcolm threw open the casements, leaned out, and shouted something lost in the January night.

Music in the form of a death-beat of drums that sounded like a funeral dirge came with her through the door.

Ellen came pounding down the hall, threw open the door, and stopped there, with the sort of portable stereo propped on her shoulder that Melrose had seen being carted about Piccadilly by gangs of thugs. Now a voice had joined the drum-bass-beat which seemed surprisingly inappropriate for the background havoc: it was grainy but soft:

> *Caroline says—*
> *as she gets up off the floor*

"Hi," said Ellen, in a general salute and with a particular look at Jury. She had not changed her clothes, although she wore different earrings: they were long overlapped triangles of dull black that looked heavy enough to anchor a small boat. There also seemed to be a different layering of chains around her neck.

> *life is meant to be more than this*
> *and this is a bum trip*

sang the mournful voice raised now against the dirge of drums and guitars.

Ellen turned the volume down, and handed the set to Melrose, general dogsbody, before she turned to Jury, who had risen from the sofa and was introducing himself as a friend of Mr. Plant.

Melrose sighed. He set the stereo on one bookcase shelf and leaned against the row of John D. MacDonalds.

> *but she's not*
> *afraid to die*
> *all of her friends call her A-las-ka*

He was getting interested in Caroline, who appeared to be mainlining drugs.

> *when she takes speed,*
> *they laugh and ask her*

". . . one of the funniest books I've ever read," Jury was saying to Ellen.

It was the first time Melrose had seen Ellen Taylor lose her cool. She gaped. "Are you saying you've actually read *Sauvage Savant?*"

"Not all of it . . ."

How, wondered Melrose, had he read *any* of it? He hadn't even *heard* of the girl until yesterday. Were they selling her books at Haworth parsonage?

Melrose turned up the volume on the stereo. There was the sound of tinkling glass. Caroline had thrust her hand through a window—

> *it's so cold in A-las-ka*

The voice suddenly blared.

"How about turning that off," Jury called over, "and joining us?"

The two of them were sitting on the sofa, comfy as long-lost friends.

Afraid that he might never know Caroline's fate, he turned the volume down, but not off.

> *it's so cold in A-las-ka*

Caroline should have a go at West Yorkshire, he thought, as he took the wing chair George Poges had vacated, trying to bury the stereo between himself and the chair arm.

". . . 'hot'?" Jury was asking. "Does that mean successful? Or absolutely famous?"

She was certainly overworking that word, he thought grumpily, twisting the volume up just a mite. The song had changed; things were getting worse, apparently. They were taking Caroline's children away.

> *because they said she was*
> *not a good mother—*

"Good question." Ellen half-smiled. "To tell the truth, it probably does mean famous, but only in the Warholian sense. . . ."

Dickensian, Shavian, Warholian. Well, thought Melrose, perhaps one could turn anyone into an adjective these days. He was beginning to feel extremely Carolinian.

"Andy Warhol?" Jury laughed. "Don't be modest—"

No danger of that, thought Melrose. "Fame," he said, and they both looked at him. "It's just as well, perhaps, you're not famous." He looked up at the ceiling moldings. "It comes from *fama,* you know." How sententious could one sound? "Do you know what that means?" They were silent. "Ill-report. Rumor." He smiled slightingly. "Better to stay away from it." Melrose returned his attention to the stereo.

because of the things she did in the streets
in the alleys and bars

Anyone can make a mistake.

"You're right, I guess. The old bitch-goddess, success."
She sighed.

"You've been biking around England, have you?"

"Umm. On a BMW. Picked it up in London."

"It's a K-100 RS. Ninety horsepower. Pretty powerful."

Good grief, thought Melrose, could the man see through
walls?

Surprised, she said, "Yeah. Very."

A bum trip, thought Melrose, definitely.

that miserable, rotten slut

So Caroline was . . . well, "loose." Melrose wrapped his
arm protectively around the stereo. The gray cat swayed
over and sat at his feet, blinking up at his benefactor. At
least, thought Melrose—part of his mind still studying Jury
studying Ellen—I inspire awe in some living creature. The
gray cat yawned and walked away.

"You weren't around to talk to the Yorkshire police," said
Jury, lighting her cigarette.

Ellen hitched an old footstool over with her foot and
propped her heavy laced-up shoes on it as she exhaled a bale
of smoke. "You know why?" She looked at Jury through
lowered lashes.

"Can't imagine."

Melrose sighed.

"Because I didn't know they were here." She flattened her
head against the sofa, blew three smoke rings toward the
ceiling.

When Jury gave him a look, Melrose turned down the
volume, but just a mite. The dreadful, sleazy, heartrending
story of Caroline and her lover or husband was too gripping.
He knew the questions Jury would ask.

Who was he kidding? No he didn't. His stomach turned over.

"Where were you, then?" Jury smiled. Melrose glowered.

"Harrogate."

"*What?*" Melrose nearly pushed Malcolm's stereo off the chair.

Ellen raised her eyebrows. "Har-ro-gate." She rounded the syllables as if she were teaching first form. "It's famous. The spa, et cetera."

"That's a distance," said Jury, "on a motorcycle."

She slapped her forehead dramatically. "My God, I just *said* I ran it all the way from London. So what's Harrogate to that? Fifty, sixty miles. Nice place. Did you know they made *Agatha*—"

"Yes," Melrose snapped as the drums and bass got slower and heavier.

"Miss Taylor—"

She sort of leaned her shoulder toward Jury. "Ellen."

"Ellen. What exact route did you take, then?" He smiled.

She stubbed out her cigarette and stuffed her hands in her jeans pockets. "You know something? You sound like a cop. I'm calling the embassy."

"Good idea," said Melrose.

Jury ignored both of them and pulled the map out again. "Let's see, now. Did you come by way of Ilkley?"

Ellen had turned her head toward the window, intent upon the distant hills and dark gray horizon. She stuffed a stick of gum in her mouth and looked at the map.

This, thought Melrose, discomfort rising in him like bile, was beginning to sound too much like the scene with Major Poges.

She shrugged. "Dunno. Probably around here—" Her finger punched at a place on the map.

Jury handed her the pencil.

Melrose felt a *frisson* of fear. He watched her, sitting there chewing her gum with her feet propped up, running the pencil across the paper as if she were doing nothing more serious than a kiddie joining dots. Melrose wanted to see the map, but he felt fettered to the chair and to the depressing song.

> *I am the waterboy*
> *the real game's*
> *not oh-vah here*

Handing the map back to Jury, she put her hands behind her head. "You dig Lou?"

His gaze on the mantle of clouds beyond the window, he heard her, but it was a moment before he realized Ellen was addressing him, not Jury.

"What?"

"Lou Reed."

He turned off the stereo; he'd have to leave the two of them to their wretched fate. Getting up, Melrose felt a stiffness in his joints, as if he were a recent accident victim.

"What *is* this tape?"

"*Berlin.*"

"East? No wonder."

Irritably, he moved to the window near the sofa, where he half-sat on the windowsill. He watched her mouth purse; she blew a pink balloon of gum in his direction until it smacked back against her face.

His eyes still on the map, Jury put out his hand to Ellen: "Mind if I have a stick of that gum? I'm all out."

Melrose had never known him to be all *in,* where chewing gum was concerned.

Ellen shrugged. "Sure." She pushed out a stick, which Jury took and put in his pocket. "Thanks."

Little tricks, little tricks, thought Melrose . . . just Jury's police tactics to raise her anxiety level and make her squirm. The suspect, however, was simply sitting there in a sloppy heap and making circles with her thumbs. She yawned like the cat. Yawned? A *woman* yawning around

Richard Jury? He squinted out the window. Were the stars all in place?

"How's Abby taking all this?"

"Very stoically." Jury turned the map around.

"She's one cool kid."

Jury turned the map back. "I agree. One cool kid."

Ellen's head snapped round. "You mean you talked to her?"

"That's right."

Melrose was getting nervous again. He left the window and sat on the arm of the cabbage-rose chair. Between the arm and the cushion was a bright card. He plucked it out. The Hanged Man. He stuffed it back.

"Well, but is there some big *secret,* or something?" Her voice deepened dramatically, exaggerating the words.

"Uh-uh."

"I mean, did she say I stuffed her in a snowdrift or tossed her over a wall and then went off she knew not where?"

"Uh-uh."

"Stop *saying* that!" Her long earrings clicked and clinked when she stood up, pressing her fingers against her breasts. "You think *I* was involved? *Moi?*"

Melrose said from under the tent of his hand, "Oh, shut up, for God's sakes; stop being dramatic; and you're talking to a fiendishly clever policeman."

"Clever," said Jury. "But fiendishly? You don't have to hang around, Ellen."

"*Thought* you were a cop."

But she seemed unwilling to go. Now her fingers were spread against her buttocks, thumbs jammed into rear pockets.

It was, Melrose thought, irritated with himself, a very sexy pose. Although with all of that black leather and those nerve-jangling chains, he couldn't see why. For Vivian Rivington, it had always been twin-sets, good wool, or some Italian designer. He shook himself. Jury was handing him the map.

Melrose looked at it, at the line George Poges had drawn across Keighley Moor, at the Oakworth Road and the Grouse Inn. He looked at Ellen's own line. He looked at Jury.

Ellen turned from one to the other. "You two going to communicate by semaphore?"

Jury smiled. "You're free to go."

" 'Free to go.' You guys actually *say* stuff like that?" Wearily, she shook her head and picked up the stereo. "Shit. I'm going upstairs and put on a little Trane."

.

2

"Dinner?" asked Melrose. They were standing in the courtyard, shoulders shrugged up against the cold.

"Afraid not. I've got to get back to London." Jury was facing the barn. At the bottom of the drawn curtain over the small window he could see a ragged edge of light. "Perhaps you should take your friend Ellen to dinner."

"All of that business about the route, Ilkley, Harrogate. You don't really think she was out on that moor . . . you know."

"Did I say that?"

"You meant that."

Jury turned up his coat collar and smiled. "Tell her I love her."

"The hell I will." Melrose's footsteps crunched across the broken shale as he turned and started back toward the house.

Jury walked to the door of the barn, took out one of his cards, folded it lengthwise twice, and wedged it in between the outside wrapper and the silver that covered the stick of gum Ellen Taylor had given him.

He knelt and shoved it under the door.

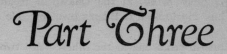

Part Three

EMPIRE
OF
LIGHT

27

It had once been a film palace. It had been an old Arthur Rank cinema, but Jury liked to remember these massive structures with their giant marquees and tiers of balconies as palatial venues that set Saturday afternoons off from the rest of a dreary wartime week. He remembered little of life before the war. Why should he? War had bred him, then killed his father, killed his mother.

Jury came up from a confusion of tunnel that reminded him of the flights to an air-raid shelter to a network of streets beneath the deadly Hammersmith flyover. In its bleakness the street looked war-torn. Scraps of newspapers, discarded tin cans, a savaged cat—all appeared to be the detritus from the last concert blown out from the doors of the Hammersmith Odeon, right down to the battered cat slinking alleywise past the announcement of Sirocco and three other groups, together with their warm-up bands. Sirocco didn't need a warm-up. There was the picture of Charles Raine that had appeared on the cover of *Time Out* magazine. The fresh poster had been crookedly pasted over the faded. Yesterday's concert was like yesterday's news.

SIROCCO rode in two-foot-high black letters on the white marquee, where a young man on a very high ladder was making a slight artistic change; the S was tilted and from its end shot a narrow black line. Jury supposed that the effect was to make it look wind-whipped.

The man climbed slowly down; he was a lad really, probably nineteen or so, wiped his dirty hands on a towel that he stuffed in the rear pocket of his jeans, all the while backing up and looking at his handiwork. Another boy, probably about this one's age, and carrying what looked like three or four instrument cases and a black amp, had crossed the street and was apparently asking directions as he hitched one of the two gig bags more comfortably over his shoulder. He wiped his windblown hair out of his face, pushed his Silva-thin sunglasses back on his nose and entered through a pair of double doors.

The artist of the marquee-board walked backward to get a better look at his artistry and nearly stepped on Jury's feet. "Oh, sorry." Then, as if Jury had come for the same reason, as adviser or overseer of this enterprise, the kid said to him, "Think it adds a bit of class, right?" He shook his longish hair from his forehead and folded his arms across his chest, hands clamped under his armpits.

"It's ingenious. Especially that line that trails off from the bottom of the S. How'd you do that?"

"With three I's, flat down. Hard to do tricky stuff with a marquee, I can tell you. See, I was trying to get the idea of a wind blowing through the name. That's what it means, you know—'sirocco'—a wind blowing," he added instructively. A stiff wind gusted from the alley the cat had bellied along, a good omen, perhaps. They both shivered. "Bleedin' cold. I been out here over an hour working on that lot. Think they'll like it, then?"

Jury smiled. "Absolutely."

"You come for tickets? Been sold out since it was announced. Listen: I'll give you a tip. Come round on Friday, day of performance, ten A.M. The doors are open, but returns don't go on sale until twelve. Mary Lee, though, she keeps back five, maybe six in case some nob comes along." The boy's laugh was wheezy. "A couple did once. I think they were some duke's kids. Mary Lee really kept 'em on the ropes. I think she permed her hair while they hung around the window looking like they had to pee. After you." With a grand gesture he opened the door.

"Thanks. And thanks for the tip."

The boy waved and hustled across the big lobby and took the wide stairs two at a time. Jury looked round at the emptiness and pictured what a crush it would be two nights from then. The deserted lobby still had that gummy smell of packed bodies, sweat, and beer. Breathing must be difficult. Did Wiggins really go to these concerts? He craned his neck upward to gaze at the huge, open circle over whose railing hundreds of beery smiles would look down on that night. And farther up in space to a baroque ceiling that brought his fancy back to those long-ago afternoons. The picture palace.

"We're sold out!" The childishly nasal voice pulled Jury from his fancies of picture palaces and he turned and saw a youngish woman with a haircut that looked done by a lawn mower on burnt grass hitting a cold-drink machine. Her face looked as parched as her hair, as if this mirage of a machine was the only thing that would keep her from dying of thirst.

"Mary Lee?"

That *did* surprise her out of her rotten mood, at least long enough to ask, "Who're you?"

Instead of answering, Jury walked over to the machine and with a hand on each side tried to sway it a little. The can plonked down into the opening. Mary Lee made a little sound, popped the cap, and then arranged her miniskirted thighs and scoop-necked sweater to their best advantage. "Well, wherever'd you learn that?"

"From when I was broke."

"How'd you know me?" Mary Lee glanced up from the Coke can she was licking her tongue around and slowly blinked her sand-colored lashes.

Poor girl, she could have done with a bit of lipstick for some color. But at least there was some glitter in the hoop earrings and the rhinestone-studded locket that lay strategically placed above the cleavage. "Friend told me you more-or-less managed the place. I just wanted a look round."

From the way she ran her long pearlescent fingernails through her half-cropped hair and tried to look like a manager, it was clear she hardly knew what to do with this information—she certainly didn't want to out-and-out deny it. "Well, I expect I wouldn't say *that,* exactly. I'm more his assistant. I can't *auth*-or-ize you going over the place. Inside's about as pretty as an airplane hangar. Whatcha want to see it for? The roadies are in there anyways, setting up. For Sirocco." Her eyes glinted like the shiny aluminum of the can. "All I want's to meet Charlie."

"Do you get to meet the stars who come here?"

"I did Eric Clapton. I nearly shook for a week." Realizing the persona might be slipping, she added, "Of course, there aren't many like him. Most are pretty run-of-the-mill."

The door to the auditorium opened and the young man, one of the "roadies" upon whom she cast an experienced and disdainful look, came through and walked over to the soft-drink machine.

As he was about to put in a coin, she called, "That's for staff, if you *don't* mind. You got your own up in the dressing rooms."

He turned, surprised, looked a little helpless, and Jury recognized him as the same person who'd passed by them under the marquee. "Sorry," he said and retreated into the auditorium.

"I don't know why they're mucking about here a day ahead of time."

"Do they use the place for practice sessions?"

"*Them?* Wouldn't be caught dead outside their *suite* at the Ritz. I expect when you're that famous you don't need to do sessions. Ever so handsome, ihn't he?"

"Who? The chap that just walked out here?"

"*No.* Charlie Raine. He's single, too."

She sighed, looked down at her obviously new shoes, and lifted an ankle. "Do you like them? Paid nearly thirty quid

for these ones and *that* was sale price." She brought the
ankle down and drew the other one in straight and bent her
head to stare at them appreciatively. "Look like glass, don't
they?"

Not precisely. More like acrylic, the uppers clear, the high
heels smoke-toned, and the ankle straps thin slivers of
acrylic dotted with tiny beads to match the heels. "Beautiful," said Jury. "They're very smart; you'd have to pay twice
that for the ones I saw in the window of—" Jury thought for
a moment. "—Fortnum and Mason."

"You never." Mary Lee breathed this out in a whispery
way.

Jury couldn't, actually, remember the last time he'd
looked in the windows of Fortnum and Mason. Much too
pricey. Yet people actually bought produce there: carrots,
lettuces, cabbages, kings, no doubt. But he merely nodded
his head solemnly.

Mary Lee turned at the sound of the telephone, disgusted,
and started off on swaying ankles to the ticket window to
answer, then came back quickly and whispered, "Look, you
just want a deco, go on in. But don't tell no one, okay?" She
gave him a wink and hurried toward the repeated *brr brr*.

That morning, before taking the tube to Hammersmith,
the first thing he had done was to start his search for the
copy of *Time Out* that he hadn't been able to find before he
went to sleep on the sofa, fully clothed.

Jury fingered through stacks of spilled magazines and papers, turned over cushions, flayed the sheets on the bed,
vandalized drawers and cupboards. If the place had been a
mess before, it was now a shambles. And he knew all the
while the search was useless; the magazine had been on top
of that pile . . . Carole-anne . . . of course.

Jury yanked off his jacket and pulled a heavy sweater over
his head, dark brown with a sort of lopsided moose woven
into its woolly strands. It was a present from Carole-anne,

who seemed to be as interested in dressing him down as she was in dressing Mrs. Wassermann up.

Down the stone front steps and right to a smaller set of steps leading to Mrs. Wassermann's basement flat Jury ran.

At his first knock, she opened the door and threw up her hands as if she'd just been delivered from a family of thieves. "At last, at last you are back." The hands then clasped beneath her chin in a gesture of thanks to the angels.

But this Mrs. Wassermann was not quite the one he'd left. Her gray hair was frizzed out with a new perm that did not strike Jury as a viable alternative to the ordinarily neat, pulled-back hair tucked in a bun at the nape of the neck. Carole-anne had obviously been raiding his flat and commandeering Mrs. Wassermann round the beauty salons. But he merely smiled and complimented her on the wave.

"No, no. *Not* a perm, Mr. Jury. It's scrunched."

"I beg your pardon?"

"Scrunched. Sassoon. They only scrunch and diffuse." She waved her hand back and forth slowly, in simulation of a hair-dryer. "No brushes, just diffusion. Sassoon believes in letting the hair be natural."

Jury leaned against the doorjamb. "Tell me, did Carole-anne sit in for some scrunching, too? Or some diffusion?"

"Oh, no. Not with *her* hair. Sassoon said it was so glorious just to let it be." Mrs. Wassermann made it sound as if Vidal himself had been in attendance.

"Of course. Well, do you think I could have the extra key to the Glorious One's flat?"

"Of course, of course." She turned to her bookshelves. "It's right behind Mr. le Carré."

Mrs. Wassermann always referred to her books by the surnames of the authors. Miss Austen. Mr. Dickens. Miss Krantz.

She placed the key in his hand and asked for no information in return. It was Mrs. Wassermann's great virtue; she never intruded with questions. She was the greatest respecter of privacy he had ever known. Too bad Miss Palutski didn't take a page from that book.

"I wish she'd stop using my room as if it were a waiting lounge between flights."

"Ah, yes, but you know she cannot afford to be on the phone."

"Why should she? She's on mine. And I wish she'd stop taking things. I had a copy of *Time Out* and I need it."

"Oh, *that*. I have it right here . . ." She swept away again. "She thought I should know what's going on around town."

That boded ill. "Thanks, Mrs. Wassermann . . ."

"Do not be too upset with Carole-anne, Mr. Jury. You know she's been under great stress lately."

Jury turned back, his foot on the steps leading upward. "Yes, she was going totally crazy when I left."

Mrs. Wassermann lowered her eyelids and made a tch-tching with her tongue as if he were speaking ill of the dead.

Looking grave, Mrs. Wassermann said, "No, she does not read her maps—"

Her maps? Everything seemed to come under Carole-anne's provenance, including the Atlantic. She shouldn't be reading the Tarot and telling fortunes down at the Starrdust; she should join up with whatever Balboas and Byrds were still around.

"—and she has grown very dismal."

"Dismal. No, *that* I'll never believe." Crazy, yes. Dismal, no. He was happy her obsession was only with maps and the schedules of the ferries from Cork and Belfast. What dangerous waters she was charting on her way to Atlantis, he couldn't imagine; he only knew that Carole-anne would skim across seas with total confidence, and God save the sharks.

"She's down-in-the-mouth, Mr. Jury. You should see her, cheer her up. It must be that she didn't get that part she'd been working so hard on."

Carole-anne had been, he thought, extremely vague about

this acting "part," except that she was doing a good bit of practicing blindness. White cane, tapping, face held slightly askew, eyes attempting to glaze over.

This (Jury thought, smiling inwardly again) was impossible. The lapis-lazuli eyes attempting to appear expressionless and empty—that would be too much for anyone, much less a part-time actress with a limited repertoire.

Actually, Carole-anne was a full-time actress with a vast repertoire, the result merely of being Carole-anne. It was extremely difficult to get down to some central core of being with the girl. Woman. Young lady. He was never sure; her age kept changing.

"Thanks." He saluted Mrs. Wassermann with the rolled-up magazine. "I'll see her."

Charlie Raine was, apparently, quite well known for his ability to avoid interviews and evade the media.

Jury read the article on Sirocco, went back and read it again. Then he read it a third time. The other members of the band—Alvaro Jiminez, Caton Rivers, a towering John Swann (sex symbol, and he knew it), the drummer, Wes Whelan—all of them had been interviewed, all of them had made comments. Jiminez scored top points for genuineness and intelligence. Swann scored only monosyllabic, self-aggrandizing points, like a man playing tennis with himself. Whelan and Rivers were fairly quiet. But Charlie Raine hadn't even been in the hotel suite, and the reporter-cum-pseudo-critic wasn't at all happy about that.

Thus the only information the reader could get about one of their lead guitarists and vocalists was whatever the others said. It was clear Jiminez was far more reliable than someone like Swann, who was being upstaged all over the place. Not even that double-necked guitar he kept on display could convince anyone that he was the main man in this outfit.

If anyone was, it was Alvaro Jiminez, the original organizer of the band, a black man from the Delta, a master of blues. Whelan was a Dubliner, Rivers from Chicago, and

Swann and Raine were British. A strange assortment, the interviewer said (with all the grace of a double-dose of *Whicker's World*). No one took him up on "assortment"; no one enlightened him as to how they'd come together. Jiminez said, "We just done fall into each other's arms."

Nor could anyone answer the jackpot question: Why was Charlie Raine leaving the band? "I expect—" (Jury smiled, sure Jiminez would leave off the *t*) "—Charlie, he just want to."

And the future of the band?

"Same as the past, mate," Swann had said (offensively, according to the thin-skinned reporter).

In various poses of self-indulgence or insouciance, they were photographed in their roughed-up clothes and booted feet, lounging in their suite at the Ritz.

It was a soppy, sappy interview. Jury liked the band, even Swann, in some old-fashioned pasteboard-hero sort of way. At least all of them were in concert when it came to this interview.

Jury put aside the magazine and folded his hands behind his head, sitting down low on his sofa. No, they'd said, they *didn't* know why Charlie was quitting. No, again. They hadn't a clue.

Jury thought he might.

28

Jury went through the middle of the set of double doors. The auditorium was empty except for a man to his right in one of the mixing bays. Sound engineer, he supposed, for Sirocco. The fellow barely grazed Jury with a glance, obviously too intent on his equipment to bother with who should or shouldn't be here. More likely, he thought Jury was one of the Odeon's staff. He probably didn't care one way or the other; his interest was the long bank of equipment, with its complex of knobs, levers, buttons, and slightly glowing lights that made Jury think of a starship.

Mary Lee's appraisal of the auditorium was as far off the mark as one could get. Far from resembling an airplane hangar or warehouse, it still held on to the remnants of its old Art Deco splendor. Probably the lighting fixtures weren't the originals, but it was hard to tell.

The distance from the center of the stage to where he was standing at the rear must have been eighty or ninety feet, and the entire stage was probably as much in width. It must have had the largest proscenium arch in all of London, he thought.

A phalanx of lights had been set up on the side and overhead a couple of technicians were working on the huge lighting strut, two or three dozen lights positioned in lines along steel bands. High up as it was, it seemed a precarious perch for the workers, unless they were trapeze artists. The big strut swayed there, twenty feet or so above the stage. They finished what they were doing, climbed down, and disappeared off to the right. Jury could see part of a metal staircase that must lead to private rooms up on the level above.

One of the humpers came in, deposited another amplifier, walked out through the stage door off to the right. It was out there that Jury had seen the vans parked.

The only one of the road crew left on the stage now was trailing some sort of cable along the side of the stage and pulling a microphone—there were five of them—over to center stage and out toward the edge. It was the fellow Mary Lee had warned off the soft-drink machine. He adjusted the mike and gave his attention to a voice that must have issued from the steps on the right. All Jury could hear was something about "lights."

The young man's answer was a laugh and a "What for?" Then he shaded his eyes and looked toward the rear of the theater—Jury thought at first he was about to get thrown out—but the fellow on the stage was apparently directing his attention to the other one in the mixing bay. The sound man raised his hand as a sign.

He picked a guitar from one of the cases, drew the strap across his shoulder, and moved into a classic introduction to a Spanish song that Jury thought he remembered as a Segovia number.

Mary Lee hadn't recognized him and it was her chief object in life to meet him. As he listened to the staccato picking and arpeggiated runs of the song, Jury thought that anonymity was not that hard to come by. Here this lad had come face-to-face with someone who had seen his picture again and again and she hadn't twigged it. Even in the context of the theater he was performing in the next night, still he'd gone unrecognized. It was perhaps not so astonishing, after all. You see what you expect to see, and you don't expect to see the lead guitarist of a famous rock group humping his own equipment or trying to get himself a Coke when a half-dozen minions—not to mention Mary Lee herself—would crawl on their knees for the privilege of supplying him with whatever he needed. And you certainly wouldn't expect to see him without the rest of his band.

And there was nothing about him that said *star.* Not his appearance (jeans and a washed-out denim shirt), not his stage presence. Rather remarkably (Jury thought) not his stage presence. Charlie Raine didn't seem to have what Wiggins and Macalvie had called "attitude." It wasn't attitude that made this classical Spanish piece take wing. The guitar might as well have been playing him rather than the other way round.

It was plain, raw exposure. He had to be more accurate and more precise than if he'd been playing electric; like nerve endings, every note was exposed.

The notes seemed to crystallize in the air, long notes arced out and kicked back and into a lightning riff, like tracer bullets, so that Jury felt he was caught in some sort of crossfire.

The music was fluid and frenetic at the same time. The piece stopped, suddenly, with a thunderous succession of sustained chords.

When the echoes stopped, Jury had the strange sensation of standing in a vacuum, air sucked out of the auditorium, walls about to collapse inward.

Charlie Raine unstrapped the guitar and returned it to its case, unbuttoned his shirt and wiped face and hair down with the shirttails. Then he pulled another guitar from another case and attached the strap to that one. It was white as blanched bone and almost glowed in the semidarkness. He attached the cord from it to one of a trail of black boxes, strummed a few chords, started making adjustments.

Quietly, Jury pushed open the nearby bay door just enough to look out into the long lobby. There was no sign of Mary Lee. Then her face appeared behind the ticket window, looking less bored than lost. Framed in the small opening, the face appeared smaller, pinched, even; and without anyone to impress it upon or intimidate it with, considerably sadder and more vulnerable. Jury let the door whish shut

behind him and went to slot coins into the drink machine.
He grabbed up the Coke can and turned to see that Mary
Lee had looked up sharply from her magazine. Jury mo-
tioned her over.

She disappeared from the window and came out through
the door to her "office," feigning again that old look of
world-weariness. "You still here?"

"Come on."

She frowned. "Come on *where?* I got me accounts to do."

"You didn't hear that?"

"Hear what?"

Jury shoved the Coke into her hand and took her arm.
And she, too surprised by this manhandling (and probably
liking it), let herself be pushed into the auditorium. She did
make a mumbled protest having to do with losing her fucking job—

"Be quiet."

He didn't have to tell her twice.

Jury tried to pull her down into the back-row seat beside
him, but she just stood there in the aisle, open-mouthed,
transfixed by the stage, the singer, the song. She was leaning
sideways, as if the gravitational pull that had bent her toward the seat was not strong enough to contend with the
force of her discovery. Holding the can, and in that odd
listing, she was like a subject in a hypnotic trance who might
keep one arm raised in the air for hours.

Charlie Raine's voice was like his guitar, each word
clearly articulated. It filled the huge, hollow room and reminded Jury of the clear sound one got from tapping crystal.

> *and yesterday's sun*
> *have all begun*
> *to fade*

Charlie did not have one of those killer voices like Otis
Redding or Presley, the sort that punch out an audience
with one note or phrase. But what got to Jury was the

sincerity, the *tone* that Wiggins had rabbited on about in
that argument with Macalvie that Jury had only half-heard.
Even Jury's uneducated ear could pick up the total emotion
that was going into this singing.

> *I watch the streetlamp down below*
> *I watch you turn, I watch you go*
> *away*
> *under yesterday's sky*

The feeling contained in the song was beyond words. It
was as if the song served as a window to some expansive
vista one hadn't raised the curtain on before. Charlie was
transparent; he was accessible. And Jury bet it was this quality that must knock out his listeners.

> *and when the leaves are blowing down the lane*
> *I know I'll see your image through*
> *yesterday's rain*
> *yesterday's rain*
> *yesterday's rain.*

It had certainly knocked out Mary Lee. She was crying in
the way he'd seen children cry sometimes, silently unaware
of the tears that dropped like waterbeads onto the top of the
can of Coke that she had clamped in her hands.

Jury got out his handkerchief, but she was still spell-
bound, even after that final chord had wavered out on the
tremolo. "Come on," he said, wiping her face for her. "He's
packing up."

When Mary Lee realized that Jury meant she was to follow him down the aisle to the stage, she became even more
fixed, immobile. Except for her head, which shook and
shook, no, no, no. The fellow in the mixing bay was gone,
probably to kick the Coke machine or go to the toilet. She
had drawn her pale lips in, clamped them shut, as if making
sure nothing would explode from her mouth. All she was

able to do was make a steady *ummmmmmmm*-ing sound like a vibrating guitar string.

Jury put his hand on her arm and gave it a little tug. He knew that later, she'd never forgive herself if she missed this chance. "I'll do the talking. You can just look at him."

At this she relented, caving in from the temptation of it all. She wobbled down the aisle after Jury on her new heels and her shaky legs.

"You're Charlie Raine?"

He turned in surprise, laden down with his two guitars, portable amp, and two small black metal boxes. He came over to the apron of the stage and looked down, squinting. "Yes. Why?"

Jury brought out his warrant card, hard to get to because Mary Lee was standing behind him, nearly melding herself to his back. He brought it out. "My name's Richard Jury. Metropolitan police." He said nothing about C.I.D., decided to let Charlie Raine think Drug Squad and then felt ashamed of himself for beginning this ridiculous lie. But if he wanted to talk to him, it seemed simpler. And he would have no reason otherwise to talk to him any more than one of Charlie's fans.

Charlie flicked a glance at the ID, his handsome face still and serious. He looked at Jury. "You didn't like my tunes?"

His smile was so high-voltage that it seemed literally to pull Mary Lee from behind the wall of Jury's back.

"This is Mary Lee," said Jury. He didn't even know her last name.

Charlie said hello and held out his hand. It was met by the Coca-Cola can in Mary Lee's. He looked from it to her.

"I brought it for you," she blurted out quickly, adding, "I'm sorry."

He understood the apology. "Thanks, Mary Lee." With his shirttail he mopped the water from the top and popped it open. Took a swig, frowned slightly.

Jury wondered if it tasted like tears. "I did like your tunes. Your music. Very much."

"What's this about, then? I've done something—?"

"I wondered if you'd heard any talk?"

He frowned, shook his head, no, he hadn't. He turned away to pick up the gig bag.

"We been having trouble, see." This came, surprisingly, from Mary Lee. Finding her voice still worked, apparently, she stepped away from Jury's protective side and embroidered: "Found a stash of coke—a kilogram, it was—up in the projection room."

Jury could not look at her, so strong was his desire to laugh. Why Mary Lee was going along with this charade— indeed, that she was swift enough to know it was a game— could only be answered by her desire to prolong the encounter. Or it might have been a desire to let him know she wasn't just any old blathering fan, but someone in a position of authority.

"Sorry. Like I said, I don't know anything about drugs. I'm not a user."

Her eyes widened. "Oh, we didn't mean that; I mean, I can tell one from miles away. But look: if your band does get any news about something going down—"

Something going down? Jury bit his lip.

"—tell me direct, okay? Don't talk to no one else." She paused, shrugged, tossed Jury a bone. "Except maybe *him*."

"I'll do that."

"Another thing . . ." Mary Lee's voice arpeggiated upward on a scale of eighth notes: "I was wondering, might I have your autograph?"

"Sure." Charlie smiled and nearly short-circuited her frenetic search for a bit of paper to write on. When Jury saw her bend down he was afraid she was going to rip the hem off her petticoat.

She reached out her high-heeled shoe to Charlie. "Here."

He laughed shortly, baffled. "Wait, it'd ruin your shoes. I

must have something . . ." But he had nothing in his pockets.

Jury had been about to get out his notebook and didn't. The intensity of Mary Lee's transaction stopped him.

"It's okay. Never mind. These ones are old; I hardly wear them."

Jury did reach over his pen to Charlie, who still seemed uncertain. "I don't think the ink will hold on the clear stuff—"

"That's all right, then. If it don't, I'll find something else," she said reasonably and watched with fascination as he carefully inked up the top of the shoe. He handed it back.

Mary Lee took it carefully, as if it were really glass. She said nothing, only looked down at the inscription. Beside her, Jury read it, too: *To Mary Lee's shoe. Charlie Raine.*

It was too much for her. Without a word Mary Lee turned and limped up the aisle into the shadows.

"Can I give you a lift to your hotel?" asked Jury.

Humping the gig bag over one shoulder Charlie said, "Thanks. But I was only just going to the pub round the corner. Haven't eaten all day. Care to join?"

"I could use a pint myself."

Charlie Raine turned up the wattage of his smile. "We can talk about drugs."

Jury carried the flanger and the delay-box—which, according to Charlie he used when he wanted distortion. The lecture on heavy distortion was pretty much lost on Jury. He was wondering about that comment on drugs.

"Because you're not the Drug Squad," Charlie said in answer to Jury's question inside the pub. "You're C.I.D."

Jury was getting the drinks, Charlie was standing at the steam table and food counter, absorbed by the large bowls of salads and rice that a girl with rusty red hair was busily covering with wrap.

The pub was a plain one, deal tables and chairs, long bar

whose only color and decoration were supplied by the rows
of bottles ranged on shelves. No handsome mirrors, no
mock Tiffany shades. But there were a number of framed
posters and pictures of musicians who'd probably played at
the Odeon.

Indeed, directly behind the food counter and the back of
the aproned girl was the by now well-known poster of the
Sirocco band.

She drew herself up, hands on hips. "It's gone two. No
food after two o'clock." She turned icy blue eyes on both of
them.

"You can't just do a ploughman's? Something cold?"

Her sigh was overwhelming, the roll of her eyes toward
the heavens the signal to God that she was a true martyr to
her job. "And what's so funny, I'd like to know?"

This was directed at Jury, who was standing at the bar
watching the porky bartender draw the pints. He had looked
up at the poster behind her, laughed, and shaken his head.

"If I were you," said Jury, "I'd give him what he wants."
His tone was mildly threatening.

It fueled her martyrdom. "If you was *me* . . . well, you
ain't, not from where I stand." Hands on hips she swiveled
from one to the other of them, displaying the hips to their
best advantage. "So where d'ya get off coming in here and
telling me—"

"Police," said Jury. He shoved his warrant card near her
face.

Under the bronze makeup, her face paled as if a mask
were sliding off. "Well, I *never* . . . oh . . ." And she set
about uncovering the cheese plate and whacking off a chunk.
Not, however, before she'd given them a dismissive wave as
if it weren't that she was scared, but that the meal was being
prepared out of her infinite largess.

Look up, Jury silently commanded her. She didn't. Charlie was looking at the face in the poster as if it belonged to
somebody else, only mildly interesting.

* * *

Sitting at a table scratched and coal-bitten by cigarette stubs Jury said to Charlie, "C.I.D. You're pretty observant."

Charlie shook his head, watched Jury over the rim of his pint of lager, said, "No. I didn't get it from your ID; it was your name."

Jury looked over at the huge poster, apparently useless as identification, and smiled. "I'm so famous?"

Charlie didn't return the smile. "I read the papers, see—"

The redhead, still haughty and tight-lipped, set Charlie's plate before him. But she did hover a bit, looking at him more studiously.

"Thanks," said Charlie.

"You're most welcome, I'm sure." The edge of sarcasm had crept back in. She rolled off, hips swaying like a sailor who hadn't found his land legs. Her own legs were in no way, however, of being lost.

"Does this happen to you often?"

"What happen?" Charlie was arranging some cheese on a piece of dark bread.

"Not being recognized? She's trying to work out where she'd seen you before and that poster's right over her flaming head."

"Happens a lot." He put a pickled onion on top of the cheese, bit down. "Recognize Alvaro more than the rest of us. But he's big and he's black. I mean, I don't think Hendrix would've been able to walk down the street without people pawing him and collapsing and . . . Or Elvis. I'm just a face in the crowd. It's nice."

"You say you read the papers—"

"Your name was right there. That murder up in Yorkshire. What happens when a policeman's the witness?"

"Nothing much. Like any other witness."

"I'll bet." Charlie put a hunk of crumbly Cheshire on another thick piece of bread, stuck on some Branston pickle, and tried to work his mouth round the clumsy sandwich. All the while he was casting glances at Jury with solder-

colored, expressionless eyes. Strangely so, given the light
they had projected back in the theater. It was as if the tints
of an impressionist painting had vanished, fled from a Mo-
net, perhaps, recalled to be used elsewhere. Jury doubted the
smile bestowed on Mary Lee was ever put to much use.

Jury had never felt so totally off-guard. The comment
about the murder was the last thing he had expected.

They both seemed to be waiting for the other to give out
with information—some signal, some clue—like poker players.

Jury called. "You've been in London for two days to give
a concert and your mind's on some obscure killing in the
West of Yorkshire?" He smiled slightly.

"I just thought it was interesting. Scotland Yard detective
as witness. You saw the whole thing."

"Yes." Jury added nothing.

"I expect you're not to talk about it?"

"What did you want to know?"

"Me?" The eyes opened wider. "Nothing." When Jury
didn't comment, he added, "Well, I expect I was interested
because I was born up there. Leeds. But you probably know
that."

"Why would I know that?"

"You're a fan." His attempt at a smile was depressing.
Jury thought his picking up the paper napkin to wipe his
mouth had more to do with wiping away the false smile.

Jury looked over to the food counter. The fiery-haired girl
was standing there, legs crossed, smoking a fag, and still
trying to sort it out. *A regular customer? Don't be stupid,
girl. You know the regulars. A busker, maybe. He has that
guitar. That could be it. Passed him in the Hammersmith
station. No, that wasn't it.* In an irritated little gesture she
flicked ash from the cigarette, recrossed her ankles, went
back to staring at Charlie Raine.

Jury could read her mind; he wished he could read Charlie's. "I think it was—a great tragedy, that killing."

Charlie returned the uneaten portion of his sandwich to

the plate, looking at it as if it were an obscure memory, some detail from the past he couldn't fit in. Then he reached into his jeans pocket and brought out some coins, got up, headed for the jukebox.

He hung there for a while, hands splayed on glass front, looking down. By the time he came back to the table, a voice both rich and ragged had started singing, *I was born . . . by a little old river . . ."* The *born* was sustained in some time warp of the singer's imagination; it was a thrilling voice.

"Otis Redding," said Charlie. He sat back, tilting his chair, looking past Jury at nothing. Then he said, "His plane went down over Wisconsin; only twenty-six, he was."

"How old are you? Twenty, twenty-one?"

"Twenty-three. Why?"

"Because you're quitting." Jury didn't expect any answer but the same one Charlie had given Jiminez.

He was surprised, then, when Charlie shoved his plate back and said, "I've gone as far as I want to go." He shifted sideways on the bench, put one grimy Reebok up, and laid his arm across his knee. The pose was listless; he was looking over toward either the redhead or the jukebox. The girl was still washing up, still watching them, still frowning slightly. "Think she'll twig it?" He slipped a cigarette from Jury's pack, thumbed the tip of a match into flame, and inhaled deeply. "Like Otis: 'too hard living, afraid to die.' " He turned with a grim smile to look at Jury, said nothing, studied his cigarette, went on smoking.

"You're at the top, and you don't want it, when you must have worked like hell to get there. You must have practiced until your fingers bled." Jury was looking at the hand holding the cigarette, the fingers hatched with tiny marks.

Charlie said nothing.

"And then what?" asked Jury.

He shrugged. "Go home for a bit."

"To Leeds?"

"To Leeds. Find a regular gig." He looked over at Jury,

his eyes narrowed against the scrim of smoke. "Dusty answers, right?"

This time, Jury didn't comment.

"I gotta go, man."

The British accent had taken on the edge of the American and the idiom he'd been used to hearing for several years. "Who plays keyboard?" asked Jury.

That surprised Charlie at least enough to make him stop counting out pounds and pence. "Caton Rivers. Why?"

"Just wondered. Do you ever play keyboard, then?"

He stacked up the pound coins, the ten- and fivepence ones, and beckoned to the redhead. "No, not much." He zipped up his jacket, started gathering his gear together.

"Nell Healey won't get off with a lecture, you know. It took all the weight of the Citrine-Healey name—not to mention money—to keep her out of custody after she killed her husband. Now—"

He froze. "She probably had one hell of a good reason for killing him." The waitress, eyes glued to him, swept the money off the table. But Charlie didn't even see her. "And it'll be God knows how long before the trial."

Jury got up. "I'm going to Haworth tomorrow. Want a lift to Leeds?"

"Sirocco's got a concert tomorrow night. Remember?"

"I remember."

"You coming?"

"I hope so. Perhaps I can talk Mary Lee into a couple of tickets."

Charlie reached into his back pocket. "I'm sure you could, but here." He handed Jury two tickets. "Friend of mine can't make it."

Jury smiled. "I'll be mugged on the way back to the Yard. They're that hard to come by."

Charlie Raine ran his hand through his long hair. "Look—" Then his eye went past Jury to the bar. Jury followed his gaze and saw the redhead, the expression on her face, standing there, her feet together, holding the money with a sadly knowing look. "Hold this, will you."

Jury watched him walk over, look around, take one of the paper plates from the stack and the pen hooked onto her belt. He wrote, handed it to her, almost had to force it on her because she stood there, stiff and wide-eyed.

He would never, thought Jury, let anyone suffer if he could do something to stop it.

"Thanks for the beer," said Jury. "Want a lift?"

They stood looking up at the cold, hard sky. "I'm not going anywhere much. Schmooze around. I like to walk in London."

"So do I," said Jury.

29

When Jury walked into his office at New Scotland Yard, Wiggins was studiously turning the pages of an uninvitingly thick book whose bindings seemed to resist this mild assault upon a volume that had lain dormant for so long.

"Hullo, Wiggins." Jury stuck his raincoat on a peg and sat down in his chair that creaked as if it had some symbiotic relationship with the old book. Books. Three others, all equally thick, were open and the pages held down by weights that Wiggins had found at his disposal: a small ceramic pot that Jury had noticed him taking spoonsful from to put in his tea; a tin of Sucrets wedged between pages of another; a black biscuit as a bookmark. In the one he was now reading he had marked several different places with Aspergum.

"What's that? *Gray's Anatomy?*"

Wiggins favored him with a crimped smile and went back to his book, marking yet another page with a cylinder that looked like a stick of incense.

He was so deep in his research that nothing was about to make Wiggins risible.

Jury pulled his In box over and rifled through the messy collection there as Wiggins looked up politely and said he'd got several reports he must sign and, incidentally, what did the doctor say?

"Hmm? The usual." Jury signed the two papers marked Urgent and tossed them in his Out box with half the other stuff he knew was red-taping its way past his eyes. Then he swiveled round and stared out of the viewless window and thought about Charlie Raine. "Get hold of that band."

Surprised, Wiggins looked across his desk. "Band?"

"Sirocco. They're at the Ritz, aren't they?"

"Yes."

"I want to talk to them—to Jiminez."

Wiggins looked pained. "Not *Jim*-inez, yhem-*in*-ez. *Yhem.*"

"You sound like you're coughing up. Ring the hotel. Tell him I want to see him. What's wrong?"

"Nothing. Sir." Wiggins said this with a good deal of snap.

"You don't have to salute."

"They have a concert *tomorrow*."

"So what? I'm talking about today. And Morpeth Duckworth and Mavis Crewes."

Wiggins looked puzzled. "What does Sirocco have to do with the others?"

"Nothing necessarily." He had decided not to tell Wiggins about Charlie Raine. Jury couldn't be certain, after all; and the less Wiggins knew, the less Chief Superintendent Racer would be inclined to beat him to a pulp with his walking stick for mucking about in someone else's manor. God, how he hated that phrase. "I'm just a fan." Jury smiled. "Big time."

Again, Jury turned away to stare at the blank concrete the window faced on. He thought about the song. He simply hadn't realized what he'd heard. "Yesterday's Rain." He put his head in his hand, looked at the blank gray squares of the building.

He could not untangle past and present. He could not focus. "Yesterday's sun . . ." His mind went to the flat in the Fulham Road, and his six-year-old life there with his mother. He could climb on a stool and spy through a wormy peephole in his bedroom into the flat next door.

Jury half-heard Wiggins on the telephone and thought

how far from the Ritz he'd been then. He'd had tea there
once with his aunt and uncle and been overwhelmed by the
luxury of dazzling lights, deep carpets, the dancers moving
effortlessly across polished floors.

But what he thought of most when he heard music was
the scratchy record that came through the bedroom wall of
the flat next door. "Yesterdays." Not the famous Beatles
song, but another one. Whenever he'd heard the old record
in the other room play "Yesterdays," he'd quickly jumped
out of bed, stood on the stool and squinted through to see
the occupant of the other room, a girl perhaps a year older
than he named Elicia Deauville.

Elicia Deauville loved to dance to "Yesterdays." It was
either the only tune she liked, or the only record she had
(though she never played the other side). Except in these
rare and wonderful dancing moments, Elicia Deauville,
when she walked down the steps and down the street to the
school, looked like an ice-maiden. Her long, tawny hair had
been worried into a tight thick braid, then severely twisted
into a pinwheel at the back of her head, into which several
pins had been plunged like sabers. It was as if the hair were
being chastised for its beauty and bounty. Jury wondered if
her dreadful caretakers—a brassy, florid man and woman—
were truly the parents his mother had assured him they
were. His own mother was beautiful and slender and had
silky blond hair and eyes the color of his own. He adored
her and never doubted what she said, except in this particular instance.

But Elicia Deauville's true self (he was sure) showed her
as something quite other at her bedtime hour (which was
also his) when she would wind up an old Victrola and dance
to "Yesterdays."

Wearing only her white nightdress, barefooted and with
her waist-length golden-brown hair, she would move swiftly
from one end of her bedroom to the other, weaving and
bowing like a sapling in the wind, moving backward and
forward in a dancing, ballerinalike run that circumscribed

less and less space. Her body would move deliriously, her hair floating and falling like blown leaves.

It was at once an act of total abandonment and a mastery of space that he had never seen repeated. Twenty years later he had seen Margot Fonteyn and thought, *You are very, very good, but you are not Elicia Deauville.*

In the middle of the night, he had watched the blitz from behind his blackout curtain chink and seen the great cones of light shoot up, waver against the night sky and thought of Elicia Deauville. Thus he had been watching when the firebomb dropped and reduced half of his block of flats to rubble. The other half, the Deauvilles' half, had remained standing.

He had found his mother in the living room, or had found, rather, her arm, clad in black velvet, extending from under what had been the plaster of ceilings and walls. The arm was in black, the hand white, upturned in a familiar *come here* gesture.

The next day, while he sat on the remaining step outside waiting for his relatives to fetch him, he watched the small collection of cases and bags grow larger next door as the loudly clothed and loud-mouthed Deauville couple, who made him think of crazy patchwork, came and went, depositing their belongings.

Sitting there, he had taken his small pocket notebook out and written *I love you. Richard.* That had not looked right and he scrubbed heavily through it as if the same heavens that had opened up and left him without a future would do it again if they saw or heard.

I will see you yesterday. Neither did that look right, and she might guess he'd been spying on her if he knew about the song. The father stomped out and plunged down a double armful of clothes, and he saw that right on top was the white nightdress that had a tiny pocket.

Good-bye, Elicia Deauville. He folded it four times and stuffed it into the pocket.

"He said six."

"What?" Jury was studying the flame of the match he had struck to light his cigarette. "Said what?"

Wiggins looked concerned. "Alvaro Jiminez. Six o'clock he said would be all right."

"Good."

"You look very white. You should be home in bed. I can work out a program of medication for you that should have you back on your feet if you get bedrest along with it."

"Thanks, but not now."

"I think he's right, sir."

"*Who's* right? You're getting elliptical."

"Commander Macalvie."

"I'm sure he'd agree. Right about what?"

Wiggins waved his hand over the lot of books, not forgetting to pluck up one of the sticks of Aspergum. "Rotten headache," he said by way of prologue. "The bone fusion. You can't absolutely determine age by means of calculating bone fusion."

Jury leaned across his desk and squinted at Wiggins more in disbelief than because of the white arc of light slicing across his face. "Dennis Dench has a wall full of degrees—"

Chewing on his gum, Wiggins waved the wall of Dench's cavelike laboratory away. "Bones, sir, except for teeth, are good indicators, but not absolute determiners." He placed his hand on each of his four books in turn. "Here's three authorities who all say the same thing, one who doesn't. But even the one who doesn't allows some margin for error. Another interesting point is, after I had a word with the forensic anthropologist here, is that the bone of the arm can help to determine right- and left-handedness. Now, I'm only saying they can be an indication. Professor Dench didn't mention that." Wiggins removed the clay pot from one of the books, closed it, patted it, and said, "So I called him up and asked what he had in his notes about the arm bones. I asked him specifically if the bone of the right arm was longer than the left. Billy Healey, you remember, was right-handed."

"As a matter of fact, I didn't remember. Most people are."

Although Wiggins's flickering glance at his superior was not at all contemptuous, neither did it register approval. "Yes. And Dr. Dench did say that there was a small difference, that the bone of the right arm was a bit longer than the left. And then he immediately said that this would not help much, since the bones were those of a child and not fully developed."

"You look as if you don't agree."

Wiggins put his hands behind his head, tilted his chair, and studied the ceiling before he handed down his decision. It was a pose that Jury recognized as one he himself often affected. "What I wonder is, why would he be so quick to try and prove me wrong?"

Jury rose from his chair and walked over to the small window that gave out onto the cheerless scene of the three other sides of the building and the courtyard below. "Perhaps because he's been at the top of his field for twenty years."

"We all make mistakes, sir."

Jury looked up at a patch of white sky. Wiggins, like Death, was the great leveler.

"What I think, sir, is that his judgment might be clouded, as happens to all of us, you must admit . . ."

Jury turned, noting the suggestive pause. "Yes?"

"Well, it could be a blind spot. In this case, Commander Macalvie could be the spot. Dench has known him for ages. They're both experts in their own ways. I don't think Dr. Dench wants Mr. Macalvie coming up with a conclusion that makes more sense than Dench's own. You must admit that's possible."

Looking down into the small square, Jury nodded. "And you think my blind spot is Billy Healey."

There was a brief silence. "Well, it's understandable. I think you don't want the boy to have been Billy Healey, that's true."

It was getting dark, and whatever leftover light there was had drained away from the courtyard down there, the high-walled building blocking it. Jury felt his stomach go queasy, drop. "I don't want it to have been *any* boy, Wiggins."

He turned to see Wiggins redden slightly as he dipped a plastic spoon into the small pot of honey mixture. "No, of course not. The thing is this, though." He looked up to make sure that he might be allowed to continue.

"Go on. You've done a good job. What's that stuff?"

Wiggins's anodynes were just the ticket for glossing over difficult moments.

"It's this dry cough. Honey, ginger, and lemon juice and a little water. It's absolutely the only thing that'll stop it." He stirred this remedy up in the ceramic pot. "The thing is that *if* you think Mr. Macalvie's whole idea about the date of the death, the proximity to the Citrine house, the disused grave-yard makes sense, then *if* the skeleton isn't the Healey boy's, whose is it? It can't be Toby Holt's because he was killed five weeks later in London. So that would mean there'd have to be a *third* boy somewhere between, say, eleven and fifteen around there, and that's too much of a coincidence, surely."

"And Macalvie's already checked that . . . did you?"

"Naturally."

"Nil?"

"Nil."

"You rang up Macalvie?"

"I did."

"And what's his theory?"

"The same. He's always thought it was Billy Healey." Wiggins's mouth pursed in his version of a smile. "He seemed a bit pleased that I faced down Professor Dench."

"Didn't it *bother* Commander Macalvie that all possibilities have been ruled out?"

"No."

" 'First we get to the truth, *then* sort out what it means.' He said something like that," Jury suggested.

" 'Shoot first, ask questions later,' I believe his words were."

"Like any gunslinger."

Jury had gone back to his desk and sat down heavily, largely oblivious to the stacks of files awaiting his inspection. "Macalvie's wrong."

Wiggins had been giving exploratory taps to his chest with his fist. Cough gone. But voice tense. "You say that as if you're quite sure."

Wiggins sat there, waiting, Jury knew, for some explanation of his superior's pigheaded behavior. "We'll talk about it later. This Stanley Keeler—"

With the injured look that always lay just beneath the surface, Wiggins said, "Stan Keeler. My eardrums will never forget him. I don't know how the landlady sticks it, except she's convinced he's some sort of Polish spy. She's big as a hoarding, nearly. I expect you'd have to be to stand up to all of those tremors."

"I want to talk to him, too. About Roger Healey."

"Suit yourself." Wiggins shut the book on osteoanatomy as if he were shutting the door on the case. "But you'll have to wear earplugs."

"Thought you said he was lying quietly on the floor during your encounter."

"He had his head on a tire." Wiggins was beginning to prefer elliptical statements, inscrutable answers.

"He was lying on the floor with his head on a tire?"

"Thassrigh," said Wiggins, duck-honking into his handkerchief. "With a Labrador. Big."

"Duckworth. I want to see him too."

Wiggins asked gravely, "Did you do your research into rock music?"

"Piles of it. What's this?" He'd just seen a pink telephone message in the Out box. "Riving——" He shut his eyes.

"Yes, sir. Miss Rivington from Long Piddleton. Where Mr. Plant lives. About an hour ago. Is something wrong?"

"No." He reached in his billfold, plucked out a ten-pound

note, reached it out to Wiggins. "Go get me some flowers."
He thought for a moment. "Tiger lilies. Something green
and brown. And toss in some white roses. There's a shop
down the street."

"That's a strange combination, sir. I don't know any
brown flower. And, anyway, you'd have to wire them . . .
sir!" Wiggins rose immediately, seeing his superior's expression.

Two days. The day after tomorrow. How could he have
been so damned stupid as to forget. "Of course I didn't
forget, Vivian. How could I have forgotten?"

"Easily," said Vivian. Her voice sounded forlorn. She
quickly picked up its tempo. "I mean, with everything that
happened to you. Your picture was in the papers. I expect
you have to testify."

"No, probably not."

"It won't keep you from seeing me off, then?"

"Never. Nothing would keep me from seeing you off. I
simply wish you weren't *going* off." He might have opened
with a lie, but this was certainly the truth. He was standing
with the receiver in his hand, looking up again at the patch
of dirty winter sky. *And sometimes I think of high windows/
The sun's*— Yesterday's sun.

"What? What did you say?"

He must have spoken aloud without realizing it. "I was
just thinking of a message I wrote a long time ago."

"What was it?"

"To a girl who loved to dance to an old Jerome Kern song
called 'Yesterdays.' " Jury asked, "Was it always better? Yesterday, I mean. There've been so many songs written about
it."

Vivian was silent for a moment. "Perhaps it was. Or perhaps it will be," she added sadly. "I'm sorry about the girl."

"I was only six." He tried to bring some lightness to this
little confession.

"Then that's sadder." She paused. "The train leaves at

eleven in the morning. The morning after tomorrow." Her tone was tentative, as if she didn't really believe he'd be there. "Victoria. I think."

Jury smiled. "The Orient Express always leaves from Victoria."

"Oh. Marshall and I are coming up to London. . . . Where's Melrose? I can't find Melrose."

Her voice was distant, as if she'd been talking away from the telephone, looking about the room, hoping to find Melrose. Hell, had Melrose Plant forgotten, too?

"Where *is* everybody?" She wept into the silence.

Quickly, Jury said, "Vivian, he's in Haworth. He stopped off there on his way back from Harrogate."

"For what?"

"He was tired, I expect. If you'd just driven Agatha over a hundred miles, wouldn't you be?" At least, she laughed at that. "I think his idea was just to stay the week until he had to collect her, rather than drive all the way back again." Before she could reflect on the location of the Old Silent, he went on lying. "Look, I'll ring him up and tell him to call you immediately. I think he said they were having trouble with the telephone service—"

"That's very good."

" 'Good'?" He heard the smile in her voice.

"That tale. Just as long as you're both there, Richard. Tell him he's forgiven."

"Forgiven—?" But she'd already hung up.

Eight years, and now she was going off to marry some smirking Italian, and it was the first time he'd heard her call him Richard.

2

"A friend gave them to me," said Jury. "Get-well gift."
He cradled the massive bunch of flowers Wiggins had
brought back and looked deadpan across Chief Superintendent Racer's desk.

Sergeant Wiggins was perched on the edge of the leather
sofa; Fiona (who'd been called in to search for Cyril) was
busy pinning a white rose from the bouquet into her plung-
ing neckline, thereby enhancing the cleavage even more.
"Still look pale to me, you do."

Wiggins agreed: "Bedrest, I told him, and proper medication—"

"Oh, *stop* it," shouted Racer. "He's about as sick as that
pint-sized panther that's lurking in here." He raised his head
slightly, as if he were sniffing the air. Then his head popped
below the surface of his desk, his voice coming back to them
hollow and brandy-soaked. "Where is he?" His head came
up again. "Stop fooling with that damned rose and *find* him,
Miss Clingmore. As for *you*—" Racer pointed his finger,
thumb turned in gun-wise, at Jury's chest. "*You* are finished.
That's the ugliest bunch of flowers I've ever seen. Who sent
it? Keighley police?"

The flowers were, indeed, a strangely unintegrated mess of
tiger lilies, white roses, rubbery green leaves, and brown
thistlelike things. Jury had no idea what they were. He said
nothing, hoping that a Racer-monologue could be hurried
along if he didn't respond unless it were absolutely necessary.

"Another call from Sanderson just this afternoon. *Again*
he told me you'd been mucking about—"

In someone else's manor, thought Jury wearily.

"—in their manor." Racer's head swiveled left to right
and back again as he yelled to Fiona that the ball of mange
was in here. Fiona was pretentiously looking behind pillows,

peering under the couch. Wiggins removed a packet of Fisherman's Friends with stealth. "You hear it? The bells?" Racer's tone was frantic.

Jury pulled at his earlobe, wondering when Racer would at last slither into a Poe-esque black tarn. "The bells" referred to the four aluminum ones sewn to Cyril's new collar, a collar that the chief superintendent demanded he wear. Fiona had insisted the collar have elastic in it in case Cyril got caught in a tree limb and hanged himself. *Do you see any trees in this office, Miss Clingmore? Wait, that's an idea. Have one planted somewhere and let the beast claw his way up it. I'll see to it he never gets down.*

What Racer was hearing was not bell-music, but tinkling bottles. Agile as Cyril was, there was no way to work his way through the glass forest of the drinks cabinet without its producing some sound. The collar, of course, had been worked off in a trice every morning after Racer had had a chance to see it was on.

"Just sign this, Jury. In triplicate." He tapped some of the Yard's business stationery with his Mont Blanc pen.

"Sign what?" Jury asked with innocently raised eyebrows. What was his chief up to now? The paper was blank.

"Your resignation." Racer showed rather yellowed, doglike teeth when he smiled his sly smile. "It can be filled in later."

Jury checked his watch beneath the flower-cover. Smart's offices closed at five, probably, and he wanted to pay a visit to the Starrdust before he went to the Ritz . . . after four now . . . He measured out times. Twenty minutes at least to get to Elizabeth Street (rush hour, too), leaving at best five minutes for one of Racer's Byzantine lectures on the reputation of the Yard and Jury's part in the ruining of it. The commissioner, of course, knew the opposite was true. No, no time.

"All right." He pulled the blank sheets over, signed the three pages swiftly with a flourish he hoped befitted Mont Blanc. "Now may I go? The flowers are wilting." He had, at the same time, seen Fiona backing up to the drinks cabinet where he knew the high heel of her shoe could catch in the latch. Consequently, he kept Racer open-mouthed and blindfolded (so to speak) until he heard a click.

Wiggins was in place at the door to Fiona's outer office and Racer quickly looked round Jury in order to salve his pride by finding some reason to yell at the sergeant. "And just where do you think *you're* going, dammit?"

Jury looked just in time to see copper fur streaking out the door. Given the speed, he assumed Cyril wouldn't have to go to a detoxification center.

"To the toilet. Sir."

The two scooted out and Jury followed with his flowers, turning at the door to give his boss a salute. "I'm always available if you need any help writing that." He bestowed a blissful smile on Racer and closed the door.

There was a thud, a splintering sound, and another paperweight hit the floor inside.

30

Flowers offered *carte blanche.* They could get you past nearly everyone but Racer, thought Jury, as the receptionist at Smart Publishing House sat with her hand vaguely reaching for the interoffice telephone, dazzled both by Jury and by Jury's huge bouquet of tiger lilies and roses.

Jury just barely stopped at her desk to draw a white rose and put it on her blotter. He now had his foot on the stair. "I'll just go up, shall I?" This short-circuited the dainty hand and it drew back from the receiver where it cupped itself on her chin. She knew true love when she saw it.

Mavis Crewes didn't. When Jury walked into her rain forest-jungle of an office with the flowers behind his back, she leapt from her chair. "How *dare* you—" and her hand reached for her own telephone either to chew out the receptionist or call New Scotland Yard.

Until she saw the massive bouquet that he produced together with an apology she could have taken for anything or everything he'd said, since he didn't want to specify what it was. "I've also read ten issues of *Travelure.*" He offered her a smile as blinding as one of Charlie Raine's riffs.

Stopped her in her tracks, that did. "If you find me a vase, I'll fill it."

"I, uh. Yes. There's one right here." She reached round an ivory bookcase and pulled out a tall crystal one etched with a jaguar in a tree. She motioned to a door. "Powder room," she said cutely.

Such convenience in the jungle as one's private toilet. For the office, like her home, was done in dark olive-green, a muddy brown, ivory, and flashes of orange. It was painted in a confusing collision of these colors, ornamented with plants and jungle fakery, like the stuffed rabbit-monkey climbing a skinny tree. One wall was a trompe-l'oeil painting of what some artist conceived as a jungle interior. A huge cat was coming right at him.

Another cat, her cat, apparently, merely spat at him. That was all it could raise its lazy head to do. It sat curled in the prime seat—a dark green velvet sofa, displaying itself before brown and ivory cushions laced with orange. Long-haired, probably Himalayan, or some other exotic breed.

He was running water in the vase in her powder room thinking of a pub called the Blue Parrot outside of Long Piddleton where Trevor Sly, the publican, had done his desert-safari look with far less money and no experience. The old film posters of the journeys of Peter O'Toole and Peggy Ashcroft, ill-fated, had struck him as sadly convincing. Then he thought of Hannah Lean. . . .

"What's taking so long?" Mavis called in a singsongish, fluting voice.

Jury looked at himself in the Art Nouveau mirror above the sink and wondered who he was. Racer's offer in triplicate might not be a bad idea. A long-overdue vacation. Another place, another country. Somewhere stark, where the rations were slim and one had to live, like Cyril, by canniness.

Unlike his cup, the vase was overflowing.

As Mavis Crewes, a cigarette in an ivory holder (this ivory was real, he suspected), rabbited on about her travels, her safari adventures, he sat at the other end of the cat's sofa and loathed her. She was shallow, overly precious in her movements, self-absorbed. She was as transparent as Mary

Lee's new shoes, made of smoke. And with her dress of the same swirling colors as her office, she could have vanished before his eyes and he'd never know it.

". . . *absolutely* four-star food. The chef was Hungarian. Would you believe it?"

She had apparently been talking about one of her safari trips. "I assumed people drank from tin bottles and ate army rations."

That made her whoop with delight, enough to make the insolent cat blink once. "Good Lord, no. One has one's entire entourage."

Jury wondered why it was that the ones who were blessed with an "entourage" were the ones who deserved them least. He thought of Nell Healey in that medieval prison of her father's; he thought of Jenny Kennington, years ago, in a huge and empty dining room where the only color was the sunlight across the varnished floor. Women like this, the ones he would remember, had no entourage; they stood in his mind like statues in snow, yet with money to burn.

"Do you take your cat with you?" He looked at the obviously indulged and spiteful cat. Cyril could stiff it with one flashing paw.

Jury winced when he heard her talk about Taffy, but smiled when he thought about Cyril. Such people as Mavis Crewes had so indulged themselves—even the starvation diet that kept her cruelly thin was an indulgence of the ego —that they became insensate. Her plants, her cat, herself thriving in the even temperature of their surroundings, would never survive in the cold world beyond her solarium. Her thermostat did her breathing for her.

". . . could stand a vacation yourself." Her wide mouth smiled slyly, her eyelids drooped, her voice lowered, probably hoping to get at Lauren Bacall's real jungle-cat image.

Jury returned the smile with one equally false. "Oh, I do. Are safaris particularly relaxing?" He eased himself down into the sofa, put his hands behind his neck, gave the impression he had all day, if she liked. He forced himself to smile a particularly seductive smile, to make it reach his eyes.

Mavis apparently "liked," all right. His look pulled her out of her chair and around the desk as effectively as Charlie Raine's had drawn Mary Lee from behind Jury's back.

Resting against the desk, both palms back on the polished surface as if for support, she said, "Well, that depends. How much relaxation were you looking for?"

"Total. Something that would take my mind off everything—this rotten city" (he loved London), "my all-hours job" (he loved his job, too, he supposed), "my solitary life" (he did not love that). "What are the sleeping arrangements? Tents?"

"Very nice ones, very cozy, really."

"Any doubles?"

Mavis Crewes was enjoying this game immensely. It was what she was good at, games. Jury hated them.

"But of course."

He did not rise to light her cigarette; it would have lost him an edge of advantage. Sleepily, he said, "I doubt I could stand up to the competition. Tigers, jaguars, you know."

"You certainly don't sound like Roger. But you're probably not a shooter. Literally, I mean."

"Oh, but I am. I've been through D-six training. I'm not a marksman, but I got a first-class rating. How good was Roger?"

"Good, though not so good as I—in most departments." Pursing her lips, she exhaled a plume of smoke. Then her face changed.

Now she realized it. Her body went slack, her expression hard, both showing her years. For a moment she stood there before she sent the vase smashing to the floor.

Taffy reared back and spat and jumped off the sofa. Jury rose, stepped over water and shards of glass, and grabbed Mavis round the waist in a gesture that in better circumstances could have been one of the furious lover.

He cupped her chin in his hand, bringing her closer. "I'm

sorry; I don't like tricks. You could easily have told me what sort of man Healey was, for God's sakes. I expect you'll be what is described as a hostile witness. I *am* sorry." He felt it, felt he had used her. But he tried to smile, to cool her rage, probably making it worse.

As he had imagined Cyril doing, she flashed her nails across his face, fortunately not connecting except at the chin line. Jury let her go.

She was screaming at him, but choked with rage. "You're a superintendent of *police*. When I tell your superiors, whoever they are, you'll be out of a job."

"Racer. Chief Superintendent Racer." Jury had drawn out his handkerchief, was wiping the blood from his chin. "But I don't think I'm the safari type, Mavis. I need a cold climate, someplace that lets you think. No abundance, just short rations, that forces you to use your wits to survive."

> *it's so cold*
> *in Alaska*

That line from the song Melrose Plant liked so much sprang to his mind and he smiled. "Like Alaska."

2

HEAVENLY SPECTACULAR
COMING
15 JANUARY

The usual mobile of planets turning on their invisible strings had been moved to one side, apparently in preparation for the "Heavenly Spectacular."

But if this wasn't already it, Jury stood in wonder at what more could be added come fifteen January. Already the window was attracting passersby, and a line of children solemn as sparrows on a fence were at the forefront.

The familiar figure of a tiny Merlin in his cape and starry coned hat had been replaced by a diminutive prince on a white horse, bearing a standard, moving slowly out on a little electrical track, stopping, then returning to the dark woodland setting from which he had emerged.

A vast sigh rose from a band of urchins who had muscled in to the front, hair spiky with the wet. From a little crystal castle in the opposite corner came a spun-glass princess, her gown ballooning icily and covering the track on which she ran. Their meeting was more symbolic than actual. The two figures did not touch, but stopped instead a hair's breadth apart, as close as the wonders of the electrician or the track could manage. Each returned to seclusion.

Then a drift of snow lifted, flew about and resettled in another part of the windowfront. There must have been a snow machine somewhere. What looked like laser lights, tiny beams in misty rainbow colors, circled the skies, beaming on Pluto and Venus, then back to cast a rainbow slick across the little snowdrifts.

And this little world of its own was yet to receive further elaboration. It seemed spectacular enough to Jury right now.

Wiggins whispered, "Will we be around the fifteenth, sir?"

Jury said, "Couldn't miss it, could we?"

As they went in the door, Wiggins stopped sneezing and put his handkerchief away. The Starrdust was the only place that Wiggins could go where things weren't catching.

The stardust twins, Meg and Joy, were the ones who were arranging something behind the velvet curtain, whispering and giggling.

When they saw who it was, they got up quickly, brushed off their black cord jeans, straightened their silver and gold braces on their shoulders. Their shirts were white satin.

"Hello."

"Hello. Were you wanting Andrew? He's with a customer."

As Wiggins looked up at the winking lights of the planetarium ceiling, Jury squinted back into the dark length of the shop. Most of the lighting was supplied by muted wall-sconces with quarter-moon shades or tall, thin, lumieres with tops like ringed planets.

Andrew Starr, a dealer in antiquarian books leaning largely toward astrology, looked up from his desk and waved. His customer was a heavy woman draped in a cape of Russian mink and a necklace of Russian amber.

"I was looking to have my fortune read," said Jury. "Who did the window?"

"We did," said Meg, somewhat breathlessly. "Joy's quite mechanical-minded."

Jury looked at Joy, surprised. Between the two of them, he wouldn't have thought they could open a lock with a key.

"But Meg thought it up," said Joy graciously. "And Andrew told us we could spend what we liked," she said proudly.

Andrew Starr would be amply rewarded, Jury knew. Hiring Joy and Meg and, especially, Carole-anne had doubled his holiday trade as it was.

As several of the urchins issued from the little hut called Horror-Scope, Jury said, "Well, Andrew'd better be good to you because if Selfridge's gets a look at that window, Goodbye, Meg and Joy."

They looked pained at this implication of possible disloyalty on their part. The Starrdust was home, after all.

The same could be said for Carole-anne Palutski now coming toward them with a plate of cake. Since Madame Zostra had got this plummy job, the universe was her home.

"Tea's up, kids," she said.

Carole-anne Palutski was dressed in her harem outfit: red pantaloons shot through with gold thread; a short, lapis-lazuli-blue blouse the color of her eyes and bound in gold;

and a flowing, filmy sleeveless coat. Had she not been wearing the gold lamé turban, Jury imagined the Princess would
have put the pattern down to unrestrained Lacroix.

"I have an acquaintance who'd love your color genre."

Carole-anne's face came up from the heavy slice of Black
Forest cake she was scooping into her mouth with far more
enthusiasm than she put in the look she gave Jury. "You
finally decided to come back. Well . . ." Her sigh was
heavier than the cake, a scapegoat sigh. "So who's this
woman?"

"The Princess Rosetta Viacinni di Belamante." Jury shut
his little notebook. "I didn't say it was a woman."

"Is she on the phone?"

"No idea."

"I can hardly wait to see you trying to look it up." With
the back of her fork she was pressing up chocolate crumbs.

"The Princess is probably seventy."

Carole-anne shrugged a filmy gold shoulder. "So when'd
that ever stop you?" Implying Jury had his own private
harem of elderly ladies. She'd put down her plate and was
putting some more records on the old phonograph. "And I
don't expect S-B-slash-H would much like that." Susan
Bredon-Hunt was still making telephone contact with Jury;
her unspeakable name was dropped in a litter of initials like
the stars now falling on Alabama in the music coming from
the phonograph.

Only terrestrial music was permitted in the Starrdust.
Pennies falling down from or stairways leading up to heavens, stars whole or trailing dust, moons of any color. Perry
Como had got his foot in the door because if his true love
had asked him for the moon he'd "go and get it." Suns,
moons, stars—the cosmos. If it were unearthly, Andrew and
his ensemble team were into it.

Meg and Joy, Andrew's sales assistants, were naturals.
They must have come from the Milky Way, W.17, with their
pretty, star-crazed faces. Now they were giggling with Wiggins in the Horror-Scope.

Jury took Carole-anne's arm and guided her to the tent where she played her Madame Zostra role. Starr himself was a serious astrologer with a shrewd eye for the commercial, and Carole-anne had caught the fever; her fever, however, was born not of real interest in the signs of the Zodiac or the rings of Saturn; it had more to do with running Jury's life, and the lives of those who crossed her own star-crossed path, such as Mrs. Wassermann. Fortunately, she eschewed Andrew's complicated horoscopes: why should she learn all that, when the *Daily Mirror* provided quite adequate ones? Vidal Sassoon had probably turned up in the column the past Tuesday.

The tent was a drapery of gauzy stuff hung over several rods protruding from the wall, the material pulled back on the outside like a curtain. Carole-anne and Jury sat opposite one another on huge cushions. On a stool in one corner sat the big stuffed monster-thing Jury had brought back to her last year from Long Piddleton. The black coned hat with the gold quarter moon was not part of its original outfit; it seemed to suit him, though.

After checking her lipstick in a crystal ball that sat on a spidery-legged gold stand—smudging her lips together, drawing them tight to look at her teeth—she picked up her Tarot pack and fanned it out over the black cloth. "Pick one."

"Not after the last time."

"Suit yourself." She shrugged, cleared a place and up-ended the Hanged Man and the Hermit, crossing them carefully with Isis. They stood.

"You look a little pale, Carole-anne; something wrong?"

Quickly, she checked her color in the crystal ball and said, "No. Except I'm overworked."

"You'd have less to do if you'd stop getting Mrs. Wassermann scrunched. Leave her looks alone. I like them."

"She needs a bit of a change. You didn't hear her complaining, did you?" Worrisome little lines appeared on her pristine forehead.

Jury smiled. "No. But give it a rest, will you? One more Sassoon treatment and her hair'll look like Romney Marsh or the Norfolk Broads."

No wonder Carole-anne looked tired. Building a house of cards from the Tarot deck probably was tiring. "We thought you were about to take a trip, what with all of those maps and train schedules and so forth. Mrs. Wassermann told me a few days ago you were making for Victoria Station."

"Oh, *that.*" She positioned three other cards delicately above the first ones. "It was just an idea."

Jury waited while "Moonlight Serenade" ran through its final bars. How different music was then, he thought, and thought about Elicia Deauville. "What idea?" he asked finally.

"That band. You wouldn't know about them. Sirocco. See, I thought they might be coming across from Ireland." As if he had laughed at her, she said defensively, "They were *in* Ireland. That's because of their drummer, I expect, Wes Whelan."

Jury was silent. "Wouldn't it make more sense they'd *fly* to *Heathrow* than take a ferry from Dublin or Cork. Or *Belfast?*"

What had supplanted the Glenn Miller record was "Yesterday's Rain." He turned his head, listened for a few moments to this music she pretended to ignore by humming herself an entirely different tune. "Or are you talking only about Sirocco's lead guitarist."

The house of cards wobbled. "I'm surprised you ever heard of him."

"That was my magazine you nicked. I read the article. Sometimes he does travel alone. But it was very unlikely. Wouldn't it have made more sense for you to go to Heath——"

"I don't go to airports," she broke in, hastily.

"You mean you're afraid of flying?"

Impatiently, she shook her red-gold hair, shining in the reflections from the starry ceiling fixtures. "No. I just don't like things you see there." She put her hands on her hips and said angrily, "Didn't you ever *notice?* You must have done when you were at Heathrow with your machine gun when that bomb went off."

This seemed to have little relationship to whatever really bothered her. "Are you afraid of getting caught in crossfire? Anyway, I didn't carry a 'machine gun.'"

"Well." As if that unraveled the whole mystery, she fixed the last card in place. "Don't breathe on it, for heaven's sakes."

Then glumly she said, "It's like airports are the last stopping place. People leaving. It's like the last . . . trench. People dying in each other's arms." She was staring at him through two squares made by the cards. "Before some of them go to the line of fire."

What, Jury wondered, was this preoccupation with metaphors of war? Perhaps her talks with Mrs. Wassermann, who had had dreadful experiences in Poland during what she called the Big War (the one she shared with Jury), except Mrs. Wassermann wouldn't have talked about this to Carole-anne. It had been too bleak.

She was telling him a story. ". . . this little girl, no, boy. His mum was holding him and they were both crying. It was there at the gate, and then other people, probably the gramps, an old man with a lot of medals on his chest, they were standing around looking terrible. The little boy was maybe three or four. And he was crying like it was the end of the world. So was his mum. Well, it *must* have been his mum." She ran a finger under the bottom cards and the house tumbled airily down as if resisting the pull of gravity. "The little boy had his face nearly up against his mum's and what really . . . what was so awful was he took his hand and even though he was hysterical he was wiping her face, wiping the tears away with his hand. Maybe it was because if she was crying, too, that meant it was real."

She stopped suddenly, the "real" hanging there, not dropping at the end. It was as if there were much more but she had neither breath nor strength.

Jury said nothing. There seemed nothing he could say. He thought of the loss of Elicia Deauville, for some reason. And he thought of all the crazy stories (that he secretly loved) Carole-anne had told to explain her apparent lack of family. That she was found inside a trunk at Victoria; that she'd been chloroformed on a train—all out of stories she had read or heard about. Except for the one about amnesia. Getting hit by a golf ball at St. Andrews was definitely her own invention.

So while Sirocco's fans were waiting to catch a glimpse of the band as they descended the metal stairs of their private plane, Carole-anne was standing on a railway platform at Victoria.

Jury swallowed. Then he took the tickets from his pocket and slid them across the table with a try at a smile.

When Carole-anne saw them, she didn't have to try. All the color rushed back into her face. "Super! Where'd you *get* them?" Her eyes narrowed. "You didn't go paying them scalper's prices, did you?" Then her blue, blue eyes widened again and she grabbed the little table, leaned across it and kissed him. "But wherever did you *get* tickets?"

Jury smiled then, got up, his legs cramped as hell. "Secret."

Carole-anne loved secrets.

31

The Ritz Hotel was still as luxurious as he had remembered it, but not as large as it had appeared to his six-year-old eyes. Few things would be. But however diminished in size, there was no diminution of sparkle, color, and splendor: the plush carpeting, crystal chandeliers, rose and gilt armchairs, columned alcoves where guests partook of coffee or cocktails, and, of course, the long, raised lounge with its white-clothed tables set for tea. Even at this late hour, there were still the partakers of afternoon tea.

Alvaro Jiminez was drinking coffee in one of the lobby's alcoves. He rose and shook hands when Jury identified himself. He was an impressive man, over six feet, black face finely chiseled, wearing designer jeans and a metal-studded denim jacket over a black turtleneck. He wore no jewelry except for a Rolex watch. He spoke with a self-deprecating air, was probably a master at it. His mother, he told Jury, was Puerto Rican; his daddy from Mississippi. His daddy was one of the best blues men he'd ever heard to this day.

"Went to school to Earl Hooker. Never did hear no one play like my daddy, except maybe Robert Johnson, Otis Rush."

Jury smiled: "How about you?"

Jiminez laughed. "Me? Hell, I'm just back-porch, back-yard blues." He poured some more coffee from the silver pot. "I never was into that manic speed picking. Not that I'm putting it down. Van Halen has the most energy of any

axeman I ever did see. I'm just not into that 'Spanish Fly'–
type solo thing. There's too much metal; more over here
than in the States. Thrash metal. The baroque stuff I
like. Our music's not just doing the chinka-chinka-chinka
rhythm or ten-bar progressions—" He moved his hand
along an imaginary fretboard. "—it's more eclectic than
that."

Not only did the diction change when Jiminez got into his
real love—blues—but the timbre of the voice dropped. Jury
had inferred from his manner that he was a sophisticated
man. And although Alvaro was really the moving force behind this band—he'd started it—when he talked about
Charlie Raine (who had taken over the tabloids, the media,
the covers of magazines), there wasn't a hint of rancor or
jealousy. It might have been because he, Charlie, wasn't trying to, didn't care. That's what Jiminez was saying.

"I got a lot of respect for Charlie. Charlie don't buy none
of this glitz. He don't seem to want fame nor money nor a
five-thousand-watt spot on him. I asked him, 'Charlie, what
do you want?' and he doesn't even smile when he says, 'To
be as good as you are.'" Alvaro chuckled and shook his
head. "I think he meant it."

Jury smiled. "Is he?"

Again Alvaro laughed as he jimmied a thin cigar from a
case on the coffee table. "Shit, no. Look at it this way: I got
fifteen years on Charles. Fifteen years of jams, club gigs"—
he looked through the spurt of flame from his lighter at Jury
—"but he would be, finally."

"You'd still be fifteen years ahead."

Alvaro shook his head, sat back. Smoke coiled upward
and he blew and dispersed it. "Because he is *the* most focused axeman I've ever come across. It's more than focus;
it's like a mission with him. You got to be able to separate
yourself from the whole rock-star attitude. You got to be one
thing on stage, you got your attitude on stage, but remember
when you pack the axe away, like Sly Stallone says, 'You
gotta go home and eat spaghetti with your mother.' When I

was a kid, I wasn't thinkin' about how did they stiff me with that contract or if my CPA made a mistake on my tax return. Back then it was just playin' for playin'. That's what I mean: you got to be able to put that stuff to one side and just play. I don't have to remind myself I was some shitty fourteen-year-old when I was trading licks with my daddy, because I got so many friends back in Mississippi askin', 'You still wanderin' around with that guitar case? What you got in it, coke? Crack?' There's one friend who can play nearly as good as Stevie Ray Vaughan reminds me I don't know nothin' and we sit around trading S.R.V. licks and I realize I jumped off the stage not a moment too soon. That's Charlie."

"The reason he's quitting?"

Jiminez shrugged. "I'm only guessing. Except for saying he's tired and wants to try something new—vague stuff like that—he just don't give no reason. No reason he got the schedule changed, either. We were supposed to be playing Munich this week. Manager nearly cut his throat over that booking."

"Doesn't make sense." Jury looked up at the ceiling, the magnificent chandelier faintly tinged by a pinkish glow. "You say he's dedicated, focused, and that sounds like 'ambitious' to me. But he's stopping at the top, or near-top of his career." He looked across the table with its silver coffee service at Jiminez.

"Tell me and we'll both know, bro'."

"Don't you think it's *strange?*"

"Strange? I think it's insane. But every man's got his own river to cross."

Jury imagined Alvaro Jiminez had crossed a number of his own. "When did Raine join up with your band?"

"First saw Charlie when we were on the road, let's see, four years ago. Doin' one-nighters in what felt like one thousand gigs from California to Florida. Charlie come in one night to a dive in the Keys. He'd already met up with Wes; was working gigs in New York. Word-of-mouth place this was, except nobody musta opened his mouth because there couldn't of been more than twenty, thirty customers and they was mostly bonged.

"Charlie would of stood out anyway. He was at the bar hardly tasting his beer, had this little bitty amp hooked on his belt, had his beat-up Fender leaning against a stool. He looked kinda familiar. Then I realized he was a follower."

Jury frowned. "He'd been going from place to place where you played?"

"Think we were the fuckin' Dead. I ask him, did he have me mixed up with Garcia, and he said, straight-faced, 'How could I do that?' " Alvaro grinned. "The way he said it, I could of been better or I could of been an asshole. Anyway, he pushed a demo at me, told me he wanted to do a number if I didn't mind. Right there, that night. I asked him what the hell's a teenage Brit doin' in Key Biscayne? 'Pickin' up work when I can.' Well, he fascinated me. I said to him, 'You play lead, of course.' Don't they all? He says, 'I play anything. Rhythm, bass, whatever you want. Whatever kind of music.' Well, he gets up there with us in the next set and I mean those twenty, thirty actually took the straws outta their noses. They did love him. He could play any of those dusty old songs they wanted. 'Georgia on My Mind'—I thought they'd died and went to heaven. Got up and danced even, some of them. He's just a natural-born crowd pleaser. Put that together with someone's got that kind of funky blues Clapton-like line and you got star quality."

Jury thought for a moment. "You changed the name of the band."

"Yeah. We all thought Bad News Coming was pretty beat, so all of us tossed a couple of names in the hat. Sirocco was Charlie's. We didn't even know what the hell it meant, but it had this nice sound."

Jury smiled. "Did Charlie know?"

" 'Hot wind that blows off the desert,' something like that. Looka there what's comin' our way."

A woman in folds of gray sable with an uptight hairdo to

match had been sweeping toward their corner and had now arrived with a young girl several paces behind. Leather opera gloves, Italian kid shoes, heavy enough with diamond-drop earrings, necklace, and bracelets that the woman reminded Jury of one of the chandeliers. "Aren't you part of that Sirocco band?" Her voice was as showy as the rest of her, low and thick with cultural attitudes. "Aren't you Mr. Jiminez?" Wiggins should have heard the "Jim—" The girl blushed and looked away. Clearly, it was she who had recognized Alvaro Jiminez.

"That's right, darlin'." He scrawled his name across one of the Ritz's hotel register cards, looked at the woman, and asked, "I guess you're comin' to the concert?"

The mother looked bemused. "What concert?"

The girl, Jury knew, could have died where she stood with embarrassment. Alvaro caught her eye, asked her name (which she said was Belle), and he said, "Tell your mama what concert, Belle."

This seemed to delight Belle; the blush receded, leaving an afterglow that brightened her face and sparked her eyes. "Hammersmith Odeon. Tomorrow night."

Jiminez grinned. "*You're* comin'."

The mother started in on a long explanation of their "schedule" for tomorrow, places they had to go, people they had to see (all important), and Jiminez kept on looking at Belle, from whose face the light had fled, listening to her mother, to whom Alvaro was paying no attention at all.

"There'll be a ticket at the box office, Belle. From me. Easy to get there on the tube, but take a cab home."

Belle's eyes were widening more and yet more as he spoke. Jiminez had plunked her down in Munchkinland where all the rules were suddenly, and marvelously, different. The mother in sable was furious, Jury could tell. Her Belle being allowed to breathe on her own, much less hightail it to Hammersmith?

Alvaro was chuckling as they walked away, the sable

bouncing as the mother tried to keep up with her daughter, who was ignoring her.

"There's one seat taken, at least," said Jiminez. "I don't guess cops have time for that kinda stuff."

"It's sold out."

Alvaro Jiminez seemed to think this was funny as hell. "You a Scotland Yard superintendent and can't get tickets? How many you want?" Before Jury could answer he said, "Hell, there'll be four at the box office. Stage manager's a nice guy. He holds some back for us. Mind if I say something?"

Jury smiled. "Of course not."

"Somehow I get the idea you ain't really into thrash security. Can't say why. And I got to go, friend." Jiminez stood up. He seemed to tower there.

As Jury stood to shake his hand, he said, "Just another fan, Alvaro. I want to thank you. You didn't have to do this."

"I like to come down here, hang out with the swells. Almost didn't get to sit down because I wasn't wearin' no tie. The reason the manager chose the Ritz is because everybody's so rich, nobody'd bother us. Excepting as long as we wore our ties." His expression was completely bland. "Why're you so interested in Charles?"

"I'm trying to save someone's life."

"Well."

Jury knew from his tone he'd say nothing to anyone about this conversation. They were walking toward the entrance, the long line of glass doors that shimmered with the reflected lights of the chandeliers. "Mind if I ask *you* one more question? About yourself?"

"Go ahead, man."

They were looking out on Piccadilly now. "You said your daddy was a great blues man from the Mississippi Delta. Was his name Jiminez?"

"Nope. That's my mama's maiden name. I went by Johnson until he died. Then I changed it." He paused. "Mama ran off when I was eight years old with a stand-up piano player. Never heard nothin' since."

As they both stood looking at the wavering circles of light reflected by the marqueelike bulbs of the Ritz, he added, "What I thought was, there's a lot of Johnsons in this world, but maybe she'd recognize her own name and come see me."

Jury didn't have to ask if she had.

2

In a warehouse on the Isle of Dogs Morpeth Duckworth sat dressed in black like a spider in his web.

When Jury and Wiggins walked in he was turning knobs, punching buttons, flipping levers right and left like a man with ten arms; he was surrounded by stacked-up amplifiers, stereo components, an elaborate sound system, digital synthesizers, video screens. His legs were outstretched, feet resting on two separate chairs on wheels like a secretary's chair. He was a man in his element.

Duckworth nodded at them, pushed the chairs toward them with his feet as an invitation to seat themselves. He flicked a few switches, adjusted the volume, so that what sounded like nothing but feedback screams was reduced to music loud enough to shimmer like a heat curtain between them. Apparently, as far as Duckworth was concerned, that level served as viable background music for conversation.

"Can you turn that down some more? My sergeant's ears bleed easily."

For once, Wiggins didn't appreciate being ministered to. He looked at Jury sternly, perhaps warning him off from comment on the quality of the soundtrack.

Morpeth Duckworth flipped a few more levers, obviously surprised that anyone in possession of his senses would make such a request, given this was prime Hendrix. " 'The Wind Cries Mary.' The, the, *the* most beautiful ballad he ever did." He talked about inversions, double inversions, fat

tones, and ghost bends like a man who'd just seen Mary
herself materialize in the shadows round the packing cases.

"You don't play with your fingers and sing with your
chords, that's what the clones don't seem to understand. Van
Halen's been cloned to kingdom come. Excuse me, that's
literally Jimmy Page. When Kingdom Come's lead guitarist
slipped out and raised that bow I nearly fell off the bed. Any
halfway decent axeman could imitate Van Halen or Yngwie
or any other technical wizard. What these clones don't see is
that they're *not* the ones they're ripping off. An obvious
point. They'd have to change their whole genetic system to
sound like Page or Knopfler or any of the others. It's this
gunslinger mentality. For one thing, most people got a tin
ear and just because you got two guitarists who are heavily
into baroque, heavily classical, and one of them does some
thrashing around with arpeggio runs and the other does
Bach progressions, the tin ear can't tell the difference. Me, I
don't knock technical wizardry." He leaned forward as if to
drive home this point. "Here's the thing: they're so good at
it, guys like Van Halen and Malsteen, that you're damned
right the technique stands out; it's so clear it sounds like it's
separated from the guys playing it. But it ain't. And that's
the reason you get some pissant sitting around doing two-
handed tapping and thinking he's Joe Pass, but he's not, so
it's nothing.

"You wanna be Riley B. King, then you get your ass out
of those studio sessions and do the chitlin' circuit just like all
the others, the real blues men. If what you really want is just
to gliss across the stage at the Grammy awards and go mul-
tiplatinum, okay, do it, but you can't ride on anybody's
coattails. You're not going to be Clapton, or B. B. King, or
Hubert Sumlin or Gatemouth Brown—"

Since Duckworth showed no signs of letting up, slowing
down, or discussing anything so mordant as a murder investigation, Jury said quickly, "How do you rate Stan Keeler,
then? I understand you know him."

"I rate him the best R-and-B guy they've got over here.

All you have to do is go to the Nine-One-Nine to see what I mean. Stan can do anything: rock, jazz, fusion, blues. Blues, blues, anarchic blues. Black Orchid, on a good day, could blow Sirocco away. But Sirocco's good. I'd like to see a triple-axe threat with Raine, Jiminez, and Keeler. The Odeon would orbit. Stan doesn't do concerts. Part of it's the way he is; part of it's he knows the way *it* is: *it* is *underground.* Fans over here are different; it's very personal. He'll go on forever. Hell, his dog's more famous than Fergie's kid. The bands in the States, they think England's the Pearly Gates because you can rocket to fame over here. What they don't know is that when you go down you go down dead. It's High Noon time. The press over here's a killer. In one column I could demolish some poor metal band that hasn't got the fans yet. It doesn't work that way in the States."

"So why was Roger Healey into your territory?"

"Because the creep was dying to trash Keeler is my guess."

"You didn't like Healey?" asked Wiggins.

Duckworth just shaved them a look.

"*Why* did this man have such a solid-gold reputation with everyone else we've talked to? Including Martin Smart?" said Jury. "He's no fool."

"He's also no musician. He gets these rags out and he's good at it. Healey—okay, I give him credit for knowing his Bach and Paganini—probably not as much as some guitarists I know. Healey was a musician, not precisely a killer pianist from what I've heard, and I think it drove him fucking crazy. You had to look close, reading his reviews, to see some of those lines were etched in acid. He was a weirdo. You been talking to our Mavie? So he was screwing her."

"Anyone else you know of?"

Morpeth Duckworth shrugged. "No one I *know.* He was obviously more discreet than that."

"Where's this club Keeler plays?"

"Mostly the Nine-One-Nine. Quint Street off Shephards Bush Road. It's a walkdown. You won't even see it unless you fall on the steps. There's no sign, just the street number."

Jury rose; Wiggins pocketed his pen.

"Thanks for the help."

Duckworth pulled the chairs back over, stuck his feet up again. "No problem."

As they were walking out, Jury turned and asked, "Who's Trane?"

Wiggins stared at Jury; Duckworth's feet hit the floor. "Trane."

"I heard someone refer to Trane the other day. Just wondered."

Dead silence.

"John Coltrane." Duckworth looked at him as if the superintendent had lost his mind.

"Oh."

"He played sax," said Duckworth.

"Oh."

"Twenty years ago."

"Something wrong?" asked Jury, as Wiggins slammed the passenger door. "You look like you could use a tourniquet; an artery's going to burst."

Wiggins unglued his thin white hand from his mouth and said grimly, "John Coltrane. John Coltrane just happened to be possibly *the* greatest saxophone player ever. Why didn't you ask *me?* It's absolutely embarrass——" Wiggins looked down at the seat where Jury was fiddling with a small machine. "What's that?"

"Sony Walkman." Jury dropped in a tape and some of the sweetest sax music this side of heaven started up. "Research."

As the car tore away from the curb, the sound that came from Wiggins was like a death-rattle and Jury was having his first real laugh in a week.

32

Abby was furious.

If someone thought she was going to die out here on the moor, they were crazy.

Snow had got down into her boots and was soaking her socks, but she'd rather have her toes freeze than risk giving herself away by making a lot of squelchy noises trying to yank them off. Anyway, with only the low wall of the shooting butt to hide her, she didn't want to do too much moving about.

It surprised her that Tim was managing to be so silent, lying here beside her. Of course, Tim was used to lying about the barn, but he seemed alert, the way he kept looking first to one side, then to the other, then to her.

Abby knew nothing about guns, nothing at all except for the few times she'd come out to these grouse butts with the Major and watched him as he scrambled up, swung his gun quickly to his shoulder, took aim, and missed an entire skein of grouse flying about two feet from his cap. The Gun: that's what the Princess called him.

Until this evening, that had been her only experience with guns. But she'd never forget the crack of the shot that had barely missed her and ricocheted off the wall. How long ago had it been? Probably only a few minutes because the sky had begun to darken as she'd been climbing the stile. The shot had come as she'd got to the top and she'd fallen back to the ground, sorting out her choices: either a dash to the stand of trees or to the line of grouse butts. Knowing what she did about her aunt's death, it didn't take long to drop the stand of pines as an alternative.

They thought she didn't know her aunt was shot. Didn't they ever stop to wonder if children listened outside doors and windows? She had an idea that the Scotland Yard policeman did because he seemed to know everything else about her. Abby had his card in her jumper pocket. She pulled it out and read it again, though it was getting too dark to read.

Where was Stranger? *Where?* She knew he wasn't shot because there'd only been the one.

Abby pulled at her damp hair, grabbed two fistfuls, and yanked it down like a lid to keep her thoughts from leaping up like flames out of control, as if she were a fiery furnace, which was what she felt like. She had been mad all her life and she didn't see any reason to stop now.

She reached out carefully from the grouse butt, scooped up snow, and rubbed it all over her face to keep the blood going. The Major liked to talk to her about "survival in the wilds" because she loved to tramp the moors. *He* wasn't in any danger of not surviving, she thought. He always made sure he had three sandwiches and a little flask of whiskey before he even put a foot out of the front door.

There was no sound, nothing now but a whisper of wind in the bog rush and bracken.

Her waterproof was yellow. Yellow. Mrs. Braithwaite had made sure she wore a bright waterproof when she walked to school so if a car came round a bend it would see her. She'd argued the roads were too narrow for any car to go fast and she'd rather have a black waterproof. This one was like those reflecting lights on Ethel's bicycle. The moon was like a spotlight, and in this bright yellow she'd be like a shooting star if she tried to dart from the butt to the wall. She looked down at Tim. A yellow slicker, a full moon, and a white dog. God hated her.

One of the reasons she'd liked Jane Eyre at first was be-

cause she'd thought God hated *her,* too; but then when Jane
went to work for Mr. Rochester, Abby knew what was coming and decided God didn't hate Jane at all; he was just
"trying" her.

Like Job. Her aunt made her go to church school where
Abby had to sit and listen to the minister talk about Job and
his three Comforters with crazy names. She'd just sat there
thinking about Job, wondering why he didn't get off his
dung heap and beat the Comforters up. After she'd said this
and a few other things in church school, her aunt had told
her she didn't have to go back.

Abby lowered her head, thinking about Aunt Ann, trying
to feel bad about her. But she couldn't, and her mind wandered off to Stranger again. Stranger had been trailing her
and Tim, straggling after them, exploring what was left of
the snowbank against the far wall over there, and had got
way behind.

He was out there, somewhere.

And here she was with a crazy person with a gun, *the
Gun,* the same Gun that had killed her aunt, she was sure.

And here *she* was with nothing. Only her crook, which
she would gladly beat the Gun to death with, smash his
brains all over the moor; Ethel's dog, a heeler that she would
gladly signal to rip the heels of the Gun to shreds, and then
all the rest of him. But her head drooped, her fisted hands
pressed her temples, and she knew neither of those weapons
could get close enough to save her.

Something glimmered in her mind and she slowly raised
her head and tented her hand over her eyes, squinting way
off across the moor.

Sheep.

2

Where in heaven's name were they all?

The Hall was virtually deserted except for Melrose and the staff, and with the exception of Ruby, they were in their rooms, Mrs. Braithwaite having decided she could be as ill as Cook, as long as she had the poor drudge Ruby Cuff to see to getting a platter of cold chicken and cheese and salad on the luncheon table.

And following luncheon, the guests had scattered like buckshot; Mrs. Braithwaite's cooking and murder had that effect on one, Melrose supposed. It made no difference that Superintendent Sanderson had given instructions that they were all to keep themselves available for questioning. The constable who had been left behind (in his orphaned, custodial position by the door) had been removed in the morning —with some help from Ellen and her BMW. The Weavers Hall inmates seemed to breathe easier.

Dinner the previous evening had consisted of some sort of stewed chicken and mushy peas and overboiled potatoes. Today's lunch had been a drier version of the dinner.

Major Poges had tossed in the towel—or the napkin—and announced that he refused to eat another meal until Cook was up and about and said he would dine at the White Lion, would anyone care to join him? Not even the Princess cared to; she had a vicious migraine and retired to her "rooms." She always made her part of Weavers Hall sound like a floor of some splendid, if decaying, Venetian palace whose façade Melrose could imagine reflected in the night-lit shimmering waters of the Grand Canal. Vivian was always gondolaing by in these fantasies. He could see Vivian's latest creation from some *couture* house as clearly as he could imagine the Princess's room strewn about with silk and bombazine, printed velvets and brocades.

Ramona Braine, throughout the meal, had remained rigidly silent, checking her turquoise watch every ten minutes, thinking, from her expression, of their ruined holiday to Cumbria and her meeting with the Emperor Hadrian— dashed now because his specter had already been hanging about there (it being well past noon), come and gone as specters do. Melrose's attempt to solace her with the suggestion that "perhaps next year" was met with a furious glance that removed him completely from the provenance of the spirit world.

Only Malcolm was making the most of things. He had exhausted the topic of the murder of "the landlady" and been chillingly silenced by George Poges. Thus what he saw as the bloody corpse was transplanted by a long description of the bloody chickens he had watched Ruby throttle and then chain-saw to death (to hear him talk). The remnants now lay coldly on the platter before them; Malcolm described this slaughter with all of the relish of Agamemnon's father, Atreus, serving up the fatal pie to his brother that contained Thyestes' children. What was impressive about the Greeks was that they never forgot anything, never let a slur pass, never let a gauntlet drop without reprisals. For family feeling, they could teach the Mafia a thing or two. The Greeks reminded him of Commander Macalvie.

Melrose pushed the pale chicken piece about his plate and took a bite of cold potato and thought of Agamemnon murdered by Aegisthus and Clytemnestra. Next generation: Orestes and Electra. Yes, it went on forever. Revenge really turned their cranks (as Ellen would probably say).

He was thinking of this as he stared out of the window at dusk. He frowned. Where in hell *was* Ellen, anyway? After breakfast she and her bike had skittered down the drive, spitting up shale and rocks on her way to some Brontë-research revel, this time in Wycoller. That had been nearly twelve hours ago.

He walked over to the fireplace, kicked at the barely burning log, looked at his reflection in the gilt mirror and found it less than inspiring. And where was Abby? He'd been checking his watch as often as had Ramona Braine and was looking through the window as if the specter might appear in its shredded graveclothes and beckon him to the pile of rocks.

Abby had been in the barn after breakfast and he hadn't seen her since. His appearance hadn't resulted in anything but her playing her Elvis record louder and stomping round the byre to medicate her cow.

He had decided to ask Ruby to fix Abby's tea, and been told, when he wandered into the kitchen that it'd do no good; Abby always did her own tea just the way she liked it.

"But she must at least come to the main house for *supplies.*" Even Admiral Byrd had to get those, though Melrose had forgotten how.

"She be all right, sir; we never worry about the lass."

He thought this so peculiar that in his abstraction he picked up a tea towel and began to wipe a platter. Ruby was doing the washing-up from their earlier meal and wasn't happy about the extra work. Her thick brows were working toward the center like burrowing moles. Clearly, she felt put upon, what with both Cook and Mrs. Braithwaite having fled the scene.

She told Melrose he needn't do the drying, but she was obviously pleased that a guest was doing scullery work and taking the load off her narrow shoulders.

Indeed, no one (including himself) had paid any more attention to Ruby Cuff than one would a lamp or a chair. He put the platter by and chose something smaller—a teacup. Police had asked Ruby a few rudimentary questions, but perhaps because Mrs. Braithwaite was clearly the head of the staff and had been there the longest, Ruby had been given short shrift. Ruby had that straight-up-and-down, tightly laced and buttonhooked look that made it hard to tell if she were twenty or forty. Had she been a beauty—like the Princess—this ageless limbo would have served her well.

"Ruby, how long have you been employed by Miss Denholme?"

"Near ten year, sir." This seemed to please her. "You needn't dry this," she said, holding up a big roasting pan.

Melrose had no intention of doing so as he watched her place it on the rack.

"But then you must have known Miss Denholme quite well."

She looked less pleased at having to admit she didn't. "You needn't try getting that bit of stain out of the egg cup. The Princess stuffed out a cigarette in it. It's the Major's."

"I take it that's why she did it." The egg cup had stubby legs and blue-dotted shoes. He frowned at it.

The smile did nothing to light up her plain features. "Cats and dogs they are."

"I expect police asked you about your relationship with Miss Denholme?" He redried the egg cup by way of avoiding the cutlery and especially the heavy skillet.

"Well, they asked how long I been here and did I know anyone'd got anything against her."

"Of course, there wouldn't be: I mean, no one you knew of?"

Since he'd appeared to have answered his own question, she saw no reason to answer it again and just kept on running a rag around a dented kettle.

Melrose sighed and picked up another egg cup. It had shoes, too, yellow ones. He had a vision of egg cups, hundreds of them, marching down Oxford Street. Blinking it away, he wondered how Jury got them to talk—the suspects, the witnesses, the children, dogs, cats. Grass, trees . . . Don't be absurd; you're just jealous. "Did Miss Taylor happen to mention when she'd be back?" Melrose hadn't meant to give voice to this speculation; it would throw him off target.

"No, sir." Ruby wiped a strand of hair back from her forehead. "She's a strange one, ain't she? Do they all dress like that in New York City?"

"Yes." He certainly had better not get into defending Ellen Taylor or her clothes or he'd never get anything out of
Ruby. He gave the shoes another shine and watched Ruby
bailing the water out of the plastic tub. Then, after she'd
plucked another tea towel from a drawer and reached for
the skillet, he beat her to it. That's what Jury would do.
He'd have done *all* the washing up. "No, Ruby, you've been
working too hard. Just have a rest." The skillet seemed to
weigh a ton. Had he been in charge of a kitchen he'd have
thrown all the heavy stuff straight out and used those plastic
disposable things.

Ruby beamed—if the expression could be called that on
her pudding face—and let out a martyred sigh and announced as how she needed a sit-down.

She made herself a mug of tea from the low-boiling kettle
on the hob and took a rocking chair by the fire where she
sipped and was silent.

"Well, I certainly admire you, Ruby. *You*" (a slight em-
phasis here) "don't crumble in a crisis." No response but a
self-satisfied little smile and a few more sighs. Martyrdom
sat well on the maid. "A horrible thing to happen," Melrose
went on. "Horrible. And on the moor. One wouldn't expect
something like that out there."

She shrugged. "Moor's as good a place as any. Better. No
one about to see him do it."

Him? He had set down the half-dried skillet and was now
half-drying the pot. "You think it was a man?"

With a slightly incredulous stare, she said, "Well, it
warn't no woman to do a thing like that."

"You mean a *woman* wouldn't? But Mrs. Healey . . ."
He tossed down the tea towel, ignoring the cutlery.

"Well, I didn't mean that." She shook her head. "Mrs.
Healey doing that . . ." She shook her head in wonder.
"*That* was a surprise. I don't know her, mind you, not to
talk to. She is a cool one. Though she did like Abby. Always
bringing her things, she was."

Melrose came over to stand by the fireplace. "You say *that* was surprising as if you weren't especially surprised by Miss Denholme's murder. And you said you didn't mean 'that'—that a woman mightn't have done it. What did you mean?"

Resolutely, Ruby clamped her lips like a penurious old lady snapping her purse shut.

He oughtn't to have been so direct. Now her eyes were beginning to close. "You know, it's rather odd Miss Denholme never married. She certainly was an attractive woman." Ruby's eyes opened, studying him carefully. "As a matter of fact"—he laughed artificially—"she had a bit of the, ah . . . well, no speaking ill of the dead and that sort of thing." His smile glittered, he hoped, like his green eyes. They had at least been said to glitter by those who didn't compare them with scarab beetles.

"Meaning her ways with men?" Ruby's smile was thin and a little mean. "Well, there was plenty of them to dance attendance."

At last his efforts were paying off. "Around *here?*" He laughed again. "It's a bit of a wasteland for romance, isn't it?"

"I never said romance. I do the rooms, you know."

With that elliptical statement and a crimped, probably jealous little smile, she was off for her own lie-down.

Ruby Cuff had a prurient mind, thank God. Ann Denholme had not apparently drawn the line at her own guests.

And who else? Melrose was wondering now, as he looked fretfully out of the front room window and yet again checked his watch. Nearly nine o'clock and no Ellen. No Abby, either. He'd just been down to the barn three times after his talk with Ruby and no sign of her.

He settled down with a large brandy to think, trying to console himself with the notion that Abby was totally unpredictable and was out with Stranger digging out sheep, or something.

Except no more snow had fallen.

Indeed, it had been melting.

But it must be sheep.

3

A blind cast.

Abby lowered her head on her folded arms and wished she'd paid more attention to Mr. Nelligan. A blind cast had to be the hardest thing to do and she didn't even know where Stranger was.

Tim nosed at her hair and whimpered. Abby raised her head and looked squarely into the eyes of this dog she'd always thought of as a lazy layabout, although she knew it was Ethel's fault. Ethel never tried to train him, no wonder. The only commands he'd ever heard he'd got came from Abby—

So it might be possible, even a blind cast. Right now, looking into Tim's sparkling eyes, she was willing enough to swallow all the tales of Babylon, Summertime, and impeccable breeding. Abby curled her fingers in Tim's coat and tried to bore, mentally, into his mind. Sheer concentration was the trick. She'd been at a lot of sheepdog trials and she'd seen what those dogs could do. She had seen the best of them head off a mob of sheep without getting a single command.

If Tim had all that royal blood in him, even if he hadn't been a working dog since Ethel got her little white uncallused hands on him, still, blood was blood and you didn't forget how to do what you'd been born to do. The Queen of England would never *forget* how to be a queen; it was like bicycle riding.

The night had grown colder, the moon surrounded by mist, the stone walls insurmountable. Her mouth was frozen more with fear than cold, her waterproof crusty with rime, her hair straggly-wet with mist.

But she was *not* going to be like Jane Eyre's friend Helen

and go round and round in a ring in sopping rain and soppy obedience to her torturers, a saint among devils.

Stranger. Well, she was going to believe he was out there waiting for a signal. Way off, the sheep were dotted about the hillside. It was more difficult now, the moon having gone misty, to see them, how distant, how far-flung. Mr. Nelligan, despite his habits, never seemed to lose one and he had over a hundred and fifty. . . . It seemed an impossible task; her heart hammered.

Then she heard—this time a little closer—the sort of rock-chinking noise someone might make scaling a wall. She turned slowly in her hideout and raised her eyes to see, over the shooting butt, a black mass slowly rising above the dry-stone.

Abby dropped her eyes, turned back to stare at Tim, the energy that had stoked her rage now massed like a fiery ball into sheer concentration. She would move Tim out to the right where he'd have at least the protection of a white back-drop, what was left of the bank of snow against the long hedgerow.

Very slowly and softly she said to Tim, "Away to me."

Tim jerked up, turned, and streaked toward the snowy rise where he turned right again and ran like a white projectile to the far moorland.

Abby huddled down. She didn't think the Gun would waste a cartridge (and also give away his or her own position) by shooting at a fleeing dog.

Thus the crack of the rifle shot totally disoriented her for a second; her mind whirled with the explosion of it; a terrifying noise that could have blown up every living thing on the moor, could have blown up the moors themselves. She squeezed her eyes shut.

Yet one part of her mind was still and told her to take advantage of the second's aftermath of that shot. With her eyes still shut, she stuck her fingers in the corners of her mouth and whistled. It was so piercing that she knew it would carry as far as the rim of the hill, way off.

Then it was quiet. Abby opened her eyes to see that Tim was still streaking toward the far fields.

The Gun had missed.

The Gun was a fool and Abby, in her excitement, was almost getting up to shout it out, to tell whoever it was: *You missed, you missed, screw you, you bloody, stupid sleazeball.* Sleazeball was one of Ellen's best words.

Everything was quiet now.

Tim was alive; she was alive; the moors remained.

4

Melrose moved the Braine woman's lap desk, still with cards outspread, and slouched down in the deep armchair that she had staked out as her territory.

He had the Tarot and Malcolm's portable stereo for company. The Magician stared up at him; the stereo squawked lightly and indecipherably with one of Malcolm's *oo-ah-oh-oh-oh* teeny-bopping tunes. He reached over and pushed the stop/eject button and looked over the several tapes to see who this brain-curdling group was. BROS. The picture in the empty plastic box showed four very young men who looked like they'd just graduated from the Beavers. He found the Lou Reed tape and slotted that in, turned up the volume, and leaned back to think.

> *Caroline says—*
> *while biting her lip*

Melrose had to admit to a fascination with Caroline's chronicle, with her drugged-out, crazy, wasted life. All of the songs were about Caroline, he was certain, though her name came up in only two. Caroline and her lover or husband and their marriage made in hell.

> *it's so cold in A-las-ka*
> *it's so cold in A-las-ka*

Endless snowy wastes. Melrose got up and went to the window again and saw the moon cast an ambient light across the misty courtyard. Where could the girl be but on the moors? Suddenly, he thought of Mr. Nelligan and relief flooded him for a few moments. Abby was probably sitting in Mr. Nelligan's van warming herself with a cup of cocoa at the very moment Caroline was being beaten.

But he didn't really believe it and walked morosely back to the armchair. Absently, he rolled the brandy around the balloon glass and thought about Ann Denholme. Ann Denholme sitting on his bed. Ruby's comments. The persistent beat of the most depressing of the songs

> *they're taking her children away*
> *because they said she was not a good mother*

A relentless dirge of guitar chords. It mimicked the repetitive, meaningless sexual encounters of Caroline—army officers, incest, she drew the line at nothing. He half-smiled thinking of Major George Poges. But even given Ruby's hints of Ann Denholme's promiscuity, Melrose couldn't imagine her trying it out on Poges.

> *miserable rotten slut couldn't turn*
> *anyone away*

Up again, he paced round the room. He stopped, went out into the hall, looked at the boots lined up there, and noticed the Princess's ermine-lined ones were missing. Perhaps she'd decided to dine with Poges after all.

What was a woman like that, with her printed velvets and figured satins, her Worths and Lady Duff Gordons . . . what was she doing here?

He returned to the front room and the fireplace and

leaned his head down on his folded arms. Police. Should he call them. About what? No one else was in the slightest way concerned that Abby hadn't eaten her tea. He sighed and paced.

Charles Citrine. Charles Citrine was a regular visitor to Weavers Hall. . . . It was ridiculous to jump to such a conclusion. He knew the man only through that brief meeting. Still.

Ann Denholme had got a phone call; she'd left and been walking in the direction of that house. When he'd stopped by on his way from Harrogate, had he seen that cloaked figure against the sky taking the same route?

But if Charles Citrine had rung up, if he were the one waiting on the moor, why? Or one of the others in that household—Nell Healey or her aunt. Had Charles Citrine thought to marry Ann Denholme? Inheritance couldn't be a motive. Had the sister, Rena, hope of her brother's money? According to Jury they didn't get on. And Nell Healey was far richer than her father. If not money, what?

Knowledge? Blackmail?

> *since she lost her daughter*
> *it's her eyes that fill with water*

That scrap of conversation during breakfast. How Ann Denholme had gone to tend her ill and pregnant sister because the doctor feared another miscarriage.

The Princess had said Ann Denholme hadn't been here when she'd made her first visit to Weavers Hall. That had been eleven years ago. *Doesn't come on as the motherly type, not to me,* George Poges had added. *Why'd she take over the child? Doesn't seem to care much about her. . . .*

> *because of the things that*
> *she did in the streets and*

5

He heard the piercing sound from down there where she
was. She hadn't come with the sound. He knew what it
meant but he was used to seeing *her,* her being there behind
the sound, aiming the crook or making the clicking and
snapping noises or, sometimes, only her eyes telling him
what to do. Or trying to. She wasn't that good, but she was
small, too, like most of the sounds she made. She couldn't
know everything.

What he *did* know was danger and that there was too
much of it in that cracking noise, the air splitting above his
head. He could sniff it like blood. Blood everywhere on the
snow.

He had not run away. He had run farther, higher, to
watch and wait.

He looked sharp to one side then to the other, his nose for
the heady smell of the Smokes. They were standing or moving silently down on the moor and round the banky hillside.
More were on the other side and he'd have to get behind
them and—

He froze. An onrush of white over there was making for
the Smokes and running faster than he believed it ever
could. It was the Deadheel, the one that never moved from
the mat in front of the fire.

That one could *run?*

The Deadheel could move that *fast?* But if she'd sent it on
a long outrun, she wanted him to work with it.

His brief howl was not pain, not Hello. It was Oh no, oh
no, oh no and he pulled it back into his throat.

Oh, *no.*

In a straight line from his point to its point, he looked at
the Starer and panted from the long outrun toward the
Clouds. He'd watched the Starer sometimes freeze a cloud

with his starey eyes and go right on until he'd frozen himself, as if he was staring at his own eyes.

It wasn't the best way to get the Clouds to obey. You had to get your teeth into them.

But they would have to do this together. Oh, no.

He started climbing the hill and so did the Deadheel. A stumbling hill of banks where the Smokes ranged wide, a hill of broken shards that made walking hard, and running awful. As he ran, some of the Smokes turned and watched.

They knew; they always knew.

Wide apart from the Starer, he'd reached the other side at the same time. He looked over at the Starer through the Clouds and caught a signal. They dashed in opposite ways.

He would have to rough them; it was better to hurl himself against several than to hang on to just one.

In widening arcs they ran until he and the Starer were behind the Clouds.

6

Carefully, Abby dragged at the bright yellow waterproof; it was blue on the inside, darker.

In the middle of getting out of one sleeve as she watched the moor and the hillside, she saw them.

A line of sheep straight across the edge of the bluff, like a platoon. Like that Zulu movie with the native tribe suddenly appearing. Her mouth had dropped open then. She was breathless, now.

She forgot everything—the cold, the danger—for she had never seen such a sight in her life.

The veiled moon rode above a tall black pillar of pine and looked like the streetlamp in the Empire of Light.

7

Ellen swung off the BMW, grabbed up the white containers from a basket she'd attached to it, and held them aloft. "You like Chinese? Sweet-and-sour pork? Lo Mein noodles—?"

"No. Abby's missing."

Ellen dropped her arms. "Missing? What d'ya mean *missing?*" Her voice was ferocious. Panther-black, she approached him.

"Missing! Disappeared! Gone."

She stopped then and looked totally confused.

"I called Superintendent Jury—"

"You expected him to find Abby in London? You think she walked to London?"

"Shut up. I rang up the Keighley police."

"Police. Wonderful. It takes them an hour just to get their bikes going." Enraged, she flung out her arm.

"This isn't New York," he yelled as the white cardboard box sailed away, noodles cascading, falling and lying in slimy drips on the stones. She took furious aim and the pork followed, this container landing inside the mesh wire of the hen yard. He heard rustles, squawks and in a moment saw flapping wings. He turned and walked toward his Bentley, cold as hoarfrost except for the anger. Let her have her tantrum, dammit.

"Where're *you* going?" she yelled at his back.

As he slid onto the seat, he yelled back: "To *look* for her, of course." He slammed the door.

She'd followed him, standing now hands on hips gazing from boot to wing of the Bentley, shaking her head. "Terrific."

"Go eat Chinese with the chickens." Melrose turned the key. The engine quietly turned over and clicked into a purr.

"Beautiful. Brilliant. Across the moors in a Bentley!" El-

len stretched out her arms and flung the words into the
night, "It's so *you!*"

"Go away." He was backing out slowly and taking her
with him because she'd clamped her hands on the windowsill. "Away, away! You're an encumbrance!" But he jammed
down on the brake.

"Listen, Wonderearl," she said, her voice dangerously
low, "you will get about forty feet in this slab. And if the
police ever *do* get here, who's to welcome them while you're
crashing around in your Batman car?"

"Malcolm. Get your hands off." Melrose tried to push
them. They were steel clamps. He nodded up toward the
dully lit window. Malcolm waved furiously.

She squinched her eyes nearly shut, looking up. "You've
got to be kidding!"

"And you." Since she'd released her grip, he backed up,
spitting gravel.

Ellen hurled herself at the car and he hit the brake again.
She yanked the door open, grabbed his arm, and jostled
Melrose away from the wheel.

"Get your damned hands *off* me!"

She didn't.

He tripped on a stone, nearly went down, thinking if he'd
fallen she'd simply have grabbed his collar and dragged him.
Now she was shoving him onto the long, leather seat of the
BMW. As she hopped on in front, he was pushed onto the
metal fender. The noise of the bike's engine was shattering.
As the bike shot away from the Hall, Melrose had to grab
for her waist. He glanced back and saw Malcolm waving
some idiot flag and could have sworn the chickens had
rushed up in a long line and were beating their wings in
applause.

8

The bike had slogged and sloshed down a green lane, come out on the Oakworth Road, then found an opening in a rotten wooden fence and they were now bucking along across the frozen field.

Melrose raised his voice, which was carried away by the wind anyway, and asked, "Do you know where you're going?"

"No." The word wailed in the onrushing wind.

"Keighley Moor." He took one arm from her waist and pointed west: "That way."

Ellen bumped across a stream and whipped the bike toward the west.

The bitter wind whipped his jacket back and he knew he would be in hospital straightaway. Still, he had to admit the race through the cold moist air, his arms hugging Ellen's waist, was exhilarating.

At least until he saw the low stone wall rushing toward them.

9

He saw the stone wall, knew the Smokes wouldn't want to move when they got there, knew he could fly over it, but they could only go through the rubble. The leader would try to hold and then to bolt.

A rush of Smokes just in front was already dithering and moving off to the left. He circled out to the left, corkscrewing to confuse them, and he got them back on course. Smokes could run. And Smokes were smart.

Something told him he shouldn't be tasting this thick salty stuff but if the Cloud wouldn't move, the others near would stop, too. Charge the whole lot. Waste of time. He

rounded on the big, stubborn one, caught its heel, clamped
down. The Cloud made its dumb angry noise, but it moved
back toward the mob and the others followed. He made a
quick zigzag line in front of his part of the mob, showing
them Teeth. Teeth, Teeth, Teeth, Teeth. Then back to his
position, running slightly behind them. He looked over at
the Starer dashing toward a Cloud way on the other side.
The Starer only had Eyes. Eyes.

He was right. The Smokes were nearly at the wall. Black-
wet, the wall ran like a river across the moor. He couldn't
see the place where he knew she was, since he'd left the
hilltop, but he knew she was only a clear field away on the
other side of this wall. The place where she'd gone with the
one in big boots and a gun who seemed to be trying to shoot
the sky down. Never got it, though.

He was right; he would have to use a powerful eye on the
old one, the leader. It was the leader who'd get the other
Smokes through and over.

Lowering his tail, he crouched as if he had a saddle on his
back, his belly nearly touching the ground.

He held the old Smoke's eye for a long time. He could
have stayed here the night, but he had to get them moving.
The Smoke stared back, then broke the look and started
moving a little to the right, then a little to the left, but he
couldn't break the look.

He moved in on it.

Deadheel was running a quarter-moon course at the rear
of the mob. Good.

The mob was crowding at the wall but the old Smoke
wouldn't move.

He couldn't waste time, because she was in danger. He
had no choice.

He shuddered. He'd have to *bark*.

The old Smoke crashed through the opening and the rest
went spilling after it.

10

It was all Abby could do to keep down because once again she couldn't believe it had worked. Worked this far, anyway.

Mr. Nelligan's sheep had been moved down the rocky hillside faster than she could believe possible. That was a hard drive. Hours, it should have taken.

Now they were cascading through the wall as if the wall were nearly invisible, no more than veils of smoke, mist, and clouds.

Again, Abby wanted to stand up and cheer and yell at this mob running toward her, driven by Stranger and Tim. The Gun would not be able to shoot, load up and shoot again and again, even if it were stupid enough to try picking off a hundred and twenty sheep.

But she did at least rise up on her knees and clasp her hands beneath her chin in a prayerful pose.

Looking up at the heavens, she thought, *Oh, why not?* and started to give thanks to Jane's, Helen's, and Charlotte's God. But then she lowered her fisted hands to her hips, and called up,

"It was *my* idea!"

She dropped back, trying to fold herself like an accordion, arms tight round her legs, but still watching the sheep running straight at her—

Oh, no!

11

The bike roared on through the underpinning of ground mist, nearly spilling Melrose as Ellen jumped a frozen stream as if it were an obstacle in a steeplechase.

They had zigzagged between drystone walls searching for the one Melrose remembered. Once the bike had skidded in loose dirt and toppled them both by a melting snowbank. She drove the BMW in ever-widening circles and through corkscrew turns at the ends of packed-down lanes.

After the second spill that had Ellen aiming mild obscenities at the BMW that seemed to sputter and grind in some sort of metallic rhythm, Melrose tried to work a boulder out of his shoe and mud off his jacket. Ellen had fanned out the ordnance map she used for her Brontë turns, paying him little attention, holding the map in front of her headlamp as she revved the engine, dying to get going again.

When Melrose had hoisted himself behind her, she tossed the map back at him and came down so hard on the pedal the bike bucked around now like an unbroken horse.

He took time out from worrying over Abby to remind himself that in spite of that incredible look of *purpose*, that intensity of eye, that frost that sparkled her hair, she was intractable, as grimy as his gardener, and probably in flagrante delicto with her BMW.

"Over there!" Melrose yelled, seeing the distant light of Nelligan's gypsy caravan.

"*Where?*"

"Straight on. Run along that wall—"

It came out as a wail, lost, but she careened the bike down the slope of the hill and another onrush of wind smacked him in the face.

Melrose unlocked his eyes to look across her shoulder as best he could. "Down there," he shouted, seeing the opening in the wall. His hand shading his eyes, he saw the hulk of what he thought might be a dead sheep until it moved sluggishly. "Don't hit that—"

She didn't. They didn't sail through the opening as much as they did *over* it. He was half-turned to look back through the rubble at the hindquarters of the moonlighting sheep and was, therefore, totally unprepared for the sudden braking of the bike.

Ellen said, "What the *hell*—" as the BMW careened into a whirling dervish-dance, tossing Melrose into the rocky furze. "—is that?" she added, bringing the bike out of its spin and stopping with a thud. Her black-clad arm pointed ahead. She rose from the bike, using the pedals like stirrups.

Melrose struggled up from the broken rocks and rime-hard heather to inspect his ripped up trouser leg and the additional damage done to his sleeve, which was hanging by little more than threads.

"Well, *look!*" Ellen called back at him.

"Sheep! Don't you know *sheep* when you see them? I think my ankle's broken."

Her voice was high and frenzied now. "I think I'll go back to Queens."

Melrose dragged himself onto the BMW, which was clearly raring to go, and said, "Stop complaining. Go!" And he slapped the fender.

Less than a minute later, the BMW slid to a stop a few feet from the herd, and Melrose thought he'd swung free of it until his bootlace caught in the wheel spokes, landing him facedown.

"Hell's bells," he mumbled, reaching up to wipe away what felt like a lacework of blood. Ellen, naturally, had managed to land on her feet and was waving him furiously on.

To where? There were sheep everywhere, two hundred or so, he judged, as he hobbled along. There was Ethel's dog, Tim, throwing himself at one of them that was about to bolt. The Kuvasc's teeth were clamped in the thick wool of the leg. He ran, negligent of the ankle that was killing him, round to the other side, where Ellen looped back and forth, running like a border collie, only aimlessly.

Melrose saw Stranger standing taut as a bow, giving an old ewe the eye. Rising from the bleats and the awful smell of wet wool came a voice from in there somewhere.

"Get me *out* of here!"

The voice was familiar, both in sound and tone. Demanding, irascible.

"It's her, it's Abby!" Ellen was jumping up and down trying to get a view.

In absolute wonderment, Melrose worked his way to the back of the low wall. A dozen sheep were standing in some sort of hypnotic trance and Melrose muscled them out of the way to get to the wall, where he reached over, dragged Abby up on her feet, and bounced her over the backs of the sheep.

She was a mess, standing there black in both body and mind, saying to Melrose, "I could have *died* out here. And Stranger's foot's bleeding . . . give me a piece of your shirt."

"I hardly have any left," said Melrose, ripping a strip from the shredded end. "Here!"

Abby reached down and bound up Stranger's foot as best she could. Then she rose, wheeled away from them, beating the mud and bits of grit from her waterproof and shawl. As both of them stood there staring from her to the sheep, she wheeled round again, saying: "Oh, leave them, just *leave* them," as if the bumping, bleating mob were a big load of dirty dishes. "It's Mr. Nelligan's sheep; he'll find them and maybe it'll teach him a lesson."

Ellen pulled her bike upright and rolled it beside her, as Abby lost no time straightening both of them out on *who* and *what* saved *whom* in this rescue mission. She began with herself, went on in great detail about Stranger and Tim, and then praised the sheep for their part. Man did not come into it.

They walked on, followed at a distance by the two tired dogs, while Melrose said he'd go to Harrogate before he'd go back to Weavers Hall if it meant hurtles through fiery hoops, dives across abysses, plummets through the air with Ellen as driver.

"I'd sooner crawl," he announced. "You must be the world's worst."

Just then they heard the distant sputter of engines and saw, across the far field, ghostly lights bobbing, appearing, disappearing as incline and uprise dictated. There were at

least three, possibly four motorcycles scattered round the
moor.

"Police!" exclaimed Melrose, wanting to tear the ragged
shirt from his body and wave it like someone marooned.
"Police! At least, thank God, I can get a ride back with
someone who knows how—"

The crash was deafening, splintering. That was to the left;
off to the right he saw what looked like a black shape wheeling in the air, coming down with a ground-shaking thud.

A little flame darted up from the match Ellen was using to
light her cigarette, which she then casually smoked, leaning
against her BMW, looking at him with a question stamped
on her grimy face. She shrugged. "Two outta three."

Melrose shrugged his shoulders and his sleeve fell off.

Thus they trudged on beneath the icy moon, fragments of
argument trailing back to the dogs as the three up front got
farther away. . . .

"*Three* of us? On *that?*" Melrose's question was lost in the
distance.

". . . the basket," Ellen shouted.

". . . not *me*. I'm not sitting . . ." Abby's voice proclaimed.

"*I'll* sit in the basket." Melrose limped along.

Stranger and Tim trotted on behind them on bloody feet
and lame legs, looking longingly behind them at the mob of
sheep who now were dispersing, searching out browse in
slightly new territory.

They turned more or less nose-to-nose, looking at one
another, both yawning and shaking themselves.

The ways of sheep were difficult, sometimes inscrutable.

The ways of man, impossible.

33

The Nine-One-Nine was a cellar walk-down where nothing at the moment was moving but the smoke from the bored-looking customers' cigarettes and cigars. At the farther end of the long, cavelike room was a cleared-out space with a small stage filled with amps, drums, a couple of micro-phones, and a keyboard. Blue lights suspended from a cross-beam were trained on the stage from which the band had departed.

Jury doubted any casuals could have found the place, thus it must have been the regulars who stood and sat about in varying stages of ennui, a curiously epicene crowd. Women with slick-backed dark hair, men with brassy curls and rings in their ears signifying (Jury bet) nothing. They stood in the aisle; they sat at the bar. In this room architecturally bland, the only hat-tipping to affluence was the very long, copper-topped bar behind which were shelved yards of bottles with optics in front. The smoke swirled, drifted, thinned, clouded above the tables, and the benches sat like church pews against the left-hand wall.

Besides this démodé crowd there were still some working-class men who sat in tightly knit little groups like clenched fists, hard knuckles grasping their pints.

The customers all looked like they belonged here because they didn't belong anyplace else. Jury remembered a café in Berlin that had looked this way: musty, furzy, with the odd gummy smell of resin and old cigars.

* * *

Jury could have picked Stan Keeler out of this haze of smoke and thirties' film backdrop even without Morpeth Duckworth's description. There was something about the man at the center table, about his posture and manner, about the several people who sat there, that told Jury who he was. He was wearing a plain black T-shirt, jeans, and low boots, his feet parked on one of the chairs, the rest of him slumped in another. There were two women and a man at his table. One of the hero-worshipping women had hair the color of port that nearly drowned her shoulders; the other was a hermetically sealed blonde who looked as if she hadn't moved a muscle in days, as if her mouth would crack and her cheekbones splinter beneath the makeup if she smiled. Leaning against the wall was another woman—tall, serpentinian, smoke curling upward from her cigarette to dissipate into the rest of the smoky scrim. Her hair and black dress looked as if they'd been done with the same shears: both were layered and slashed. Her eyes were nearly shut, weighted with kohl liner and deep shadow sunken in a powder-white face.

As Jury wedged his way through a tight knot of customers, the leather-vested fellow with a sunburst guitar was arguing, leaning forward toward Keeler like a man trying to shoulder into a tree that wouldn't give: ". . . can you say that git can play blues? He's heavy-metal and a Bach/baroque freak that couldn't do a twelve-bar boogie if his life depended on it." As he spoke he was slapping the guitar up to his knee and doing a *wumpa wumpa wumpa wumpa wumpa* progression that earned him a tiny rustle of applause and an urging on to play more. Someone called him Dickie. Dickie didn't notice or didn't care. "So the dumb git's fast—" His fingers slid down the neck to pick the strings at what sounded to Jury like lightning speed, and there was more between-tables applause. "So he's fast? You're fast; I'm fast; and I know a blues baseline when I hear one. He's got nothing to do with that kinda thing. Come on, admit it, Stan."

Stan Keeler just sat there staring at him.

"Either you or me could blow him off the stage. Why don't you admit I'm right?"

"Because, number one, you don't know shit, and number two, you don't know it in Swedish."

Dickie swore under his breath, grabbed up his guitar, and did one of those rolling-thunder John Wayne walks back to the stage at the end of the room. As Jury came up to the table he saw the black Labrador, face on paws and apparently asleep. He seemed happy to be propping up a black guitar case, the neck of which lay across his back as if it were another dog.

"You're Stan Keeler?" said Jury, watching the heads of the girls swivel to gaze up at him. The redhead smiled. The blonde couldn't seem to make it. The one against the wall lowered her lids even more.

Stan Keeler looked at him and Jury knew the meaning of burning eyes. They reminded Jury of brandy just as someone touched a flame to it. The indolent expression beneath the black curly hair was given the lie by those eyes that could have singed Jury where he stood and by the luminous, child-like skin. He was in some way the apotheosis of the gaunt woman behind him; he had the coloring and intensity that she had tried to find in the pots on the dressing table. The high-cheekboned face looked a little emaciated under the tight, dark curls. And the expression on Stan Keeler's face seemed completely passive.

He said in a tone-dead voice: "I'm thirty-two, live in a bed-sit in Clapham. It sucks. Black Orchid's next club date is two weeks hence. I was born in Chiswick; my mum still lives there. My favorite food is jellied eels. I stopped doing drugs when I fell off the stage three years ago. I got a land-lady with a nose you could hang your pants on. She sucks. The reason I don't move is because most of London sucks. I smoke some, drink some. That's all. Print it. Good-bye."

"I hardly said hello."

"Hello. Good-bye. Bugger back to Fleet Street. You're from *New Dimensions,* right?"

"Wrong. I'm from the C.I.D." Jury showed him his warrant card.

Stan Keeler's expression still didn't change as he flicked his eyes over the card and his cigarette at the ashtray. At the same time he took his boots off the chair, motioning Jury to sit, he turned to the redhead and blonde and said, "Go away." He said nothing to the domino leaning against the wall; Jury had the impression she wasn't interested anyway.

The two girls rose as a team and moved their blank eyes off through the customers toward the end of the room. Dickie seemed to be tuning up; a sallow-faced youth with long crimped hair was fooling with the drums; a gaunt-looking black man was sitting with an instrument case by his side.

Stan Keeler crossed one low boot over the other knee and rubbed at it with fingers that looked agile enough to catch butterflies without dusting a wing. He looked almost pleased. "I belt my old lady and they send round the C.I.D.? She deserved it." He scratched his hair into an even greater tangle of curls. "The only guy she missed in Clapham was the flasher on the common and I ain't sure he's telling the truth."

"Your old lady? I was afraid you meant your mum."

"Mum lives in Chiswick. I managed to shock just about everyone except her. God knows I tried. It makes no difference if I go double platinum or what. She just says, 'Stanley, you been to mass?'" His voice was a high-pitched squeal. "So what kind of shit you're laying down here? You mad at me because I messed up Delia?"

"Not particularly."

"You guys are sadists. Hey." He snapped his fingers. "I already talked to your friend. He was cool." Stan laughed, choked on smoke, and wiped away some spittle. "Your friend got by Nose. She thinks she's protecting me from the press. It's got nothing to do with my band; it's because she thinks I'm a Pole. An *agent provocateur,* or something. She saw me in this newspaper photo with Lech Walesa."

"What were you doing in a photo with Walesa?"

Stan looked disgusted, searching Jury's face for signs of intelligent life, apparently. "What the hell would I be in a picture with Walesa for? Do I play Gdansk? It was just some cretin who looked like me. I told Mum this story and she told me Lech goes to mass all the time, and why ain't I more like him? Want a beer? If you drink bottled, I can send Stone. Hey, Stone, man—" He raised his bottle of Abbott's and the Labrador rose, yawning. Keeler held up one finger. The dog burrowed off through the crowd. "He can only get one at a time." He sounded apologetic.

"I can only drink one at a time. Look, Mr. Keeler—"

"Call me Stanislaw. Nose does. Wanna go to Brixton? There's a pub there I play at for free some nights. They're in kind of deep shit, and I help the manager out."

"You're very humane."

"No humanity to it. I'm trying to get it on with his wife."

"Sorry. Brixton's out. I want some information." Two other women had more or less oozed into the empty chairs. They looked like twins. Stan told them to get lost.

"You knew Roger Healey, the music critic."

"I didn't know him and I wouldn't call him a critic."

"According to my sergeant, you did." Jury heard Dickie run something by the microphone and the band started up. "Healey didn't seem to care for your music very much. As a matter of fact, the reviews I read made it sound like a vendetta. Why would he be devoting a column to you, anyway. *Segue*'s pop, jazz, rock critic is Morpeth Duckworth."

"You been talking to Rubber Ducky?" His head was turned to watch the band and his eyes squeezed in pain at the high whine of the slide guitar. "Oh, we have *certainly* got a double platinum."

The customers were beginning to wake up and inch nearer the stage. Stone was back with a bottle clamped in his jaws and Stan took it and snapped the cap off with an opener on his keychain. The dog lay back down again. Stan shoved the Abbott's toward Jury.

"Again, why?"

"Huh?"

"Roger Healey. Why was he trying to get at you?"

"I expect because he was coming on to my old lady."

"Are you saying Healey was having an affair with your wife?"

"Aren't you old-fashioned? I never said she was my wife." He was searching out a butt in the littered tin ashtray. Jury tossed his own packet on the table, but Stan said, "Thanks, but new ones don't taste as schmuzzy." He found half a cigarette and lit it. "Deli's not my wife, though I think she might be several other guys'. She said, no, she wasn't screwing Healey, but Deli couldn't open her mouth without lying. She even lied about the weather. Pathological, right?"

"Deli who?"

Stan's eyes were on the group bathed in blue light. He didn't answer.

"Mr. Keeler?"

His fingers were beating a rhythmic tattoo on the table.

"Deli's last name?" asked Jury patiently.

"I never asked. Dickie's getting better; he must've cleaned the moss off that slide."

"Sounds great to me, but we won't stick around for it. Come on." Jury rose and the lady whom one of the customers had called Karla turned her head slowly to stare at him. People didn't order her boy around, it seemed.

"Come where, for God's sake?"

"New Scotland Yard. You can't seem to keep your mind on answers here."

"You're a real happening guy."

"That's me."

"Look, I don't know if it's her real name." Stan motioned him to sit back down. Karla looked off into the unfiltered air again. "She said it was Magloire. Delia Magloire. No one knew how to say it right, so we just called her Deli MacGee."

Jury had his notebook out. "Where was she from?"

"Martinique. So she said. Well, she did look like she might of come from the islands. Honey-colored skin, hair as black as Stone here." He reached down to scratch the dog's head. "Don't ask me where she went to . . ." His voice trailed off as he concentrated on the inert dog. Stone was a good name.

"Pretty?"

"Oh, yes. Thick as two planks, but pretty, oh, yes."

"How'd she meet Healey?"

Stan mashed out the butt, searched for another. "She was on her way to the Hammersmith Odeon and stumbled into the Royal Albert Hall by mistake. You believe that, you believe anything. About two A.M. she weaves past Nose and up to the flat and says, 'Love, Eric's got this big new band . . .'" He raised his eyebrows above the tiny match-flame. "The London Symphony. She wanted me to think she was that dumb. Then she starts talking about this famous music critic and kind of oomphing round the old bed-sit, puts on Robert hootchi-koo Plant and wants to dance. I never could figure out what possible centrifugal force could blow Deli across the path of that pissant Healey."

"When did Deli leave?"

Stan shrugged. "Year ago." He glanced at the small stage where the blue lights made the group look cyanosed. Dick-ie's slide screamed in Jury's ears. He wondered how Wiggins could make it through a concert without a nosebleed. "If that slide's got moss on it, you couldn't prove it by me," he shouted across the table. "Did you believe her? About Hea-ley?"

Stan shrugged. "Why not? The guy was a lech."

It was getting harder to talk and to hear. The riffs were ear-splitting and the drummer had gone into an epileptic frenzy. Jury's ears seemed to have closed up, as if he were in a plummeting airplane. Stan was pulling a black Stratocaster from the case on the floor.

As he fastened the leather strap around his neck, the dog gave a terse bark. "Sounds like Dickie's picking with the top of a tin again. I think I'll join. Stick around.

"Where's the picks, Stone?"

The dog snuffled in the long arm of the case and brought out a tortoiseshell pick.

"Not *that,* for chrissakes. Thinner."

Stone spat out the one in his mouth, rooted again, brought out a black one nearly thin enough to see through.

"Thanks." He stuck the pick beneath the strings.

"Did Deli MacGee dump Healey?"

"I'd say so. She made some comment about him 'trading licks' that wasn't—how'd she put it?—'within my venue.' " Stan smiled. "I kinda liked that."

"What did she mean?"

Stan brought his hand away from the tuning knobs, hit a chord. "Come *on,* man. What'd'ya *think?* Healey wasn't an axeman. At best a ladies' man, at second best a lech, at worst a sado. You look surprised. You're a cop; you've seen these squirrely types before."

"And were those reviews written after Deli walked out?"

"You got it."

"Jealousy?"

"Who knows?" Stan shrugged. "Who cares?"

You do, thought Jury, sadly, looking at the smudges under Stan Keeler's eyes. "Martin Smart seems to think he was knowledgeable. How could the man you describe keep such a reputation as a critic?"

Stan reached out his arms slightly, inviting Jury to survey the room. "You see any critics in here? They're sitting in Italian leather swivel chairs in their 'study' recycling shit in their PCs. The only one that comes to Nine-One-Nine is Duckworth. Listen, man, Healey didn't know sod-all about rock, jazz, nothing. What's all this about, anyway?"

"Mrs. Healey. She shot him."

"She deserves a medal, not a fucking police investigation."

Jury rose. "Thanks for your help. But I'm wondering why you didn't tell all of this to my sergeant."

"I had a chain-saw hangover, man. I didn't feel like jamming with a cop. Listen, stick around. We can go to that Brixton place I was saying."

Jury shook his head, smiled, and extended his hand.

The band had slipped into a blues number and the old man by the piano had opened his case and was fitting the mouthpiece to a sax. Several couples had wandered onto the dance floor and stood in dreamy proximity to one another.

"Hey, Stone." The dog was up in a flash. Stan turned and said to Jury, "You going to look for Deli?"

Jury smiled. "If I find her I'll let you know."

"Hell, find me a landlady instead. Come on, Stone, let's lay some shit down."

Stan pushed his way through a crowd that willingly parted for him, followed by the black dog. He leapt onto the raised platform beneath the blue lights, and nearly before his feet hit the floor he let go with a sizzling riff followed by some staccato picking that made Jury's skin prickle, it was that fast. Then he switched over to a murky ghost bend, picking up the blues line of the old man with the sax. Its languor made him feel the poisonous losses of the past were working their way through his bloodstream.

He turned to go, throwing a look at Karla, who was still leaning against the wall, still looking wanton and sad as a long rainy Berlin night.

34

Only the Princess (and Ruby, who opened the door to him) appeared to be in attendance at Weavers Hall when Jury turned up early the next morning.

Ruby said she imagined Mr. Plant was still asleep, as he always tended to be the last one down for breakfast: a look of disapproval accompanied this.

Plant was not, however, in his room. On the way down the hall he saw the Princess, in hers. The door was open; she was packing an old steamer trunk full of her elegant garments. One of these she was holding against her, assessing the effect in a cheval mirror. The blue dress was of crepe and chiffon, loose and languid, something the pre-Raphaelites would have admired.

Seeing Jury's reflection in her mirror, she turned, unsurprised, to ask: "What do you think?"

"Beautiful. You're leaving?"

"Oh, yes. The Major and I are going up to London for a month or two. Or three. I'm weary of death . . ." She sighed.

(As she might have sighed over the London season or the tag-end of summer in Cannes, thought Jury.)

"It seems to be making the rounds like a virus." She flashed a smile at him in the mirror, then turned to toss the blue dress over the open trunk, and to pick another garment from the wardrobe. "And we see no one these days but police." The Princess held the printed velvet jacket, sleeves bound in dark green satin, to her shoulders. "That poor child," she went on, as she caught her reflection from different angles, "alone out there on the moors. I simply *cannot* believe anyone would want to do her mischief." She tossed the jacket across the trunk beside the dress. "The trouble is it's so difficult to know what to take. *You've* just been there. What are they showing? Givenchy? Lacroix? I heard Saint Laurent was changing his hemlines again. I hope not too short: he does such lovely long skirts." At the moment she was holding one of her own against her waist, black and falling in a thousand narrow pleats. "And you needn't look at me that way," she said to the reflection in the mirror.

"What way?"

"Patronizing. Disapproving. Because I'm not at the funeral."

"*Funeral?*"

She was turning this way and that, kicking the skirt about. "Some cat or other. You should have heard the screaming this morning." When Jury looked a question at her, she went on. "Ruby: she found the cat in the freezer. Mrs. Braithwaite gave Abby quite a tongue-lashing. Didn't make any impression."

She gave Jury an impatient, yet pearly glance. "*I* didn't know the cat, for heaven's sakes."

2

Behind the barn, the service was in progress. The four people there were framed like a picture by the big open doors at that end of the threshing floor. Jury stood in the shadow it cast, hesitant to join them, somehow feeling he hadn't the right to participate. He hadn't, after all, been around when tragedy had struck.

Melrose and Ellen stood solemnly on one side of the small grave, still open, into which the box containing Buster (under its black cloth) had been lowered. Six votive candles outlined the opening. On the other side sat Tim and Stranger, close together, with bandaged paws, both with the sort of blue and green ribbons presented at dog shows fastened to their collars. Tim kept trying to get at his blue one with his teeth. Stranger was looking up at Abby with sorrowful eyes, and then farther up at the sky as if, in her words, were some intimation of an animal heaven.

A little girl in powder blue and with a fresh ribbon in her hair (whom Jury assumed to be the friend Ethel) stood there by the dogs. Her head was bowed, her small hands folded against her starched skirt. She looked far more angelic and heaven-bent than Abby, planted firmly at the head of the grave in a black slicker and wellingtons with her Bible, looking dark and retributive and wild with the wind blowing her black hair. She had that controlled expression of one who accepts pain and death as if they were unbridled, poorly trained hounds that would follow her to the end, gouging her heels.

Whether she was looking at him or through him, Jury couldn't tell. When she started reading again, he realized it wasn't a Bible, but a dark-covered, flimsy-paged book of poetry.

> *No more I'll see your splendid outward sweep*
> *With ears erect and drooping head and tail*
> *Nor view your gliding turns in front of sheep.*

He saw the frown cross Ethel's face at the recitation of this verse. Then Abby snapped the book shut and the marker fluttered to the ground. It was his card, the one he had given her before he left. Surely, that had been longer than yesterday?

Picking up a handful of dirt, she let it trickle on top of the black cloth.

Ethel mewled: "Oh, Buster, I'll miss you soooo. . . ." That sentiment earned her a glare from Buster's mistress, and a warning-off of whatever specious words Melrose Plant was about to say. He shut his mouth.

Abby turned her face to the grave and nodded slightly and said, as if some terrible accounting between Buster and the wretched forces of this earth had been settled, "Goodbye."

And keep cold, thought Jury.

Abby retrieved his card from the ground, stuck it in her pocket, and then handed Melrose the shovel.

Ethel was playing hostess, handing out cups of tea and roughly cut slices of brown bread and butter. It was she (Ethel informed them) who had had to remind Abby that people had to be *fed* after funerals. It was the proper thing to do. And it took her all yesterday to make the cake.

Abby sat in her rocking chair, white-knuckled hands round the ends of the arms, gazing at the floor. Ethel skipped lightly across the floor, wanting, apparently, to bounce the full skirt of her dress and show off her lace petticoat.

As she put the piece of cake on the bookcase-crate she whispered, "That poem was about a *dog;* Buster never ran around *sheep.*"

Abby gave her a look that would have flattened an entire mob.

Then Ethel twirled off, skipping back to Melrose, Ellen, and the dogs. She removed the ribbons from their collars and went over to the bulletin board to pin them up. They were old ribbons, weather-worn and faded. Tim, Jury noticed, had had the blue one. Stranger's was green. Second prize.

Abby stared at her, one hand removed from the chair arm and curling in a fist in her lap. "That's Ethel," she said with a sigh, the first words she'd spoken to Jury. He was sitting on her bed deep in the comforters.

"That's Ethel." He smiled.

Her mouth hooked up at the corners, but she quickly

stopped the grin that threatened. Grinning was not on, not at Buster's funeral. "The earl was there when I got Buster." When Jury looked puzzled, she said, "At Loving Kindness. The vet's. He had his cat but I don't know what he did with it."

The notion of Melrose Plant wrestling a cat into the vet's made Jury smile. It had to have been a stray. The only animal that Plant had ever bothered to develop a rapport with was his old dog, Mindy.

"I'm sure the cat wasn't his," said Jury. "He must have found it by the road, or somewhere."

"Oh." Abby rocked a bit harder, absorbing this new information. The earl wasn't a heartless wretch who'd dump his cat and never go back. "Anyway, he's pretty smart." The corners of her mouth hooked up in a smug little grin. "He found Ethel's hiding place." She gave Jury a look. "And he's not a policeman, either."

"Where was it?"

"Over behind the medicine bottles. It was just another bottle that had a Present from Brighton written on it."

"Incredible. How did he know?"

She shrugged. "I don't know, except he told her he knew, and right away she looked over there."

Holding back a smile, Jury studied the runners of the rocking chair, moving fast as a swing. After a few moments, he said, "I'm sorry you had to go out on the moor again this morning. It must have been hard."

"Not as hard as the first time," she said with a wonderful note of *je ne sais quoi.*

"Do you mind talking about it?"

With a pretense of world-weariness not even the Princess could have matched, Abby told him. About the phone call, the voice muffled, coughing, saying something about Stranger and Mr. Nelligan's sheep. She told Jury about the whole dreadful experience.

He asked her nothing further; there was no sense in making her repeat answers she'd already had to give a dozen times over. Jury said, "I'm sorry. I'm sorry I wasn't here."

He followed her gaze to the bulletin board, where Ethel was carefully pinning blue ribbons up. "It doesn't matter. I had Stranger and Tim. And sheep."

In that, there wasn't a hint of accusation, not a shred of irony. It was a statement of fact: this is the way the world is.

Jury sat there watching her eat her cake, feeling her disappointment.

3

"Her daughter." Jury shook his head as he jammed in the Volvo's cigarette lighter.

"Everyone who saw them *did* think Ann Denholme was Abby's mother. That's the irony." In the passenger seat, Melrose was fiddling with the radio. The doors on both sides were open, the car sitting in the drive where Jury had left it.

"Finding Trevor Cable wasn't hard. Wiggins said he sounded like a nice fellow, said he was helpful, if 'a bit croupy,' to quote my sergeant. It wasn't he who wanted to get rid of Abby. That row with Trevor Cable Mrs. Braithwaite overheard was Ann Denholme's demanding Abby come back here."

"She wanted her back so Abby could live in a barn?" Melrose shook his head. "I feel as cold right now as I think I'll ever feel." He gazed through the thin, drifting rain toward the barn from which they had just come. "Medea would have won the Mum-of-the-Year award compared with Ann Denholme. Jocasta would be an absolute *plum*. And Clytemnestra, good grief, a veritable *heroine*. People seem to forget that Agamemnon did offer up their daughter on that dismal island to appease the gods. Wouldn't you think they'd have got tired of all that patricide, matricide, infanticide, and incest? And isn't anyone going to tell Abby? Wouldn't it be better if she were undeceived?"

"Wouldn't it only mean her having to work through yet another deception?"

"What about the uncle? Trevor Cable? Sounds as if he wants her back."

"Would she *go* back? If you thought your real father had given you up, would you want him back?"

Melrose replaced the car's radio handset, sat back, said nothing for a while. Then, "But she's only a little girl, Richard. She has to have *someone.*"

"By that you mean some blood relation. Since when was blood really thicker than water? I've yet to hear relations who really cared *ever* utter those words. Which is why it's a cliché, I expect."

Melrose opened the glove box. "Superintendent Sanderson will think it provides Nell Healey with one hell of a motive for murdering Ann Denholme if Roger was the father."

Jury slumped down in his seat. "I smell money in all of this."

"I smell *The Scarlet Letter.*"

"Ann Denholme didn't strike me as a martyr. Far from it. She struck me much more as a blackmailer."

"What I meant was, in this case it's little Pearl who suffers. I'm talking about Abby as a constant reminder to Healey. Ann was flaunting her would be my guess." Melrose closed the glove box. "Perhaps something happened with the 'arrangement.' Perhaps the original idea was that if Ann got rid of Abby, Healey would divorce his wife and marry her. Something like that. But she must have been a very foolish woman to let it go on for over ten years."

"It makes sense." Jury stopped. "Are you looking for something?"

Melrose had bent down to peer under the dashboard.

"Me? No."

Jury sat back. "Emotional blackmail, though, would work with the guilty minister in your book. But it certainly wouldn't work with Healey."

"There're other ways of keeping someone on a string. And telling the wife would make for a very heavy piece of rope."

"And then she kills him? Nell Healey knew what he was like. He must have been incredibly smooth, incredibly plausible with others. But she wouldn't have killed him because of his affairs with other women."

"But if she found out Abby was his daughter—?"

Jury shook his head.

"Then why?" Melrose was running his hand under the dashboard.

"It's beginning to look—what in the *hell* are you doing?"

"Doesn't this car have a tape deck?"

Jury shut his eyes. "Judas *priest.*"

"Not them. Ellen found a copy of *Rock 'n' Roll Animal.* But there's something wrong with Malcolm's stereo."

Jury reached round to the back seat and shucked the Sony to Melrose. "Here. I'm going over to the Citrine house."

Melrose slid out of the car and shut the door. He opened the cassette player, took out the tape, inspected it. "Who's this?"

Jury took it. "Coltrane. Good-bye." Jury put the car in gear, started driving slowly.

Melrose did a little run, hand on the sill. "You wouldn't have the earphones to this, would you?"

Jury braked and nearly sent him to the ground. *"Here!"* He tossed them out the window and the car lurched forward, stopped, and he called back, "Did you ring up Vivian?"

"Vivian? Of *course* I rang Vivian."

As the Volvo drove off, Melrose plugged in the earphones and walked in the Hall to ring Vivian.

35

"I can find my way," Jury said to the silent servant who had just opened the heavy door on the depressing sight of the cold entrance room and the dim hall that reached away from it into darkness. "Don't bother announcing me."

Carefully folding his coat over her arm, she looked at him doubtfully. Jury merely smiled and waited. As unused as she apparently was to requests either to or not to announce, she shuffled off with his coat.

In the Great Hall a fire blazed in the hearth and the brasserie. But only in these two pockets did the room seem warm, for the rest was still cold, like stepping from the heat of the sun into the shadows. In the shadow of the archway Jury now stood.

Given the positions of Charles and Rena Citrine in the magisterial chairs at the end of the long table, they might have been facing off for an argument. Yet their low voices, their ignorance of the presence of another person might have brought them together not as enemies but as conspirators. It might have been his imagination but his sense of their relationship, seeing them thus, was turned around.

When he said *good morning,* their heads turned together. It wasn't long, though, before Charles Citrine was on his feet and displaying as much hostility as he probably ever let show. Jury expected he prized that cool, shambling manner of his above all else.

It must have taken steely control to limit his anger at Jury's appearance to a mere "Just what are you doing here?"

"Trying to help your daughter."

Citrine slumped back in his chair and said nothing.

His sister looked from him to Jury. "And do you think we're *not?*" Her smile was a trifle arch.

"I don't know, do I?"

Citrine shot him a vitriolic glance.

"Charles . . ." Rena leaned forward a bit.

Jury would never have pictured Rena Citrine as a peacemaker. Certainly not for the brother she had so often referred to as "Saint Charles." But the circumstances here were rather more serious than what part of the house she felt she had been permitted to occupy.

She said to him, gesturing toward the heavy walnut chair positioned several feet in front of the brasserie, "You needn't stand, Superintendent." The brandy decanter that she and her brother had been sharing she lifted, as invitation to join them. Jury shook his head. The glasses from which they drank were cut glass, heavily pointed. The decanter itself looked like old pressed glass, smooth. She shoved it across the table toward Charles, who poured a half inch into his glass. The lines round his mouth had deepened since Jury had seen him, as heavily cut as the glass in his hand.

Jury said, "Ann Denholme got a telephone call before she set out across Keighley Moor. Doubtful it was a friend since the housekeeper says Miss Denholme barely said a word. Might have been a message from the milk-float man about a delivery. Might have been Nelligan about stray sheep. Might have been anyone." Jury watched a large log roll down, split, send up sparks. He did not bother watching their faces, for they had heard all of this before.

As Charles Citrine wearily reminded him. "But more likely someone from this house. We've been through this again and again with police from Wakefield and that detective, Sanderson."

"What you think," said Rena, "is that someone in this house lured poor Ann Denholme to her death. Given we're rather short on family at the moment, the suspects are few. And I don't expect you think our servant was the gun-wielder." Her arm went toward Charles as she gestured for the decanter. For just past eleven in the morning, the decanter appeared to have done quite a bit of traveling. But neither of them seemed in the least drunk.

"And Mrs. Healey, of course," said Jury mildly.

Citrine dropped his head in his hands. But his sister turned, as he had done earlier, and flashed Jury a look of rage. "Don't be absurd. You don't believe that for a minute!" Her glass went down with a thump.

In the same mild tone, Jury said, "Anyone could have made both of those calls to Ann Denholme and to Abby from a public call box."

Rena picked up her glass again without replying.

"Except we know it wasn't the milk-float man. Abby lived to talk about it."

Neither of them said a word, nor did they look at one another.

Finally, having cleared his throat perhaps to see if his voice was in working order, Charles said, "The same person?"

"Would you imagine two people were playing the game?"

Charles shook his head. Rena looked stonily across at him, seeing him or not seeing him, Jury had no idea. She finally said, "In the case of Ann Denholme, there might have been a number of candidates. Men."

Citrine's voice rose a notch, a cautionary notch. "Rena."

For a moment there was silence, and then she got up to stand before the fire, hands thrust into the large pockets of her quilted skirt. It was a patchwork of squares and crescents, satins and silks and wools, a kaleidoscope of greens and blues and golds that shimmered in the firelight. With her heel, she kicked angrily at the log that had fallen, sending up yet more blue flame, and gold sparks that made her red hair glimmer with silvery highlights, her amber eyes take on a reddish glow.

This square of the cheerless hall seemed to flame up around him; the brasserie behind, the sparking logs before, Rena in her flaming crescent colors. Jury looked at her, at her fiery pose, and knew that the slapdash, comic role as the madwoman in the tower, the outcast, the prodigal was illusory.

And he saw it:

Not the bits and pieces, not that last part of dark, leafy tree, not the scalloped edge of pale blue sky, nor the symmetry of the little windows, dark or lit. It was not the beautifully framed square of the Magritte print, but the light cast by the streetlamp in Abby's picture. In that he saw it.

36

"She's German."

Ellen was tinkering with the BMW; it had taken less of a battering than one would have thought possible. "German? *Who's* German?" She was squinting up at him over her shoulder.

Although she was holding a spanner in her raised hand he answered her. "Caroline. She's his 'Germanic Queen.' "

The seat of the bike must have been very strong; he was surprised the leather didn't split when she smashed the spanner down on it. "Will you *stop* with that fucking tape! I wish I'd never mentioned Lou Reed."

"They met in Berlin. This whole round of songs is about their relationship." The earphones went up again. Unfortunately they didn't cut out her voice.

"Who *cares* where they fucking *met?*" She started wheeling round and round, reminding him of Abby. Goading Ellen was almost as much fun as goading Agatha.

"You look really fucking stupid with those earphones on," she shouted.

"It that all you think about?" he asked mildly.

She stopped her dervish-turn two feet from him and looked at him suspiciously. "Is what?"

Melrose reached out his hand, shoved the fingers in the neck of her black jersey, and pulled her to him. As he kissed her, harder than he'd ever kissed anyone, she made a strangling sound—perhaps, one part of his mind told him, because his fingers were looping the neck of the jersey too tightly. Still with his mouth on hers, he let the jersey go, put his hand instead on the back of her head; her hair was softer than it looked, given the tangled and crinkly style. After a certain amount of pounding her fists against his heavy sweater, she went limp. That part of his mind into which blood was still pouring (all the rest was going off in different directions) thought that perhaps she was dead. Strangled. He went on kissing her.

But he must have let her go at some point because she was standing back, getting her breath, and muttering. He seemed to see this through a filament as if there were a wavering, clear waterfall between them. Or possibly he was getting cataracts.

Ellen wandered drunkenly over to her BMW and lay across the leather seat, still mumbling.

"Are you being sick?" asked Melrose. "Did we stop too soon?"

She raised herself and wheeled on him. "*No!* My Lord, I have *never* been kissed like that—"

"That's because you've manacled yourself to Manhattan men. They're all dolts who spend their lives chasing the elusive shadow of success instead of women—"

Her hands, like headphones, leapt to her head. "Shut up shut up shut up. I wasn't *complimenting* you. My God, I was nearly raped by an earl."

"Is that the trouble then, I mean the 'nearly' part?"

Her hands dropped away. She stared at him. "What *conceit.* How does any woman *manage* around you? Why don't they tear off their earlobes, or something?"

Melrose thought of Vivian, leaving tomorrow. She hadn't wasted time on Manhattan men. Only Italian, he thought woefully. He was floundering. He didn't know what was happening to him. He was listening to the bedroom scene where Caroline had cut her wrists, and he felt like weeping. But he came round in a minute as if he'd just had a fever-flash and saw Ellen looking at him with real concern.

"Ellen, you're too smart, too young, too much wanting to be another Brontë. Get out of this place; you'll die of illusion." Melrose restationed his earphones. "Let's go to Berlin."

"I don't know what you're talking about." It was hopelessness rather than dismissal in her tone. "I have deadlines to meet."

Melrose shrugged. "Let's go to New York, then, and meet them. Stop talking. I think another clue about Caroline just went missing." He pressed the 'phones to his head.

Calmly, Ellen went back to adjusting the lugs on her BMW wheel.

37

The WPC brought her into the wood-paneled room that might have been the library of a home, except for the lack of books and that it was furnished only with a long table and a chair at either end. Jury turned from the barred window where he'd been staring out at a snow-threatening sky only a shade lighter than the room itself. No burning logs, no turkey carpets relieved its unblemished paint. The room was clean in that way of places that few people stop at. Jury shut his eyes and opened them again, childishly surprised that the scene hadn't changed. That in its place there wasn't a tall tree, a weak slant of sunlight, a rotting gate.

Nell Healey herself was dressed in a square-necked prison dress, and looked like a figure in a tintype, where the faces take on the tincture of the amorphous, steely gray edging. Because of their unsmiling complicity with the camera, the faces seem all to look the same.

She was looking at him, waiting. Neither of them sat down. It was not a room to linger in, to look over the photograph album, to reminisce about the past. They stood nearly the width of the room apart.

"It's nice of you to come."

Her voice was threadbare, unraveling. She coughed slightly.

He rejected the usual openings—I hope you're not catching cold; I've just seen your father, your aunt; are they treating you well. Perhaps her own silences were infecting him.

He began to see the uselessness of that sort of talk. So he said, "I was talking to Commander Macalvie. You remember him, I know. There's probably no way he can avoid testifying."

Was that all? Her vague smile was a little dismissive. "With the Lloyd's banker dead *and* the superintendent in charge, you mean that he's the only one left who knows about the ransom."

"Knowing him, I don't think the prosecution will relish the testimony, even though they might think they're pulling a plum from the Christmas pudding. They'll be wrong."

She frowned. "Won't this have got him in trouble? To say nothing of you. I know Father called the Wakefield head-quarters—"

"I'm always in trouble. At least with my chief."

"Commander Macalvie is very convincing."

"Very."

"And is he usually right?"

"Nearly always." *You tell her, Jury. Go ahead.* The shots of the boy's skeleton passed before his eyes. "Nearly," Jury repeated. He felt ill. The temptation to show her the maga-zine, to tell her about the lunch with Charlie, was strong. But he didn't; he couldn't. Partly, it was Macalvie, but partly something else. He couldn't pin down the something else.

"Is that what you came here to tell me?"

"No. I want you to tell me what happened."

Is *that* all? her little smile said. She had turned her head toward the window. Did she care there were bars? He doubted it. She was no more prisoner in here than she'd been that afternoon a week ago, standing and searching the crippled orchard.

"Friend of mine," said Jury, "was talking about the Greeks. Medea, Jocasta, Clytemnestra. You remember the tale of Clytemnestra and Agamemnon? I mean the whole of it? Agamemnon has always been considered the husband betrayed and murdered."

She seemed amused in his telling of this tale. "And that's true. Are you drawing an analogy with me? Does your friend think I'm as evil as Clytemnestra, then?"

"He was talking about Ann Denholme."

Her expression changed very swiftly, became impassive.

"You knew Abby was her daughter. You also knew Roger was her father. I'm not sure how, but you knew."

She actually smiled. "I murdered him in a fit of jealous rage. Is that it?"

"No. You murdered him because you thought he murdered your son. And not for the reason Agamemnon nearly sacrificed Iphigenia. In that case, it was a sacrifice demanded by the gods. Fortunately, the gods gave him a last-minute reprieve. In this case, there were no gods to appease. And no reprieve. Healey wanted the money."

Her mouth slightly open, she watched his face.

Nell just avoided stumbling as she took a step toward the nearby chair and put her hand on its back. She was too careful to stumble, too controlled to lean.

"Commander Macalvie always thought that you suspected something, that you came to that decision not to pay up with extraordinary swiftness and decisiveness. The kidnapper had to have been someone Billy would have gone with willingly; there wasn't a sound, not even from the dog. You never thought they were taken by force. But who would have believed you, given your husband's near-unimpeachable reputation and your own 'highly susceptible nervous condition'? Obviously, not even your own father. And I wonder who put that idea in his head? You're the only one *in* that family whose nerves are about as strong as nerves can get. There was no way you could be absolutely certain it was Roger who was behind the kidnapping, but that suspicion together with Commander Macalvie's advice made up your mind.

"You were fairly certain if you paid up, you'd never see Billy again. Or Toby. And you'd never be able to prove it," Jury added. "But if something went wrong, and Roger failed, Billy would be able to identify him. That must have occurred to you."

"Roger never failed," was her bleak response. "If he wanted something."

"Then why did you wait all of these years?"

She looked down at her hands. "It might sound—frivolous. But one reason was that Billy and Toby had been declared 'officially' dead. In that, there was something dreadfully final."

When she stopped, Jury prompted her. "You said 'one reason.' Was there another?"

"Oh, yes. It's the reason I met Roger at the Old Silent. He wrote to me from London, said he wanted to talk about Billy, and he thought it would 'be pleasant' to have dinner at the Old Silent." She raised her eyes. "Absolutely nothing incriminating in such a letter; he phrased it carefully."

"The letter that went into the fire?"

She nodded. "Obviously, he did not want to have dinner. What he wanted was a million pounds." She turned her head to look at the barred window. "In return for information about Billy. He thought he knew, you see, what had happened."

Jury frowned. "But surely the man wasn't reckless enough to admit—"

"Oh, no." With that she rose.

He looked at her for a long moment and said, "You were never, then, one-hundred-percent sure."

"Oh, no." Folding her arms across her breast she half-smiled. "But what would you do to a father who would extort money for information about the disappearance of his own son?"

They stood there with the pale sun throwing shadows of the bars across the table that separated them.

Jury didn't need to answer.

38

Marshall Trueblood was overjoyed.

He told Melrose over the telephone that all was well with Viv, that she'd forgiven them, that they were to consider themselves reinvited to the wedding. There were, oh, a few little stipulations. . . . They were to promise they would not put into operation one or two of the plans that had apparently been hatching in "those chicken coops you and Melrose call your 'minds.'" *That's the way she put it. She's merely polishing up a few ripostes for that epicene count she's intending to let drag her to an early grave. . . .*

What plan? What was she talking about? They had hatched so many between the two of them, Melrose couldn't remember them all.

Vivian had apparently overheard that whispered conversation about "bricks" and "wine cellar," *and, of course, since the wedding is during Carnivale, she put two and two together. I told her not to be silly, that I'd have to be a lunatic to try walling up Franco—"I rest my case." That's what she said: "I rest my case."*

. . . Dior, or Saint Laurent. The gown she's considering buying in London. I told her to wait until she got to Italy and go for an Utrillo. Now I, of course, shall have a right rave up in the Armani shop. You should get rid of those knobbly old tweeds and try Giorgio. Ah, his elegance, his understatement.

Understatement? Not when Trueblood got through with Giorgio.

Must they talk about *clothes,* for God's sakes? Melrose felt he'd been wardrobed to death this afternoon, listening to the Princess, who, with the Major (still spit-polishing his boots), was now waiting with her steamer trunk for the Haworth cab. Now how the devil was she to get that thing on the train in Leeds? She'd been trying all through breakfast to get Ellen into a perfectly *divine* frock that Ellen said would make her look as shapely as a tree trunk as she dropped Mrs. Gaskill's life of Charlotte Brontë on the table and pulled on her black leather jacket.

Melrose had helped a rosy-smiling Ruby take out the dishes and cutlery and had carefully arranged napkins round the two egg cups, dropped them in his pockets, and started toward the door. He stopped, pictured Jury's questioning look, and sighed. He went back to the table and wrapped Mrs. Gaskill in his handkerchief.

2

In the Old Silent there was a better-than-average lunchtime crowd in the dining room. Jury walked through the lounge and saloon bar and asked the proprietor for a pint of Abbott's, a cheese sandwich, and the use of the telephone.

Sitting near the fire were a young man and woman with a distinctly newlywed look about them paying no attention to Jury.

Jury was halfway through his drink, thinking again about that argument between Macalvie and Gilly Thwaite in the forensics lab. His call to Bradford station having gone through the hands and ears of three policemen, before Chief Superintendent Sanderson decided to pick up. "What is it, Superintendent?" Sanderson asked edgily, making it clear he didn't want to know the answer.

The young waitress put Jury's sandwich before him—a slab of cheddar between slices of richly grained bread, the platter nicely done up with cress and tomato. He thanked her.

"For what?" asked Sanderson.

"Nothing. The waitress. I'm at the Old Silent having a sandwich."

"Unfortunately I haven't time for lunch. We could sit here and have a meal together. Why're you calling, Mr. Jury?"

"About the telephone kiosk along the Oakworth Road. About a mile from the Grouse—"

Roughly, Sanderson cut in. "I know where it is. And so do my forensics people. Next question?"

Jury smiled as he bit into the end of the sandwich. Very good, but he wasn't really hungry. Sanderson certainly didn't dawdle along with preliminaries. "None. I wanted to apologize."

The silence meant that he'd caught the superintendent slightly off-guard, as Jury hoped he would: not that an "apology" meant a damned thing; it was that Sanderson was gearing up to stomp on Jury's next words. Now, of course, he had to refute the apology. Jury pushed the cress off the sandwich and took another mouthful that he didn't want.

"Mr. Jury, your apology is noted and means sod-all to me and my department. You happen to witness a crime in a jurisdiction you've nothing at all to do with and you persist in investigating same. All of this has, as I'm sure you know by now, been reported to your superiors. You've been getting in our way—"

Not *mucking about in our manor*. Jury wouldn't mind working for Sanderson.

"—so if I were you, I'd stop chewing in my ear."

Again, Jury smiled. "I was wondering." Jury took a drink of his beer.

Another brief silence. "Wondering what?"

"About that call box—"

Sanderson must have been leaning back in his chair, for the sudden thump sounded like something hitting the floor. He was probably furious with himself for having forgotten the original thread of this conversation. "Listen to me: you know goddamned well that we're not rubes and that we don't need London to tell us how to lift fingerprints. That kiosk was gone over so thoroughly it'll probably need a paint job. We are routinely putting a trace on any prints we found." He lowered his voice. "But I doubt very much that a killer would forget to wipe the receiver, the door handle, the entire damned *thing* if he wanted to."

"Except the coins. No way to get to the coins you've slotted into the box. As long as Telecom doesn't go at it with an axe."

Sanderson was silent.

They hadn't done it; Jury knew it would click into place in Sanderson's mind much faster than it had in Gilly Thwaite's. It would probably be one or more of the coins lying on top. The calls had been made only within the last thirty-six hours.

Jury thought he'd give him breathing time by becoming obnoxious. "I'm not stupid, Chief Superintendent. I know that the last time you asked for help was with the Ripper case. That man is brilliant; Yorkshire police made things so difficult for him he threw up his arms and went back to London." Jury was depending on Sanderson's being the professional that Racer wasn't. He'd know what Jury was saying.

He did. "The only prints we have are Nell Healey's, the ones taken when she was charged."

"There's a brandy decanter that was getting some heavy use at the Citrine house. I'm sure you could find some reason to take something from that house. As for prints, I have some others. A package will be delivered to headquarters this afternoon. Do you want the details?"

"Hell, no." The line went dead.

Jury drank off the dregs of his beer, as he dialed the Holts' number. Fortunately, it was Owen who answered. Yes, he supposed he could meet the superintendent at the inn if it was important.

Jury rang off and sat regarding the largely uneaten sandwich and felt Sergeant Wiggins was looking over his shoulder—*have to keep your strength up, sir.* He stared down at the table, wondering what it was he had missed. Some detail, some small detail seemed to have lodged beneath his consciousness like a figure under thick ice, the contours of which one couldn't make out. He went back over the conversation with Sanderson, tried to chip away at it. Nothing would surface. He sighed and picked up the sandwich and ate it as he looked at the notes Plant had made in his straight-up-and-down, rather elegant hand.

The Princess was a "possible" *(Poss.).* She might have been in her room since tea with one of her "sick headaches" (as she had said), but the ermine-lined boots had been missing when Plant had walked through the hall. George Poges: *verified dinner O.S.I. but after? Poss.* Ramona Braine: *TL to bed early. Snores.* And Malcolm, well, highly unlikely, although he had the temperament for it. By his name was an *X.* Impossible. Same for Mrs. Braithwaite and Ruby, both of whom were either in their rooms or the kitchen. But Jury had to grin at the way the handwriting changed when it came to Ellen Taylor. One could actually feel the grudging tone in the hand that had grown stiffer, tighter, almost at the end shriveling into indecipherability. It must have killed Plant to strike out the *X* and pen in *Poss.* (since Ellen hadn't shown up at Weavers Hall until long after Abby appeared to have left). But Plant could not resist the editorializing: *Absolutely ridiculous!*

Jury sat for a few moments thinking of Dench and Macalvie. He dialed the Exeter number.

He picked up on the first ring, interrupted the first ring. "Macalvie here."

It was amazing. Macalvie managed to be both out and in simultaneously; Jury knew he seldom hung round his office, yet he always managed to be at the telephone. He seemed to have doubled himself in some magical way.

Before Jury could say anything but his name, the receiver was moved and the commander was yelling at someone. Since Jury could hear a sharp voice return the thrust, it must have been Gilly Thwaite.

"She's got scissors for a mouth. Yeah, Jury what?"

"She's probably the best person you have. You'll push her so far she'll put in for a transfer."

A sound between a gargle and a laugh came over the wire. "Are you *kidding?*"

It sounded much like Melrose Plant's *Absolutely ridiculous!* Jury smiled, and said straightaway, "You're making no allowance at all that Dennis Dench is right?"

"No. He's wrong."

Jury heard a slight creak and a small thud: Macalvie leaning back and planting his feet on the desk. Jury could see him there, probably sitting in his coat.

"You ever heard of W. B. Yeats?" Macalvie asked. Before Jury could answer, Macalvie put him on Hold to deal with another call.

Macalvie was an omnivorous reader, a habit picked up from standing by bookshelves in suspects' homes. It had paid off several times, once in particular when he'd come across one of Polly Praed's mysteries, among the tooled-leather volumes of a Greek scholar who was suspected of having coshed a fellow-academic with an easing knife, but who had claimed not even to know what an easing knife was. Polly's book was titled *Murder in the Thatched Barn.* While his D.I. questioned the professor, who'd done masterful translations of Pliny the Younger, Macalvie speed-read the first half of the book. He later informed Melrose Plant that his lady mystery-writing friend didn't have exactly the wings of Pegasus, indeed must have been writing with horse's hooves, so turgid was the plot and so asinine the policework. But he was now a rabid fan, since she'd helped him out, all unknowingly.

"Dear Miss Praed: The rifle you claim to have killed Doris Quick (p. 134) in Sussex would have blown her all the way to Cornwall, fired from that angle. Enclosed, please find . . ."

Stuff like that. And Polly shot a letter, like the bullet, right back.

Jury wondered, while Macalvie was giving "instructions" to some poor forensics clod probably also wed to the God of Inaccuracy, how the Praed–Macalvie correspondence was going. It was certain, given Polly's books, she didn't read the material the commander helpfully sent her.

Thus Jury smoked his cigarette and wondered how Yeats had got into all of this.

" 'A terrible beauty is born,' " said Macalvie. "That Yeats."

"Macalvie, there's only *one* W. B. Yeats."

"True. And what do you know about his bones?"

Jury frowned. *Bones?* A line swam into his mind. " 'The old rag and bone shop of the heart'?"

"The rag and bone shop is where I work, Jury. No—"

Jury could hear drawers opening and slamming and then a paper rattling. "I kept this; I tossed it in Dench's face. Now we're talking about W. B. Yeats, remember? So you can imagine how those bones would have been gone over to prove they were his."

"Yeats was buried in County Sligo."

"France. In a temporary grave before they could get the bones back to Ireland. Someone comes along and says the bones were tossed into a huge paupers' grave and no one really knew if the remains were the poet's. Naturally, the family went nuts. Who can blame them? My point is: the expert said that after all that time it would be impossible to prove they were or weren't W. B. Yeats's bones."

"Meaning Dennis Dench could be wrong."

"He *is* wrong. Too many coincidences, *too many.* The time frame, the burial place, the dog—the little *dog*, Jury— the remnants of metal, et cetera, et cetera—"

"Speaking of poetry, Macalvie: when we were at the house in Cornwall I found a little paperback book in Billy's room. American poetry—Frost, Whitman, Dickinson, et cetera. Emily Dickinson is one of Nell Healey's favorite poets. It was a copy of the same book she had in her pocket when I was talking to her. She sent her copy to Abby Cable, little girl at Weavers Hall. Nell Healey's very fond of poetry; she used to read it to Billy and Toby, especially Frost and Dickinson."

"What's all this in aid of?"

"Several poems in this paperback are heavily scored or X'd. One in particular is interesting:

> *It was not death for I stood up*
> *and all the dead lay down—*"

"Sounds like headquarters—"

"Listen, Macalvie:

> *It was not frost, for on my skin*
> *I felt siroccos crawl.*"

Jury stopped and there was a brief silence on Macalvie's end.

"In the margin there's a little notation, '*a desert wind, hot.*' " Jury paused. "You know a band called Sirocco?"

"Yes. . . ."

"Have you read the latest *London Weekend* or *Time Out?*"

"I'm fully booked. I have an opening to attend in the Haymarket, front-row tickets for Derek Jacobi. Then there's Wembley Arena and Jimmy Page. And I *always* catch Michael Jackson. Hell *no*, I haven't read them."

"The name of the band used to be Bad News Coming. Then they changed it; Alvaro Jiminez said they wanted a new identity, or something. Sirocco was Charlie's idea. It was also Charlie's idea to change the tour date for the

Odeon. Sirocco was supposed to do a concert in Munich first. Do you know how hard that is? To rearrange tour dates? The manager went through hell."

"Why'd they change it? Not that any of this means sod-all because I know where you're headed and you're wrong."

"No, you don't know where I'm headed, Macalvie. I'll get to that in a minute. Do you know their tunes? Or do you only listen to Elvis?"

"I've heard a few of their cuts. Weren't we playing one on the way to Cornwall?"

" 'Yesterday's Rain.' "

"Don't sing to me. The poetry was enough."

"The words wouldn't mean anything to you unless you'd seen a Magritte painting called 'Empire of Light.' There's a print hanging in—never mind, only that it was one of Nell Healey's favorite paintings. The words to that song are extremely resonant of both Cornwall and that painting."

Macalvie sighed. "At least Denny has a few bones to fool with."

"I talked to Charlie Raine. I went to the Odeon, took him to a pub for some lunch. He knew about the Healey case—"

"As does half the country."

"The kid's been out of England, Macalvie. With all he's got to do, why would he be so taken up with this case? He knew every detail. More than that, he thought I'd come to the Odeon because I knew who he was. He got the concert date changed because he wanted to be here."

"Um-hmm."

"Meaning?"

"We're back to the Unknown Kid, the third-party solution, or . . . oh, let me guess. Next you're going to tell me the skeleton in that grave was—"

"Toby Holt."

Macalvie's silence was so total that Jury could hear, from across the room, the black cat's twitchy little snores coming from the sedan chair.

"Toby Holt. Brilliant. Aren't you forgetting one crucial

piece of evidence? Toby Holt was run down by a lorry five weeks later. Owen Holt identified the body."

"Who said he was telling the truth?"

"Why in hell *wouldn't* he?"

"Ten thousand pounds. A trust fund set up for Toby's schooling by Nell Healey. You didn't know about it; you were taken off the case." Jury told him what the Holts had said. "You know how the odds go down every day, every hour a kid is missing that he'll ever be found. It's not that coldblooded—"

"Just a tad illegal, for Christ's sakes. And how do you know this?"

"I don't, yet. But I think I will after I talk to Owen Holt."

Jury heard a drawer open, slam shut. Macalvie was getting out the paper cups. "It wasn't your case, Macalvie."

"Obviously. It never got solved."

"The lead guitarist, Charlie Raine." Jury paused. "I think he's Billy Healey."

In that cat-pad, quiet voice Macalvie used when he was really disturbed, he said, "Jury. Billy Healey is *dead.*"

"I was afraid you'd say that. Listen—"

"No. I'd rather talk to Denny. At least he serves wine."

"Listen: say I'm crazy—"

"No problem."

"Security at those concerts is nil. It's only laid on to keep the peace. The loudmouths, the beer-guzzlers, the snorters, the ardent fans. Wiggins has rounded up a few men who aren't on rota."

"Are you telling me you think someone's going to try to off your boy in the middle of a *concert* with—hell, you've seen too many Hitchcock films."

Jury was getting impatient, but still kept his voice low. "Come on, Brian, goddammit, I'm not talking about the London Symphony or the Royal Albert Hall. This is the Hammersmith Odeon, and these aren't people who toss on their gowns and tails to make sure they're seen. These are *fans.* These are people who don't eye the box seats to see if there's someone they've missed who's wearing a coronet. These are fans who plunk down ten pounds to see some of the greatest musicians in the world and they *listen*—"

"You should be reviewing for *Juke Blues*. Okay, okay, I get the point. There's so much noise you couldn't even hear Gilly if she was standing next to you. So you want reinforcements. Yeah, so go ahead. What time tonight?"

"Eight."

"Wonderful. That's all of six hours to round up whoever's stupid enough to buy this act and get them there. Great. Except it isn't Billy Healey, Jury."

"So what've we lost?"

"Probably our jobs. Not that that means anything."

Jury could almost hear the grin. "Thanks. I'm sending photos of six people on the wire. One in London, five here. One in particular. There's a mass exodus to London from West Yorkshire."

The silence lengthened until Jury wondered if Macalvie had rung off.

"And did you tell Nell Healey that you think her son's alive? That he turned out to be famous, which is what that bastard of a husband always wanted?"

Jury didn't answer.

"Billy Healey was a *pianist,* Jury, not a guitarist."

For Macalvie, that was pretty weak. "He could play anything put in his hands, according to several people. And I imagine Charlie plays keyboard, though he said 'not much.' "

"Like your theory. Psychologically it's lousy, Jury. Here's a kid who doesn't get in touch with his much-beloved stepmother for eight years."

"If someone tried to bury you alive, I imagine you wouldn't be too eager to take a chance on being found."

"So Billy Healey *somehow* becomes a hot, young guitarist in New York. Ridiculous. Absolutely ridiculous." The phone slammed down.

Jury sat there with the dead receiver knowing Macalvie

had serious doubts about his own theory and thinking of Plant's list.

Absolutely ridiculous.

Jury replaced the receiver and thought of Plant's hot, young, New York writer.

Poss.

3

Far from giving the impression of a man who frequented pubs, Owen Holt stood just inside the door of the Old Silent, turning his cap in his hands and looking round him as if he'd wandered onto some foreign shore where he didn't speak the language. His slight smile when he saw Jury was uncertain, his expression baffled.

Jury led him to a chair in the lounge bar, saying, "Thanks for coming so quickly." The man merely nodded and waited. "Sit down; let me get you a drink."

"Half pint of Guinness'll do for me. Helps me sleep."

Jury watched Owen Holt as he waited for the drinks. He was studying the room and its unfamiliar furnishings, looking about naïvely as if he seldom left his front parlor. For some reason, Holt put Jury in mind of a stodgy fairy-tale figure: the trusty woodsman, perhaps, or one of the kind but utterly unimaginative couple who had taken in some waif. Weren't children in fairy tales so often disenfranchised?

As he set down the drinks, Jury said, "I hope your wife wasn't too annoyed by my dragging you away."

"Dihn't tell her, did I? Just said I was going along to the Black Bush to see one of my mates." He took a long, slow drink, wiped his hand across his mouth and leaned forward. "I expect this is about the money."

"Yes and no. What I wonder about is why you don't seem to be far more bitter toward the Citrines. Didn't you feel it was high-handed of them to make the decision about that ransom money considering it was your son, too, who was in danger?"

Holt sighed, raised his glass again, put it down. "Police come to t'house, told us what happened, told us it hardly ever did good to pay ransom money. Well, whistling down a well with us, anyway, weren't they? As if we had that kind of money."

"A little over five weeks later you did have some, though," Jury said, blandly. "You must have wondered why Toby'd gone to London."

"Aye." Holt kept his hands clamped round the glass and didn't meet Jury's eyes.

Jury leaned forward. "Mr. Holt, you must have wondered even more why Toby didn't try to get in touch with you for five whole weeks." He waited. Holt sat there slowly drawing his hands away from his glass and dropping them in his lap. "Were you absolutely sure that was Toby's body?"

"Well, you're right there: I couldn't see why Toby never tried to ring up, at least. Never a word. Never a word. Never a word."

He ignored the last question and kept his eyes on his hands, kneading the knuckles as if the hands pained him.

Jury tried through sheer will to draw Holt's eyes up to meet his own. He wanted to see their expression. But the man's head was resolutely downcast. The silence went on for some moments. "A lot of children go missing and they're never found. Most, probably. Every day, every *hour* that goes by reduces the chances they'll ever be found. Perhaps you thought Toby never would."

Finally Owen Holt looked up and said, with a fleeting smile, "You're right smart. 'Twarn't Toby. But if you think it were to get the money, you're wrong."

"Then why, Mr. Holt?"

"Alice." His gaze returned to his half pint, half full. "The pore woman kept hopin' and hopin'. You'd not think she was that fond of the lad, but you'd be wrong there. Day after day she'd be cleaning the kitchen windows. Pretending she was cleaning, when what she was doing was watching the little path back there that Toby always came up. I sat there in t'kitchen once and counted six times she washed off the same little pane." He shook and shook his head. "Eight years. I think it were the right thing I done." He gave Jury a fleeting smile. "At least now she just cleans to clean, not to hope."

"I'm sorry."

Owen Holt drew in breath and puffed out his cheeks as if he were the North Wind in the old story. "What happens to me, now?"

"Nothing."

Holt raised his eyebrows, surprised. "Nothing?"

"Why should it?"

There was silence again. "He's dead, I expect."

The rising inflection made it a question, not a statement. Jury thought of Dennis Dench and that grave in Cornwall. He could think of nothing to say to the man as he watched Owen Holt turn his head toward the Old Silent's window where the panes were black.

39

The driver of Brontë Taxi, together with George Poges and Melrose Plant, was attempting to jostle the steamer trunk up onto the top of the car, since it could not, by any means, be maneuvered inside or strapped on the boot.

They all sweated as the Princess Rosetta Viacinni di Belamante stood about in her Chanel suit, living up to her name and delivering a wistful account to Ellen of a past symbolized by each of the faded stickers on the trunk, emblems of hers and the prince's travels (or "escapades," as she liked to call them), across several continents. Ah, Saigon, ah, Kenya, ah, Siena, ah, Orlando.

Ellen just looked at her: "You mean Disneyworld and not Virginia Woolf, I guess." Over Ellen's arm lay a darkish green gown, given her by the Princess, who said it was a very rare find, one of her own favorites, and that Ellen must have it; it suited her and she would see once she put it on. The Princess had purchased it on that Venetian street of fashion dreams, the Calle Regina. Designed by an Indian.

Probably, thought Melrose, with some irritation, by a Tibetan monk. He only wished the Princess would shut up about Venice.

Said George Poges, "Why the devil can't you have *ordinary* cases like the rest of us?" Even in the crisp and icy air he was perspiring, wiping the back of his neck with a handkerchief.

"I do not advertise makers' wares: no scribbled names on

my luggage and no swans on my arse, as it were. Can you imagine Madame Vionnet sticking a logo on a lapel? Vulgarity knows no bounds in this world. Believe me, that gown"—here she touched her hand to the wilting, dark thing over Ellen's arm—"is worth half of Venice. But not on everyone." The Princess put her arm round Ellen's shoulders and kissed her cheek, not kissing air (in that odious way that some highly sociable women do, Melrose thought) but firmly.

Major Poges, rather gruffly did the same.

Neither of them, however, felt the need of a physical display of *adieux* with the Braines, who had just come through the door.

Ellen sat, looking disconsolate, on one of the rocks in the courtyard, smoking.

"I don't see why you refuse to come to London with Richard Jury and me."

Ignoring this she said, "Charlotte Brontë said all of her books pained her."

Melrose had been arguing with her at breakfast, before breakfast, at lunch, after lunch. "She should have written about delicatessens."

Ellen sat mournfully looking at the ground. "That school near Kirksby Londale—it was probably the model for Lowood School. The discipline was fierce; Marie Brontë died of consumption when she was eleven and Eliza died when she was ten a month later." The train of her thought became apparent to Melrose when she added, "So what's going to happen to Abby?"

"She's certainly not going to die of consumption. She owns—"

Ellen ground out a cigarette. "A bullet in the back, that's what. For fu—for Pete's sake! How can you sleazeballs leave her here *alone?*"

"She's not *going* to be alone! How many times do I have to tell you, Keighley police are protect——"

"Ah, ha! Ha! Ha!" She paused in her dismissal of the Yorkshire constabulary and asked, "When do you see your Great Friend off, anyway?"

Vivian. It had been great friend this, and great friend that until the phrase had grown capitals. He told her again. "Tomorrow morning at eleven o'clock. She's taking the Orient Express to Venice."

"I guess she's got money."

"So do you, if that means anything."

But she wasn't listening; she was holding the gift from the Princess up before her, trying to mold it to the leather jacket, the cord jeans. "What do you think?"

Said Melrose, "I'm not sure. Do you *wear* dresses?" He was still irritated with her for bringing up the Great Friend once again. Then he looked at her downturned head and felt ashamed. As to the gown, its purpose and shape seemed fathomless, its color grungy—some fog-washed shade of green, dark and faded. "Well, perhaps you have to put it on. She said it takes on the shape of the person who wears it." The Princess had sounded a bit like Ramona Braine, as if there were auras hanging about certain gowns that the wrong person daren't meddle with.

Melrose was so engrossed in his conflict that he scarcely heard the other car, Jury's car, until it came to a standstill at the side of the Hall.

Jury got out and walked over to them, and in so doing set up a bit of a flurry amongst the few ducks that waddled over to the fence.

"We were just talking," said Ellen, "about leaving Abby here and the rest of you hightailing it to London."

Naturally, she would make it sound as if Melrose had agreed with her.

Instead of reassuring her, Jury asked, "What about you, Ellen? Aren't you going, too?"

"*Me? I'm* not leaving her *alone.*"

Jury looked off toward the barn and back to Ellen.

"Thought you had things to do in London before you went home. Don't you have a booking on the QE Two?"

She thrust her hands in her jacket pockets and toed through some gravel. "I can always Concorde it."

"There's a concert tonight. Sirocco. You don't want to miss that, do you?"

Melrose disliked the form this was taking; it sounded less like an inquiry than an interrogation. "Come on, Ellen; we can have dinner with my Great Friend and my Great Aunt and the local antiques dealer. He alone is worth the trip." Melrose smiled brightly.

"No."

Jury paused. "I don't think Abby is in any present danger here."

"You could've fooled me." Ellen turned away, stuck her fingers in the mesh wire of the fence, and ignored both of them.

Ethel emerged from the barn carrying a basket, followed by Abby with her feed bucket.

Ethel had changed her funeral finery for a more workaday gingham dress, the skirt flaring with starch like a brightly checkered tent where her jacket ended. The skirt standing out and the pink jacket ballooned with goose down and her wispy reddish curls the substance of angel hair made her appear as if she'd lift off and float away, strewing rose petals from her basket.

By contrast, Abby might as well have worn wellingtons filled with lead. Her yellow slicker was inside out, the lining the color of her eyes, a deep inky blue.

Ethel skipped; Abby trudged. They were followed by Stranger and Tim. Coming upon this little cluster of people in the courtyard, they stopped. Stranger tried a creep toward Malcolm, who recoiled slightly, but the *click* of Abby's tongue brought him back. He sat and stared round.

There was the noise and confusion that often augments departures, that seeming desire to get off in a cloud of dust and irrelevant chatter to avoid the fact of separation, the *you must come to us next week, next month, next year;* or the promises that one usually can't eventually keep, *see you next winter, next Michaelmas holiday;* the hubbub of arranging cases, of ordering trunks and bags placed just *there;* the handshakes, the stiff smiles. And yet no one actually *leaving.*

Ramona Braine stood awkwardly by the taxi with a perplexed look as if this weren't in the cards; the Major, about to light a cigar, stopped in the act; the Princess, having said her adieux, stood, one hand on hip looking about the little circle with an uncertain smile; Ellen refusing to meet any of their eyes, leaning against her BMW, a study in black-on-black; Ruby in her cap behind Mrs. Braithwaite's shoulder, the two of them in the doorway looking like figures in a Breughel painting.

They made, this small gathering drawn together in outrageous circumstances, a sort of closed circle.

The dog Stranger sat close to the center, eyeing each of them as if he'd managed to catch and hold them, by transfixing them with his hypnotic eye.

It was Abby who broke the ring; she walked over to a spot not quite within Jury's reach, and put out her hand. Abby, with her black hair unevenly cut around a face pale as a moonbeam, and those navy blue eyes, reached out a hand that lay for a moment in Jury's like a white moth.

Then she walked over to Melrose, again extended her hand and looked up at him gravely.

It was the Deep Blue Good-bye.

Part Four

LIKE
ALASKA

40

Jury was glad he'd seen the theater empty before he saw it packed. The crowd that had flowed from the Underground tunnel and jumped the iron railings in the slanting rain, diamond-splinters in the reflection of the bright marquee, were jammed in the lobby and packed upstairs where the bar was open.

Jostled by the line in front of the poster and T-shirt concession, Jury looked up at the huge oval, peopleless yesterday, tonight thronged with faces peering over the railing and above them the flashy chandelier that tossed tiny squares of light across some of the faces and hands. He wished he were here just for the show. It was wonderful, this climate of expectancy; the ring of faces looked down as if from a height where they breathed headier air. And from the boozy appearance of some of them, the air up there was decidedly winey. They talked, laughed, giggled, yelled down at their mates below, for it seemed in that magical way that certain occasions afforded, they were all mates.

Mary Lee was in her element down here and secured behind her window, where she could, given the line of hopefuls waiting for no-shows, dispense with infinite largesse what tickets there were to be had. For the begging, Jury imagined. Mary Lee was dressed in purple silky stuff, blue shadow with gold glitter on her eyelids.

Wiggins had asked Jury why her shoe was sitting behind the window on the ticket counter.

It had always been a wonder to Jury and Carole-anne—no matter how packed the crowd, how large the room—that Carole-anne could always be seen across or through it, as if people instinctively moved back a little to allow a clearer view of Miss Palutski, this evening wearing her Chinese stop-light-red dress over which she'd tossed a short little silver-sequined coat that gave off fire and glitter like the domed chandelier. To give off fire and glitter though, Carole-anne only needed that flaming red-gold hair, those blue eyes.

"Super!" She threw up her hand, jumped up a bit, and seemed oblivious to the synchronized turn of male heads. Carole-anne, oddly enough, was not really vain. If you look like that (thought Jury, pushing his way through the crowd), vanity is redundant.

He searched the people crushed against her for Andrew Starr or one of the dozen or so males Jury would sometimes pass on the steps of his digs.

A couple of feet away he heard his name. It was a breathless Mrs. Wassermann, who had just, apparently, beat her way from the concession line. Mrs. Wassermann held up a T-shirt. *Sirocco* was scrawled across the front in silver, and a picture of the members of the band was outlined in a square on the back. "I do not know if it will fit, Mr. Jury. It seems small." She held it up to him.

Mrs. Wassermann also looked once again almost like Mrs. Wassermann. It had been impossible to get the scrunch completely out, but the hair had been combed back, frizz only round the face; she was dressed in one of her well-tailored, comfortably familiar dark dresses, with her silver brooch.

Jury thanked her for the T-shirt, looked at Carole-anne, and bent down and kissed her. This drew an appreciative little round of applause from a few itinerant musicians (perhaps hoping some Sirocco magic would rub off on their gig bags).

"Wait outside the front door when this is over; there's someone I want you to meet."

"Meet? Who?"

"It's a man . . . musician-type."

Carole-anne tried not to seem pleased by either the kiss or the mystery and pulled Mrs. Wassermann along.

In the bun at the nape of her neck were two hot pink, sequined Spanish combs.

With the crowd shoving round him toward the sets of double doors, Jury felt a tap on his shoulder.

"If you must send me on another mission, make it Lourdes," said Melrose Plant, who had his cosher under his arm and was peeling off leather gloves supple enough for a surgeon. "First of all, Trueblood blackmailed me into going on one of his London shopping sprees, and I can only thank God it was Upper Sloane Street and not Harrods; he insisted I buy this." Melrose shook out the lapels of a new overcoat.

"You look like Armani himself. Did you get our man?"

As Melrose wedged himself between a girl with rainbow hair and a leather-jacketed one who ogled his coat and reminded him a little of Ellen, he said, "Yes, but I had to leave my Rolex behind."

Over his shoulder, Jury said, "You don't wear a Rolex."

"I bought one for the occasion. Traded it off for this on the way out." He held up a pair of mother-of-pearl opera glasses. "I think she's running a pawnshop."

Jury pulled him over to one side of the stalls and let the crowd stream by, making for their seats.

"Where's Sergeant Wiggins?" asked Plant.

"Up there." He nodded toward the balcony. "Projection room."

"You've been seeing too many reruns—uh!" His stomach was prodded by the elbow of a boozy fan. "—of *The Manchurian Candidate*. God!" The heel of a boot had just crunched down on his shoe.

"Probably," said Jury, checking the Exit signs and the double doors at the rear. Five men, that was all he could muster, one at the stage door, one in front, one operating as a scalper, the other two inside. It was hardly mounting a battalion. The two huge spotlights on each end of the circle suddenly switched on and started crisscrossing the stage, which sent up cheers from the audience.

Plant had raised his voice at the next onslaught from a couple of punches on the shoulder. "For God's sakes, you could get killed in here just from standing about."

"So you're both down here waiting for some shooter to stand up on a front-row seat, for chrissakes." The owner of the elbow sounded disgusted.

"Macalvie?" Jury couldn't believe it.

"Well, you wanted help, didn't you? Lord knows you could use it." He shoved a couple back who were blowing smoke in his face. "I don't know anyone at headquarters who likes rock music. So here I am. How many men have you got here? Not that it'd make much difference, judging from the crowd."

"Five," said Jury, raising his eyes to the balcony where he was blinded momentarily by the spotlights. The crisscrossing of the spots on the stage made him think of the air raids. He remembered that this theater was the meeting place for Operation Overlord. The audience, hundreds of people, all of them still standing, might have been waiting for the last briefing before D-Day.

The stage was empty except for the amplifying equipment, a deep, double-tiered black platform, and, at the rear of the stage, a long black backdrop of a curtain with *SIROCCO* spelled out in silver letters. Behind or offstage must have been a wind machine, for the curtain rippled and swayed, moving the cursive letters.

All five of them walked on stage together to an explosion of applause. They were dressed in basic black, shirts and cords. John Swann was bare-chested except for a glittery silver jacket, sleeveless and short, that gave the audience a good look at his biceps and pectorals. Jiminez's loose black jacket had a red satin lining, and Wes Whelan wore a red satin shirt and a cap made of the same silvery stuff as

Swann's waistcoat. Whelan quickly took his place behind the drums on the second tier and Caton Rivers was half-surrounded by keyboards on the first.

While the spotlights up in the dress circle dropped huge coins on the stage, a switch thrown somewhere flooded the stage with a rainbowlike iridescence from the lighting truss. It was the sign to begin.

This band didn't wind up its audience, didn't grandstand, didn't preen. As soon as those lights hit them, Wes Whelan hit the drums for his sizzling solo introduction to the band's signature song, "Windfall." And the crowd, simultaneously, went crazy. Jiminez kicked in with that one-note riff building his bass line, and Charlie Raine stepped a few feet forward and started one of his arpeggio runs. The huge hall reverberated with the lightning of the music and the thunder of the crowd echoing it.

"I think I see," said Plant, picking some foreign object from his new coat, "what you mean."

He looked up, momentarily blinded by the spotlight.

The dress circle was an amorphous mass of moving bodies . . . except for Carole-anne's, whose glittery jacket was just caught by the spotlight's edge in the middle of the second or third row of the circle.

Height, he thought.

Obviously, the killer would need height. "Lobby," he said to Plant and Macalvie.

Mary Lee was holding sway behind her window over an intrepid group still trying to get in. When the wave of music issuing out through the doors thwacked shut behind Jury and Plant, she snatched her shoe off the counter and shouted, "That's *it,* luv!" to a leathery-skinned couple and secured the little window. The leftover Sirocco disciples were flapping their arms in gestures signaling distress.

"You got another one of those?" asked Macalvie, when

Jury yanked up the antennae on his radio. He shook his head as Wiggins's voice crackled over the receiver.

"Fine, sir, so far. There're two projectionists up here, there's no way anyone could get in without being seen. I even checked out the old spotlight that looks like it must've been here when the place opened. Big enough to hide a body in." He paused to chuckle at his own inventiveness. "It's a warren of rooms and stairways; we checked out what we could."

"How much can you see of the theater? The circle?"

A pause as Wiggins apparently looked round. "Nothing much."

"Get down to the dress circle and try to cover the rear."

"Yes, sir."

Music hit them in a wave as the double door slapped open and shut after Macalvie, who came through talking: "Great band. One thing that worries me—"

"May I see your ticket, if you pul-*eez*," said Mary Lee, her tone clearly suggesting he'd sneaked in.

"It's all right dear. I'm from *Juke Blues.*"

Her eyebrows shot up. "The mag?"

Macalvie handed her a card that seemed to impress her.

"Well, all right. But they should let us know."

The lobby was not empty. The two fellows who worked the T-shirt concession were standing at the other set of doors, listening; the squatters were sitting in surliness near the ticket booth as if extra tickets might miraculously walk out of Mary Lee's window; a few fans were wandering toward the open air, stoned.

"Mary Lee—" He looked at her, wondered if she'd have the nerve to walk out on the stage if he needed her. "Mary Lee. There's something I might want you to do." He handed her a two-way radio.

"What's this, then?"

"Take this, go backstage."

"*Back*stage. Whatever for?"

"I'll tell you when, *if* the time comes." He showed her how to work the radio. "You'll love it."

Mary Lee frowned; she didn't look as if she were about to fall in love with this contraption. "Well, I dunno—"

Macalvie said, "Just do it, right? *Juke Blues* is doing a big feature on this concert, *big,* and we're gonna want to include some behind-the-scenes people." He winked and tapped her shoulder.

Mary Lee's eyes widened.

Jury went on. "First of all, I want you to get up to the dress circle, and tell the lady in silver and red—she'll be sitting in the middle of the second, third row—"

"Oh, I seen *'er,* all right." Mary Lee adjusted her own décolletage as if competing with the Chinese neckline. "What about 'er?"

"Tell her I want my own personal cheering section if something happens. Applaud, yell, jump up and down—"

"Won't work, Jury," said Macalvie. "For five seconds, maybe. No more."

"All I need is five seconds."

"All I need is an explanation," said Melrose.

That the swell beside her apparently wasn't in on this operation galvanized Mary Lee into action. "Right, luv." And she left to churn up the stairs.

"Come on," said Macalvie, "let's get up there."

The Odeon might as well have sold Standing Room Only because no one was sitting down. The rows of seats were superfluous. Jury bet they'd stand all the way through the concert, given their enthusiasm for the next two numbers.

Then, keyboard-led by Caton Rivers, John Swann gave himself over to a solo called "Sunday's Gone Again." Swann had enough available attitude to spread around a dozen bands, but he also had a nightingale's voice and an incredible range. The top notes he hit were as silvery as the jacket he wore. No wonder Jiminez (who kept his own attitude under subtle wraps) wanted him in the band.

Jury was holding his breath for Charlie Raine's solo. Charlie didn't move like the others; he didn't wheel round like Jiminez, who was graceful as a dancer; he wasn't all over the stage like Swann, marking out each section of the clamoring audience as his provenance. Charlie was both shy and cool; he stayed still.

As he was doing now, swamped in light by the doubled-spot playing on him, standing with his amplified acoustic singing "Yesterday's Rain" into the hush of the theater. He ended with a return to the last verse, stopped, and there was a silence as heavy as the applause, foot-stomping, and yelling that followed.

Jury breathed again and looked over to Macalvie near the stairwell, then to Plant, who was sweeping the balcony with his opera glasses.

The band had been at it now for nearly an hour . . . another forty, fifty minutes to go. They didn't break.

Jiminez and the keyboardist, Rivers, traded a few improvisational, intuitive licks that gave the audience some breathing space and Charlie time to towel off his head. The two spots separated now, one following Jiminez and one Raine as they broke into a trade-off of technical wizardry, Alvaro on a funky blues line that backed off into a classical progression—Bach, it sounded like. Jury smiled in spite of the tension that made his arms, his back ache. The old "back-porch blues man"; it was an ear-bending mix of perfectly amplified acoustic and heavy slide distortion on Jiminez's electric.

Jury felt the crush of people behind him, people before him, people standing in the aisle, backs against the wall, cheering. He edged forward to stand beneath the Exit sign, couldn't see because of the reflection from the spot. Both of the lighting technicians were following their targets with the light—

From his position by the stairwell, Macalvie frowned, squinted at the stage. The spotlights were out of sync. The one light was following the black guy, Jiminez, who was moving all over. The other was fixed; it wasn't on Raine, wasn't following him, though his movements were sparse. He stepped into it and stepped out. Hunched down, Macalvie started moving along the aisle, toward Jury.

Plant whipped the opera glasses quickly from the stage back to the spotlight. It was in a pool of darkness, and all he could see of the operator was a chap in a leather jacket and a cap who seemed to be adjusting something near the bottom of the huge spot. Beside it was a gig bag.

The noise as Macalvie tried to muscle his way through the knots of devotees turned the Odeon into a compression chamber. For chrissakes—

Jury saw both of them coming, had his hand on the revolver in his shoulder holster, moved slowly along the wall.

He should have realized it: of course it wouldn't be Charlie's solo, where the audience was as hushed as a sleeping baby; it would be like this, a trade-off of technique between Charlie and Alvaro that whipped the house up into a frenzy. They were playing together but they stood absolutely apart.

Charlie was sending fiery arpeggio runs across the long stage; Jiminez was addressing them with those heavily distorted power chords. It was a complex, killer duet that kept the audience in a state of controlled havoc with little spills of applause all along the way for Charlie's shot, for Alvaro's return.

Plant couldn't move all the way up to the rear, cross it, and go down again. There wasn't time. He jumped up on the empty seat and used the whole row as a clattering path to the other side, followed by outraged shouts to get the fuck down and the bloody hell out of the way. Along the way he sent at least one illegal tape recorder, a couple of beer cans, and a waving Sirocco T-shirt flying into the air with his cosher and might (given the crack) have broken the wrist that tried to pull him down.

It wasn't a gig bag.

The folding stock of the rifle clicked into place and she raised it so that the barrel jutted through the bars of the circle. It was the perfect hiding place, with herself in a pool of darkness, the light huge and blinding. And who would pay much attention to whoever was operating the Super Trooper? She was between it and the wall anyway.

Jury was crouched, holding the Wembley with both hands. "Rena." The word cut through the noise just like the snick of a safety.

"Hold it right there," said Macalvie, who'd drawn out a .38.

Rena fired a half second before the commands, out into the theater, toward the stage.

Wes Whelan did a total turn, and yet still came down on the one, hitting all the punches, not missing a lick.

The others hesitated, looked at him, and hit their instruments again, following his lead.

As she swung the rifle, catching Jury in the sight, Melrose tossed his coat at the gun. Macalvie threw himself at her legs and raised the butt of his pistol. The spotlight fell across Rena Citrine and hit the floor with a hideous crash.

And now, thought Jury, comes the hard part.

Panic in a theater filled with over a thousand people.

In the second row, Carole-anne and Mrs. Wassermann were yelling, jumping, applauding the drummer and Jiminez, who had picked up on this improvisational mix. The people round them were distracted momentarily. But those nearest were staring in frozen silence for what Jury knew would last only seconds before the panic started. The audience in the stalls hadn't picked it up yet, but bad news travels fast. He pressed the radio button, spoke into it.

Melrose Plant, seeing Macalvie and Jury throw themselves at Rena Citrine, calmly lit a cigarette and turned to the several dozen people nearest and said, "That's show biz, ladies and gentlemen."

A woman screamed. It was one of the shrillest noises Jury had ever heard.

He got off his knees, looked down at the stage, and as soon as he thought it—for God's sakes, Mary Lee!—here she came . . .

Nervous, hobbling on the stiltlike heels of her glass slippers. The people in the stalls were looking from her up to the dress circle, where there seemed to be something rather nasty going on.

Wes Whelan was hugging his arm; the rest of the band was momentarily stunned at the appearance of this girl.

Come on, Mary Lee, *do it!*

She did it. Grabbed at a mike and shouted, "Ladies and gentlemen! Staaaan *KEELER!*"

When Stan Keeler moved, he moved. He came out of the wings at such speed he covered the last several feet on his knees, sliding to a stop, and playing on his way up from the floor.

Near him, the ones in the worst state were now moving between fear and astonished delight.

All Keeler had to play was that famous chord progression to "Main Line Lady" and he had them cold.

People had stopped moving for the exits, stopped crushing against each other, and when the woman screamed again, Jury saw a hand flash out and slap her down in her chair.

In the meantime, the band was backing up Stan.

Stan Keeler in person, in *concert,* and with *Sirocco?*

What sort of competition was a crazy killer with that?

41

The police ambulance *sans* siren had just left the alley with its cargo and left the faces of the limo driver and a few of the roadies open-mouthed, staring after it. Security police were in their element, although they weren't too sure what the element was: they seemed disappointed that there wasn't a crowd to be cordoned off and held back, that there wasn't a mob of funky punk rock fans all jostling for a front-row view. Aside from the single stretcher borne by two orderlies in plain clothes and a youngish man held up by two more, it was the slickest exit made from a stage door they had seen, slicker than the exit of the stars themselves.

. . . who were still performing. Jury, Plant, Macalvie, and Wiggins were sitting in one of the equipment vans on amps and crates, being brought mugs of tea and stale sandwiches by Mary Lee, who was also in her element. When one of the roadies kept after her, grabbing her to tell him what was going on, she strong-armed him and told him and the limo driver, *Get out of my face,* as she sashayed back in the stage door with the tin tray that had held the food.

She stopped, however, for a photo session with a young man who claimed to be the photographer from *Kregarrand* and who was actually Jury's Scene-of-Crimes man, enjoying his double role.

When Jury saw the police pathologist come out of the stage door, he jumped down from the lorry.

Dr. Phyllis Nancy was, in Jury's mind, the crème de la

crème of doctors, the one he had searched out not only because she could work with lightning speed, but because she had an imaginative grasp of a situation that was lacking in her colleagues.

Phyllis Nancy was, on the other hand, a conflicted personality; she pretended to disdain her femininity and looks by wearing harshly cut suits and little string ties. On the other hand, she went all out when she was off-duty.

As she walked—or strolled—toward Jury, it was clear that she was definitely off-duty. Beneath a fur coat she wore a long gown, green and slit up the front. The conflict also extended to her having been called away.

"From a performance of *La Bohème,* Superintendent, Pavarotti singing. Box seat, bottle of superior Chablis—"

"I know. About the seat, I mean, not the wine." He smiled.

Phyllis Nancy looked first to the right, then the left, then at the sky. Anywhere but at Jury, as she clutched the collar of her fur coat round her neck. In the other hand was her black bag. "The victim is in critical condition. One of what I would imagine to be at least four broken ribs penetrated the lung and started hemorrhaging, with blood coming out of both the ear and the mouth. The right wrist is broken, compound fracture, you can see the bone protruding. One side of the skull endured a blow with a blunt object, bits of the cheekbone adhering to the blood . . ."

Jury listened patiently as Dr. Nancy went on. Ordinarily, her reports were like her no-nonsense, crisp suits: brief, staccato, atonal. Dismembered bodily parts were inspected and collected like shells. But for some reason, she seemed to enjoy whatever Grand Guignol touches she could bring into play when she gave Jury her reports. She ended hers now by asking Jury just what the hell was going on; at the same time, she extracted from her pocket a cigarette case, removed a cigarette, and snapped the little lighter before Jury could produce a match. She did not seem to notice she was standing in a drizzling rain that was matting her fur coat and taking the wave out of what looked like a pricey hairdo.

Before Jury could answer her, she exhaled a thin stream of smoke and said, "That police photographer"—she motioned to the young fellow at the stage door who was still taking photos of a couple of the road crew, who were enjoying it immensely—"was in the balcony popping his flashbulbs at the curious and telling them he was the photographer from *Kregarrand*."

Jury smiled: "A distraction, Phyllis. How's the member of the lighting crew? We found him in a storage room, tied up and out cold. Why he wasn't dead is beyond me."

"I brought him round. He said about twenty or twenty-five minutes before the show, a woman came up to him when he was adjusting the spotlight, said she was from the supply equipment company and that the spot was defective. He said it wasn't—"

"And showed her, I take it."

"His leather jacket gone, his cap gone, and she was gone. Well, we know where she was. She looked like she'd been set upon by a gang of punks. Those blows to the head weren't all caused by the spotlight falling—"

"Beer bottle, maybe?" asked Macalvie, who'd descended from the lorry.

Phyllis Nancy looked at him, mouth open, and when she didn't reply, he shrugged and offered, "Couple of beer bottles?"

She dropped her cigarette on the pavement, scrubbed at it with a green satin shoe. "Who are *you?*"

"Macalvie, Brian. Devon-Cornwall constabulary." He flicked out his ID. "I've been working on a case."

She looked at him, looked back at Jury, squinted into the shadows of the lorry. "Who else is in there?"

"You know how crazy fans get at these concerts," said Macalvie. "Anything can happen."

As if to augment that statement, Sergeant Wiggins came out of the stage door in a rush as if he were being blown thither by the swell of music and thunder of applause. "I got hold of Sanderson—"

Phyllis Nancy said, "Well, if it isn't Sergeant Wiggins, our karate expert."

"Kung fu," he corrected her. "And I'm not," he said modestly, "an expert."

"Just enough to break a wrist or arm, I expect. What are you all sitting in that lorry for? Is that the getaway car?"

"Waiting for autographs," said Jury. "I'll tell you all about it later."

"This should be one of the more interesting reports I've written up." She checked her tiny watch. "Well, I might be able to catch the final aria." She collected her black bag and started toward the police car.

"You should have come to the concert, Phyllis," called Jury after her. "Better than listening to 'O Sole Mio.' "

She stopped, called back: "I couldn't get tickets." Dr. Nancy slammed the door and the car lurched toward the Hammersmith Road.

"What did Sanderson say?"

Wiggins was blowing on his hands. "That he was sending someone from Wakefield headquarters. And that the coins from the call box matched the prints on the brandy decanter—Irene Citrine's. He added it didn't prove *when* the calls had been made."

"He's as hard to convince as Commander Macalvie," said Jury.

"Good for Sanderson. I take it this Citrine woman was one of Roger Healey's ladies?"

"It might have been pure greed and not love and greed. Rena's the poor Citrine. Everyone else in the family had money. Roger and Rena must have made a divine pair, both after his wife's money. They meant to kidnap Billy; Toby was there; they had two boys to deal with. Somehow Billy Healey got away. But they couldn't let Toby live to identify them later—"

"So Toby Holt goes into the grave," said Wiggins. "Dr. Dench was right about the age, then." Wiggins sounded almost disappointed.

Macalvie cut a look round at all of them. "No, he isn't."

"Why are you still arguing, Macalvie? The woman tried to kill him. You sound like Sanderson talking about the *time* the calls were made. That's a little after-the-fact, isn't it?"

"That is, but this isn't. So she tried to shoot *someone*—"

"You're worse than a pit bull."

Macalvie steamrolled on: "Psychologically, your theory won't wash, Jury. I told you. Instead of running home to his mum, which would be the natural thing, he disappears—"

"Can't we assume he was scared out of his mind?"

"Which is why he'd go running home. Or to *some* kind of sanctuary. Instead he goes off to Ireland. To *Ireland?*"

Jury sighed. "I'm not saying at twelve he—"

"Some sanctuary." Macalvie sat with arms binding his chest, the brim of his loose tweed cap shown over his eyes. "This twelve-year-old piano prodigy just dusts himself off, grabs the ferry for Larne, becomes a guitarist, and lets his beloved step-mum sweat it out for eight years thinking he's dead. You got any Fisherman's Friends, Wiggins? I think I'll choke myself." Back and forth, back and forth, Macalvie slowly shook his head. "Uh-uh." He got up, drained the cup of tea. "I'm supposed to be in Sidmouth. Let me know what happens when the music dies." He nodded toward Melrose. "Plant's really into this; he's reading *Segue.*"

Melrose looked up. "Jimi Hendrix was left-handed."

"So?" Macalvie rose just as Mary Lee came out of the stage door again, moving between security police. She carried a tray with fresh cups and a plate of stale-looking sandwiches.

She shoved the tray onto the floor of the van: "Want another cuppa? And there's someone rung up to talk to—just a tic . . ." She pulled a scrap of paper from her shoe, which she seemed to regard as the only proper place for safekeeping, like a safety deposit box, and read "—Chief Superintendent Macalver." She emphasized the second syllable.

"*Mac*-al-vie," he said. "What someone?"

"A woman. Said to call right away."

Muttering imprecations, Macalvie jumped down from the van, nearly upsetting the tray and definitely upsetting Mary Lee who said, "*You? You* said you was from *Juke Blues.*"

"I do that part time because I can't make a living as a cop." He patted her cheek. "Don't worry; your picture will be all over the papers. Where's the nearest phone?"

With some show of hostility she said, "I expect you could use my office."

Macalvie turned to leave, turned back again and called to Jury, "If you're so sure, Jury, why aren't you on the phone to Wakefield headquarters? I imagine Mrs. Healey would like to know he's alive."

He went off through the driving rain.

The first to come out was Stan Keeler, followed by Stone. The drizzle had turned to a steady downpour and the cigarette turned soggy in his mouth. "*That* was some play, man." He dropped the cigarette on the ground. "Am I nuts or was that a bullet that spun Wes around? Is some crazy trying to make a statement they don't like Sirocco? What the hell was going on in there?" He didn't seem to expect any answers. "Your friend was very persuasive. So where's this new landlady he was telling me about?"

"Front of the theater. You can't miss her. Red hair, silver jacket, beautiful nose."

Stan grinned. "Aw-*right.*" He turned to the black Labrador.

Stone was already halfway down the alley.

"The last number; they'll be out in a minute," said Wiggins in answer to Jury's question. "Got to keep your strength up, sir." The sergeant pushed the paper plate toward him. Wiggins was munching on one of Mary Lee's cheese sandwiches. The bread was curling up on the edges. Jury picked up a pale-looking round and then put it down.

He imagined himself sitting in the lounge of the Old Silent, staring down at his plate after the conversation with Sanderson. It wasn't, he realized now, anything Sanderson or he had said, it was the plate. The detail which then had tried to surface now did.

Wiggins was talking to him about the chap whose job it had been to monitor the spotlight. "He could identify her, sir. Why didn't she kill him if she was that desperate?"

Jury stared at his sergeant without answering. He had his own personal allergist sitting right there before him. "Wiggins, people can outgrow allergies, can't they?"

Wiggins looked perplexed by his superior's interest in a subject Jury generally considered as fascinating as one of Racer's preachments. He was, nonetheless, delighted to hold forth at some length about the various *types* of allergic reactions. "Billy Healey's?" Wiggins frowned. "Doubtful. His was very serious."

"Then I don't imagine he'd be eating a ploughman's." He looked from the sandwiches to his sergeant. "Lunch. Consisting mainly of cheese."

Wiggins stopped the cup of tea on the way to his mouth. "If you'd only told *me* what he had for lunch—"

"Duckworth's column," said Melrose, "mentions the eccentricities of some guitarists. Hendrix was left-handed and restrung right-handed guitars because he thought they were probably superior."

"What's the point? Charlie Raine's a right-handed guitarist."

"He taught himself to play by looking at instruction books and naïvely assumed the guitar had to be held that way. Mirror-image." He tossed Jury the magazine. "By now, he's ambidextrous. But he was born left-handed."

"Remind me to ring up Dr. Dench," said Wiggins, smugly.

* * *

The band came out.

Jury jumped down from the van and walked over to Wes Whelan. One arm of his red shirt was caked with blood. "You amaze me. You didn't even drop a beat. That was the most acrobatic turn I've ever seen." He shook his hand.

Grinning, he said, "You forgot? I grew up in Derry with the IRA." He looked at his shirt. "This is but a scratch. Nothing a tall a tall. It only grazed me."

"You all showed incredible presence of mind."

Jiminez laughed; it was very deep, very throaty. "Man, we were so into things I doubt we even knew what was goin' on until Stan Keeler came out on that stage. Don't give us no credit."

Jury smiled. "No, of course not. Where's Charlie?"

Swann motioned over his shoulder. "In there. Hates to leave the stage, Charlie does." He pushed back his golden hair and smiled.

"Don't wait for him," said Jury as they started piling into the limousine.

"If you're going to the Ritz," said Melrose, "may I hitch a ride?"

42

He was sitting on the bottom level of the black platform in the center of the stage, a towel round his neck, holding the white Fender, plucking a string, plucking another, playing a chord as if some ghostly remnant of that shouting, ecstatic audience still sat out there in the rows of empty seats, as if there were the lingering echo of applause.

Perhaps because of the way he sat there, looking out, the theater seemed not so much empty as abandoned. In the aisles a couple of lads were cleaning up the detritus of the concert, but they left, lugging plastic bags behind them. A clutch of roadies were standing at the rear of the stage looking out, smoking, talking. Wondering, probably, what the hell had gone on in here tonight.

When Jury sat down beside him, he didn't turn to look. "Wes is a great drummer. He's got the quickest reaction time of anyone I know."

"Quicker than mine, certainly."

"I never knew anyone to pull off anything like that."

"What about you, Charlie?"

He looked down, strummed one chord, then another. He looked out through the semidarkness much the way Nell Healey had stared beyond that broken wall, as if someone might materialize before her eyes.

" 'I was trying to pull myself up by my bootstraps and the bootstraps broke.' Stevie Ray Vaughan said that. Great guitarist."

"Stevie Ray Vaughan mended the bootstraps. You're quitting at the height of your career as some sort of penance, that it?"

He didn't answer, just picked a few more notes, struck a few quick chords.

"Or was the penance learning to play that"—Jury nodded toward the guitar—"in the first place?"

There was a long silence, and then he said: "Every morning, sometimes twice a day, since I've been in London I've gone to Waterloo. Go into the buffet, get a cup of tea, go out, walk around and look at the departures. There must be a train to Leeds nearly every hour." He took his hand from the strings and reached into the back pocket of his jeans. "I bought these." He fanned out four tickets—day-returns to Leeds. "For eight years I tried to come back and tell her what happened." He was silent. "I couldn't face her."

Jury waited, let him hold on to his guitar, strum the chords to "Yesterday's Rain," and stare out over the emptiness as blighted, perhaps, to him as Haworth Moor.

"The last time I saw her was when I was looking down from my window that faced the sea and she stopped on that cliff path and looked up and waved. She had a way of waving and smiling that was so"—he shrugged—"joyful you'd think she hadn't seen you in ages. Like mums on station platforms when the kids come down from school on their holidays. You know." He looked over at Jury then, who was looking down. "I really loved her. Hard to believe, but I'd have died for her."

Jury raised his eyes and looked out over the empty seats. "You did."

"I was getting my clothes on when I looked out the other window, the one facing the rear and saw *her*"—he looked up toward the corner of the circle—"walking down that back road. I wondered what in hell the aunt was here for; no one said she was coming. Then she disappeared inside, into the kitchen. I started down the stairs—the room was at the top of the kitchen stairs—but then I stopped. I still don't know why I didn't just clatter on down. I could only hear muffled voices and in a minute the door slammed. The kitchen door. I went back into my room and saw his Aunt Irene and Billy walking up the road, and Gnasher, his terrier, padding behind him. I nearly raised the window and shouted but something stopped me, again. It was just, I don't know, *wrong*.

"Then I ran down and looked for Mrs. Healey. Nell. She must have walked farther along the cliff and I thought, no, I'd just waste time looking for her. So I went round the house and up the road, trying to catch up and stay out of sight at the same time. Then I saw the car, the aunt's car; I recognized it from seeing it at the Citrine house. It was parked nearly all the way up to the entrance and they got in. It looked like they were having an argument about the dog, but Billy pulled it in. Anyway, it gave me a chance to get to the shed and get the bike and an old slicker. It was getting dark fast. Where the car ended up—"

He stopped. He looked down at the guitar as if he'd never seen it before.

Jury turned and said, "Was a disused graveyard."

He nodded. "It came on suddenly, the dark. The only light came from the car's headlamps and an electric torch. It was held by a man but I couldn't make him out; it was like the torch was shining right in my eyes, had me pinned down. But they hadn't heard me. The rest was like broken-off images in a dream. I could hear Billy, saying something, and then crying. I could hear Gnasher, he just barked once and then nothing. But I didn't hear *them,* I mean they went about all of this in silence while I was ducked down behind a grave marker. It was all so nightmarish I read over and over the words on the marker.

"Billy was lying on the ground, and the little dog was lying beside him. His aunt pushed the dog down into the ground." He stopped. "Did you ever have one of those feelings you become two different people? It's as if one part of you is sitting in a chair and the other part gets up and walks across the room? That's what happened to me. It was like part of me still hid behind that stone and the other part ran toward the grave. I was yelling; but even my voice didn't sound like my voice. I still couldn't see his face, the man's, because he was down in the grave, but hers—good God, I'll never forget that look.

"And then it all happened in slow motion: she brought out a gun, a small one, from her pocket and turned it on me; I backed up against a tree and she fired. But she must be as good a shot with a revolver as she is with a rifle—" He laughed ruefully. "—because she missed. Missed killing me, I mean. The bullet only nicked my ear, but, my God, the blood . . ."

He stopped to pluck a few more notes on the Fender, then to search for a cigarette. Jury shook one out of his packet. "She thought she'd killed me, though, I think. I slid down the tree and crumpled. He was running over now, shoving her back, calling her a bloody stupid bitch and while they were exchanging names, I managed to edge myself away from the tree, get up, and run. You've got to understand, I thought Billy was dead. I ran back to the road, thinking maybe I could stop someone. I was holding a piece of my ripped-off shirt up to stop the blood with one hand and hailing a car with the other. Brilliant." Here he played a flashy riff in a burst of anger at himself. "Did you ever try to outrun headlamps?"

"No. I take it the car was theirs."

"I don't know how she missed me again, but she did. This time with the car. What would I have been but another hit and run?"

"You'd have been hard to explain, in the circumstances."

"I veered off the road and ran toward the coast, toward the cliffs. There wasn't much she—or he—could do by way of following in the car. I probably wasn't losing as much blood as I thought. I managed to stagger along for a mile, maybe two, maybe more; I wasn't counting. And then I had the best piece of luck I've ever had: ran into a party of campers. There were five of them, sitting round a campfire. They were Americans, backpacking round the British Isles. All of them young, in their twenties." Charlie grinned. "And all of them stoned. They were absolutely fascinated by this bloody—literally—Brit who stumbled into them. Again, literally. I'll never forget them: Katie, Miles, Dobby, Helena, Colin. They had some stuff in their backpacks to take care of the wound. They thought I was hallucinating, they really did, when I kept talking about getting the police, told them I'd just seen someone murdered. I'll never forget Miles looking at me, blinking. He handed me a roach-clip and said, 'Hey, man, mellow out.'

"I mellowed out, all right. I *passed* out. Slept through the next day and when I woke up, Dobby and Miles were jamming on their guitars. Still stoned. Only the girls were beginning to take me seriously, but just as seriously they told me to stay away from the cops. I didn't see a newspaper for six days and didn't know about the ransom demand. And I don't mind saying I was terrified. I was a *witness* and I suppose I'd seen too much telly."

Jury said, "Whose idea was it to identify somebody else's body?"

"Mine and Uncle Owen's. I couldn't stand him thinking I was dead, like Billy, so I rang up, finally."

"You mean he knew Irene Citrine had done this and didn't go to the police?" Somehow that didn't sound like Owen Holt.

"He didn't know. I didn't tell him. I was afraid for him and Aunt Alice. I told him . . . I didn't know who they were."

"But your aunt didn't know. Your uncle didn't tell her. Why?"

There was a silence. "He was going to, but then he thought, in the long run, it might be easier for her just to think I was dead than that she'd never see me again, probably." He looked at his guitar. "And you've met Aunt Alice.

Do you think she'd really have been able to keep it to herself? Uncle Owen was afraid she'd go to the police. She'd hardly have been able to talk to you without telling you. Maybe it was cold-blooded, I don't know."

"None of you strike me as that. Go on."

"Uncle Owen said not to worry. To leave things to him, to lie low—he'd find some way of getting money to me. He did. A lot."

Jury smiled. "Your uncle never did strike me as a gambler."

"What?" The boy frowned.

"Nothing. You went to Ireland?"

"I did. From Stranraer to Larne. And I met Wes." He smiled. "Wes had more than talent. He had contacts—like someone in the U.D.C. who knew someone who knew *someone* who could forge passports."

Back at the rear of the auditorium, light fanned briefly across the wall as one of the doors swung open and shut. Whoever it was was standing back there or had sat down.

Mary Lee, Jury bet, and smiled. Then the memory of Charlie writing on the clear surface of the shoe came back to him.

"The longer I kept quiet about it, the more guilty I felt," Charlie was saying. "And the more guilty I felt, the harder it was to do anything, to come back, to tell the story. The old vicious circle of guilt. Why didn't I do something to save him?"

The question was rhetorical, but Jury answered it anyway. "Because you knew damned well they'd kill you."

Charlie rested his forehead against the guitar frets, eyes closed. "But not to do anything about it later—"

"You did. You thought if he'd lived, Billy Healey would have gone on to have a highly successful career as a concert pianist—"

"He would have." Charlie brought the guitar back up to his lap.

"I doubt it."

Charlie looked round, sharply. "That was the whole idea."

"His father's idea. Not Billy's. And not necessarily Nell Healey's. Wasn't it hard to get him to practice?"

"Yes. But he was a natural."

"Come on, Toby. You, of all people, would know that even a 'natural' has to practice like hell to get where Roger Healey wanted his son to go. Billy was lazy. Irene Citrine said that. On the other hand *you* were just the opposite. Determined. Or as your aunt put it, pigheaded."

He had to smile. "I expect I was."

"You 'expect' you were? You *weren't* a 'natural'; you couldn't play anything. That is, you couldn't play anything until you were so driven by guilt to pick up on a career that Nell's son had lost; there must have been times when you wished you could have died in his place."

"There were."

"And you did. In a sense you became Billy. It must have been hell. No musical inclination, no background, presumably no talent. I *thought* you were Billy."

"You thought *I* was—why?"

Jury told him about the poetry, the picture, and the impression Charlie himself had given him about the Healey case. "Let's say I thought you were Billy because you couldn't possibly have been Toby Holt. And Toby would have been the only other one who knew all of that."

"If you practice twelve, thirteen hours a day, you don't need background. Sometimes the fingers of my left hand would bleed and I'd just wrap gauze round them and put on a surgical glove and keep going. Some martyrdom, right?"

"Which you apparently plan to complete by quitting at the top. You told me you'd got as far as you needed to and I wondered what that could possibly mean. So now you're quitting. And to do what? Live in West Yorkshire and become a shepherd? A groundsman?"

"I have to go back; I have to tell them what really happened; I want to see her."

"Yes, I know. But for God's sakes, don't think of staying there. It's not meant for you, Charlie. This time, it could really kill you."

"That's pretty dramatic. I was thinking about Abby. With her aunt dead, well, she could use some help."

Abby. Yes, she could have used it a long time ago. "Nell Healey will see to that." Jury turned from trying to see into the shadows of the back to look at Charlie. "You've paid up, Charlie. And, anyway, you haven't done what you'd sworn you'd do."

Charlie cut a bleak smile in Jury's direction. "I haven't?"

"No. You haven't quite peaked. Sirocco hasn't played Wembley Stadium." Jury called to the rear of the auditorium, "Isn't that the order, Mary Lee? The Marquise, Town and Country, Odeon, Arena, Stadium?"

A shadow moved and she started down the aisle. "What about the Ritz?"

Jury shaded his eyes and looked back.

"Remember me?" asked Vivian.

Vivian had Marshall Trueblood's Armani coat slung about her shoulders. Underneath was a gown Jury could see as she moved closer to the stage that the Princess would have approved. It was burgundy, fluid, semitransparent and fit her body like a second skin to just below the hips where it flared out. It had a languid, pre-Raphaelite look. Her hair was done up partly on top of her head, partly down, as if the hair had escaped its entrapment on top. She wore long emerald earrings.

The combination of her appearance (which was gorgeous) and the surprise of seeing her here made Jury's mind go blank. "Why in hell are you wearing Trueblood's Armani coat?" *That* was a sporty question, he thought, cursing himself.

But she took it in stride. "Because I had the coat-check

ticket for it in my bag. I'm supposed to have gone to powder
my nose during the entree; we started dinner without you,
but no one will have finished, not if Agatha had her way
about the seven-course meal and Melrose orders one more
bottle of wine. He told me you were here." Vivian beamed
up at Charlie Raine, whose own smile would have lit up the
Embankment. "I was cheated. They got to hear you; I
didn't."

"I can always fix that."

"You wouldn't!"

"I would." Charlie strapped the Fender round his neck.
"What do you want to hear?"

Vivian thought for a moment. " 'Yesterdays'—not the
Beatles' one, the one by Jerome Kern. Do you know it?"

Charlie thought for a moment, shook his head, "I know
the Beatles'. Will that do?"

"It'll do," said Jury, sitting down in the front row with
Vivian beside him. He wrapped his arm over the back of her
seat.

As Charlie, twenty-three years old, sang about a day
when his troubles had been far away, here in the building
where the last briefing for D-Day had taken place, Jury was
drawn back to the flat on the Fulham Road, Elicia Deauville, and the rubble that once had been his and his mother's
parlor.

He was just as glad he hadn't been there on the moor to
see the black-clad arm of Ann Denholme lying against the
white backdrop of snow.

He feared, as the song said, that all his troubles might be
here to stay.

43

"Toby Holt?" said Melrose. "My God, that shows determination equal only to Agatha's trying to knock off every eligible female in sight."

Sitting at a table as far from the small stage as he could, Jury smiled. "Thanks for not beginning with 'So Commander Macalvie was right.'" His head was throbbing from a combination of no sleep, Wiggins's report from the hospital, and the slashing licks of Dickie's rendition of "Déjà Vu" (determined, according to Stan, to prove he was as fast as Yngwie).

Melrose squinted through the smoke-filled room. "How did *Vivian* get here?"

Jury put his hand to his head as Dickie let go with another ravaging chord progression and wished for once he had access to Wiggins's pocket pharmacy. "It was her idea." He waved his hand toward the blue-lit stage of the Nine-One-Nine, where Vivian, pumps off, was churning and applauding. "Have any of those cigars?"

"This was *Vivian's* idea?" Melrose fumbled inside his jacket pocket for his cigar case.

"One of London's best-kept secrets. One of those underground places you hear about through word-of-mouth, and not much of that. The regulars want to keep it to themselves. Vivian wanted to see the 'real' London."

"I don't want to go back to the Ritz and a lot of rich, boring tourists. You must know some nice, sleazy club." To

which Jury had said he didn't do much club-hopping. "*Well, you must raid them sometimes.*" She seemed sure he knew every club in London's underbelly.

"She kept reminding me it's her last night in London. Exact words, 'my last night on English soil.' " He smiled at Melrose.

"How dramatic." Melrose draped his black dinner jacket with its ribbed satin facing over the wooden chairback. "If we keep her drinking she'll forget and go all the way to Istanbul."

"I think the Orient Express stops in Venice. They'll chuck her out."

"Is Wiggins still at hospital?" Jury nodded. Melrose asked, "What's her condition?"

"As bad as can be expected. Slips in and out of a coma. Wiggins said she was talking like someone in a dream. About Healey, Ann Denholme. Some things we'd deduced."

"Extortion, blackmail, that sort of thing?"

Jury swallowed some of the club soda. The headache was lessening. "Unfortunately, she chose Rena instead of Charles. 'Pay up or I'll tell his wife about Abby.' My God, she might as well have put a gun to her head as let Rena Citrine know Abby was Roger's daughter."

"And if Nell Healey had found out about Abby, the Fury would have got the lot, wouldn't she?"

"The entire inheritance, is my guess."

"My Lord, but Healey took chances. Involved with two women up there right under his wife's nose? Not to mention Mavis Crewes."

"I think his involvement with Rena might have been pure greed. And she certainly tried to steer me away from revenge as a motive—wanted me to think it was adultery." Jury shrugged. "But then again, who was she actually with on Bimini? I'm having Wiggins check to see if there's a record of a marriage between Citrine and Littlejohn. Roger might have decided to run through what money Rena had. We'll probably never know. But Rena certainly had expectations insofar as Nell was concerned; Rena was careful to champion her cause, to stick by her." Jury looked through a film of smoke toward the right-hand wall. "I see Trueblood's found a friend."

Marshall Trueblood had been in the place for all of fifteen minutes and he was already having an animated discussion with Karla. At least, Trueblood's part was animated. Karla was standing in the same spot, in the same position, holding up the wall against which Marshall Trueblood was leaning his elbow, his head against one hand and his other gesticulating wildly. In answer, Karla merely smoked and gave Trueblood the best of her profile. Her lips, otherwise, did not move. Trueblood was wearing a paisley dinner jacket, black cummerbund, and a cerise bow-tie, butterfly fashion, beneath a wing collar.

"But to try and kill *Abby?* The very night after Ann Denholme? She had plenty of time for that—" Melrose paused. "No, she wouldn't. Because Nell Healey was to be taken into custody the very next morning. And all three of those killings were to look like her revenge on her husband having not just an affair but a child by that affair."

"Try to imagine Irene Citrine's state of mind when she walked into Abby's barn and saw that Sirocco poster," Jury said.

"Why did she recognize him when no one else did? Had he changed that much since he was fifteen?"

"She was the only one who *knew* Toby Holt was alive; not even his uncle could be certain. Three years ago the band was playing clubs in the Florida Keys. Remember, she spent several months on Bimini. But it's not only that. It's *context.* Rena saw that poster in a context she could hardly have forgotten. A young man against a tree right beside a view of the Cornwall coast. The only person who could identify her, and he's right here in London."

"Look at that, would you?" Melrose nodded toward the tiny dance floor. Trueblood and Karla were dancing to a bluesy, jazzy version of "Limehouse Blues." Arms shot straight out to the side and holding each other at arm's length, Karla's hand on Trueblood's shoulder. They were staring into each other's eyes. The other couples on the floor didn't seem to notice and were hanging on to one another for dear life, moving in a hag's dream.

"Oh, to be young," said Melrose. Then he half-rose from his seat. "Who's Vivian dancing with? If you call it dancing. She's got her arms round his neck."

"Incidentally, where's your beloved aunt?" He looked round at the door of the Nine-One-Nine, as if Agatha might march through it.

"In Wanstead somewhere." Melrose was half out of his seat, watching the dance floor.

"*Wanstead?* What's she doing in *Wanstead?*"

He sat down again. "Because she insisted on coming with us. After you called the hotel, we tried to shake her off and couldn't. Trueblood told her this was a dreadful dive where cocaine and crack dealers met. Nothing would do but Agatha *had* to come along. So Trueblood and I fixed it up that when the doorman got her into a cab, Trueblood would get in while I bumbled about on the pavement, hand the cabbie an address, and then suddenly remember he'd left his money in his room, get out, slam the door and say, 'Go on without us; we'll be along in a minute.' "

"You mean you abandoned poor Agatha to wander in Wanstead?"

"We did not abandon poor Agatha. We're gentlemen, aren't we? There was a note to the cab driver that if he had trouble with the address to drive his fare straight back to the Ritz. Well, of course, he had trouble. There was no such address." Melrose smirked. "We're not heartless, just fast on our feet."

"Christ," breathed Jury. "Speaking of being fast on your feet, I think I'll cut in." Perhaps it was the soothing sound coming from the old sax player, but his headache had all but disappeared.

"You mean you *dance?*"

"I can certainly do *that*." He flung his arm toward the floor where the cyanosed couples were hanging onto one another as if rigor were passing off.

Melrose started to get up. "*I* dance. I'm quite expert."

Jury shoved him down. "What's this to you? You've got your American lady." Jury sat back down again. "Whom, I might add, you actually suspected of these killings. 'I'm glad Ellen's in Yorkshire, I'm glad Ellen's in Yorkshire.' "

"Shut up. Naturally, I suspected she stayed behind—the only one who did—just to throw us off. That she jumped on that damnable bike ten minutes after we left and careened down the M-one."

"I'm surprised you didn't call Weavers Hall to check up on her."

"I did," said Melrose morosely. "She left. Gone. Vanished."

"Suspecting your lady?" Jury clicked his tongue. "And what would be her connection with the Citrines and Charlie Raine?"

"The New York—Yawk—connection. Obviously, I couldn't sort out a motive. And who says she's *my* 'lady'?"

Jury took out several color brochures stamped *Sloane Street Travel* and dumped them on the table. "The Chrysler Building fell out of your coat."

Melrose snatched them up. "The place was near the Armani shop. I just popped in for a moment."

"Um-hmm." Jury stood up. "If you pop off the QE Two or the Concorde in New Yawk, you'll have to walk a hell of a long way. She's from Maryland."

Melrose stopped in the act of stuffing the travel agent's agenda back in his pocket. "What? Don't be ridiculous. What makes you think—"

Like a sleight-of-hand artist, Jury now dropped a book on the table. *Sauvage Savant*, paperback edition. He flipped open the back cover. The picture of Ellen was taken on a windy day and she looked exactly as she had the first . . .

and last time he saw her. Jury tapped the caption. "Baltimore." He smiled.

Casually, Melrose drew his cigarette case out, tapped a cigarette before lighting it and said, "I knew the accent was a put-on. No one really talks like that."

44

Against the splendid backdrop of the brown and cream Pullman cars of the Orient Express, Vivian stood self-con-
sciously smiling as Jury and Melrose took turns with the
camera. Vivian alone; Vivian with Jury; Vivian with Melrose; Vivian with Trueblood's hands positioned bat-wing-
like behind her head (of which, Vivian, smiling self-con-
sciously, was unaware). Vivian with Agatha; Agatha alone;
Agatha alone; Agatha alone—snap, snap, snap, snap.

Compared with Vivian's flawlessly cut and fluid creamy-
wool dress and brimmed hat, her fellow travelers, walking
by with chins high, pretending they weren't attracting attention, looked as if they'd been turned out by some of the
Princess's favorite designers—Worth, Mme. Vionnet, Chanel, even Lady Duff Gordon, with their long draped skirts,
printed velvets and silks, crepe-de-chines and low-slung
waistlines, fluttering printed scarves, ropes of pearls, cloche
hats and headbands. They might have been headed for a
'twenties bistro.

The gentlemen were no less dressed to the nines in peacock blue and salmon striped jackets, doeskin trousers, bot-
tle-green waistcoats and double-breasted dark blue reefers
aplenty. In the midst of them, Marshall Trueblood, who had
turned up with Karla on his arm (or he on hers, given the
difference in their heights) was absolutely the quintessence
of taste amongst all of the (what he called) "reefer mad-
ness." He was wearing his new Armani jacket with its low-

sloping shoulders and loose-cut sleeves. Armani's clothes always had that comfortable, broken-in look from the very moment one put them on. Melrose almost wished he'd bought more. Would he cut a swathe in the Jack and Hammer, looking comfortable and creased?

He heard his name barked. Agatha, again, positioned by the gold crest on the Pullman car, looked fairly broken-in herself after her sojourn in Wanstead, for which she said she'd never speak to them again. Unfortunately, she never kept her word and here she was yelling, "Trueblood! Leave *that person* and come here for another picture."

That person, Karla, who evinced no interest in the handsome people or the handsomely appointed train compartments—the little tables set for luncheon, the upholstery, the passengers in motley—wandered off to stand against the wall of the café and smoke the Eternal Cigarette. Given her marvelous shingled haircut and that same sheared-up dress that fell at odd angles, she was a natural for the present company. Karla stood, staring off across the tracks of Victoria Station as if she'd only been looking for a wall to hold up.

Melrose instructed Agatha (who'd put herself firmly in the middle of the camera's lens) to move away from Jury over to the end because given Jury's height (and her girth, he didn't add) she'd look like a toad. That moved her. Melrose carefully adjusted the camera's prospect to cut her out, although the ostrich feather in her hat managed to land in front of Trueblood's chin.

It was exactly ten-forty and the passengers were lining up in the reception area, and people bound for their second-class seats on other, less-colorful platforms flowed round this elite group, some smiling at the peacock clothes, some shaking their heads as if to dismiss this homage to rampant conspicuous consumption.

The Orient Express personnel, most in brown livery, wore smiles that betokened the most personal service this side of

Charing Cross Hospital's intensive-care unit. They were presently seeing to the tickets and luggage.

Melrose spotted the tag on Vivian's single trunk. "Good Lord, Vivian, is this *all*? The one trunk? What it holds wouldn't last Agatha a day in Harrogate." Agatha was going, she said, straight back to Harrogate, was going to hail a cab ("*No, Mr. Trueblood, I do* not *need your help!*") and zip straight to Waterloo as soon as the Orient Express chugged out, spot on eleven. She had told Melrose that she had no intention of accompanying him back to Long Piddleton, not after last night. He must suffer the consequences of his tricks.

Trueblood folded his arms and pursed his lips, looking at the trunk. "Oh, I don't know, Melrose. I think it'll do. It looks quite long enough. Heavy, of course, but that's just English soil. Vivian was out shoveling half the—"

Vivian, made even more beautiful by the bright flush rising to her cheeks, thrust her face so close to Trueblood's, he leaned back. He quickly pulled and wound his striped scarf about his neck, shrieking, in a mockery of fear, "No closer! No closer!"

"Oh, shut up! I don't know if I *dare* have you to the wedding. God *knows* what you'll get up to." Her fiery gaze included Melrose.

"Don't look at *me!* Have I said a word? No."

"Keep it that way." Then she turned to Jury. "You're being very silent," she said softly.

"I can't stand train stations." He thought of Carole-anne. "Or airports. Or partings."

Agatha was too busy pulling at Melrose to bother with her nemesis, Marshall Trueblood. "*Who,*" she demanded, pointing toward the station café, "is *that* woman?"

"Karla. She's—it's—Trueblood's friend."

"Not *her.* That person *inside* the café. She's been staring at us for the last half hour. At you, for some reason. I was watching her when you were taking my picture."

Melrose looked, squinted, moved closer to the plate glass

behind which a young woman in dark green was standing on the other side of the glass, as still as Karla on this side.

Melrose put on his spectacles, squinted through them . . . *Ellen!*

He loosened Agatha's viselike grip and pushed through the surge of passengers rushing for their trains.

Ellen immediately turned and sat down in one of the plastic-form chairs and sipped her cup of tea.

Melrose tapped and tapped on the pane. Finally, she turned round, giving him a speculative look. Where on earth had they met?

He motioned her outside with several furious waves.

When finally she emerged, both of them ignored by Karla, Melrose decided that the Princess was right. "You look indescribable." Actually, it was true. The dress was totally shapeless, except where Ellen lent it shape (and that considerable); it was a swampy green that did nothing whatever to light up her face. Ah, but the face was clean, the nails actually manicured, the hair combed and possibly Sassooned. And the legs and high heels visible. *There* was a view the Lido would have a hard time matching. Melrose reconsidered dying in a deck chair.

Holding her hand, he dragged her over to the train, where he smiled brilliantly at Jury, haltingly at Agatha (whose own mouth was agape), and uncertainly at Vivian, who was now in her compartment—barely two minutes to go—and who reached down her slim hand to take Ellen's.

She released it and grabbed at Melrose's and with the other hand for Jury. Trueblood was quick-walking beside the liveried porter who was pulling the luggage. Marshall held up a decal of the British flag, smiled and thwacked it on her trunk, taking his time pressing it in place. He waved the porter on and came running back. "Viv-viv, darling! Watch those canals, be careful of the Giopinnos' cellar . . . ah, but, of course, he doesn't drink wine, does . . . owwww!" (Vivian had thrown her paperback book at him.) "My dearest, darling, Viv. I shall *never* say another word. . . . Oh, God, it's moving, it's moving."

Say another word, no. Melrose looked at the departing rack of luggage. There was the British flag! And right next to it was stuck the cut-out of Dracula swinging in his gondola. Melrose shut his eyes.

"Don't do anything foolish, Vivian!" was Agatha's last word. "Mind those gondoliers! Have you any Italian *at all?*"

"Arrivederci, that's about it." She was wiping away tears that trailed slowly down her face.

Still holding her hands, Melrose and Jury were half-running beside the train which finally gained so much speed, they had to release her.

Good-byes were shouted, cried, flung all down the line until the train heaved itself out into the sooty light of a London January day.

Jury stood there, unconscious of a pram that barked his shin and a couple of punks with mohawks who shoved him aside.

He dragged his eyes from the track when he heard Trueblood beside him. Karla had reengaged his arm. "Come on, old trout. We're off to see a rerun of *The Untouchables.*"

"What? Why in God's name would anyone who'd just seen Vivian off want to see Al Capone?"

"Don't be dense. We'll only stay for the credits."

"That makes sense." Jury looked down the track. The end of the train was a cinder now.

Trueblood drew a banner in air between thumb and forefinger. " '*Wardrobe by Armani.*' Everyone applauds. Then we leave, go somewhere and get drunk."

Jury smiled, looked at Karla, whose mouth hitched up on one end. "You two go along. I'll see you later."

Trueblood looked at him with concern. "We'll all get together at Nine-One-Nine. How's that?"

"Hmm? Fine."

Jury was looking at Melrose and Ellen, who in some sort

of twosome metamorphosis had walked over to take the place of Trueblood and Karla. "Luncheon at the Ritz. What do you say? Agatha's taken herself off to Waterloo. Sorry about that." Melrose grinned.

Boyishly. It was the first time Jury ever remembered seeing his friend actually grin. "No, you two go on."

"Not without you. And I've something for you." Melrose reached into the deep pocket of his overcoat and brought out the Sony Walkman. He smiled. "Here." Then he reached in the other and brought out some tapes. Six of them.

Transformer. Lou Reed; *Rock n Roll Animal.* Lou Reed; *Berlin.* Lou Reed; *Live in Italy.* Lou Reed; *Mistrial.* Lou Reed; *New York.* Lou Reed.

"I'm sorry," said Melrose, "I couldn't find *Metal Machine Music.*"

Ellen sighed. "You've got to be a real Lou Reed fanatic to dig that one. Feedback screams."

"I dig feedback screams. I'm with you, aren't I?"

"I can't thank you enough," Jury said, looking at Melrose Plant's enthusiastic face. "I've got some work to clear up; these'll help." He held up the tapes.

"Work? For God's sakes, that's all you've been doing! Come with us."

"Yeah, come on." One hand pulled on Jury's arm; the other was in Melrose's.

"What is it you say in the U.S.? 'Later days'?"

Ellen smiled. "Later days, then."

He shoved both of them gently: "Go."

Jury watched them walk away, heads close together.

He turned to look back at the empty track and then in the other direction over the heads of Victoria's crowded railway station. Over there was the old, dependable Underground sign. Jury held on to the tapes Melrose had given him and brought out another tape from his pocket, looked at it, shoved it back.

He might as well go home and put on a little Trane.

I wish I could promise to lie in the night
And think of an orchard's arboreal plight
When slowly (and nobody comes with a light)
Its heart sinks lower under the sod.
But something has to be left to God.

—Robert Frost
"Good-bye and Keep Cold"

You need a Busload of Faith to get by.

—Lou Reed
New York

Match wits with Richard Jury of Scotland Yard. And solve these cunning murders by

MARTHA GRIMES

___	The Anodyne Necklace	10280-4	$4.99
___	The Deer Leap	11938-3	$4.95
___	The Dirty Duck	12050-0	$4.95
___	The Five Bells and Bladebone	20133-0	$4.99
___	Help The Poor Struggler	13584-2	$4.99
___	I Am The Only Running Footman	13924-4	$4.99
___	Jerusalem Inn	14181-8	$4.95
___	The Man With A Load Of Mischief	15327-1	$4.99
___	The Old Silent	20492-5	$5.95